HOLIDAY CHEER

December is here and it's time to celebrate with holiday cheer and a romantic collection of contemporary stories from three of Arabesque's favorite authors. Each of these talented authors will introduce us to a special couple who have discovered the magic of true love mingled with a passion that cannot be denied. Enjoy Donna Hill's tales of a Christmas time love, share the spirit of Kwanzaa with Margie Walker and delight in Francis Ray's New Year's Eve miracle. These three unforgettable novellas will touch your heart and are bound to warm your heart during the chilly winter season.

SPIRIT OF THE SEASON

Spirit of the Season

Donna Hill
Francis Ray
Margie Walker

PINNACLE BOOKS
KENSINGTON PUBLISHING CORP.
http://www.pinnaclebooks.com

PINNACLE BOOKS are published by

Kensington Publishing Corp.
850 Third Avenue
New York, NY 10022

First Printing: December, 1994
10 9 8 7 6 5 4 3 2

Printed in the United States of America

TABLE OF CONTENTS

The Choice

by
Donna Hill

He was tall, and handsome in an exotic, decidedly sensual kind of way. His warm hazel eyes, an almost identical match to hers, seemed able to peer into her very soul. His shoulder-length dredlocks framed a face of smooth rich chocolate, a face that any woman could fall in love with. And that's exactly what Jewel Avery had done. She'd fallen head over heels in love with Taj Burrell.

A wistful smile tilted her full, bow-shaped lips as she momentarily relived the feel of his mouth trailing tantalizing kisses along her neck. So what was the problem? she asked herself, shaking away the vision with a toss of her dark brown head, as she busied herself making a quick breakfast for her daughter, Danielle. With swift, precise movements Jewel smoothly prepared a plate of scrambled eggs, wheat toast, and a glass of orange juice and placed them on the smoked-glass dining room table.

The problem was, Taj was five years her junior. He was a struggling musician and she was a thirty-seven-year-old independently wealthy divorcée with one of the fastest growing real estate and development agencies in the state of Connecticut. She had yet to introduce him to her family. Her daughter Danielle didn't even know that Taj existed.

Why was introducing him such a problem? she questioned. After all, *age ain't nothin' but a number.* How many times had she heard that line? Yet an admonishing voice echoed in her head that a grown woman with a child did not "run around" with a younger man, and a *musician* no less. What would people say?

Jewel frowned and turned away from the table. Other people's reactions were the least of her problems. It was Danielle who was her greatest source of concern.

She returned to the kitchen and walked toward the polished cherry wood cupboard. Automatically she reached for a jar of coffee. Her slender hand halted in midair and changed direction. She reached instead for a box of herbal tea, hearing Taj's warning about the effects of caffeine. She smiled. He had changed her life in so many ways.

She sighed heavily. It wasn't fair to Taj to keep him a secret from her family. They'd been seeing each other for nearly three months, almost from the first day that they met, when he'd walked into her office and asked for help in finding a loft apartment. Since then, he'd asked her repeatedly to introduce him to her family, especially Danielle. But each time, Jewel made some excuse, and then Taj had just stopped asking. If she didn't quickly come to terms with her dilemma, she knew she would lose him.

She walked to the bottom of the spiral staircase that led to the bedrooms above.

"Dani! Breakfast is ready," she called. "Hurry up or you'll be late for class."

"I'm comin', I'm comin'," fifteen-year-old Danielle yelled back.

Moments later she heard her daughter bounding down the stairs. She turned as Dani bustled into the dining room. Her straight, shoulder-length black hair hung evenly around her pretty, almond-toned face. Her best friend, Kim, had wrapped Dani's hair the night before. Her electric blue backpack was slung over her right shoulder.

Jewel's smile of greeting froze on her face as her large hazel eyes scanned her daughter's attire.

"Must you dress like that every day Danielle?" Jewel cried plaintively, sounding, she knew, much like her own mother.

"Like what?" Dani countered, taking a seat at the table. She frowned at her mother, gearing up for their usual debate.

"Like—like you're ready to go to a yard sale. Your shirts are too big, your jeans are two sizes too large, those sneakers look like space boots." Jewel inhaled, then quickly expelled an exasperated breath as she put her hands on her round hips.

"You'll be sixteen years old in a couple of months. A young lady," she added in a gentler tone. "It's about time you started dressing like one." Jewel turned away and picked up her cup of tea from the counter. Dani rolled her eyes.

"Everybody dresses like this," Dani said. "I don't see the problem. Daddy wouldn't have had a problem with how I dress," she added accusingly.

Jewel swallowed back the lump of frustration that had risen in her throat. Slowly she turned toward her daughter. "Your father isn't here, Dani," she said evenly.

"No, he isn't."

Jewel felt as if she'd been slapped even as she heard the barest hint of pain beneath the angry words.

Danielle sprung up from her seat, tossing her napkin across the uneaten food. "I've got to go," she mumbled. She rounded the table and gave her mother a perfunctory kiss on the cheek. "Bye." She spun away, snatching her backpack from the chair.

Jewel took a calming breath. "Dani," she called softly.

Dani halted and reluctantly turned back. "Yes?"

"It isn't my fault, Dani, that your father

moved out." She took a step forward. "I don't know what else I can do to make you understand that. Things didn't work out. It happens, even in the best of families."

Dani sighed. "Maybe if you didn't try to be so perfect and expect perfection from everyone else then Daddy wouldn't have left."

Jewel stared wordlessly at her departing daughter. Perfection. How many times had she had that word thrown in her face?

She sat down heavily in the gold and black chair, unconsciously straightening the place mats and salt and pepper shakers. Then just as quickly, returning them all the way they were. Another Taj Burrell influence, she thought wryly. He had subtly and lovingly tried to exorcise some of the idiosyncrasies that permeated Jewel's life.

Ever since she was a little girl, her parents had demanded her absolute best at everything, from the way she dressed and combed her hair to the straight A's that she maintained throughout her school years.

Any deviation from perfection was met with chilling remarks, withdrawal of affection, and questions about her character. As a result, Jewel had grown up meticulous, afraid of confrontation and starved for affection. So when she met Steven Avery in her freshman year of college, she envisioned him as her knight in shining armor.

Jewel strove to please him in the only way she knew how—by being perfect at everything. But Steven demanded more than even she was capable of giving. When he couldn't get it, he turned to others.

At first he was discreet about his affairs and then he became blatant with his dalliances. He never really wanted her, Jewel had painfully come to realize; he only wanted someone to warm his bed at night. She could never have done enough to satisfy Dr. Steven Avery.

Jewel slowly rose from her seat and placed her teacup in the sink. She'd promised herself from the day he'd walked out of the door that she'd protect his image in his daughter's eyes. As a result, Danielle believed that Jewel had driven her father away. Jewel had spent the past year, since the divorce, trying to make it up to Dani. Tears welled in her eyes. All to no avail, she sighed.

And now with the Christmas holidays rapidly approaching, she had to find a way to introduce the new man in her life to Danielle. The thought of that confrontation chilled her almost as much as the numbing December air. Deep inside, she knew that Dani would be adamantly against anyone attempting to fill her father's shoes. Dani still maintained the childlike hope that her mother and father would be miraculously reunited.

Jewel slipped on her mint green, wool suit

jacket and retrieved her ankle-length mink coat from the hall closet.

As she drove to the office, thoughts of Taj penetrated her troubling musings. Despite herself, she smiled. Taj had planned on an early lunch at his loft apartment for the two of them. Her heart began to race. It was the thoughtful things like that about Taj that had endeared him to her from the beginning.

Moments later she pulled up in front of her office. She stepped out of her BMW and quickly crossed the parking lot, eager to find refuge from the blistering winter wind. She had two houses to show before she could leave for her rendezvous with Taj as well as make some final decisions on the purchase and renovation of a string of abandoned buildings in New Haven. Another full day, she mused.

When she entered her office, she was surprised to find her assistant, Tricia Monroe, already at her desk.

"Mornin' Jewel," Tricia greeted. "You have a visitor," she added. Tricia angled her auburn head in the direction of Jewel's private office.

Jewel frowned. "I don't recall making any private appointments for this morning," she replied. "Who is it?"

"See for yourself."

Jewel stood up straighter and gave Tricia a puzzled glance, then headed down the corridor.

Jewel opened the frosted glass door to her office, ready to apologize for her oversight but was instead swept up in a breathtaking embrace.

Before she had a chance to respond, Taj's strong hands found their way beneath her coat and pulled her solidly against him. His warm mouth found hers, covering it in an intoxicating kiss that left her weak in the knees. His fingers played along her spine, sliding downward to pull her hips closer to his pulsing center.

"I couldn't wait till lunch," he moaned against her mouth. "I dreamed about you all night long."

"Taj," she whispered breathlessly, arching her neck to receive the rain of scintillating kisses as his feather-soft dredlocks whispered tauntingly against her cheek. "What about Tricia?"

"What about her?" he teased. "This is just between us." He looked down into her upturned face and grinned, flashing even, white teeth. Reluctantly he took a step back and slowly released his hold.

Jewel struggled to control the rapid beat of her heart. "What on earth are you doing here?" she was finally able to ask. She pushed the door closed and with much effort crossed the mauve, carpeted floor to her desk, needing to put some barrier between her and Taj if only for a moment.

"I thought I'd surprise you. I know what a stickler you are for order and I just felt that a little spontaneity was way overdue."

"You've certainly accomplished that," she said, slowly regaining control of her breathing as she took in the sight of the gorgeous man in front of her. It took all of her willpower to keep from unbuttoning the tiny white buttons on his pale blue denim shirt and to keep from stroking the hard, muscular thighs that were encased in his blue jeans.

Taj flounced down on the soft, black leather sofa, stretching his long, muscular arm across its length. He crossed his right ankle over his left knee and gave Jewel a penetrating stare. "What's the problem?" he asked, intuitively sensing her uneasiness.

With a long sigh, Jewel slipped out of her coat and hung it on the brass coatrack.

"Dani and I had another falling out this morning." She took a seat behind her desk.

Taj pursed his lips and briefly shut his eyes. "About what?"

"The usual. Her father, me . . . everything."

"Don't you think it's about time that you told her the truth about her father, Jewel?"

"Of course I've thought about it. But knowing my daughter, I'm sure she'd find some way to use that against me as well."

Taj closed his eyes and sighed, then abruptly stood up. "When am I going to get to *know* this daughter?"

She looked up at him, her eyes pleading with him to understand. "Soon Taj. I promise. It's just that—"

"Just what, Jewel?" His voice rose in frustration. "Is it *just* that you're ashamed of me? Is it *just* that I don't fit into your world? What? Because I'd really like to know. Once and for all."

"Taj, please try to understand. It's not easy for me either."

He crossed the short space to her desk, leaned down, bracing his hands against the hard wood, his hair falling on either side of his dark face. The heady scent of his cologne wafted around his body, assaulting her senses.

"We've been together for close to three months now, Jewel," he said evenly. "In that time, you've come up with every excuse in the book to keep me away from your family and your friends. What am I supposed to think? I may be younger than you, but I'm not stupid." He straightened. "I think it's about time that you decided what it is that you want to do about us."

He turned, snatched up his black leather trench coat and his saxophone case, keeping his back to her as he spoke. "I have an audition in an hour. I don't want to be late." He walked toward the door. "You can give me a call when you reach a decision. I'll be waiting." He pulled open the door and left without another word.

Jewel sat motionless. Her heart ached. There was no doubt about it, Taj had finally had enough and had given her an ultimatum. Slowly, she stood up and crossed her arms in front of her. She had a choice to make. Save her relationship by coming to terms with her trepidations and her daughter, or once again, avoid a head on conflict with Danielle and risk further estrangement and lose the man she loved. She couldn't avoid making a decision any longer.

Jewel sighed heavily, pressing her right fist against her lips. If only she had the same control and self-confidence in her personal life as she did in her business dealings, everything would be so much different.

The ringing of her private line intruded on her thoughts.

"Yes, Tricia?"

"Mr. Hamilton is here with his attorney."

"Send them right in."

Jewel straightened and smoothed down her suit. She had put together a master plan for the development of a stretch of abandoned property that was sure to make the unflappable Donald Hamilton drool with longing. Her problems with Taj would have to wait.

Moments later Tricia opened the office door. Following on her heels was Don Hamilton and his attorney, Sam Connelly.

She'd met Donald Hamilton only on one other occasion and once again, his striking good looks caught her off guard. He was at least six-foot-three-inches tall, with a warm honey-brown complexion. His close-cropped hair was the only indication of his age as it was sprinkled with flecks of grey. However, the grey only intensified his distinguished appearance. It was easy to tell that his suits were custom made and fit as though he were the only man on earth who could wear them. Broad shoulders fanned the dark blue suit jacket, contrasting sharply against a stark white shirt. He moved with an easy grace, yet gave off bursts of energy that seemed barely contained. His wife was a very lucky woman, Jewel thought absently.

"Good morning, gentleman," Jewel greeted warmly, stretching her hand to shake each of theirs in turn. "Please have a seat, we have a lot to talk about this morning."

"I certainly hope so, Mrs. Avery," Don intoned, giving her an appreciative once over.

"You peaked my interest with this project. I'm eager to see what you have to offer."

Donald Hamilton was reputed to be one of the wealthiest men in the state. He had holdings in several major corporations around the country and had begun to dabble in real estate over the past year. Word had it that he was determined to buy up as much property as was available. Jewel also knew, from inside sources, that Donald Hamilton was a major player in the President's health care plan. Her vision for the development of the land met all of Don Hamilton's needs.

"In that case," Jewel responded, "let me get right to the point. The land in question is in an ideal location, easily accessible by car or public transportation. What I envision, Mr. Hamilton, is an extensive complex which will include not only major shopping sites but a medical and dental facility and a day care center for shoppers." Before any response could be made, Jewel pulled out a sketch that she'd had an architect draft for her. Expertly, she pointed out the locations of the various buildings and detailed how they would all fit in together.

"This is just the kind of economic boost that Connecticut needs," she concluded.

Don sat back and viewed the sketches. Abruptly he looked across the table at her. "I think you have a marvelous plan. If I didn't know better, I'd say you read my mind." His smile was slow and warm.

Sam Connelly, who had remained silent up to that point, broke in. "Don, I think you need to take these plans over to our people and have them take a look. I wouldn't advise making any decision until then." He looked at Jewel with skeptical green eyes.

The corner of Don's mouth inched up in a grin. "I don't think there will be a need for that, Sam. Mrs. Avery's plan is exactly what I've been looking for." He turned his gaze on Jewel. "Why don't you and I continue this conversation over lunch? I'd also like to take another look at the site. Then, if I still like what I see, just show me where to sign."

"But Don!" Sam sputtered. "You can't just—"

Don turned hard eyes on his attorney. His voice was calm. "I appreciate your advice, Sam. But that's all that it is, advice. The decision is mine to make. And I believe I've made it." He returned his gaze to Jewel. "Lunch?"

She hesitated, thinking of Taj and their aborted plans. "Lunch sounds fine," she said finally.

"Wonderful." Donald checked his watch. "Why don't I pick you up at one o'clock. Is that good for you?"

"Perfect. I have two houses to show, but I should be finished by then."

Both men rose. "I'll see you then." He shook

Jewel's hand. Sam gave her a curt nod and they departed.

It took all she had not to burst out laughing from the look of absolute disgust on the face of Sam Connelly. Unfortunately, her brief moment of gaiety was quickly replaced with an onset of nerves. What was she going to do about Taj? She couldn't leave their situation unresolved.

Jewel reached for her phone and punched in Taj's number. The phone rang four times, then the answering machine clicked on. Jewel hung up with a mixture of relief and disappointment. She'd try again later. Mechanically, she straightened her desk, collected her purse and coat and left her office.

"Tricia, I'm going over to pick up my clients to show the house on Melrose. Then it's off to Hudson Street. I should be back by one."

"No problem," Tricia gave a shallow smile.

"Thanks." Jewel turned to leave, then stopped. "Oh, Don Hamilton is going to stop back by. If he should arrive before I do, just ask him to wait in my office."

"Will do. Anything else?" Tricia asked with an inquisitive glimmer in her eyes.

"Anything like what?"

"Like an exquisitely tall, dark, fine man deserving to be cherished who may call in your absence."

Jewel pursed her lips. "*If* Taj should call,

tell him I'll call him back." Without waiting for further comment, Jewel walked out.

Taj had just finished his second set with the band. He put his saxophone back in the case and walked in the direction of the club owner, Nick Hunter.

"That was great, man!" Nick said enthusiastically. Nick slapped Taj's back and shook his free hand.

"Thanks."

"Let's go into my office and talk."

Taj followed Nick into a small back room off the bar. Nick quickly cleared away a stack of music sheets that occupied the one available chair.

"Have a seat," Nick instructed, then sat down behind his cluttered desk.

Taj sat down, stretching his long legs out in front of him.

"Now, this is the deal," Nick began. "I'm only in town one night a week. Which is usually the night that I play," he grinned. "I have another club in New York and one I'm opening in Los Angeles," he added proudly. "What I'd like to offer you are the other six nights." He quoted a salary. "How does that sound?"

"Almost too good to be true," Taj chuckled.

"Hey, listen, I know talent when I hear it, and you've got it. I wouldn't want anybody else snatching you up while I'm haggling over a few dollars. So?"

Taj thought about the offer. If he accepted, it would greatly cut into his time with Jewel. But then again, as things stood between them . . . well, he didn't know where things stood between them.

"I'm in," he said finally.

Nick stood up and stretched his hand across to Taj. They shook in agreement.

"Then it's a deal. I'll have my partner, Neal, get you all of the necessary forms and give you a schedule. You start tomorrow night, seven o'clock."

"I'll be here."

"Glad to have you aboard. Your sound is just the lift the band needs." Nick came around the desk. "Where did you study?"

Taj laughed "I didn't. At least not in the traditional sense. I taught myself."

"No kiddin'?" Nick said, suitably impressed. "You did a helluva teaching job."

"It just seemed like it came natural to me," Taj shrugged. "And it was a way for me to stay out of trouble, especially on Chicago's southside. My mother didn't have the money for lessons, so I just listened and copied from the masters."

"Well, you stick with me and there may be a lot more doors opened for you. I just negotiated a record deal for my wife, Parris. I do all of her management."

"You're Parris McKay's husband?" Taj asked, suitably surprised.

"Yeah." Nick chuckled. "That woman's been ridin' my coattails long enough," he added playfully. "Had to get her those deals or she would have worn me out singing in the shower."

It was all coming together now. Taj recalled reading an article a couple of years back that talked about Parris' debut in New York. And now that he thought about it, her opening night was at *Rhythms* in Manhattan.

"Seems like I'm in pretty classy company," Taj said.

"Yeah, well, we try to keep a low profile. Otherwise life would be unbearable. Next time Parris is in town, I'll make sure I introduce you."

"That would be great."

Nick nodded. "Actually, I've always wanted to get one of the bands really launched but I never found the right combination." He paused. "Until now."

"It's definitely something to look forward to," Taj said.

"Let's talk again later," Nick said. "I'll be back sometime next week. Neal will give me the lowdown on how things went. Any problems, whatever, you go to him. He'll take care of it."

"Thanks, Nick."

"Don't thank me yet," Nick grinned.

Taj was on cloud nine. Things were finally starting to come together. He had a full time job, paying good money and the possibility of a record deal. What more could he ask for? Maybe now Jewel would take him more seriously. He still believed that although she said she loved him, she still thought of him as someone who needed looking after. Now he could show her that he could make it on his own. He could be all of the things that he felt she needed.

He strolled down Main Street, oblivious to the biting December wind. He spotted a phone booth up ahead and decided to give Jewel a call to share his news.

He dropped a quarter in the slot and started to dial Jewel's office number when something caught his eye. He hung up the phone and stared through the plate glass window of the restaurant opposite the phone booth.

The well-dressed man was looking intensely at his lunch companion. The man spoke to the woman as if she were the only woman in the world. Jewel looked as though she were enjoying every bit of the man's undivided attention.

Taj's jaw tightened to a point where his head began to ache. He took a step toward the restaurant, intent on just walking in on the apparently intimate meeting. Good sense prevailed and he stopped just short of the door. He wouldn't reduce himself to causing a scene, or worse, risk being humiliated by Jewel and her lover.

Taj turned away and strode across the busy intersection, unconscious of the rush of afternoon traffic. All he wanted to do was get away from the two of them as quickly as possible.

So that was it, he fumed, Jewel was seeing someone else. No wonder she didn't want to introduce him to her daughter. What if she simply used Danielle as an excuse, that her daughter wasn't the issue—the other man was. In the short time they've known each other he really believed that the two of them had something special. Obviously he'd been very wrong.

On the next corner Taj hailed a cab and directed the driver to his apartment. Through the entire ride he replayed the scene he'd witnessed over and over again in his mind. And with each vision his hurt intensified to compete with his anger.

He thought Jewel was different. She made *him* feel different, special, but apparently he wasn't special enough, he thought, sticking his key in the door. He stepped into the enormous space and the first thing that caught his eye was the cozy lunch setting he had arranged especially for the two of them. The small, round table was set for two, with a scented candle as the centerpiece. He had prepared a special vegetarian meal that Jewel had come to love. His anger threatened to overpower him.

He breathed heavily as he took off his coat and tossed it on the overstuffed couch that he and Jewel had selected together. If that's the way she wanted it, then that's the way it would be, he decided. He would confine his energies to his music and let Jewel live her life.

"I didn't mean to lay my troubles on you, Don," Jewel confessed softly. "It—you're just so easy to talk with."

"I've been where you are, Jewel. My second wife, Linda, and I had similar problems with my son. He hated her on sight. It took time but I had to decide that if I wanted to preserve my marriage, I had to put my cards on the table with my son."

"What was the turning point for you?" she asked.

"I don't know, really, I guess it was when I realized that one day my son would be out on his own, living his life. If I sat back and allowed him to dictate my life, I knew I wouldn't have one. I slowly began to understand that it wasn't so much that he hated Linda, but that he was afraid of losing me to someone else."

Jewel stared at her partially eaten lunch. "It's just that Dani's been through so much in the past year. First her father and I break up, then we move to a new neighborhood, she has to change schools and make new friends. I just don't know if I can add any more to what she's already had to deal with."

"You're going to have to decide sooner or later. And whether you believe it or not, kids are a lot more resilient than we give them credit for."

"Thanks," she said softly. She sighed. "Enough of my problems." She forced herself to smile. "We're supposed to be conducting business."

"You're absolutely correct. But," he added, "if you ever need to talk, don't hesitate."

"I'll keep that in mind."

After taking him on a tour of the development site, Jewel returned with Don to his office, where he readily signed the preliminary agreement.

"I'll be in touch after the holidays," Don

said. "I'm taking the family down to Florida until the first of the year."

"How wonderful. Have a great time."

"You do the same. And good luck with everything. I'm sure you'll make the right decision. If your instincts for your personal life are as good as they are for business, you won't have any problem." He walked her to the door. "See you next year. And don't forget what I said."

"I won't," she smiled warmly. "And thanks again."

After her meeting with Don, Jewel decided to cut her day short. Suddenly, the holiday spirit had captured her. With Christmas only a week away, there were still so many things she had to do, and the first thing on her agenda was buying something special for Taj. He deserved it.

Jewel spent the next few hours selecting the perfect gifts for her loved ones. She'd found an exquisite jade brooch for her mother, a brilliant piece of African artwork for her eclectic sister, Amber, a CD player for Dani, a silk scarf for Tricia, and for Taj, an original collection of early compositions by Miles Davis.

Satisfied with her purchases, she hurried to the outdoor parking lot and deposited her treasures in the trunk of her car just as the first sprinkles of snow began to fall.

There was still so much to be done, she thought, as she put the car in gear. She wanted—needed—this holiday to be special. But even as she thought of the plans still to be made, her heart tripped with foreboding. She'd have to prepare Danielle for meeting Taj. She wanted this Christmas season to be extra special and she dare not risk an ugly scene on Christmas day.

Don Hamilton's words of advice ran through her head. "Put your cards on the table." That's when she decided on a plan.

Several times Taj reached for the phone, intending to call Jewel. But each time, he stopped. He'd debated with himself for hours over the scene that he'd witnessed earlier, and had eventually come to the conclusion that he knew Jewel well enough to know that she was not the type of woman who played both sides of the fence. His ego and his pride had temporarily blinded him to that fact. Jewel meant too much to him to let his irrational feelings get in the way of their relationship. They had enough to deal with, without him adding to it with his unfounded assumptions.

Taj reached for the phone again, but at the last minute he changed his mind. He was never one for discussing private matters over the phone. Today would be no exception.

With new found resolve, he called the local cab service, grabbed his coat, and took the ten minute ride to Jewel's office.

Tricia had just finished inputting the agency's most recent sales figures into the computer when Taj walked through the door. When Tricia saw him, her pulse immediately quickened. Over the past few months, her secret attraction to Taj had grown by leaps and bounds. Each time that she saw Taj and Jewel together her heart constricted as if the very life was being squeezed out of it.

She knew Jewel was trying her best to keep Taj a secret from everyone, including her. That fact irked Tricia to no end. Taj was the kind of man that deserved to be flaunted. If only she had a chance, she would show him how he deserved to be treated.

"Taj," Tricia greeted with an inviting smile. She stood up and instantly wished that she'd worn something more revealing, rather than her winter white knit pantsuit. The full jacket and flowing pants successfully hid the voluptuous curves beneath. "What a pleasant surprise."

Taj stepped fully into the warm reception area. "Hi, Tricia," he said in a slow, lazy voice. He returned her smile and her stomach did a slow somersault. "I thought I'd surprise Jewel. Is she here?"

"No, she's not," Tricia replied almost too enthusiastically.

"Then I guess the surprise is on me." He tried to laugh it off but it came out hollow. "Do you know where she is?"

Tricia intentionally avoided his gaze. "I would guess she's still with Don Hamilton. They had lunch together." Her eyes finally met his. "I can't imagine what's taking her so long. They've been gone for hours."

Taj fought the urge to allow his imagination to shift into overdrive. "I see," he said tightly. "Maybe the weather is holding her up," he said, giving himself an explanation as well as Tricia.

"You're probably right," Tricia replied. "Well, I was getting ready to lock up, but I'd be happy to stay awhile if you want to wait."

"That won't be necessary. I'll catch up with her later. It wasn't important." He turned to leave.

Tricia thought quickly. "Can I give you a lift? The weather is starting to look pretty bad."

Taj turned back in Tricia's direction and hesitated a moment. "Sure. I'd appreciate it. That's if it's not out of your way."

"No problem. I'm in no real hurry. Let me just get my coat."

By the time Taj and Tricia had left the office, the ground was blanketed with at least an inch of brilliant white snow, making walking treacherous.

"My car is around the corner," Tricia said, pulling her wool coat collar up around her neck. She took a step and slipped. Taj instinctively grabbed her around the waist to steady her.

"That was a close one," he grinned.

"I wouldn't have made a pretty sight sprawled out on the ground," she laughed back, immensely enjoying the pressure of his arm around her waist.

He gave her an appraising once over, taking in her full head of bouncy auburn curls, brown eyes and full pouty lips.

"You would make a lovely sight no matter what," he assured her simply.

"There's my car over there," Tricia pointed, her words sounding breathless to her own ears.

Behind the wheel she tried to recover her composure, but Taj's close proximity only heightened her anxiety.

"I'm over on Auburn Avenue and South Street," Taj offered as he buckled up.

She nodded knowingly as she maneuvered the sky blue Jetta into traffic.

By this time, the snow was coming down so heavily that visibility was near zero. They crawled through the streets at no more than ten miles per hour. A trip that would have normally taken ten minutes, took a half hour.

"I usually see you with a music case," Tricia commented, needing to break the long silence that hung between them. "What do you play?"

"Saxophone," he said with a hint of pride.

"Really? Are you any good?" she teased.

Taj chuckled. "Some people think so. As a matter of fact, I just got a full time gig playing with the band at Rhythms." His voice took on an empty tone. "That was one of the reasons why I stopped by the office. I wanted to tell Jewel. She was the one who suggested that I check out some of the local clubs," he added, realizing that he'd said too much. Although Tricia had seen him and Jewel together, it was never outside of the office and they always maintained a sense that his visits were business related. However, Taj sensed that Tricia knew exactly what was going on, whether Jewel wanted to believe that or not. He looked off toward the swirling snow.

"I'm sure she'll be sorry she missed you," Tricia said.

"Hmm."

"Well, I hope you'll accept congratulations from me." She smiled.

"Of course. Thanks."

Tricia swallowed. "I'd love to hear you play sometime."

"I start tomorrow night. You're welcome to stop by. Bring your boyfriend."

She flashed a tremulous smile. "I'll be by myself." She paused for effect. "I'm not seeing anyone right now."

"Sometimes that's best," he replied absently. He peered out of the snow encrusted window. "Well, this is where I get off."

Tricia pulled the car to the curb. Taj turned to her and caught a look of longing in Tricia's eyes that startled him with its intensity. Maybe he was just imagining things he reasoned. "Thanks for the ride, Tricia. I really appreciate it. Maybe I'll see you at the club." He reached for the door handle and felt Tricia's hand on his thigh.

"Wait, Taj," she said softly.

Taj looked down at her hand then upward to her eyes. Before he had a chance to respond, Tricia leaned over and kissed him full on the mouth.

"I've wanted to do that for a long time," she said breathlessly. Her eyes roved longingly over his face as she silently prayed that he would somehow feel the same way.

Taj's jaw clenched. He clasped her shoulders in his hands. "Listen, Tricia," he began gently, "I'm in love with someone, and I wouldn't want to mess that up."

"Jewel," she said in a flat voice.

He nodded. "She means a lot to me, Tricia." As the words came out, he realized the truth in them more than ever.

"We could be good for each other," she nearly pleaded. "I know we could."

Damn. What had he walked into? "Tricia please," he shook his head as he spoke, "I'm sorry, but it just couldn't work. Jewel is too important to me."

"It'll never work between you and Jewel," Tricia cried, struggling against her tears. "Else she wouldn't hide her relationship with you."

That jab hurt more than he wanted to admit. "I'm sorry Tricia," Taj said gently. "I hope that this incident won't interfere with your work. We can just put it aside and go on from here." He opened the door. "Thanks for the ride. Drive carefully." He gave her a parting smile and darted for the doorway.

Tricia sat for several moments after Taj had entered his building. She was trembling all over. She kept reliving the feel of his lips against hers. It wouldn't end here, she determined. It couldn't. She firmly believed that, given time, Taj would realize that he and Jewel would never last and that only she could love him like he deserved. If only there was a way to rush the inevitability . . .

Taj stepped into his apartment and took a shuddering, relieved breath. The last thing he had expected was a declaration of love from Tricia! He shook his head in disbelief, pulled off his coat and tossed it on the chair. What was he going to tell Jewel? He paced across the hardwood floor. *Nothing.* He wouldn't tell Jewel a thing about this. It would just make things very uncomfortable for everyone. Tricia was a sensible woman. Obviously she thought there was a clear path or else she would have never come on to him like that. He ran his fingers through his dreds, tossing them behind his ears. "I just hope I handled it right," he said out loud.

Jewel eased her BMW into the garage, then quickly unloaded her purchases and stashed them away from Dani's prying eyes. She entered the house through the door that connected the garage to the house.

"Dani! I'm home." Jewel put down her purse and hung up her coat on the brass coatrack.

Dani emerged from the living room looking dreamy-eyed and yawning. "Hi," she mumbled. "I fell asleep on the couch. The last thing I remember was Oprah introducing a woman who was acquitted of stabbing her husband by blaming it on PMS." She yawned again.

"Hmm. Heavy topic. I think I saw that one. How was your day?"

"Not bad. We had a Spanish exam, but I know I aced it."

"Don't you always? Language and every other subject just come naturally to you."

Danielle had skipped grades twice. At fifteen, she was already a senior in high school. She looked and spoke like a twenty year old. That was one reason it was so difficult for Jewel to remember that Dani was biologically still a girl. Intellectually, Dani had the mind of an adult, but emotionally she was still a child in many respects.

"I suppose," Dani shrugged dismissively. "Ma," she began.

Jewel turned toward her, a questioning smile on her lips. "Yes?"

"I just wanted to apologize about this morning. I was way out of line."

"It's all right, angel. I know it's hard sometimes." Jewel kissed Dani's cheek and stroked her hair.

"Yeah. Maybe it was PMS or something," she joked.

Jewel laughed softly. "May-*be*. Worse things have been known to happen."

"Is it all right if I spend the night at Kim's house? Today was the last day of school for the Christmas break. Her mother said it was fine with her."

"So that's what that apology was all about.

Trying to soften me up," Jewel chided playfully.

"Oh, Ma. Come on."

"Sure you can go. Do you want to eat first?"

"No. I'll have dinner over there. I think Kim's ordering pizza."

Jewel thought of her impending free evening. "In that case I think I'll go out, myself, for a while," Jewel said, thinking of an uninterrupted evening with Taj.

"Are you going to aunt Amber's house?"

"No. Believe me, I can wait to see my dear sister on Christmas and not a minute before."

They both laughed. Amber Sinclair was a bundle of nervous energy. Anytime she was in your presence for more than ten minutes you began to feel as though you'd been on a wild roller coaster ride.

"So, where are you going?" Dani asked as she walked toward the hall closet.

"Maybe I'll take in a movie, or do some Christmas shopping. This place could use some cheering up."

"Well, have fun." Dani retrieved her coat from the closet.

"Don't you need your overnight bag?" Jewel asked.

"Already packed," Dani grinned, pulling the large tapestry bag out of the closet.

Jewel shook her head in amusement. "See you tomorrow."

"Bye."

As soon as Dani had departed, Jewel dialed Taj's number and prayed that the answering machine wouldn't pick up.

"Hello?"

The simple sound of his voice traveled through her like a good brandy, warming her thoroughly.

"Taj. It's me, Jewel."

"Hey baby," he crooned. "I was hoping that you'd call."

Her heart skipped in relief. "I'm free tonight. Feel like some company?"

"I can't think of anything I'd like better," he said in a decidedly intimate voice.

Jewel felt tingles creep through her veins like a thief in the night. "I can be there in an hour."

"I'll be waiting."

Jewel took a quick shower and selected a brand-new set of lingerie that she'd ordered from a catalog. She dabbed Taj's favorite body oil, Volumpte, behind her ears, her wrists and all of the very private places that never remain private with Taj. She selected a canary yellow silk shirt and matching straight-legged pants. She accented the outfit with a wide, soft brown and gold scarf which she draped around her hips, leaving the loose ends to trail at her right side, and covered her feet in ankle length calf-skin boots.

Jewel took a final look in the full-length mirror, ran a comb through her precision haircut and dabbed her lips with coral lipstick. Satisfied, she hurried downstairs, grabbed her coat and was about to walk out of the door, just as the phone rang.

She hesitated, debating on whether or not to answer. It could be important, she concluded. She quickly crossed the gleaming wood floors and picked up the phone on the fourth ring.

"Hello," she answered in a rush.

"Sounds like I caught you at a bad time?" responded the voice that instantly unnerved her.

"Steven."

"You remember," he chuckled sarcastically. "How are you, Jewel?"

"Fine, thank you," she answered in a strained voice. She hadn't heard from her ex-husband in nearly six months. And she especially didn't want to hear from him now. "What is it, Steven? I'm in a hurry."

"Then I guess I'll get right to the point. I'll be in town next week and I want to spend some time with Dani, take her shopping, whatever she wants."

Jewel blinked back her disbelief. "You what?" she exploded. "How dare you call here as though nothing has happened and casually ask to see your daughter," she railed, completely losing the control she struggled to maintain. "Where have you been for the last six months of her life?"

"I know it's been a while, but I wanted the dust to settle first," he said in the cool patronizing tone that she despised. "Are you saying that I can't see her?" he asked calmly.

She knew that tone all too well. Steven was ready to go for the jugular. If it took wearing her down in anyway he saw fit, he'd do it to get what he wanted.

Jewel swallowed. This was the last thing she needed. Tonight she planned to tell Taj that she wanted him to meet Dani to break the ice before Christmas then ask if he'd like to share Christmas dinner with them. Now, Steven pops out of the woodwork. His reappearance in Dani's life was sure to ruin any chance that Taj and Dani would hit it off. But she couldn't, in good conscience, refuse to let Steven see his daughter. He may have been a bastard of a husband but he loved Danielle and was always good to her.

"Jewel? Are you there?"

"Yes," she said weakly. "When did you want to see her?"

"I'll be driving down to New York on Monday evening. With Christmas being next Sunday, I wanted as much time as possible."

"Will you be coming alone?" she asked cattily, unable to resist the barb.

Steven let out a hearty laugh. "Come on, Jewel, what kind of man do you think I am?"

"It's best if I don't answer that question, Steven."

His joviality quickly changed. He said in a menacing voice, "Let's not dredge up old soil. If you were half the woman you pretended to be, we wouldn't be having this conversation."

Jewel bit back a response, knowing that retaliation was futile. Steven would just dig and dig at her emotions until she was raw. She forced calm into her voice.

"I'll have to speak with Dani first and see what she says."

"I can't imagine that she wouldn't want to see me," Steven replied with his usual confidence.

"I've got to go, Steven. Where can you be reached?"

He gave her the number of the hotel he'd registered in. "Are you planning on the big, family Christmas dinner, as usual?"

"Yes."

"I hope I'm invited," he taunted.

"Goodbye, Steven."

"I'll be expecting your call Monday night." He broke the connection.

Jewel's hands were shaking when she finally replaced the receiver. What was she going to do? Burning tears of frustration threatened to overflow. She blinked them back and took deep, cleansing breaths.

Mindlessly, she made her way to the garage and headed, at a snail's pace, to Taj's apartment.

Jewel plastered a smile on her face as she stood in front of Taj's apartment door. Taking a deep breath, she rang the bell.

Seconds later the door was flung open and Taj stood before her in all of his magnificence. Immediately, her spirits lifted and her plastered smile took on real life.

He was bare from the waist up, wearing only a pair of faded gray sweatpants that did nothing to camouflage his bulging thighs. His entire upper body formed a perfect V, tapering to a board-flat stomach and narrow hips. His broad chest was clearly defined by his rigid exercise and martial arts regime. The muscles of his chest and forearms rippled like undulating waves as he reached across the threshold and captured her in his embrace.

Painfully slowly, his mouth descended and covered hers, tentatively at first, and then deepening with every beat of her heart. Her lips opened like a blooming flower, receiving the sweet nectar of his kiss.

"I'm sorry about this morning, baby," he whispered against her lips. "It's not my style to issue ultimatums." He took a step back and looked down into her upturned face without completely letting go of his hold on her.

"Maybe that was the push that I needed," Jewel said softly.

Taj searched her face, then took her hand and walked her to the couch, closing the door behind them.

"Did something happen?" he asked once they were seated. He draped his arm across her shoulders.

"I came to a decision today." She smiled wistfully. "With the help of Don Hamilton."

Taj felt his muscles tighten at the mention of Hamilton's name. "Really. Who's Don Hamilton?" he asked as if he didn't know.

"He's a new client. I thought I mentioned him to you." She shook her head. "Anyway, he's buying that abandoned property. We had lunch today, and before I knew it, I was telling him about my problems with Dani. I came to find out, he went through the same thing with his son and his second wife." Jewel looked deep into Taj's eyes. She took his hand in both of hers. "He said that I had to put my cards on the table and that soon Dani would be on her own and my life would be mine again."

She stroked his cheek and he captured her hand and held it against his lips. "I decided that I want you to meet Dani—before Christmas—and come what may, I'll deal with it."

He kissed her palm. "I guess I owe Don Hamilton a favor," he said, realizing what a fool he'd been to have been jealous of the man. At least he wouldn't have to make that confession to Jewel.

"I don't want to ever lose you, Taj."

"You won't. I promise you that." He leaned closer and lightly kissed her eyes, her cheeks, her lips, then trailed downward to her neck, causing a soft moan to break through her parted mouth. All the while his deft fingers unbuttoned the tiny white buttons of her shirt to expose the satiny skin beneath.

Taj buried his head deep between the swell of her breasts as his own breathing became one with the rapid beat of her heart. He peeled away the lacy yellow bra, slipping it beneath the full, heavy breasts causing the tender mounds to jut out before him, taunting him to take each one in turn.

The hot and cold contact of his mouth made Jewel cry out with shocking pleasure, his own deep moans of longing, blending with hers in perfect harmony.

"I've missed you, Jewel," he groaned against her breast, his warm mouth encompassing the hardened bud.

Jewel's eyes slammed shut, her head involuntarily dropped back as she clasped her fingers behind his head, urging him further.

Skillfully, almost magically, he slid her blouse

from her shoulders and down her arms, never once ceasing his assault of her heated body.

The force of his body edged her down onto the couch. Taj kneeled beside her, his dark eyes raking over her, continuing to stoke the flames of passion that raged within. Slowly, Taj removed the last remnants of her clothing until she lay bare and beautiful before him.

He stood up and loosened the tie at the waist of his pants. Jewel reached out and finished what he had begun. Her breath caught in her throat as the full power of his virility loomed before her.

Gently Taj lowered himself above her, resting the full force of his weight on his hands. "It's been too long, baby," he said softly. He lowered his head. His mouth teasingly caressed her lips. The silky strands of his hair brushed her cheek, sending tingles of electricity ripping through her.

"Taj," she cried, as the initial moment of union broke through the final barrier.

Jewel's long, slender fingers dug into his back as Taj buried himself deep within the liquid fire that bathed him, enveloped him. Together they found the perfect, age-old rhythm that held them captive within and around each other.

To Jewel, the act of being with Taj was more glorious than with any man she'd ever known. He, with every word, every breath, every movement, made her feel worthwhile, needed, and truly loved for the first time in her life.

Jewel was everything Taj had ever wished for or dreamed about. He wanted to give her more than just physical love. He wanted to give her all of himself—the best that he could be. She made him feel that he could move mountains. And with her at his side, he knew that he could.

The snow continued to swirl, buffeting all in its path, seeming to summon the forces of nature within the confines of the torrid room. Jewel and Taj merged with the heavens, building in tempo with the beat of the howling winds. Nature released an outpouring of purity that exploded between them in crystalline synchronism.

They found their way to the enclosed area that Taj had sectioned off for his bedroom. On the king-sized bed, they lay nestled in each other's embrace, quietly relishing the afterglow of their loving.

Taj tenderly brushed the damp tendrils of hair from Jewel's face. "I have some good news," he said softly into her hair.

Her eyes fluttered open and rested on his face. "What? Tell me."

"I got that job today."

Jewel sprung up and then planted herself

solidly atop of Taj. "Really? That's fabulous. Where? When?" she rushed on.

"Over at Rhythms on State Street."

"Nick Hunter's place?" she asked with renewed enthusiasm.

"The very one," he grinned.

"I love that place *and* the music," she exclaimed.

"You know Nick?"

"As a matter of fact, I do. I helped him locate that space and connected him with the designer who did the layout."

"No kiddin'. I should have mentioned your name. Maybe he would have upped the pay scale," Taj joked.

Jewel tapped him playfully on the head. "You got this job on your own, without any name dropping. Why didn't you tell me that's where you were going?"

"Well, I didn't want to get my hopes up or yours."

"When are you going to realize just how talented you are? Your music is about as close to heaven as you can get." Then she smiled wickedly. "Except for your other talents. Now that's heaven." She kissed him solidly on the lips.

"You think so, huh?" he said, grabbing her bottom and pressing her firmly against his growing arousal. "You ain't seen nothin' yet."

* * *

Tricia sat alone in her apartment, curled up on the sofa, stoically drinking a glass of wine. She couldn't seem to shake the vision of Taj out of her head. The harder she tried, the worse it became. Maybe if she just had another chance to talk with him she could make him see the light. She sighed heavily and took another sip of wine.

She sat straight up as a plan began to materialize. Maybe there was something she could do. She sprung up from the couch and dashed to her bedroom to the small section she used as an office.

Sitting behind her computer she switched it on and brought up the data base file. Quickly she scanned the files until she found the name she wanted. Steven Avery.

Taj and Jewel sat at the dining table finishing off the last of the meal they'd prepared together.

"That was delicious," Jewel announced. "If I may say so myself."

"Compliments to the *chefs,*" Taj added.

"We make a great team," she said, looking at him with loving eyes.

"I know. And it can only get better with time." Taj sat back and looked squarely at Jewel. "Now that you've been loved and fed, do you want to tell me what's on your mind?"

Jewel shook her head in disbelief. His intuitiveness never ceased to amaze her. No matter how hard she tried to camouflage her emotions, Taj saw through every barrier that she erected.

"Am I that transparent?" she asked, stalling for time.

"Not at all. But I can always sense the tension in your body even when that gorgeous smile is planted on your lips. You give off vibrations, and I happen to be very attuned to your vibes." He gave her a wink that made her laugh in spite of the seriousness of her dilemma.

"Steven called me this evening," she blurted out. She looked at Taj to gauge his reaction, but got nothing more than an arched eyebrow. "He wants to see Danielle. He'll be in town next week," she added quickly.

"Is that a problem?" Taj asked calmly.

Jewel's shoulders slumped. "Right now it is. When Steven gets Dani back under his fatherly spell, I know it will be nearly impossible for her to accept you in my life." She took a breath. "And then he had the audacity to ask if he was invited to Christmas dinner!"

"I think you're making this more complicated than it is. You made a decision. All you have to do now is follow through. Give Dani some credit, Jewel. Me, too, for that matter," he said evenly.

"You're right," she said with conviction. "And the sooner the better." She looked at him with a gleam in her eye. "Are you free for dinner tomorrow?"

"Let me just check my social calendar." He put his index finger to his temple. "It just so happens that I am totally at your disposal."

Jewel laughed. "Then dinner it is."

Jewel arrived back at her house just after sunrise. Although she knew that Dani wouldn't be back before noon, she wasn't quite ready for Dani to discover that she'd spent the night out. She felt that it was essential that she be a credible role model and exhibit a sense of discreetness about her relationships.

With Dani blooming into womanhood, it was important that she get the right messages. Jewel may not have done a great job with Steven, in Dani's eyes, but she had no intention of making the same mistakes with Taj.

Between the two of them, Taj and Jewel had decided to form a united front with Dani. It was not going to be open season on either of them.

With that notion in mind, Jewel plunged into preparing for the evening. She did a thorough cleaning of the house, which was totally unnecessary, as she always kept the modest home in immaculate condition. Some old habits are hard to break, she thought as she took a final look at her handiwork.

Next on the agenda was planning the meal. She sat down at her antique, Queen Anne desk and made a list of the necessary items she needed from the market. As Taj didn't eat red meat, she planned a sumptuous seafood menu with a crab meat, shrimp, and scallop soufflé as the main course. She wanted everything to be perfect.

It was nearly noon by the time Jewel returned from the market. Loaded down with packages, she was happy to find her daughter home. Dani hurried to the door when she heard her mother.

"Wow, Christmas dinner shopping already?" Dani asked as she helped bring in the array of bags.

"Something like that," Jewel replied.

"Hi, Mrs. Avery," Kim greeted as Dani and Jewel entered the kitchen.

"Hello, Kim," Jewel responded to the pretty teenager. "How are you?"

"Fine. My mom put us out," Kim complained. "Hope you don't mind me hangin' out over here for a while."

"Of course not. You know you're always welcome." Jewel began putting the groceries away. "As a matter of fact, why don't you stay for dinner?" Jewel asked, the beginnings of a plan germinating in her head. If Kim was around for dinner, she thought, the whole event wouldn't appear so formal and no one would be put on the spot.

"Love it," Kim responded enthusiastically.

"Just let your mother know."

Kim shrugged. "Believe me, she won't care," she said, her voice taking cynical edge. "Some guy she's dating is coming over and I know she won't want me around." The hurt was evident in Kim's voice that Jewel turned quickly toward Kim to see her looking dejectedly at her sneakers. Dani had a comforting hand on Kim's shoulders.

Jewel took a cautious step forward and tilted Kim's chin up with the tip of her finger. Kim's dark eyes glistened with unshed tears.

"Kim, sweetheart, I know your mother cares about you. Just because she has someone in her life doesn't mean she loves you any less." She intended the statement as much for Kim's benefit as for Dani's.

"It doesn't seem that way," Kim said in a shaky voice. "Whenever *he's* around she barely gives me the time of day. And he acts like I'm in the way."

"Maybe you should give them both a chance, Kim," Jewel said gently.

"For what?" Dani jumped to her friend's defense. "What kind of chance have they given her?"

"Dani!" Jewel admonished.

"Well, it's true," Dani added with a touch of vehemence.

This was not going well, Jewel realized with alarm. Instead of Kim being the support system that she had hoped for Dani, Kim's situation would only complicate her own.

"Maybe you should talk with your mother about how you feel," Jewel said gently.

Kim shrugged. "I guess."

"That's better." Jewel patted Kim's shoulder, then looked at Dani. "Dani, I need to talk with you for a minute." It was now or never, Jewel thought.

Jewel walked through the archway into the living room. Danielle followed moments later.

"What's up?"

"Sit down a minute, angel." Jewel took a deep breath. "There's someone I want you to meet," she began, measuring her words carefully.

Dani tensed. "Who?"

"His name is Taj Burrell."

Dani frowned. "Who's he?"

"Someone who's become very important to me," she said softly.

Jewel saw her daughter's face change expression from bewilderment to anger.

Dani sprung up from her seat. "Well that's just great. Sure, Ma, do what you want. It's your life."

"Danielle," Jewel started.

"I don't want another father," Dani continued.

"Danielle, no one is going to try to take your father's place."

"I don't understand," Dani's voice took on a childish tone. "I don't know why you and daddy can't work things out, Ma," she cried. "I don't want to end up like Kim." She angled her chin in the direction of the kitchen.

"I'd never let that happen, baby," Jewel assured, taking Dani's hand in her own. "I thought you knew me better than that."

Dani pressed her lips together and turned her head away.

Jewel pressed forward. "Taj will be here for dinner tonight and he's anxious to meet you. I've told him wonderful things about you."

"Where'd you meet him?" Dani asked in a flat voice.

"At my office. I helped him find an apartment."

"Mmm." She kept her gaze from Jewel. "What does he look like?"

Jewel grinned despite herself. "Why don't you be the judge of that this evening?"

Dani heaved a sigh and nodded.

"There's one more thing, Dani."

"I know, be nice."

"That too, but that's not what I meant." Jewel took a deep breath. "Your father called last night."

"Dani whirled around, her eyes lit up like two Roman candles. "He did! What did he say? Where is he?"

"He's still in Chicago, but he'll be here next week." She paused. "He wants to see you."

Dani's smile nearly broke Jewel's heart, knowing how Steven had literally abandoned Dani. Yet she still worshipped the ground he walked on.

"I can't wait," Dani gushed. "I'm gonna tell Kim." She ran out of the room before Jewel could say anything else.

All Jewel could do now was hope for the best.

Steven put the last of his clothing in his suitcase. The phone call from Tricia the previous night had put a new spin on things.

So his dear ex-wife was sleeping around with some long-haired musician who was young enough for Dani. What kind of an example was Jewel trying to set? He may not have been a lot of things, he admitted grudgingly, but he was always a decent father. The last thing he wanted for his daughter was to see a string of men running in and out of her mother's life.

It was apparent that he was going to have to step back into the picture. He'd even go so far as to sue Jewel for custody if that's what was needed. He'd do whatever he had to in order to protect Danielle.

Jewel had obviously gone over the edge after the divorce and this was her way of asserting her independence. "We'll just see about that," he said.

He snatched up his coat and his suitcase and headed for the door. He'd put a stop to this quick, fast and in a hurry.

"I spoke to Dani," Jewel said to Taj over the phone.

"And?"

"It went better than I expected. No histrionics."

Taj laughed. "Great. I told you to give your daughter some credit. What time do you want me there?"

"About five?"

"Sounds good." Then he remembered. "I have to be at the club tonight at seven."

"Hmm. That doesn't give us much time."

He thought about some options. "How about this? We have an early dinner and then you all come to the club and hear me make my debut."

Again Jewel was struck by Taj's sensitivity and smiled brightly. "Perfect! Then why don't you come over at four, help me with dinner and get acquainted. We can eat about five-thirty."

"No problem. I'll be there. And Jewel . . ."

"Yes?"

"Don't worry. I hear the anxiety in your voice. Believe me, if I can charm you, I can charm anybody."

"Gee, thanks," she laughed.

"See you later, baby." He hung up.

Jewel replaced the receiver, a contented smile framing her lips. She sighed softly. She really did love that man. She turned away from the phone and walked to the bottom of the staircase.

"Dani! Kim!"

"Yes!" they replied in unison.

"Come down, I have some errands I need for you to run."

"Listen, girls," Jewel began when they'd both arrived in the kitchen. "I need you two to go down to the mall and pick up some holiday decorations."

"Okay," Dani agreed.

"And," Jewel continued, "I have a treat for you young ladies. We're going out for a night on the town after dinner."

"Where?" they squealed in unison.

"To a club called Rhythms."

"You're taking us to a club, Mrs. Avery?" Kim asked in astonishment.

"Yes, missy. A friend of mine is playing there tonight for the first time. I want to give him some moral support."

"Who?" Dani asked, her face clouding over.

"Taj."

"He's a musician?" Dani asked, plainly surprised.

Jewel nodded.

"What does he play?" Dani asked.

"The sax."

"Oh man, sax players are so cool," Kim said.

"Well you'll both get to meet him in a few hours. He's coming for dinner."

"Mrs. Avery," Kim teased, giving her a sidelong glance.

"Don't 'Mrs. Avery,' me," Jewel tossed back with a smile. "Come on you two. I want to get this house in a festive mood. So hurry up."

After Danielle and Kim had left for the mall, Jewel took a moment to assess the situation. Although Dani was unusually quiet after the news, everything was turning out better than she'd expected. Things were going to work out just fine. She hoped.

The telephone call replayed in Tricia's mind. Calling Steven Avery was a desperate move. At the time, she'd felt compelled. Now all she felt was guilt. Even though Steven had sworn to her that he'd never reveal what she'd told him, her conscience still nagged at her. Steven had sounded furious. She wanted to talk with Taj before things got out of hand. But then again, maybe she should just leave things alone, yet something told her, she'd made a big mistake.

By the time that Kim and Dani had returned from the mall, the aroma of dinner filled the air.

"Smells good, Ma," Dani said.

"Why, thank you," Jewel answered, relieved at Dani's casual tone of voice. "Were you able to get everything?"

"Yep. We went to this really great store with all sorts of African art and stuff. I thought we could do something a little different this year."

"Like what?" Jewel asked with interest, knowing that Dani had an innate talent for creativity.

"Decorate in kente colors for Christmas. Maybe we could carry it through to Kwanzaa. It might be nice."

"Sounds fine with me. Maybe Taj could help," Jewel offered. "He celebrates Kwanzaa."

"I see. Taj seems to do everything," Dani said, her tone sarcastic.

Kim poked her in the ribs. "Chill," she said through the corner of her mouth.

Dani sucked her teeth. "Come on. Let's get busy." She snatched up the bags and marched off to the living room.

Jewel watched Dani's departure and her spirits slowly sunk.

Kim lingered behind. "Mrs. Avery?"

"Yes, Kim," Jewel sighed.

Kim looked over her shoulder to see if Dani was out of earshot. "Me and Dani were talking and, well, she's real upset about meeting your . . . friend. Even though she's trying to hide it."

Jewel pursed her lips as she noted Dani wasn't hiding it well. "Could you tell me why? I had really hoped that she was all right with this."

"She thinks things are gonna be different."

Jewel sat down on the stool at the counter. "Different how?"

"Well, like how things are between me and my mother. And"— Kim lowered her eyes— "she still wants you and her father to get back together."

Jewel sighed and patted Kim's shoulder. "Thanks, Kim. I'm sure everything will work out for the best. Go on and help Dani."

Jewel watched Kim depart, but before she had the opportunity to think about what she'd been told, the doorbell rang. Instinctively she checked the overhead clock in the kitchen. Taj was an hour early, she mused. Her pulse beat faster as she turned toward the living room.

She was on her way to the door, but Dani beat her to it. Instead of the subdued greeting that she'd expected to hear, the screams of joy from Dani caused Jewel to race into the foyer.

Steven looked over his daughter's head, as she held him in a bear hug embrace.

"Hello, Jewel," Steven said as though standing in her living room, unannounced, was the most ordinary thing in the world.

Jewel felt as if she'd been slammed against a brick wall. She took a deep breath, willing the trembling in her body to cease. She took one step forward and then another until she stood no more than a foot away.

The look of absolute adoration glowing from Dani's face was almost more than Jewel could stand.

"Steven," she said in a flat monotone, her eyes defiant and cold. "I wasn't expecting you today," she added, enunciating every syllable.

Steven's lips curled into a sheepish grin as he gave Dani a kiss on the cheek. He stepped out of her embrace and over to Jewel. Jewel's heart thudded madly.

Steven bent down and kissed her chastely on the lips. She did everything she could not to visibly cringe at the contact.

"You know me, Jewel, when the spirit hits

me, I just go with it." His grin widened. "You, on the other hand, were never so creative or impulsive," he said in a voice so low only she could hear the mocking words. "Maybe that's what our problem was."

Jewel stood stiffly before Steven wondering if Dani could feel the tension and hostility that snapped and sparked between them.

Jewel took a step back. "We're—I'm expecting a guest for dinner, Steven. I don't think this is a good time."

Dani quickly jumped into the conversation, took her father's arm and looked imploringly into his eyes. "Stay, Daddy. Please. There's plenty of food." She turned to Jewel. "Ma?" She hadn't heard from her father in six months and she wanted him to share Christmas more than anything.

Jewel swallowed hard, knowing that the minutes were ticking away. If she said no, she'd immediately be seen as the heavy. If she gave in, there was sure to be a fiasco when Taj arrived. She was trapped.

"Fine," she said finally. "Stay. But just for dinner." She turned away, halting any further discussion, and almost ran up the stairs to her bedroom.

Leaning against her closed bedroom door, she shut her eyes and tried to calm her rapid breathing. Her thoughts raced in confusion. What in the world was she going to do? And what was Steven doing here nearly three days early? This was the type of nightmare that only happened in romance novels and soap operas—not to real people!

Taj put his sax in its carrying case and reached in the closet for his jacket. He'd decided to wear all black for his debut at the club. He checked his watch. Three-fifteen. If he left now, he'd reach Jewel's house right on schedule.

All night he'd struggled again with the notion of telling Jewel about his encounter with Tricia. Again he'd decided against it. There was no need to stir up trouble.

He put on his jacket and loosened an extra button on his shirt. Feeling confident about his appearance, he picked up the small bouquet of flowers that he'd purchased for Jewel. He'd debated about getting something for Danielle but thought that it would appear that he was coming on too strong. He really wanted to make a good first impression on her. So much hinged on how she would react to him.

He took a deep breath, and grabbed his coat and his sax case. "It's show time," he said to his reflection in the hallway mirror.

Just as he opened the door, the phone rang. He didn't have time for a conversation. He'd let the machine pick it up then call in for his messages later. With a dismissive wave of his hand, he closed the door behind him.

Jewel listened to Taj's phone ring until the answering machine clicked on. She hung up. There was no point in leaving a message. It was too late now to warn him. Was there any chance of a freak earthquake? she wondered morosely.

She stood at the top of the staircase, listening to Danielle, Kim, and Steven engaged in animated conversation below. Jewel was so nervous, she nearly fell down the staircase when the doorbell chimed.

"I'll get it," Dani called out.

Before Jewel had the presence of mind to react, Dani had the door opened. Jewel suddenly felt as if everything was moving in slow motion. She stood stock still on the stairs as Taj and Dani met for the first time. She wished she could see Dani's expression.

"Hi. You must be Dani," Taj said. "You look a lot like your mother." He gave her his most engaging smile.

Dani felt her cheeks flame, and she couldn't find her voice.

"Dani," Jewel said, walking briskly toward the door. "You're letting all of the cold air into the house."

"Sorry," Dani mumbled.

Jewel walked closer to Taj and he immediately saw the panic in her hazel eyes as they darted between him, Dani, and the living room. "Come in, Taj."

"These are for you," he said softly, giving her the bouquet of flowers. He stepped across the threshold as Steven rose from the couch and turned in his direction. If he thought Dani looked like her mother, that idea was swiftly eliminated. Even at a brief glance there was no denying that this was Dani's father. Steven Avery and Danielle bore a striking resemblance from the same chiseled features, wide eyes, to the strong chin defined by an unmistakable cleft.

Taj crossed the foyer in long measured strides until he was within breathing distance of Steven. He stuck out his hand. "Taj Burrell."

"Steven Avery," came the modulated response.

If Steven expected to spark a reaction at the mention of his name, he didn't get one, Jewel noted in silent pleasure. The hard set to Steven's chin was a familiar indication that he was ticked off by that fact.

"I've heard a lot about you," Taj said evenly, looking Steven straight in the eye.

Steven's eyebrow's arched. "Is that right?" He released the hand that gripped his. "I can't say the same."

Taj shrugged nonchalantly. "It happens,"

he smiled. "I guess it all depends on the level of communication."

Steven looked like he wanted to explode. But before he could toss back a response, Taj turned his attention toward Jewel who had watched the exchange with her heart lodged firmly in her throat.

"Something smells great," Taj said, flashing Jewel a smile that said, *I have everything under control.* She released a long held breath. "Is there anything I can help you with?" Taj asked, slipping out of his coat, which Dani quickly took from him. Jewel raised her eyebrows in surprise.

She swallowed hard. "There are just a few things left to do, if you wouldn't mind."

"Of course not. Lead the way."

As soon as they were out of range, Jewel nearly burst into tears as she tried to explain her ex-husband's impromptu appearance.

"Oh, Taj, I'm so sorry. I had no idea that Steven was going to show up today. This is just a mess," she cried in a strangled voice.

Taj gently pulled her into his arms and brushed comforting kisses across her face. "It's okay, Jewel," he whispered into her hair. "We'll handle it."

"This is not the way it was supposed to happen," she continued, apparently unmoved by Taj's reassurances.

"Did he say why he's here so early?"

" 'Oh, you know how I am, Jewel,' " she mimicked in Steven's patronizing tone, " 'when the mood hits me I just go with it.' "

Taj wanted to laugh at the brilliant rendition, but fought off the impulse. He eased her away, holding her at arm's length. He looked down into her brimming eyes. "We'll get through this, babe. It's no big deal."

"Dammit, Taj!" she shouted, breaking free of his hold. "He just makes me so furious, as though he has some right to just saunter in here and commandeer my life like he's always done."

"Maybe it's about time you stood up to him, Jewel," Taj said calmly. "Instead of venting your anger out into the air, let him hear it once and for all. Otherwise, he'll always think he can do whatever he wants to you."

She went back into Taj's embrace. "You're right," she said weakly, then with more conviction. "You're absolutely right. This has got to stop. Tonight."

Taj smiled broadly. "Now that's the woman I know you can be."

Taj was the center of attention at dinner. From every direction he was bombarded with questions; from why he decided to grow dreds to his musical career. All of which he graciously answered with a touch of his usual humor and charm. Surprisingly, most of the questions came from Danielle, Jewel noticed with a sense of relief. Maybe things would work out after all, she thought.

Steven also noticed the flurry of attention that his daughter directed at Taj. How could Danielle fall for this musician's smooth talk? And what about me? he thought jealously. Although she sat next to him, all of Dani's attention seemed to be on Taj. He'd put a stop to this once and for all.

Steven loudly cleared his throat and pushed his chair away from the table. "Dinner was delicious, Jewel. I see you haven't lost your touch."

"Thank you," she answered graciously.

He leaned toward Jewel, who sat at the head of the table. "I'd like to speak with you briefly before I go," he said in a near whisper, intentionally giving the impression that they still maintained an intimate relationship. His gaze included everyone at the table. "If you'll excuse us for a moment."

Jewel glanced at Taj, who gave her a reassuring wink. She excused herself and walked into the kitchen.

Practically before she could turn around to face him, Steven began his attack. "What the hell is going on around here, Jewel?" he hissed. "You have some *boy* coming in here to see you and your daughter falling all over him as though he were some *god* and you just sit by and allow it! What's happened to you? Have you lost your mind?"

"I haven't, but apparently you've lost yours!" she tossed back with a vehemence that surprised them both. "How dare you come in here and talk to me that way. How I run my life or who I see is not up for discussion, Steven. Taj is not here for you to approve or disapprove of. No matter what you may conclude about him, he makes me happy, which is more than you were ever able to do." Her eyes narrowed into two slits. "Maybe *that* was our problem," she added nastily, giving him a taste of his own venom. "And another thing," she continued, finally feeling the power of her emotions, "this is *my* house. I pay the mortgage. The next time you decide you want to visit, I strongly suggest that you call first."

Her heart was pounding so loudly she thought it would explode. But she refused to back down. Her eyes locked firmly on his as they continued their staring contest.

Steven was so taken aback by Jewel's outburst, he was at a loss for words. Never in their seventeen years of marriage had she ever stood up to him. If he wasn't so furious and, he hated to think it, jealous, he could actually admire her new found backbone. This wasn't the same woman he left over a year ago. It was obvious that this new man in her life had had a great impact on her.

"This isn't the end of it, Jewel," he said, finally finding his voice. "I won't stand by and have you traipse one man after another in front of my daughter. What kind of example is that? If I have to file a suit to get Dani away from you in order to protect her, then I will." He knew he'd hit home when he saw the lights in her eyes suddenly go dim.

Jewel felt the floor sway beneath her feet.

"I'll prove that you're unfit, Jewel. And you know I'll do whatever I have to, to get what I want."

Jewel's fury rose again. "What is it that you want, Steven? Do you want me to always be the meek, subservient woman that you married? Do you want me to never have love again? Do you want to make sure that no one else ever cares about me? Are you that selfish, Steven? You don't want me, but you don't want anyone else to have me. Fine. If it's a fight you want, then it's a fight you're going to get. I'm not backing down from you, Steven." She spun away from him, the tears of anger ready to overflow. But she wouldn't give him the satisfaction of seeing her cry. She took a deep breath, and pushed open the kitchen door.

"This isn't over, Jewel," he tossed at her back. "Not by a long shot. You better decide what it is you want; that man or your daughter. Or else I'll be happy to make the choice for you."

Jewel's back stiffened. She pushed through the door and back into the dining room, relieved to see that only Taj remained at the table.

Taj immediately rose when he saw her enter. Although she wore a smile, he knew it was empty. He could feel the pent up tension vibrating around her body, ready to explode.

"Are you all right?" he asked softly.

She nodded. "We'll talk later. Where are the girls?"

"They went upstairs to find something to wear for tonight."

Steven came through the swinging door. They both turned in his direction.

"I guess I'll be going." He stuck out his hand. "It was a pleasure to meet you, Taj. Good luck with your musical career."

Jewel felt nauseous.

"Thank you."

He inclined his head in Jewel's direction. "Jewel, I'll be in touch. Tell Dani I'll pick her up tomorrow around one o'clock."

Taj put his arm protectively around Jewel's shoulder as they watched Steven put on his coat and leave.

Jewel nearly collapsed when the door closed behind Steven. Taj ushered her over to a chair, while taking glances over his shoulder toward the staircase. The last thing Danielle needed to see was her mother falling apart.

He stroked her face as the tears rolled unchecked down her cheeks. "I didn't want to eavesdrop, so tell me what happened? What did he say to you?"

Jewel sniffed back her tears, her body trembling. "He threatened to take Dani away if I didn't get you out of my life."

"Jewel, listen to me," Taj said gently, brushing away her tears with his thumbs, "I can't let you make a decision like that. I love you. You know that. But I'd never be so selfish as to jeopardize your relationship with your daughter for my sake."

She looked lovingly into his eyes. "I can't back down. You taught me that. This is too important, Taj. If I let Steven threaten me every time he doesn't like something, I'll never have any peace."

"You know I'm behind you a hundred percent, no matter what you decide to do."

Jewel nodded sadly then brightened. "Well, it seems as though Danielle liked you."

Taj smiled. "She's a brilliant girl." He knew that Dani had lavished him with attention, but as dinner progressed her interest became genuine, not flamed by some teenage infatuation. He really believed that they had hit it off.

"I've made up my mind, Taj. If it's a fight Steven wants, then he's got it." She stood up and wiped her eyes. "Now, let's get ready to get out of here before you're late for your opening night." She walked over to the bottom of the staircase. "Dani! Kim! Hurry up or we'll be late. I want to be out of here in the next fifteen minutes."

Jewel turned away to see Taj smiling broadly at her.

"What?" she asked suspiciously.

Taj walked right up to her. "You're an amazing woman, Jewel Avery." He lowered his head until his lips brushed hers. "I'm happy that you're mine." His mouth covered hers, tempting her lips open with the force of his tongue. His hands slid up and down her back, the strong fingers kneading out the knots of tension and replacing them with a tingling warmth. She slid her arms around his neck, pulling him closer to her, their bodies melting into one. For those brief moments that they clung to each other, nothing else mattered.

"So, how did you like the show?" Jewel asked, as she stood at the door to Dani's bedroom.

"It was great," she reluctantly admitted. "I

didn't even realize that I liked jazz," she grinned. She sat on her bed and looked up at her mother. "Ma?"

"What baby?" Jewel stepped into the room and sat on the edge of the bed.

"You really like him?"

Jewel nodded.

"Well, Taj is all right. I mean, I didn't intend to like him, but I do. He's real. When we were talking at the dinner table he really listened to the things I was saying. He didn't treat me like a kid, but a real person. Even when I tried to trip him up with a bunch of hip hop talk, he was right there with me understanding every thing I said. Even you don't understand half the things I say sometimes." She looked up at her mother with a *you're hopeless* expression. "He just might do you some good," she grinned. She sighed and studied her entwined fingers. "It's just that," she hesitated, "I don't want to neglect Daddy. He's still my daddy." She looked up at her mother and twisted her lips in concentration. "But I guess the most important thing is that *you're* happy."

Jewel moved closer to Danielle. "The important thing is that we're *both* happy. Taj is a decent man. He cares a great deal about me and it's important to me that you like him, too."

"If I ask you a question, would you tell me the truth?" Dani asked.

"Sure."

"Suppose I didn't like Taj. Would you have kept on seeing him?"

Jewel breathed deeply. "That's a question I've been wrestling with for the past three months. I finally came to terms with it yesterday. If you were really dead set against him, and had legitimate reasons, I wouldn't keep seeing him. But, I just prayed that you were really growing up and would see what a good man he is."

Danielle smiled at her mother's glow as she spoke about Taj. She leaned back on her elbows and eyed her mother skeptically. "How old is Taj?"

"None of your business, young lady," Jewel teased, tweaking Dani on the nose.

"I know he's younger than you, Ma. Come on, tell me. This could be my big break for television. Older woman dating younger man. Daughter tells all, today on *Oprah!*"

"Danielle Nichole Avery! Don't even think about it."

Danielle fell back on her bed in a fit of laughter. "I wonder if they'll pay airfare for friends of the guests?"

Jewel shook her head. "You're impossible. Good night." She gave Dani a kiss on the cheek. "And don't forget, your father is planning on picking you up at one o'clock tomorrow."

"I'll be ready. Kim wants me to go with her downtown in the morning. But we'll be back in time."

"Where is Kim?"

"In the bathroom taking a shower."

"All right. See you in the morning." Jewel closed the door and walked slowly to her room. Taj had been right when he said to give Dani a little credit. She had certainly underestimated her daughter. All things considered, what could have been a fiasco turned out to be a wonderful evening. She was definitely looking forward to Christmas and sharing it with her family and the man she loved.

As soon as she reached her bedroom, she went for the phone and dialed Taj's number. He answered on the third ring.

"Hello?"

"You were wonderful tonight. On stage and off," Jewel said.

"I'm glad you approve," he chuckled. "Listen, it's still early," he coaxed in his most persuasive voice, "why don't you come over?"

She ran the possibility over in her head. The office was closed until after the holidays. Plus, she had no pressing engagements for the next day. Finishing off the night with Taj would be the perfect ending to an almost perfect evening.

"I can't stay long," she hedged.

"I know. It's no problem. But I'd still love to spend some quiet time with you. To celebrate."

"Well, it's eleven-thirty. I can be there by midnight. Kim is here to keep Dani company."

"So I'll see you shortly?"

"I'm on my way."

Jewel went back to Danielle's room and told her that she was going out with Taj for a while. The girls were more than happy to have the house to themselves and were already making plans to stay up all night watching videos before Jewel stepped out of the room.

Steven sat in his hotel suite, silently fuming over the events of the evening. He still couldn't get over the change in Jewel. And to think that she found a younger man to replace him was almost more than he could tolerate. He had to find a way to put a stop to this once and for all. His pride was at stake. He had prided himself on his playboy persona and for others to see Jewel with the likes of that musician, even though they were no longer married, would make Swiss cheese out of his reputation. Besides, Danielle liked him just a little too much.

Well, he'd have his chance with his daughter tomorrow. Jewel may have changed in some respects, but he knew that Danielle was the most important person in her life. If he could convince Dani that her mother was making the wrong decision, his battle would be won without a fight. His daughter adored him and he was confident that she still believed every word he said. He sighed. He didn't relish having to resort to suing for custody although he knew he could make a winning case. However, a victory was not what he really wanted. While he loved and missed Dani, having full custody would put a serious crimp in his own life. Yet he was sure he wouldn't have to go that route. Not after talking with Danielle.

"You handled Steven beautifully," Jewel said, wrapping her arms tightly around Taj's bare waist.

"You didn't do too badly yourself," he returned. "I'm proud of you." He kissed the tip of her nose. "Do you really think Steven is serious about his threat to sue for custody?"

"I wouldn't underestimate him. It may have been a scare tactic, but when Steven is pushed, especially when his ego is at stake, he's liable to do anything."

She released him and turned away. Taj clasped her shoulder and spun her around to face him.

"It's your call, Jewel. Whatever you decide, I'm behind you."

She smiled tightly. "And I love you for it. But I don't want to think or talk about Steven. I'm just so happy that you and Dani hit it off. She really surprised me. I think she surprised herself."

"Dani is really a together young lady. You've done a great job with her, Jewel."

She smiled at the compliment.

"I promised her that she and Kim could come down to the club on Sunday for brunch and hear the band rehearse. I hope that's okay."

Jewel smiled in amazement. "You two really *did* hit it off."

Taj shrugged, the beginnings of a smile tilting his lips. He winked at her. "I told you I was a charmer."

"We'll see about that. The next hurdle is the rest of family—particularly my mother."

"Oooh, the dreaded mother-in-law," he said, twisting his face into a feigned grimace.

They both laughed at the image.

"She's not that bad," Jewel admitted. "Just set in her ways."

"Well," he brushed her lips with his, "if she produced something as special as you, she can't be all bad."

His warm hazel eyes gently caressed her face, telegraphing the depth of emotion that beat inside of him. Each and every day he realized how much Jewel meant to him, how much he needed her.

Jewel gave him something that no woman had ever been able to give him, a sense of being needed. She filled a void that had been a part of his everyday existence. Before meeting her he'd only lived for his music and the moment. Now, he had really begun to think about the future and a family—permanency. Jewel had become his anchor. Without her, he knew he would be adrift again. And although he'd projected the gallant image, he really couldn't imagine what he would do if she chose to let him go.

He pulled her tightly against him, needing to feel her nearness and force away the shadow of foreboding that he'd struggled to keep at bay. Unceremoniously, he picked her up, cradled her against him and carried her to his bed.

When her body arched and trembled in fulfillment and the last shuddering pitch sprang from his body, he knew that together they could conquer anything.

Jewel sighed and snuggled closer to Taj's warm body. Absolutely perfect, she thought. Maybe one day soon they wouldn't have to settle for stolen moments, but could wake up in each other's arms every morning. They hadn't talked about marriage, specifically, but she knew that she wasn't quite liberated enough to have a live-in relationship. With the lifestyle that Taj was used to living, that may be all that he expected or wanted. It was something that they would have to discuss at some point.

"It's almost two a.m.," he whispered into her tousled hair.

"I know," she replied with a hint of regret filtering through her voice. "I should be getting home."

"I'll turn on the shower for you."

"Are you going to join me?" she asked, turning to him with a wicked gleam in her eyes.

"I guess you don't intend to leave anytime soon," he said in a low voice that vibrated through her veins.

"I wish I didn't have to."

"One day, you won't." He kissed her slowly, stirring the embers that still glowed hot between them. "I promise you that. But until then," he patted her bottom and got up, "it's off to the showers with you."

He popped up out of bed and strode across the hardwood floor, giving Jewel an ample view of what she was leaving behind.

She pulled the sheet up to her chin and sunk deeper into the fluffy pillow. Did he really mean what he said? she wondered. And what exactly did he mean?

Moments later she heard the rush of water and Taj's deep voice humming a tune over the rushing water. She pulled herself into a sitting position, just as the phone rang.

"Taj! Telephone!" she called, but he couldn't hear her. She'd never answered his phone before and she wouldn't start now although she couldn't help but wonder who would be calling at this hour?

On the fourth ring the machine picked up.

"Hi, Taj. It's me, Tricia." Jewel sat as if frozen as the all too familiar voice continued. "I know I shouldn't be calling you, but I just wanted to say that I didn't mean for anything to happen between us yesterday. It just did. I guess it was the only way I could show you how much I cared." Jewel's head began to pound. "I feel foolish. I know I can't face Jewel, not after what I've done. I'm sending in my letter of resignation. There's no way that I can continue to work with Jewel, see the two of you together, and the both of us knowing how I feel. Please take care and I hope that when you think of me, it will be kindly."

Jewel felt as if she were going to faint. *Taj and Tricia. Yesterday. It just happened* . . . What did she mean? Suddenly she didn't want to hear Taj's explanation. She didn't have the strength to stand there and watch him lie, just like Steven had always lied. Like a robot, she found her clothes that were scattered around the room, dressed and was out of the door by the time Taj returned.

She felt as if someone had her by the throat. Jewel struggled for air as she made her way to her car. Behind the wheel she momentarily squeezed her eyes shut and forced herself to calm down long enough to start the engine and get the car onto the darkened streets.

How long had it been going on? her mind screamed in agony. Maybe Tricia was really what Taj needed. Her own life was so complicated. Tricia was young, attractive, single, and didn't have the responsibility of a child.

Her throat constricted. She shook her head and wiped away the tears with the back of her hand. How could she not have known? The question tumbled around in her head clashing viciously against the realities. Taj seemed so sincere. He showed such an interest in Danielle. "He told me he wanted to be a part of my life," she shouted to herself. "The way he made love to me . . . Oh God." The tears streamed down her cheeks unchecked.

She took a shuddering breath. Maybe all the months of secrecy had been too much for him and he just never admitted it, and he turned to Tricia. Or worse, maybe this was just the way Taj was.

Even with all of Steven's infidelities, she had never felt so betrayed as she did now. She thought Tricia was her friend. She thought that Taj loved her totally. How wrong she'd been. And to think that she was willing to do battle with Steven in defense of her relationship with Taj, and all the while he was . . .

A sense of hopelessness settled over her like a blanket as she pulled up in front of her house. All of her dreams seemed to melt away like the snow that ran in puddles on the ground.

Taj returned to the bedroom with all the intentions of fulfilling Jewel's earlier request to join her in the shower. The teasing smile on his face dissolved by degrees when he returned to the bedroom alcove.

"Jewel?" He quickly scanned the expanse of the loft. He walked into the enclosed kitchen sure to find her busying herself with something. Nothing.

"What the . . . ?" He ran his hands across his face in frustration. "Why would she leave just like that?" He expelled a breath. It was too late to call her house at that hour. He'd wait until morning—bright and early—and he truly hoped she had something to tell him that would explain her abrupt departure. Confused and annoyed, he stomped back to the bathroom and turned off the steaming shower.

It wasn't until he stretched out on the bed and saw the flashing light of the answering machine that the pieces began to fit together.

By the time that Jewel walked through her door, stripped out of her clothes, and scrubbed her body free of all traces of Taj, her hurt at his betrayal had transformed itself into anger.

She'd been a fool. She'd been taken in by his sweet words and attention. She'd been so starved for affection after her divorce that she was easy prey.

She sat down in front of her vanity and stared at her reflection, angry at herself for being so naive. At her age, she should have known better, been more aware. But what did she know? she thought miserably, some of the self-condemnation ebbing. Steven was the first man she'd ever been with. After the divorce there had been brief, platonic dinners with business associates, but she'd been wary of any relationships because of Danielle. Until Taj. Her throat tightened.

Slowly she rose, suddenly bone weary. She crossed the room, switched off the ringer on her phone and stretched out on top of the bed, not even bothering to turn down the quilt. For several moments she just stared sightlessly up at the ceiling. She flung her arm across her eyes, but it didn't stem the tears from trickling down her cheeks.

For hours she drifted in and out of sleep with images of Taj and Tricia playing havoc with her head. Realizing that sleep was not hers to have, she got up when Danielle's and Kim's laughter drifted to her room. Then reality struck another blow. What would she tell Danielle?

"Ma!" Dani called from downstairs. "Telephone!"

Jewel's heart thumped. It was Taj. She just knew it. He'd try to explain and she didn't want to hear it. But then again, she did.

She walked to her bedroom door and opened it. "Thanks, hon." She retraced her steps and for several seconds she stood staring at the phone. She let out a shuddering breath and snatched up the receiver, ready to administer the verbal lashing that had cemented itself on her tongue.

"Yes," she snapped.

"That's a fine way to greet your mother," Nora Sinclair replied.

Jewel's shoulders slumped and she sat down on the edge of her bed. A flash of disappointment swept through her. She rested her head on the palm of her hand.

"Mom, I'm sorry. I was just getting out of the shower," she lied easily. "How are you?"

"Wonderful. I was just calling to find out if you needed me to do anything for Christmas dinner."

"I can't think of anything," she said in a distant voice. Christmas was the last thing she had on her mind at the moment.

"Are you all right, Jewel? You don't sound like yourself."

"I'm fine," she answered almost too quickly, forcing cheer into her voice. "Maybe a little tired, but I'm fine."

Nora could easily detect the false note of gaiety in her daughter's voice. Jewel never believed that she understood her, but Nora knew her daughters better than they knew themselves, especially Jewel. Maybe this wasn't a good time to share her news. Hopefully Jewel would be in a better mood on Christmas.

"Well dear, if there's anything you need, just call me. I know that no-cookin' sister of yours won't be any help."

Jewel chuckled. Her sister Amber's ineptness in the kitchen was the family joke, although her mother never thought it was very funny. "Ma, be nice."

"No harm intended, but that Amber doesn't have a drop of domesticity in her. No wonder she can't keep a man for a hot minute. She probably starves them to death." Nora laughed lightly.

"Anyway, sweetheart, you take care. You're

probably working too hard. Tell that granddaughter of mine to give you a hand. You know how lazy teenagers can be if you're not firm."

"Yes, mother, I know," Jewel said in a singsong voice.

"Ugh, there's that tone that I hate. I'm hanging up. See you next week, sweetie. And Jewel?"

"Yes?"

"This too shall pass," Nora said gently.

Startled, Jewel paused before speaking. "Thanks. Bye, Mom."

After Nora had hung up the phone, she remembered that she didn't tell Jewel to set an extra place. Oh well, the surprise would do her good.

He didn't even bother to call, Jewel fumed. He probably didn't have any explanation. That was just fine! The hell with him. She wasn't interested in any of his lame excuses anyway. If and when he did call, she would be unavailable. Furious with herself for feeling that momentary sensation of disappointment, and furious at Taj for creating the problem, she stomped out of her room, slamming the door in the process.

She entered the kitchen to find Dani and Kim at the table huddled over enormous bowls of cereal.

"Hey, Ma," Dani greeted with her mouth full.

"Hey, baby. Morning, Kim." She tried to smile but it felt more like a grimace. Thankfully, neither girl seemed to notice.

"How was your date with Taj?" Danielle asked.

Jewel bit down on her lip and turned toward the cupboard. She put the kettle on to boil. "Fine," she said tightly.

Dani and Kim gave each other a quick, "wonder what happened" look.

"If he should call, I'm not in," Jewel said in a tone that left no room for discussion.

Dani's eyes widened in surprise, but she knew her mother well enough to know not to pry.

Jewel pulled open the cupboard door and in an act of defiance she snatched up the jar of coffee, scooped up a heaping teaspoon and dumped it into her cup. Somehow she felt mildly satisfied.

"Ma, is it okay if I go to Kim's house for a while before Daddy comes?"

Damn. She'd forgotten all about Steven. He was the next to last person she wanted to see.

In that same short, snapping tone she replied. "Go ahead. Just be sure to be home in plenty of time. I may go out and won't be here to let your father in."

The girls got up from the table and put their empty bowls in the dishwasher. Dani eased up next to her mother. "Are you all right, Ma?" she asked gently.

Her daughter's concern nearly did her in. She felt the tears that rested just beneath the surface sting her eyes with warning. She swallowed and blinked quickly. "Sure," she answered in a steady voice that surprised her. "You go ahead."

Dani gave her mother a last questioning look, then kissed her cheek. "Um, maybe this isn't a good time to ask, but is it still okay for me and Kim to go to the club tomorrow? If not," she added quickly, "it's no problem."

She'd forgotten that, too. She couldn't very well say no. But of course she could. Dani didn't need to be around him anyway, having one philanderer in her young life was enough. But then again, she really wasn't prepared to explain her sudden change of attitude toward Taj. Denying Dani, would only draw attention to a problem that she wasn't ready to handle. She sighed.

"Sure you can go. But don't make it a habit. Understood?"

Dani nodded. "Thanks, Ma. See you later." Dani dashed out.

"Don't forget your keys," Jewel called. She

looked up at the kitchen clock. Nine-fifteen. She had absolutely nothing to do today, except think about things she didn't want to think about. The kettle began to whistle in concert with the ringing phone. She felt the hot flush of nerves envelop her. She stood in front of the kitchen phone staring at it as though it were a foreign object. The phone rang for the fourth time and the answering machine, connected to her bedroom phone, clicked on. She ran up the stairs to her room.

"Please leave a message after the tone."

"Jewel, if you're there, please pick up."

Jewel listened to the voice that was still like a song in her heart. She trembled with hurt and anger. But she couldn't—wouldn't pick up the phone, even as the sound of his voice seemed to magically erase the stream of accusations and condemnations that she'd planned. She wasn't willing, emotionally, to allow herself to fall victim to his words of explanation.

He waited several seconds, willing her to pick up the phone. "Please, Jewel, call me."

The pleading sincerity of his voice almost convinced her, but she held her ground.

"We have to talk, Jewel. It's important. I can explain everything. Call me."

"Explain!" she yelled as if he could hear her. "What is there to explain?"

He called three more times within the next two hours, sounding more urgent with each call. Jewel couldn't bear to hear anymore and she certainly didn't want to be home when Steven arrived. What she wanted was to turn back the clock before everything got so ugly. But that was impossible. What she could do was get in her car and drive as far away as possible. At least for a while.

She erased the telltale messages from the machine, put on an old sweatsuit and sneakers, got her coat and went out.

Taj's mood shifted between misery and outrage. If he'd only followed his instincts and told Jewel what had happened with Tricia, none of this would have happened. He could kick himself for being so stupid! Now Jewel thought the worst. He couldn't really blame her. If he'd heard a similar message he would have undoubtedly jumped to conclusions. But at least he would have given her the opportunity to explain. That's what infuriated him the most, the fact that Jewel had so little confidence in him—in their relationship—that she would think he was capable of cheating on her.

He sat down heavily on the couch. Maybe the relationship wasn't all he thought it was. Maybe he'd just wanted it so badly he couldn't see it for what it was. Talk about love being blind.

Well, he wasn't going to run behind her like some lovesick puppy. If she wanted to be stubborn, so could he. He hadn't done anything wrong.

He sprung up from the couch, grabbed his sax case and coat. He needed to get her off of his mind and the only way he knew how was through his music. He'd go over to the club for a while and warm up for the early dinner crowd.

Steven picked up Danielle promptly at one o'clock.

"So, what would you like to do today, sweetheart?" Steven asked as they pulled out of the driveway.

"I could really use some new clothes," she said coyly.

Steven grinned. "Is that right? So I guess it's the mall, then."

"Sounds good to me."

"I bet it does." Steven drove in the direction of downtown New Haven. He cleared his throat. "So what do you think about your mother's new friend?"

Dani shifted uncomfortably in her seat. Her shoulders lifted then dropped. She kept her eyes glued to her knees. "He's nice."

"Does your mother really like him?"

Dani thought about her mother's earlier behavior. Based on that she really didn't know anymore. But no one gets that upset over somebody if they don't really care, she decided. "I guess."

Steven pursed his lips. "I've seen his type before, and believe me, he's nothing but trouble."

Dani turned her head to look at her father. Steven kept his eyes on the road.

"I can't understand what your mother could possibly see in him. He's young enough to be your older brother, for Chrissake," he added, his injured ego inciting him. "He's the type of guy that will come and go. You know musicians. And if your mother's hooked on that type then who knows how many men she'll be involved with. I don't want you in that kind of environment. Your mother is obviously too blind to see what's going on. If I have to," he paused for breath, "I'll take you out of there and bring you to Chicago."

"What?" For the first time Dani thought about her situation. Her mother had done everything possible to make Dani happy and all she did was complain about a father who had totally disappeared out of her life for the past six months. While she missed her father desperately, she would not have him cast judgment on her mother.

"Mom is happy for the first time in I don't know how long and she deserves it. I like seeing her happy." she said clearly. "Taj is not that kind of man. Not at all. You haven't been around. You haven't even called and suddenly you want me to go live with you? You don't have a clue, Dad."

"Dani, honey," he said in his most cajoling tone, "I just want what's best for you—to protect you."

She looked at him with new eyes. "Did you want what was best for me when you had all of those other women in your life?"

The question was so unexpected, he nearly lost control of the car. "Dani, what are you talking about?"

"You think I didn't hear the arguments, or hear Ma crying to Aunt Amber on the phone?" She swallowed hard and tried to control the trembling that had taken over her body. "I wanted to believe that it was Ma's fault. I blamed her when you left because I didn't want to believe those things about you. But you know, no matter how horrible I was to my mother she never said an ugly thing about you! Ever."

Steven had never felt so small as he did at that moment. He'd always wanted his daughter to see him as a knight in shining armor. Even though she had known the real him, she had loved him anyway. And Jewel had never allowed her own pain to cloud Dani's opinion of him. How wrong he'd been.

"I'm—sorry Dani. For everything," he said humbly.

Dani swallowed down the knot in her throat and sniffed back her tears. Now that she had finally gotten the words out, she realized that the person she was angry with for so long was not her mother, but her father. She'd only lashed out at the person who was available. She sucked on her bottom lip and turned to face the window. "Forget it," she said in a strained voice.

"I can't do that. It's about time I admit that I was wrong. I was wrong, Dani. I allowed your mother to take the blame for everything, just so that I could keep up a good front with you." He blew out a heavy breath. "I never allowed myself the opportunity to appreciate what kind of woman your mother really is. You're right, your mother deserves to be happy. I'm sorry I'm not the one to do it."

Dani's lip trembled as she struggled not to cry. "Can you take me home, please?" she asked in a tiny voice.

Steven pulled the car to the curb and unfastened his seatbelt. He reached over the stick shift and gathered Dani, gently into his arms. "I'm sorry, baby," he said softly into her hair, stroking her back as he spoke.

Dani nodded feebly against his chest, then eased herself away. "Can we go now?"

"Are you sure?"

"Yes."

Steven turned the car around. They made the return trip in silence. When they pulled to a stop in front of the door, Steven turned to Danielle. "Listen to me a minute. Okay? I might have really blown everything between us. But I hope that, in time, you'll find a way to forgive me, Dani. I wouldn't ever do anything to intentionally hurt you. You know that. I've made a lot of mistakes, maybe sometime soon you'll give me a second chance."

Dani turned shimmering eyes on her father. "I know things can't be the way they were," she said sadly, giving him a crooked smile, "but maybe they can just be different."

He returned her smile and gently stroked her hair. "Deal," he agreed softly.

"You still owe me a shopping trip," she added with a wavering grin.

"Call in your I.O.U. whenever you're ready."

"Will I see you before you leave?"

"Of course. Do you think it would be all right if I stopped by on Christmas? I think I owe your mother a big gift and a big apology."

"You'd better ask Ma."

"Put in a good word for me."

She smiled. "I will." She leaned over and

kissed his cheek then turned to open the car door.

"I'll call you during the week."

"Okay," she said, shutting the door behind her. She stood on the curb and waved as Steven drove away and quietly realized that she had grown up quite a bit.

"Taj," Nick greeted, walking up to the bottom of the stage. "I'm glad you're here. I have a proposition for you."

Taj put down his sax and hopped down off of the stage. "Hey, Nick" he stuck out his hand for Nick to shake. "I didn't expect to see you until tomorrow night. What's up?"

Nick put his arm around Taj's shoulder. "Come on in my office so we can talk in private."

Once they were inside, Nick wasted no time in getting to the point.

"There are some people in New York that I want you to meet," he began, taking a seat on the edge of his desk. I told you that I'd been thinking about getting a group together to cut a record deal."

Taj nodded and took a seat opposite Nick's desk. He crossed his left ankle over his right knee. His adrenaline began a slow, steady build up.

"A couple of guys are interested in hearing

what I've got. They offered me studio time to cut a demo tape." He paused for effect. "And I want you in on it."

A slow smile eased across Taj's face, even as he tried to contain his growing excitement. "You don't waste any time," he chuckled, shaking his head.

"There's no time to waste. So what do you say?"

"I say, if you want me, I'm in," Taj said without hesitation.

"Now, when I said there's no time to waste, I meant that. We have to be in New York by tomorrow night."

Taj's eyes widened in surprise. "Tomorrow?"

"Is that a problem?"

He thought about his unresolved situation with Jewel. Leaving now would only widen the bridge between them. But if he didn't go, he may ruin a chance of a lifetime. "No. No problem. I just didn't think you meant immediately."

"I promise to have you back before Christmas. How's that?"

Christmas. He didn't even want to think about it. "Sounds fine."

"Great. That's what I was hoping you'd say." Nick hopped down from the desk, smiling broadly. He clasped Taj's hand in both of his. "I have a good feeling about this," he said, his dark brown eyes sparkling with excitement that was barely contained. "It's what I've been dreaming about."

So have I, Taj thought. I had only hoped that I'd have someone to share that dream with.

Jewel drove for hours, stopping occasionally at the boutiques along the shopping district to pick up additional gifts for her family to put under the tree. Valiantly, she'd tried to push thoughts of Taj to the back of her mind, but images of him nipped at her as powerfully as the biting December wind.

By the time she began the long drive back home, a light snow had begun to fall. All around her couples huddled together, twinkling lights glistened against the darkening skies, music could be heard in concert with the gay voices of the holiday crowds. All painful reminders of how alone she felt.

The shock of what had transpired between Taj and Tricia had yet to wear off. She still vacillated between anger and impending tears. *This too shall pass,* she kept reminding herself, playing her mother's favorite phrase in her head like a mantra. But when? she asked of her reflection in the rearview mirror. When?

Entering the house Jewel was surprised to find that Dani had already returned and was stretched out on her favorite spot on the couch, fast asleep. Then her antennae went up. She quickly scanned the living room as she crossed the foyer and deposited her bundles then took a quick peek in the kitchen. No sign of Steven. Thank heaven.

She walked over to the couch and lightly tapped Dani's shoulder. "Hi, hon," she said softly.

Dani's eyes fluttered open. She gave a sleepy smile.

"How was your day?" Jewel took off her coat, hung it on the rack and stepped out of her boots. "I didn't expect you home so early." She plopped down on the love seat facing Danielle.

Dani pulled herself up into a sitting position. "I've been home for a while."

Jewel's brow creased. "That doesn't sound like you. You can shop for hours. I assume that's what you'd planned."

Dani cleared her throat. "We didn't go shopping."

"So what did you do?"

"We talked."

Jewel leaned back, angling her head speculatively. "Do you want to tell me about it?"

"Let's just say we got a lot of things straight." She looked away and then let her eyes rest on her mother. "I made a big decision today."

Jewel felt her pulse quicken. *Please don't let her leave me,* she thought frantically, Steven's threat reverberating in her head. "What decision was that?"

"That I have to stop pretending that I don't know what really went on before Daddy moved out. That I had to decide if I was going to be a grown up and face it, or stay a little girl and believe in fairy tales."

"Dani . . . I—" Jewel leaned forward, her throat burned with the tears that she held in check. Danielle got up and squeezed next to her mother on the love seat. Jewel wrapped her arm around her, hugging her fiercely. "You knew?"

Dani nodded. "I didn't want to believe it."

"What—what made you change your mind?"

"When I was faced with the choice of having to decide if I would defend you, or listen to Daddy."

Jewel squeezed her eyes shut as joy washed over her. "Thank you," she whispered.

"Dad and I got a lot of things aired out. He finally admitted how wrong he had been. He also said he never really appreciated you." She looked up into her mother's face. "And that you deserved to be happy. He just wasn't the one to do it."

Jewel blinked back her surprise. "Your father, Steven Avery, actually said that?"

Dani smiled. "Yep."

"Will wonders never cease?"

"He asked me to put in a good word for

him. He wants to stop by on Christmas. Would that be all right?"

Jewel instantly thought about Taj. "How could I say no?" she answered.

Dani hesitated a moment. "What about Taj?"

Jewel got up. "What about him?"

"Is he going to be here?"

"I really don't know," Jewel answered tightly, turning away.

Danielle watched her mother's reaction and knew that something was definitely wrong. If her mother didn't tell her, maybe she'd find out for herself when she went to the club. It seemed like the adults were having a hard time communicating.

After his last set at the club, Taj returned to his apartment, charged with the excitement of anticipation. A budding new career loomed on the horizon. All of his years of struggling to perfect his craft may finally pay off.

He tossed his coat on the chair and followed behind it, kicked off his boots and stretched out his long legs in front of him. Automatically he looked at the answering machine that sat on the small table by the couch. No message.

He heaved a sigh, and was tempted to call Jewel again. But, he reasoned, it was apparent that she had no intention of returning his numerous calls.

It continued to irk him that Jewel thought so little of him. He'd never been the type of man who ran around. If anything, he was the complete opposite. He'd spent most of his adult life trying to carve a niche for himself in the music world. His social life had taken a back seat as a result. Sure, there'd been women. Occasionally, but never anything serious. He'd never met anyone who could compete with his first love: his music. Until Jewel. She'd changed him. She gave him reason to want to plant roots, to have a family. All of the things he hadn't had since he was ten years old and woke up to find that his mother had left him alone, in a cold, shabby apartment to fend for himself. Neighbors had found him wandering in the street and had contacted the authorities.

Sure he'd told Nick that his mother couldn't afford lessons. It was just a story that he'd brainwashed himself to believe over the years, as he was shuttled from one foster home to another. His mother's desertion had made him feel unworthy and he carried that burden with him throughout his life. The only stable thing he'd had was the beat-up saxophone that he'd found in an alley. It had comforted him when he felt alone in the world. It was his constant companion. But there was still that great big hole in his soul that all of the music in the world couldn't fill. Until Jewel became a part of his life.

He stood up. He'd gotten over other hurts and disappointment. He'd get over this too, he tried to convince himself. In time.

Jewel lay in bed and stared up at the ceiling. So many things had happened in the past few days. Her mind was reeling. It was at times like this that she would reach out to call Taj and share her thoughts. He would ease her troubles away with his earthy wisdom and genuine concern.

It was remarkable, she thought, that a man with such a troubling beginning could have turned out to be so compassionate to others and so giving of himself. She expelled a shuddering breath and closed her eyes. That's probably what attracted Tricia, she thought miserably.

Jewel knew that at some point she would have to confront him, let him know how much he'd hurt her. But she dreaded the moment. But maybe she should give him more credit, as she should have with Dani.

You've got to put your cards on the table. The words rang so clearly in her head that she flinched in surprise.

"Yes, I will," she said out loud. "How soon, is the question."

"Ma! Kim and I are leaving now," Dani called out from the bottom of the staircase.

Jewel came to the top of the landing, still dressed in her nightgown. She'd debated all night whether or not to accompany Dani and Kim to the club, but finally decided that the club was not the place for a personal discussion. And she didn't want to be a distraction to Taj while he played. Once she'd finally made up her mind to talk with Taj, she decided to wait until he'd returned home.

"Be home before dark," Jewel instructed.

"See you later."

"You two be careful."

"Any messages for Taj?" Dani asked hopefully.

"You've done enough delivering for a while," Jewel said lightly, referring to Dani's request on her father's behalf.

Dani shrugged. "Bye."

Jewel returned to her room, got dressed and went downstairs. She opened the cupboard and reached for a jar of coffee. Momentarily, she hesitated. She took the box of herb tea instead. A fleeting smile curved her lips. Somehow she knew that things were going to be all right. She took the jar of coffee and dropped it in the garbage can.

Taj joined Dani and Kim at their table. "I'm glad you two came down," Taj said, surprised that Jewel had allowed it. "How did you like what you heard?"

"Great," Dani said, between bites of buffalo wings. "I was telling my mother that I didn't realize that jazz was so cool."

The mention of Jewel caused Taj's jaw to tighten. "How is your mother?" he asked with hesitation.

"Excuse me," Kim interrupted. Taj and Dani turned their attention toward Kim. "I'm going to the ladies' room. Be right back."

"She likes to make announcements," Dani explained, looking down at her plate of food. "Maybe you should call and find out," she said quietly, easing back to his question with finesse.

Taj leaned back and gave Danielle a long assessing gaze. His instincts told him that she knew more than she would tell, and he wouldn't push her. It would never be his style to pry her for information about her mother. Now or in the future. If there was a future.

"Do you think that's a good idea?" he asked in a slow, probing voice.

"Absolutely." She looked across at him from beneath long, thick lashes. "Sometimes people need a push. Know what I mean?"

"I think I get the picture," he said, struggling not to smile. "Uh, in your professional opinion, would a personal visit be too pushy?"

The corner of her lip quivered in a grin. "Sometimes personal is best."

His smile was open now, enveloping Dani in its glow. He reached across the tabletop and placed his hand over hers. "Thanks," he said softly.

Dani brought a wing to her mouth with her free hand. "No problem," she said giving him a conspiratorial wink.

Taj pushed away from the table and stood up just as Kim returned. "You two should be getting home. It'll be dark soon."

"Yeah," Dani said, finishing off the last of her soda. "Aren't you coming with us?"

"No." He shook his head. "I've got to go home and pack."

"Pack?" Dani asked. Her smooth brow creased in bewilderment.

"I'm leaving for New York tonight. My boss is trying to put together a record deal. I should be back by Sunday."

"A record deal!" Kim piped in. "So you mean we'll see your video on *Video Music Box?*"

Taj tossed his head back and laughed heartily. "That's probably a long way off," he said.

"So when are you coming over?" Dani wanted to know.

"Let's say soon. How's that?"

Dani twisted her lips. "Whatever," she said dismissively, feeling disappointment. "Come on Kim, let's go." She got up from her seat, avoiding Taj's watchful eye. "Thanks for inviting us," she said to her shoes.

Taj tipped her chin up with the tip of his finger and peered down into her face. "Everything's gonna be cool. Okay?"

She nodded. "Sure." All she could think about was that she should have stuck to her convictions. She allowed herself to like him and now he was going to wind up being like all the other guys that her friends complained about. How could she have believed he was special? She hated him!

She pulled her head away from his touch. "Bye," she said sullenly. She snatched up her coat from the back of her chair and stomped off toward the door with Kim on her heels.

Taj watched them leave and tried to figure out where he'd gone wrong.

"How'd it go?" Jewel asked, almost too anxiously, when the girls returned.

"Fine," Dani said shortly.

Jewel came to stand beside Danielle, her face

clouded with concern. "Dani? Are you all right?"

"I'm fine," she snapped, her dark eyes burning when she looked at her mother.

"Dani." Jewel reached out and braced her shoulders. "What is it?"

"Just forget it. Okay?"

"No. I won't forget it. That's your response to everything you don't want to discuss. Now you tell me what happened," she demanded, her panic rising as thoughts of Steven's accusations about Taj raced through her mind.

"It's nothing," Dani insisted. "Sometimes you just let your guard down and it isn't worth it." She pulled away from her mother and ran upstairs.

"Dani!" But the only response Jewel got was the sound of the slamming door.

"What on earth happened, Kim?" Jewel asked, whirling toward Kim like a top.

"I don't know, Mrs. Avery. She's been pissed off—I mean, upset—since we left the club."

Jewel pressed her palm to her forehead. "If he did anything to hurt my child. I swear . . ." she seethed under her breath.

"I guess I'd better go and let my mother know I'm back."

Jewel nodded absently as Kim slipped soundlessly out of the house. She looked up the staircase, debating on whether or not to go up, or give Dani some time to collect her thoughts. She was sure that whatever was bothering her daughter, Dani would eventually tell her. It was the waiting and the not knowing that was so difficult. Then suddenly she made up her mind. She marched over to the phone and punched in the seven digits. Somebody was going to tell her something, she fumed.

The phone rang until the machine clicked on. Jewel slammed down the receiver and issued an expletive just as the doorbell rang.

Kim probably had forgotten something. She briskly crossed the room and snatched the door open, ready to send the girl back home to her mama.

"Taj!" A million thoughts and feelings converged and collided into one large lump in her throat that seemed to keep her from breathing. She tried to swallow but her mouth went dry when she saw the suitcase that rested at his feet.

"I know I should have called," he began slowly, prepared if she slammed the door in his face, "but I didn't want you to hang up on me."

Jewel folded her arms protectively beneath her breasts as if the act could somehow contain the torrent of emotions that tumbled within her.

"Can I come in, or should we talk right

here? Because we *are* going to talk," he said in a tone that left no room for argument.

Jewel tugged on her bottom lip with her teeth and stepped slightly aside. Taj picked up his bag and brushed past her, the scent of him rushing to her brain and scrambling her thoughts.

He walked halfway into the living room, then turned abruptly around, nearly colliding with Jewel on her approach. He instinctively reached out and grabbed her by the shoulders. The instantaneous flash of heat raced from her body and shot straight up his fingers to his heart.

She shuddered and it wasn't from the cold, she realized, staring up into the eyes that matched hers. Her heart fluttered and pounded as if she'd been running and was desperate for air.

"Jewel," he said in a strangled whisper. His hand slid up her shoulders to stroke her cheeks, then angled upward through her hair, pulling her forward until they were only a breath apart. He looked down into her eyes, his own slowly caressing her face. "I love you," he said softly. "I'd never do anything to hurt you. Nothing happened between Tricia and me. Nothing ever could."

"But the phone call," she said between tiny gulps of air. "She said—"

"I don't give a damn what she said. I know

what she meant." His lips brushed tantalizingly across hers and her knees weakened. "She was apologizing for kissing me."

"What?" She tried to pull away, but Taj tightened his grip, locking his body to hers.

"Yes," he said huskily, "a kiss. Like this." She held her breath. Taj pressed his lips almost dispassionately against hers, and released her mouth, but not his hold. He looked down into her startled eyes. "Not like this," he said, in a throaty whisper. He lowered his head by degrees, until his lips fluttered across her eyelids, slid down to her cheeks, seared her long neck, raised up to her chin where he nipped her with the tip of his teeth. He cupped her face in his hands and grazed her lips with the pads of his thumbs. Languidly his tongue traced a pattern across her parted mouth. She let out a gasp of pleasure as the slow heat of desire built a fire in her belly.

His mouth captured hers in a total act of possession. He delved deep into the warmth that awaited him. A moan rose deep from within him as she clung to him, curving her body to match his. All of her worry and hurt seemed to evaporate like melting crystals of snow.

Dani stood at the top of the landing, peeking down at the scene below. Slowly she smiled and tiptoed back to her room. Maybe he wasn't so bad after all, she smiled happily.

* * *

Taj and Jewel were settled on the couch, with Taj's arm draped across her shoulder. He played with her hair as he spoke.

"You have a very special daughter. I hope you know that. She was in there pitching for you. Indirectly, of course."

"Every time I think I understand Danielle, she surprises me. I truly underestimated her. She's growing up so fast, it's frightening."

"You've done a great job. You don't have anything to worry about." He turned her head to face him. He looked steadily into her questioning eyes. "I don't ever want anything to come between us again," Taj said softly. "Have faith in me. I'm not Steven."

Jewel looked away. "I know that now. I guess my confidence in relationships has been trampled on so badly that I just ignored my better judgment." She curved closer into his embrace and looked up at him. "Don't ever worry about my mistrusting you again."

"If you promise me that if you ever have any doubts, any fears, and flashes of jealousy, you'll tell me."

"I promise," she said smiling. "I promise."

"That's better." He kissed the tip of her nose, and reluctantly pulled himself up, just as Dani entered the room.

"What's the big grin for?" her mother asked.

"Just wondering if it was safe to come in now?" she teased.

Jewel felt the hot flush of embarrassment sweep through her. She worried just how much Dani witnessed.

"The coast is clear," Taj said, grinning. He walked over to where Danielle stood and chucked her under her chin. "Thanks for the advice, Doc."

"My bill is in the mail."

"Ugh."

"What are you two whispering about?" Jewel crossed the room and boldly slipped her arm around Taj's waist. She looked suspiciously from one to the other.

"Family secret," Dani said.

Taj smiled warmly at her. "I like the sound of that."

Dani grinned at them both and skipped back up the stairs.

"See you when I get back," Taj called out.

"Bring me something!"

Taj chuckled, then turned his full attention back to Jewel. "I hate to say this, baby, but I've got to go. Nick is picking me up at the club in a half hour."

"I'll drive you."

Taj winked. "I knew you were going to say that."

She swatted him on the shoulder. "Oh, yeah. Don't get too comfortable in predicting my behavior," she challenged, taking her coat from the rack.

"Ooh, sounds like a threat," he countered, following her to the door.

"Trust me. It's a promise. I intend to keep you on your toes."

He spun her around and into his arms. His eyes burned down into hers. "You'd better," he warned, before his lips covered hers.

The next few days were a race against the clock. Every hour seemed to be crammed with activity as Jewel and Danielle prepared for Christmas dinner.

"Taj told me he doesn't really celebrate Christmas," Dani said, dipping her finger in the chocolate icing that Jewel lathered on the three-layer cake. She shooed Dani's hand away.

"I know. His holiday starts the day after. But he said he'll come for dinner. He just won't be exchanging gifts."

"I like seven days of getting gifts. Maybe we should start celebrating Kwanzaa," Dani suggested hopefully.

Jewel gave her a sidelong glance. "You would," she said, her tone ripe with sarcasm. "But Kwanzaa is a lot more than just receiving gifts for a week."

"I know," she said in a singsong voice. "I've been reading up on it."

"Good. Now pass me that apple pie so I can put it in the oven," Jewel instructed. "Is Kim coming over tomorrow?"

"She said she was, after she gets back from her grandmother's house. Speaking of grandmothers, did you tell grandma about Taj?"

Jewel sighed "No. But I will."

"When?"

"When she gets here."

They both laughed, imaging the look on Nora's face.

Jewel surveyed her kitchen. Every available counter space was covered with prepared dishes ready for the oven or the refrigerator. She had something for everyone. Collard greens seasoned hot and sweet for her mother. Candied yams loaded with maple syrup and marshmallows for Amber. And for everyone, french cut string beans and carrots, a huge garden salad, macaroni and cheese, a twenty pound turkey, her seafood casserole, and enough dessert to send everyone into diabetic shock.

The house was filled with the fragrant scent of evergreen. Poinsettias decorated in kente colors adorned the tabletops. Brilliant African fabric, twisted into intricate knots, draped the banisters of the staircase and twinkling lights gave the entire scene a picture postcard appeal.

Instead of the traditional tree, the stacks of gifts were arranged in front of the fireplace. Everything looked beautiful, she thought, pleased with herself and her talented daughter's handiwork. Now for the grand finale. The arrival of her family. Her heart skipped in anticipation of what tomorrow would bring.

When she finally settled down for the night, she felt every muscle of her body give a relieved sigh. As she lay there, she replayed her last phone conversation with Taj. She smiled. The executives from the record company were thrilled with what they'd heard, and were ready to sign them on the spot. "Nick wants his lawyer to look everything over first," Taj had said. "He doesn't want us falling into any traps."

"I'm so proud of you," she'd said, her own excitement for him barely contained. "You're going to really make it. I can feel it."

"I needed to hear you say that. That you believe in me."

Her heart pinched. She knew how desperately he had longed for someone to really feel that way about him. And she promised herself that she would do everything in her power to keep reminding him of just how important he was.

"So I hope you won't mind being married to a superstar. You don't look like the live together type."

Shock slammed against her and her hand began to shake. "What?"

"You heard me." She could feel the laughter in his voice. "We'll talk about it when I get back tomorrow. Think of me until then."

He'd hung up before she had a chance to catch her breath and respond. Her heart was racing so fast she thought she was going to have one of those conniption fits that she'd heard about.

All she could do was repeat the word over and again in her mind, just like she was doing now. Marriage. A smile of pure joy lifted her lips as she drifted off to sleep filled with beautiful dreams of her future.

Squeals of delight and the sound of pounding footsteps pulled Jewel out of her sleep with a start. Seconds later, Dani jumped on her bed and smothered her with kisses.

"Thank you, thank you, thank you," she chanted. "You got me everything I wanted."

Jewel sat up and rubbed the sleep from her eyes. "Hmm. I'm glad, honey," she said drowsily.

Dani plopped a large, beautifully decorated box on her lap. Jewel squeezed her eyes shut then opened them. She must be tired, she thought, she hadn't even seen Dani bring the box in the room.

"Open it," she said, her eyes bright with anticipation.

Jewel did as she was instructed. She gasped with delight as she pulled out the silky pink kimono and matching gown. "Dani!" she exclaimed in awe. "This is beautiful. Where on earth did you get the money for this?"

"I've been saving my allowance," she announced proudly. "You like it?"

"I love it." She slipped the kimono over her arms, relishing the feel of the feather-light fabric as it glided over her skin. She gave Danielle a tight hug. "Thanks, sweetie."

Dani popped off of the bed. "I'm going to hook up my CD player, put on my new coat and boots and *Paarty!*" she giggled.

Jewel smiled. "Go right ahead."

When Dani reached the door she stopped and tossed over her shoulder, "All those skirts and tops were nice, too."

"Right." Jewel immediately lay back down as soon as Dani was out of the door, only to jump back up again when she realized all that she had to do.

She took a quick shower and dressed in comfortable jeans and a tee shirt. All the better to hustle around the kitchen in, she thought merrily.

In no time, the house was filled with the delicious aromas of Christmas dinner. When she'd finished mixing up the ingredients for the stuffing, she checked the clock. Taj said he'd be back by noon. It was nearly that. Her heart picked up a beat. *Married.* She wanted to change before he arrived.

She quickly cleared her countertops and checked the progress of the turkey. Everything was right on schedule. Except whoever was ringing the doorbell. She wiped her hands on the red and green kitchen towel and went to the door, knowing that it could be none other than her mother, who always arrived three hours early so that she could supervise. Well at least she'd have time to tell her about Taj before he arrived, she reasoned, pushing her stomach back in place with a deep swallow.

She took a deep breath, put on a warm smile of greeting and opened the door.

"Merry Christmas, Jewel."

"Steven." Her smile vanished.

"May I come in? I promise I won't stay. I just wanted to drop these off." He indicated two large shopping bags, that sat at his feet, with a nod of his head.

"Sure. Come on in." She stepped aside to let him pass.

"The place looks real good," he said, turning toward her with a smile that hovered between regret and longing.

He was still so devilishly handsome, she thought, annoyed with the observation. "Thank you. Can I get you something? Apple cider, coffee?" She started toward the kitchen.

"No. But you can sit down for a minute."

"I really have a lot to do," she protested. "If you want to see Dani, I'll get her. I—"

"No, Jewel." He put a restraining hand on her arm. "I want to talk with you. Please. Sit down. Just for a minute."

She nodded reluctantly and took a seat opposite him on the armchair.

"I just wanted to say that I'm sorry, Jewel." Her eyes widened in disbelief. She'd never heard Steven apologize for anything. "Sorry for the way I treated you," he continued. "Sorry for the things that I've done that hurt you. There's no excuse." He looked down at his hands as if searching for answers. He linked them together and looked across at her. "You didn't deserve the things I've done to you. Even though I tried to make you believe it was your fault."

If he wanted a response, she thought wildly, she couldn't give him one. She was stunned into complete silence.

"I know I can never make it up to you. I know we can't go back. I made certain choices in my life and I'll have to live with them. I just wanted you to know that you were the best choice I've ever made."

He stood up, and heaved a sigh. "I want you to be happy, Jewel. You deserve it more than anyone I know." He tried to smile. "Putting up with my B.S. for seventeen years should earn you sainthood."

"Steven, I—"

"Ssh. Please don't say anything. There's no need. I just wanted you to know that at any time for whatever reason, if you need, you tell me. No matter what it is."

Jewel stood up and pursed her lips. "Are you the same man I married?"

"And divorced," he reminded her. He chuckled. "The new and improved version. Now, where's that daughter of ours? By the sound of the racket, she must be upstairs. I want out of here before the troops arrive. You know how they always want to be diagnosed."

"Steven." She took his hand in hers. "Thank you," she said softly.

"For what?"

"For finally setting me free."

The corner of his mouth inched up in a smile as he nodded in understanding. "It's about time. Don't you think?"

* * *

Jewel was still reeling from the shock of Steven's confession when the doorbell rang. The Christmas celebration had begun.

Nora Sinclair was a stunning woman in anybody's book. She was a personal testament to self-preservation. She worked out every day. Played tennis twice a week. Saw her doctor regularly. Had her hair always styled in the latest fashion, and shopped for clothes incessantly. And for a woman who knew her way around any kitchen, she was still a size ten. At sixty-three, Nora Sinclair could still turn the heads of men half her age.

Which she'd apparently done.

The tall, handsome man on her arm must have been forty, Jewel thought, as shock gave way to amused bewilderment. Was this her mother, who as far as she knew hadn't dated a man since her father died nearly ten years ago?

"Well, are you just going to stand there with your mouth open, or are you going to let us in? It's freezing out here." Nora did all she could to keep the grin off her face when she saw Jewel's expression.

Nora breezed in with her escort and an armful of gifts, leaving Jewel standing at the door. Nora spun around.

"Jewel, I'd like you to meet James Monroe."

Nora cast adoring eyes on James. "James, my daughter Jewel."

Jewel was finally able to move. She closed the door and stepped into the foyer. James stepped forward and gave her the most engaging smile she'd ever seen, next to Taj's. He extended his hand.

"Nice to finally meet you, Jewel," he said in a voice that sounded surprisingly like James Earl Jones. "Your mother has told me a lot about you."

Jewel took his hand and felt like a complete fool as she kept staring at him trying to frame something coherent to say. She cleared her throat. "I hope it was all good things," she said lamely.

"Most of it," he teased, giving her that smile again.

"I came early to help," Nora said, hanging up her coat. "James, make yourself at home while I help Jewel in the kitchen."

Dutifully, Jewel followed her mother into the kitchen. Before she could get a word in, Nora cut her off.

"I know what you're going to say. He's too young for me. Well, I thought so at first, too. But after ten years of being around men my own age, I found they couldn't keep up with me," she said defiantly. She walked over and took both of Jewel's hands in hers. "I know this is a shock, sweetheart. But I think I'm in love again. And he loves me." Her soft brown eyes begged for understanding.

Jewel grinned with delight and a hint of mischief as she hooked her arm around her mother's shoulders. "Mom, there's something I think you ought to know . . ."

Christmas dinner was more than she could have ever hoped for. It was filled with laughter, acceptance and an abundance of love that flowed as freely as the falling snow. Even her sister Amber seemed to have added a new dimension to her character. It was a time of change, for everyone.

Long after the last dish was washed and dried and all of the guests had departed, Jewel and Taj sat in front of the fireplace, finally sharing a quiet moment together.

"You have some family," he said, twisting a lock of her hair around his finger.

"You can say that again. This week has been a true revelation to me. All of my beliefs about everyone I thought I knew were blown out of the window." She shook her head, remembering her mother's parting words, "I'll see you when I get back," Nora had said wickedly. "We're going to the Bahamas for the weekend."

"A new year is on the horizon, baby," Taj

whispered softly. "Time to make changes." He looked into her eyes. "Are you ready for that?"

She thought about the person that she had been and the person that she'd become with Taj at her side and she knew what he was asking of her. Was she ready to make that choice?

She cupped his face in her hands and looked at him with all of the love and passion that filled her soul. "Yes," she said without further hesitation. *"Yes."*

whispered softly. "Time to make changes." He looked into her eyes. "Are you ready for that?"

She thought about the person that she had been and the person that she'd become within a few weeks and she knew what he was asking of her. Was she ready to make that choice?

She cupped his face in her hands and looked at him with all of the love and passion that filled her soul. "Yes," she said without further hesitation. "Yes."

Harvest the Fruits

by
Margie Walker

Selinae noticed she was not the only runner taking advantage of the spring-like evening. Enticed by the pleasant weather, several joggers traversed the trail that twisted over the sloping landscape high above MacGregor Bayou. Though it was now dusk, it had been sunny and bright all day. Not atypical in Houston, even in late December.

As if unaffected by the change in seasons, oaks, pines, and magnolia trees stood tall and proud in well-tended grounds around grand, two-story homes strategically located on either side of the bayou in a predominantly African American neighborhood. Decorations featuring Santas, snowmen, and reindeers graced practically every yard.

A professional-looking runner passed Selinae easily and continued across the Scott Street light. Selinae smirked as she watched him go. She turned up the paved sidewalk, crossing to the other side of the bayou on the return run to her original destination, MacGregor Park. She had no idea the distance she had come, and she was beginning to regret that she had ever set out. She hated running. It hadn't always been that way.

But she didn't have anything else to do, she reasoned to herself and wasn't up to being in the company of others. And in the privacy of her own house, there was too much temptation to wallow in despair. She had to get out.

Her sense of alienation and loss was always amplified during the holidays, a time when suicides were high. In that regard, she was not alone. The day after Christmas was always a letdown, even to the happiest of people.

But the day before, Christmas Day, had been no joyous occasion, either, she remembered.

"Forget it," Selinae said, the command instantly carried away on the wind.

With the back of her hand, she wiped at the sweat dripping from her forehead, then rubbed her hand dry on her pants. Pumping her arms in sync with the moderate tempo she'd set, her mind jogged back in time.

At the start of the year, one of her resolutions had been to bridge the gap between herself and her parents. Olive branch gestures made during the year were to culminate in a Christmas truce. Her brothers and their families planned to come in from out of town. She was going to spend the whole day celebrating the holiday with her family. It would have been a first in many, many years.

While there had been no major blow-up

with her father, she almost wished there had been. It would have been better than the facade of cheer and grudging politeness that permeated the affair. She left shortly after the elaborate dinner her mother and sister-in-laws had prepared.

But not soon enough, she remembered. Not before her mother caught Selinae staring at her father, bouncing his chubby eight-month-old grandson on his knees. His face was as animated as the baby's; it was hard to tell which one of them was enjoying the moment the most.

Selinae hadn't needed a mirror to see her expression. She was certain it fully conveyed her lachrymose spirits. She was on the precipice of dredging up even more painful memories.

"It's time you put your bitterness aside," her mother had whispered in her ear.

Mission unaccomplished, Selinae thought. Whoever said time healed all wounds apparently never knew the depths of pain her indiscretion had wrought. It defied forgiveness.

Since she couldn't have the latter, she'd better work harder on forgetting and building herself a new emotional life, she told herself. The cycle of guilt, regret, and despair had been with her for too long.

Yet, letting go was hard.

Suddenly, Selinae picked up her run in an

all-out sprint. Almost there, she told her legs, which were burning at the calves from the effort. *Almost there.*

Finally, she reached the corner of Calhoun and North MacGregor. She ran in place, waiting for the light to change before crossing the street.

When the oncoming traffic stopped, she sprinted across the street and over the grassy landscape of the park. With only yards left to go, she set her sights on her car, a black convertible Mustang. It was the only car parked in the lot across from the fenced-in swimming pool, which was closed for the winter.

Nearing the lot, she slowed to a walk, drawing deep breaths of oxygen into her lungs. Glad the run was finally over, she planned a nice, long bubble bath for when she got home.

No more than twenty feet from her car, she spotted several young men walking toward her from the opposite direction. They were coming from the basketball court. She paid them no particular attention, fiddling for her keys in the small pocket of her jogging pants. They reached the car at about the same time she did.

"This your car?"

The key now clutched in her hand, Selinae looked up. She counted heads, noting quickly that there were five of them. They were sweaty looking, but nowhere near as exhausted as she was.

On the surface, the question was innocent enough. But a sidelong gaze, revealed one of the gangly youths eyeing her car covetously, rubbing a proprietary hand across the hood. Selinae immediately felt threatened. A shiver ran down her spine; it had nothing to do with her body temperature.

Her gaze split between the adorer of her car and the speaker. A slender, tough-looking youngster of about thirteen, he was the smallest and the shortest in the group. He returned her curious look with practiced cockiness. She assumed he was the leader by his stance and the menacing smile curled on his lips.

Trepidation replaced exhaustion. She thought about turning around and running in the opposite direction. Reasoning that she probably couldn't outrun them, she decided to hold her ground.

"It's my car, yes," she replied at last.

"Nice," he said.

She wanted to hurry and open the door, but was hesitant to approach them. Realizing she was convicting them in her thoughts, she felt a twinge of guilt. Innocent until proven guilty, she reminded herself. These were kids, after all, and they had done nothing criminal . . . yet.

"How 'bout giving us a ride?"

His tone posed more of a challenge than a request, and it caught Selinae by surprise. She shifted uneasily, not sure how to answer. Despite their youth, these young boys were potentially dangerous to her health.

"Not today."

She tried for a friendly, firm tone; instead, her voice sounded scared. Holding the key defensively before her, she casually took a step toward the door. She could feel her legs shaking.

"But we tired," the youngster declared, stepping into her path.

Though she could look down into his face, standing so close he seemed taller; his boldness defied his size. The other boys closed in around them, and a hard fist of fear clenched in the pit of her stomach. She railed herself silently for not running when she had the chance.

Street lamps automatically popped on around the park. Selinae looked, but saw no one in the area to call to for help.

Sterling saw them as he crossed the street on his way to the hillside jogging trail above the bayou. A female—he couldn't tell much about her from this distance—surrounded by a gang of youth.

Returning from a three-day out-of-town trip, he was feeling pretty tired, but it was too early to call it a night. He intended to run a couple of miles, then return home for a big meal, a beer, and bed.

It may be nothing, Sterling told himself. And then again, he'd feel awful if tomorrow's headlines informed him that a woman had been assaulted right across the street from his front door.

It wouldn't hurt to check it out, he decided, cutting across the yard toward the side-street parking lot.

The circle of young men was closing in on her. He saw the woman's head, a mass of soft black curls, moving from side to side, and knew she was searching for a way out. Sizing up the situation, he recognized it as one he'd seen the world over in his photographic jaunts. A gang of youth emboldened by their power in numbers, looking to take out their frustrations.

Standing at about five-six or five-seven, the woman towered over the lead bully by a good three or four inches. She could have stood a chance against them had there been only one, but together, they were like Michael Crichton's velociraptors. She didn't have a prayer if they all decided to strike.

He wished he had Hannibal with him to even up the odds in case the situation turned violent. His ninety-pound Rottweiler could teach them a lesson or two about terror and fear. But there would only be the two of them if things got ugly. Hopefully, it wouldn't come to that. He felt his adrenaline level rising, and hoped they weren't packing.

Sterling slowed his gait and settled on an approach strategy. The woman had assumed a "last stand" position as she poised to defend herself.

An attractive woman of about thirty, maybe younger, she had a quiet oval face, dark and delicate. She had a small mouth with full, pursed lips. Her chin jutted out bravely. Her deep brown complexion glistened with perspiration.

As Sterling approached, she looked up, over the head of her aggressors and into his face. Sterling stopped in his tracks. She was beautiful. Her most remarkable feature was her eyes. A light brown flecked with gold, they were bejeweled amber buttons. He wished for a moment that he had his camera with him, but then, he remembered his purpose.

Excitement mounted within him. He felt dually motivated. An aggressive band of youths to be reckoned with; a chocolate darling, he suddenly dubbed her, in distress.

So intent in their terror-tactics, the youths neither saw nor heard him walk up on them from the front of the car. When one standing on the outskirts of the circle noticed his presence, it was too late.

Sterling broke their circle, as if oblivious to

their ill intent, and sauntered straight to the woman. "Hi, babe. I see you beat me back."

He lowered his head to kiss her cheek as he took her hand in his. It was ice cold with the same fear that blazed in her big, doe-shaped eyes. Conscious they were under the watchful gazes of the human velociraptors, he gave her a reassuring smile, a look that implored her to play along, before turning his attention to the group's young leader, who stared at him with a decidedly displeased look.

Selinae stared, speechless. He'd addressed her in an unmistakably intimate tone, pecked her cheek like a lover, then stood at her side like a protective warrior. Her heart was hammering in her chest, but now it wasn't fear she was feeling.

She was mesmerized by the stranger with the dark, liquid voice. He moved with the languid grace of a cheetah. He had a light brown complexion and deep-set eyes whose color she couldn't discern in the light. He wasn't very tall, a few inches shy of six feet. In a blue and white body shirt and running shorts that revealed muscular everything, she only saw a black knight in shining bronze armor.

"You can gloat if you want to," he said, prompting her.

She met his eyes, caught and received their message. It brought her wits sharply together.

"I told you I was faster," she replied sweetly, taking up the game.

"That you did," he said, winking at her.

Then he turned to the youngsters. They had already backed up a step. Noticing the curiosity and disappointment on their faces, Selinae realized she had nearly forgotten all about them.

"Yo, little brothers, what's up?" the knight said.

"This yo' woman, man?" the leader asked, folding an arm across his chest, a fist under his chin.

"That's my woman," he said, with proud ownership in his tone.

Selinae could feel the giveaway heat rush to her face as a torrent of warmth coursed though her.

"Man, you let a woman beat you?" another of the youths asked.

"Sometimes they do that," her knight replied, reaching for her hand again.

Not only was she grateful for his timely appearance, Selinae was happy to let him take charge. She basked in the sudden turn of events and her elevation to a stature of importance, blithely ignoring the voice that told her it was only a temporary game.

"I wouldn't let no woman beat me," one said.

The leader, Selinae noticed, appeared skeptical. "Well, if she yo' woman, how come yawl coming from two different directions?"

Selinae couldn't think of an answer. She sought the eyes of her knight, her mouth open. She watched his eyes rake her with a possessive look before he lifted her hand, still balled in a fist, to his mouth, and kissed it. A jolt of desire forced her to look down at her feet which suddenly seemed suspended two feet off the ground.

"It's our way of giving each other space," he replied. "Couples have to do that sometimes to keep the relationship from getting boring." As he angled his body to unlock the car door, he said, "Now, if you gents will excuse us, we're going home for a long shower and dinner." He opened the door and helped Selinae into the driver's seat. "You might want to do the same. Be careful going home."

"Why don't you give us a ride?" the young leader asked. Selinae saw that he was not convinced by her and her knight's performance.

"Sorry," the knight replied with no apology in his voice as he walked around to the passenger side of the car. Opening the door, he said over the top of the car, "Ask your own woman to give you a ride."

Once he was in, Selinae locked the doors.

"Looks like we're going to have to leave together to convince our little friend," he said.

Having escaped the immediate danger, Selinae stopped to think. She was now in a locked car with a stranger. What if her situation had merely gone from bad to worse? Her hands trembled as she put the key in the ignition.

"My name is Sterling Washington," he said. "You don't have to be afraid of me. I'm not going to hurt you."

Selinae didn't trust herself to speak. She nodded, eyed the lingering youths, then backed out of the lot.

"That could've been a bad situation," he said. "I know how you must feel. I've been there, too. I live right across the street on Calhoun. You can drop me off and be on your way."

"They're still hanging around," she said, looking out her side mirror. Still slightly shaken—she didn't know which encounter was affecting her more—she could barely lift her voice above a whisper.

"Drive up North MacGregor, down to Cullen, and turn left, then circle back up," he instructed. "They should be gone by then."

"Thank you," Selinae said as she drove off. "I mean, for stopping. Most people wouldn't." Good, she thought, strength was returning to her voice.

"You're welcome," he replied.

"My name is Selinae Rogers," she said.

"Selinae Rogers," he repeated, as if testing

the name on his tongue. "I don't think I've met a Selinae before."

"I'm glad you decided to meet one today," she said with a hint of relief in her voice. Then she was silent again. She wasn't out of the woods yet, she reminded herself.

In the lingering quiet, Selinae felt herself growing calmer, her hands steady on the steering wheel and her eyes on the street. Questions about her handsome passenger began to surface in her head, but she asked none of them. Sterling's voice finally broke the silence.

"So, how did you happen to run into the homies?"

"They ran into me," she replied. "When I first saw them, I was just finishing a run I wished I hadn't started, so I wasn't paying them too much attention. That was my first mistake. Then when I reached the car and the little guy asked for a ride, I thought about all the things I should have done."

"You can never prepare for those situations," he said. "You just make do and hope for the best."

He'd spoken as if it were his philosophy of life, she thought, and somehow it gave her a peaceful feeling.

"Kids aren't what they used to be," he said.

"That's true," she said with a hint of sad fatalism in her voice. Neither are families, she added to herself.

The fading light outside and darkness creeping into the car afforded Selinae a moment to chance a stealthy glance at the handsome profile of her passenger. His slim, powerful build filled the bucket seat. Though dressed for running, it was clear he hadn't even started.

"Sorry about interrupting your workout."

"That's all right," he said. "I really wasn't up to it, anyway. I was just doing something to get out of the house for a while. Do you run often?"

"No," she said with a laugh. "I needed to get out of the house, too." She turned back onto Calhoun and slowed the car to a crawl.

"It's the next one," he said, pointing toward a newly paved driveway.

Following his directions, she pulled up to the front of a closed double-car garage. It was connected to a recently constructed two-story contemporary home. Work was still being done to the yard, where small mounds of dirt had been dumped.

She put the car in park and let it idle. "Thanks again, Sterling Washington," she said, feeling suddenly shy. They had come to the end of their journey, and she felt reluctant to part.

"You're more than welcome, Selinae Rogers," he said, his hand on the door handle. "Take care of yourself." He started to open it, then changed his mind. "Hey, look, if you don't have anything planned, why don't you come in and have a drink or something?"

"I wouldn't want to impose on your generosity any more than I have already," she said half-heartedly. Even though she wasn't eager to return to her empty house and morose thoughts, which had sent her away in the first place, she was still guarded where he was concerned.

"It's no imposition at all," he replied. "Come on. You're still safe. I don't turn into a vampire until midnight."

He flashed a broad grin at her that made her stomach flip. It was so tempting, she seriously thought about accepting his invitation. But in her silent debate, caution and common sense ruled.

"No, I don't think so," she said. "Besides, I need to go home and shower."

"Selinae, I know we didn't meet under ideal circumstances." He spoke slowly, feeling his way, "but the truth is, I'd like to see you again. That is, if you're not already involved."

"I'm not involved," she replied, too quickly, perhaps.

"Okay, that's one down," he said with a smile. "Since I'm on a roll, I might as well keep going. If I give you my number, will you call me?"

"Yes," she replied, again without hesitation,

then wondered what it was about this man that made her want to take risks she normally wouldn't consider.

"When?"

"When what?"

"When can I expect to hear from you?" he asked. "I don't want to jump every time the phone rings. Can you give me some idea when you might call?"

"You're persistent, aren't you?" she asked, though she was more than a little flattered by his interest.

"Aggressive," he quipped. "A trait expected of men, I'm told."

He was too good to be true, Selinae thought. First appearing out of nowhere to rescue her, then pursuing her as if any woman couldn't be his for the asking. Selinae suddenly became suspicious. "How do I know you don't have a wife waiting for you inside?" she asked, nodding toward the house.

"If I had a wife, she would be out that front door by now demanding to know what happened. Then she'd invite you in and insist you stay until you truly felt safe. But there is no wife, inside or any place else. I'm the one that has to insist you stay. And you are safe with me," he emphasized. "You'll just have to take my word on it."

"Where on earth did you come from?" she asked laughingly, when she really wanted to ask, *Where have you been all my life?* "I didn't think a man like you would have to work so hard for a date."

"I don't know what you mean by a man like me," he replied, "but I believe that if you want something, you have to work hard for it. I don't have any problem with hard work. So," he said, brushing his hands together, "when are you going to call me?"

She stared at the clock in the dashboard. It was 6:05. Hours before she could reasonably expect sleep to claim her; that meant hours of thinking and rethinking the things she wanted to forget. It was time to look to the future, she reminded herself.

Selinae gazed directly at Sterling. Yes, there was humor glinting in his eyes, but there was also something else. She was hard pressed to define it, but the look infused her with new hope. She was anxious to see, to know the color of his eyes in a clear light.

"Right after I clean up," she replied. "Want to go celebrate Kwanzaa with me?" She spoke fast, as if fearing she'd change her mind and rescind the invitation. He stared at her in surprise, and she laughed, simply because it felt good to do so. "You *do* know what Kwanzaa is, don't you?"

"What time shall I be ready?"

* * *

Despite all the books on the wall-to-wall bookshelf behind him—two full shelves devoted to photography—not a one was on Kwanzaa.

While the study was complete, it appeared his library wasn't, Sterling mused. He was sitting in a soft, black leather chair behind a massive cherry desk in the bluish-gray-walled room, a copy of *Our Texas* clutched in his hands. He was reading an article on Kwanzaa.

The study and the kitchen were the only rooms downstairs he'd had time to completely decorate. It was only three months ago that the house had been ready for its owner to take up residence.

Since then, he hadn't been home for more than two weeks at a time. He didn't complain about the long absences because they meant he was working. Since going off on his own as a freelance photographer, he was happy to get as many assignments as he could.

In truth, he was tired of being on the go, but resigned to it, especially if the position he was pursuing with a local paper didn't come through. At thirty-six, he wanted more than the satisfaction he'd enjoyed from his career. He wanted a home. Not a big empty house, but a place that teemed with warmth and welcome and love.

And he wanted it in Houston, the city of his birth, he mused, a faraway look alight in his eyes. With his thoughts embracing the image of Selinae Rogers, he stared unseeingly across the room, a dreamy expression on his face.

Shaking his head to clear her image from his mind, he forced his attention back to the article. It wasn't easy, but finally he was able to concentrate on his reading.

Shutting his eyes tight, Sterling tried to visualize the words he'd just read.

"*Matunde ya Kwanzaa* means first fruits," he quoted from memory. "The seven principles are called *nguzo saba. Umoja* means unity. Uh, what's that next one? Come on, you can see it," he cajoled himself. "*Ku . . . kuji . . .*" he strained, biting down on his bottom lip.

"Ahh," he muttered with disgust, opening his eyes to look down at the words. "*Kujichagulia* means self-determination."

He dropped the magazine on the desk before him and leaned over it, poring over the information as if preparing for a test. He hadn't studied this hard since high school, when Mr. Churchwell, his physics teacher, had told him that if he didn't pass the final, he wouldn't graduate.

The instant Selinae had driven off, he'd rushed inside to look for information about Kwanzaa. He'd heard of it, had even read about it. But that was a long time ago, and his memory was stale. What he remembered wasn't much.

He knew it grew out of the 1960s movement and was designed to be more than a symbolic gesture to instill blacks in America with a sense of pride, self-worth, and values that they could call their own. But as far as the rituals and practices were concerned, he was ignorant, having never celebrated the holiday.

Lucky for him, the magazine had done an article on Kwanzaa celebrations across Texas. Now if only he could digest everything—he looked up at the elegant gold-rimmed clock on the wall—within the next thirty minutes, he should be reasonably informed.

He wanted to impress Selinae with his knowledge about something she apparently cared about. She promised to pick him up at 6:45; the celebration began at 7. It was going to be held at the Harambee Community Center, only a short ride away.

Sidetracked by the reminders of her eminent return, he thought about the short ride they had shared from the park to his house. He knew she was still shaken by her encounter with the young hoods and sensibly afraid of him. She must have wondered whether she'd jumped out of the fire and into the frying pan, he thought.

He didn't believe she was the talkative type, even when at ease. Rather, he guessed she had a fiercely protective way about her. She hadn't parted with her phone number, though she had his.

Still, he wondered, what had changed her mind about him? Curiosity or attraction?

He wasn't entirely oblivious to the effect he had on women. Some women, anyway, he amended. He had long years of practice, honing his charm. It served him well in his profession, but he wasn't so foolish as to think that charm alone made him highly sought after by the opposite sex.

If he picked up that attitude from a woman, he wasn't interested in getting to know her past her name. His one-night-stand years were over.

He didn't get that impression from Selinae. There was something he instinctively liked about her and how it made him feel, like a promise of something wonderful about to happen. He was both curious about and attracted to the woman with the beautiful name.

"Selinae," he said, an unconscious smile stealing across his face.

The very first time he locked gazes with her, he'd seen a fire in her eyes that hinted at a woman of unlimited passions. Recalling how she'd been prepared to defend herself in what would have been a futile effort, he was impressed by her courage.

Still, there was something else about her,

he mused. He couldn't define it, the sensibility he felt emanating from her. Maybe she'd let him photograph her and he could capture and study that elusive quality that shone in her eyes.

The first night of Kwanzaa always drew a big crowd. The parking lots surrounding the Harambee Community Center in the predominantly black Third Ward community were filled to capacity.

Cars lined Almeda Street three and four blocks in either direction. Sterling and Selinae joined a throng of other arrivals, heading toward the Center four blocks away.

Though Sterling did most of the talking, joy bubbled in her voice when she spoke and shone in her eyes, as bright as the stars twinkling overhead in the clear, black night.

She wasn't ready to concede Sterling had anything to do with this blissful happiness that made her feel fully alive. She couldn't stop looking at him as if expecting horns to sprout from his head and fangs to protrude from his firm mouth.

"You know, Kwanzaa is celebrated practically all over Africa, even though it was founded here," Sterling said. "The names are different, and they're agricultural in nature, but they're still harvest celebrations. I read someplace that even the ancient Egyptians had a first-fruits celebration."

Selinae was familiar with his recitation because she had written several stories about Kwanzaa over the years. But she wasn't going to interrupt a lesson from Sterling. She just liked hearing him talk. His voice was so mesmeric, she would just have happily listened to him recite the alphabet.

He had been entertaining and attentive from the time she picked him up. She felt herself being drawn to him with every passing second in his presence. No man had ever spoiled her with such eager attention before. If she weren't careful, it could go to her head.

"I don't know if they celebrate for seven days, though," he said, as if puzzled by the thought. "I wonder how he came up with seven."

The "he" to whom Sterling referred was Dr. Maulana Karenga, the creator of Kwanzaa, Selinae knew. Even though the seven-day African American holiday had been celebrated since 1966 in the United States, all the angles had not been covered in news and feature articles about the holiday. But it was generally known that the celebration ran from December 26 to January 1 of the new year, and that one of the Seven Principles was honored each day.

"As I understand it," Selinae replied plainly,

"the number seven has a cultural and spiritual significance in African culture. Dr. Karenga wanted to develop an Afrocentric value system in which to rebuild the black community. The Nguzo Saba, or Seven Principles," she said, looking up at him, "are geared toward that end, of highlighting the importance of community over the individual."

He flashed her a shamed-face little grin. "I must have been boring you to death," he said almost apologetically. "You already know all this stuff."

"Not at all," she replied. "Besides, I wouldn't want to be guilty of gloating twice in the same day. It's not good for your image with the homies." She smiled.

"Well, I guess I'm going to have to redeem myself," he replied with challenge in his voice. "Do you know the Seven Principles by heart?" he asked, then emphasized, "In Swahili?"

"I warn you," she said, "I'm up on matunda ya Kwanzaa. Matunda means fruits and ya Kwanzaa means first."

"Aw, she reverts to the old stalling tactic," Sterling teased. "That was not the question, Ms. Rogers."

She smacked her lips at him in jest. "Want to make a small wager?" she asked.

"I wouldn't want to let the brothers down," he replied with bravura. "Count me in."

"What's to be my prize?" she asked saucily.

"Hmm," he muttered, as if in deep thought. "If," a finger pointing heaven-bound, "you can name the Seven Principles . . ."

Cutting him off, she interjected, "Nguzo Saba."

"Same thing," he quipped. "*If* you can name them all in Swahili, dinner is my treat for a week."

"I hope you're a good cook," she said.

"Start naming," he chortled.

"*Umoja;* Unity," she said, counting them off on her fingers as she spoke. "*Kujichagulia;* Self-determination. *Ujima;* Collective work and responsibility. *Ujamaa;* Cooperative economics. *Nia;* Purpose. *Kuumba;* Creativity. *Imani;* Faith." Looking up at him smugly, she asked, "When do I collect my first meal?"

Just feet from the door to the entrance of the center, the inside light and a chorus of drums spilled out onto the sidewalk. Sterling pulled Selinae aside to let others pass, then looked at her, his bottom lip folded in his smiling mouth.

His eyes were the color of root beer, she now knew. The look he sent her implied she could very likely be on the menu. The thought sent a barely imperceptible shiver through her.

"Anytime you want it," he replied quietly.

Selinae couldn't find her voice; his was resonating in her ear and creating havoc with her senses. He shouldn't be allowed to speak in public. That voice belonged in the bedroom, she thought, unable to stop herself from imagining the two of them in her own. Shaking the wayward thought from her head, she let him usher her into the lobby of the center.

"You'll have to be my teacher tonight," he said, lowering his head to her ear. "This is my first Kwanzaa."

Casting a sidelong, suspicious glance up at him, Selinae didn't know whether or not to believe him.

Without even looking at her, he said, "I read a lot."

His disclosure was so insignificant, Selinae thought, she didn't know why she felt as if he'd shared a long-held secret with her. As she struggled to quell her skittering pulses, she wondered where were those horns.

The gathering in the lobby of the Center resembled a high school or family reunion. One could always count on seeing people whom she hadn't seen in a long time. While a chant of "Harambee" reverberated from the adjoining room, Selinae stopped to speak to longtime friends and associates.

Hearing the phrase, "Habari gani?" and a roaring reply of "Umoja," she excused herself. "We've missed the opening," she explained to Sterling, leading the way.

They reached the entrance, which was the

back of a room that had once been the showroom of a furniture store. As big as a high school gym, it was capable of seating hundreds, with standing room for hundreds more. Tonight, every square inch of it was packed.

"Wow," Sterling exclaimed softly.

"We give thanks to the Creator for bringing us together in Umoja, for we are the most valuable fruit of the nation," the speaker was saying. "On this first night of Kwanzaa, we commemorate our ancestors who have brought us this far. We recommit ourselves to the dreams we have and the actions we must take to uplift our families, our communities, our nation. Unity!" he cried extollingly.

"Unity!" the crowd echoed.

"Umoja!" he refrained.

Under the two-worded chant, "Umoja! Unity!", echoing through the room, Sterling and Selinae looked for two seats. Finding none, they searched for a spot alongside the wall where several others had already assembled near the stage. Room was made by them to snuggle in a tight space, with Selinae standing in front of Sterling.

As the speaker lit a black candle in the center of the candle holder, Sterling recalled his reading. According to the article, wine or grape juice was poured into the unity cup, then the liberation statement was made. It was followed by the lighting of the candle to represent the principle that was being celebrated. Because the black candle represented African Americans in unity, as well as the first principle of the seven that were recognized, it was always lit first.

They wouldn't be late tomorrow night, he declared to himself, placing his hands on Selinae's slender shoulders. He felt the muscles in her shoulders rise and tense under the tempered weight of his hands. Then they settled under the light pressure, and he too, relaxed, realizing just how anxious he'd been about their date, afraid he'd scare her away with his eagerness.

When she'd arrived at his door in her red African-styled outfit, a subtle and intriguing fragrance surrounding her, he wanted to take her in his arms and just hold her. She'd been wise to decline an invitation inside. But the prohibition against touching only fueled his desire. He felt a response as age-old as the sea threatening to rise in him.

It was best not to think about that right now, he counseled himself, forcing his attentions elsewhere.

Impressed by the ceremony, Sterling swelled with pride. The colors matched those of an island carnival. Even though it was a serious occasion, an aura of festive reverence permeated the room.

His photographer's eyes scanned the room,

focusing on the faces of the people. A joyous anticipation shone in their features. He imagined the expressions were the same Sojourner Truth saw when she successfully guided enslaved Africans into freedom.

Some were garbed in African attire; others dressed as casually as if they were going to a movie. It was like attending a church with a come-as-you-are policy, he thought.

Down center of the platform stage, a kente cloth displaying the symbolic colors of liberation—black, red, and green—was draped over the sides of a table. Atop it were items he recognized, but he couldn't recall all their Swahili names or remember their significance. But even without that information, Sterling could see that Kwanzaa was no different from any other holiday, in that symbols were part of the ritual.

The speaker sat down to applause and the emcee, whom he recognized as a local news anchor, introduced a performance by a percussion ensemble of young boys. As the instruments were set up, he bent to ask Selinae a question.

"Is the kente cloth merely for decoration, or does it have symbolic significance to the celebration?" he whispered.

"The selection of kente is decorative," Selinae replied softly, angling her body to look up into his face, "but the cloth is traditional. It's called the *bendera ya taifa,* which means 'national flag.' I'm sure you recognize the colors."

"Yes," he replied, "black for the people, red for the struggle, and green for the future. I believe Marcus Garvey had something to do with it." Selinae nodded in the affirmative. "What's that straw mat?" he asked, noticing a woven floor covering, atop of which were several fresh ears of corn and a large basket of fruit.

"It's called the *mkeke,*" she replied. "And the corn and fruit represent the crops, called *mazao.* You'll also notice those wrapped boxes. They represent the gifts, called *zawadi.*"

"I remember that," he said. "And that big brass cup is the unity cup, right?"

"Yes," she replied. "It's the *kikombe cha umoja.* You already know about the *kinara* and the *mishumaa saba,*" she said.

"Yes," he nodded. Hearing the names, he recalled that the kinara, or candle holder, was the symbol of ancestry. It contained seven holes for each of the seven candles, three red and three green ones on either side of a black one. The candles symbolized the *nguzo saba.*

The young percussion ensemble began to play, effectively ending Selinae and Sterling's conversation. The program continued with entertainers interspersed between speakers. They all expounded on the values of Kwanzaa and encouraged living the *nguzo saba* beyond the seven-day holiday.

Nearing the program's end, a hush settled over the room. The emcee held an extinguisher over the still burning black candle.

"Umoja," she said reverently, and the word was repeated in that same reverent tone by the audience. She put out the light.

Selinae turned to look up into his face, peace shadowing her expression. "Happy Kwanzaa," she said softly.

He was humbled by the experience, but never more so than by the woman who'd introduced him to this warm gathering. He felt enjoined to her in the spirit of *Umoja.*

A diverse selection of Christmas music played by the college radio station flowed continuously from the tall floor speakers in the sun-bright orange room. The KTSU announcer deftly segued from Charles Lloyd's "Merry Christmas Baby" into the mastery of John Coltrane blowing the tenor in a rendition of "My Favorite Things."

Selinae became aware of the music for the first time since she'd sat down to work. She pressed the save key on her keyboard, and as the computer safely stored her document, she took a sip of lukewarm coffee and glanced at the polished wood, Africa-shaped clock on the wall. It read 10:55.

She was in her home office, formerly the master bedroom in an old A-frame house. She'd purchased it five years ago when she was a reporter with one of the local dailies. It wasn't wholly hers yet; she shared ownership with the mortgage company.

Setting her cup down, she double-checked the printer for paper, pressed the print command, then settled back in her chair. The printer quietly went about its work.

With the exception of the computer workstation, stereo entertainment center, and a few art items, the furnishings were Salvation Army and garage sale purchases. The teacher's desk, twin bookshelves, daybed, and army-green file cabinets had been either refinished, recovered, or simply washed and cleaned. The thin beige carpet covering the floor had come with the house.

The room was streetside, perpendicular to the living room separated by a hallway. The four windows, two each on the front and side walls, were covered by the same heavy black-and-white fabric featuring African animals as the comforter on the bed and seat cushion in the wooden armchair.

Normally an early riser, she had slept late this morning, but had gotten more work done in a few hours than she had in weeks. It was amazing what a little sleep could do, she thought, picking up a sheet of paper that the printer spit onto the holding tray.

"You can call it what you want," she smiled to herself with a chuckle, replacing the page.

Sitting back with her feet on the edge of her chair and mug in her hands, the image of Sterling Washington appeared full blown in her mind. A blush of pleasure rose to her cheeks, and she felt a tingling sensation in the pit of her stomach.

As their evening wound to a close, he had seemed as reluctant as she to part, she recalled. She hadn't trusted herself to go inside his house, though he'd invited her. Instead, they had sat talking in her car, parked in his driveway.

Sitting a bucket-seat away from each other had altered her definition of a romantic setting. It could be anywhere, requiring only one ingredient—a sexually attracted couple.

While outside, the temperature dropped several degrees, inside the car, the atmosphere had teemed with the electric sparks of their mutual attraction. She had been hungering for his touch from the time they left the center.

And even before that, she told herself. In fact, she felt her passion on a low boil even now, just thinking about him. She knew what would have happened had they gone inside the house.

But the boldness that propelled her to ask him to Kwanzaa vanished in spite of her desires. She was paralyzed by a caution that carried with it endless arguments against fulfilling the desires running wild and rampart in her. It was too soon, she thought. She really didn't know him; nor he, her. He might think her too forward, and she feared being labeled a tease, or any of the names she'd been called before by someone of whom she least expected.

Besides, she reflected, slow and methodical, rather than brash and brazen were more in keeping with her nature.

When they finally called it a night and he went inside, she had driven home with the heavy ache of an insatiable hunger. After a warm shower, she fell in bed. Sterling was the last waking thought before sleep claimed her.

Swallowing a sip of coffee, she stared absently at the computer screen and began to wonder what Sterling was doing now.

A loud shot erupted outside her window. Startled, Selinae jumped, spilling coffee on her work clothes, a purple blousey top and black lycra pants. When silence rather than screams and chaos followed, she realized it was merely a car backfiring. She drew a deep calming breath, but the minor incident evoked her memory of the perilous situation she'd gotten herself into the day before.

"God takes care of babies and fools," she mumbled in the mug as she took a sip of coffee.

She'd put her life in danger at the hands of a gang of teenagers who were out to prove their manhood, she recalled. She never had to contemplate suicide again. All she had to do was make herself visible and some nut would be happy to oblige, she mused sarcastically.

"I'll never do that again," she said, setting the cup on the desk. Sterling Washington, her black Adonis, might not happen along again, she thought.

With her head cocked to the side, her expression smiling and thoughtful, she supplanted the name Horus in her thoughts. Horus, the Avenger. It was more appropriate, she decided, and an appreciative sigh that began in her chest seeped past her lips.

It had been a while since a man had noticed her. Or maybe it was the other way around. One thing was for certain, she'd never felt such an exhilarating response to any man as she did for Sterling Washington.

Feeling herself getting carried away, Selinae cleared her throat and busied herself collecting the sheets from the printer tray. Nothing had changed the arguments for caution, she reminded herself.

Besides, Sterling Washington was as dangerous to her as the young thugs that had surrounded her had been. If, she told herself with emphasis, she couldn't control her response to him.

Maybe she was making a big deal out of nothing, she mused, inserting the typed pages into file folders. One date does not a future make, she told herself.

But then again, she thought, holding the stack of folders, to be on the safe side, maybe she'd better reconsider collecting any of the meals she'd won and forget him altogether.

The doorbell rang, interrupting her silent debate. Wondering who was calling on her, she lay the folders on the corner of the desk and rose to traipse down the hall on her way to the front door in the living room.

"Who is it?" she asked before looking through the peephole.

"It's us, Sel."

Only one person in the world called her Sel, and that was her baby brother, Anthony, whose own name had been shortened to Tony. Confirming her visitors' identities through the peephole, she saw her brothers Tony and Oscar, Jr., and her nephew, Andrew.

They were the last people she expected to call on her. Infrequent visitors to Houston, when they did come home, their parents hardly let them out of their sight.

Opening the door, she asked, "What brings you guys this way?"

Tony, carrying Andrew, Oscar Jr.'s son, walked in and promptly deposited the baby into her arms. "We figured you weren't working today, so we thought we'd drop by," he replied.

"Hi, lil sis," Oscar said as he walked inside, a blue and white baby bag hanging from one shoulder, a gift bag in his other hand.

"Have a seat," she offered, dropping onto the couch, the baby propped on her knee.

Instead of sitting down, however, Tony meandered about the room, looking at and touching items of interest. Nosy, Selinae thought. Oscar, Jr. was more subtle in his perusal. She freed them both to be openly inquisitive with a nod of her head. With the baby in her lap, she examined her brothers as they examined her home.

Tony had a slim build like Selinae and their mother. Oscar junior was a big, muscular man becoming heavy in the middle, though he, like Tony, had inherited their mother's caramel complexion. Their grandmother used to say their parents had practiced on Selinae and Oscar, Jr. before getting it right when they had Tony, she recalled. He was good looking and knew it. But luckily, he'd grown out of his teenage conceit.

Oscar Jr. was the complete opposite. Staid

and steady, he had always been old-acting and old-thinking. When he spoke, he sounded as if he'd rehearsed his words in front of a mirror. A labor attorney with a prominent law firm, the temperament suited his profession well.

"I like what you've done to the place," Tony said from the door separating the kitchen from the dining room.

"I like it, too," Oscar, Jr. echoed.

From where Selinae sat, she could see clearly into the dining room, as far as Oscar had ventured. The room featured a glass-topped wood table with matching high-back chairs and a china cabinet. The room led into the kitchen, the door of which was open as well.

"It's rather appealing," he added, retracing his steps to the living room.

Selinae couldn't tell whether or not he was sincere. Not that she cared. The room revealed an Afrocentric-minded owner. It was decorated to satisfy her recognition of and appreciation for her two cultures—on a budget.

A waist-high wooden bust featuring big eyes and thick lips stood on the polished hardwood floor in the space between the couch and love seat, which was upholstered in a gray, black, and peach African-print fabric. A hanbel rug of Moroccan origin lay under the wood and glass coffee table, decorated with porcelain-sculptured animal figurines. Colorful paintings and prints depicting black lifestyles adorned the white walls. There was plenty of greenery from plants both potted and hanging.

"Mama said it looked like a jungle," Tony said, dropping onto the couch next to her. "But I like it."

"No tree," Oscar, Jr. observed, raising a questionable brow at her.

"Yeah, you don't have a Christmas tree," Tony echoed.

"No," she replied, laughing inside. They *would* notice that, she thought, but not the symbols of Kwanzaa she'd neglected to put out for the same reason she hadn't gotten a tree. Sterling would notice, she thought: *if,* she gave him a chance. With a fond light of memory in her eyes, she decided to put up the kinara and mishumaa later.

The baby began to squirm in Selinae's lap. "I guess visitation time is up," she said, handing the child to Oscar, Jr.

"Come here, Daddy's big boy," Oscar, Jr. said. He settled on the love seat, Andrew in his arms.

"We tried to reach you yesterday, but you weren't home," Tony said. "You forgot to leave your answering machine on."

No, she didn't forget, Selinae thought. She'd deliberately turned it off and muted the phone bell so she wouldn't have to hear it ring, though she hadn't expected to hear from her family.

"And, you forgot your gift at the house the other day," Oscar, Jr. said, glancing around him. "What did I do with that bag?"

Selinae looked puzzled. "I got everything."

"Here it is," Tony replied, reaching over the side of the couch for the bag. He dropped it in Selinae's lap.

"Well, Mama told us to drop it off if we stopped by," Oscar, Jr. said.

Peering into the bag, Selinae recognized the gift immediately. It was a cashmere sweater, pretty, pink, and expensive. "Your dad picked it out," she recalled her mother boasting proudly, and a spark of hope sprang in her chest. But it was extinguished quickly. A glance at her father's expression revealed the truth. Her mother had lied.

"Can I get you guys something?" she asked as she got to her feet, gripping the thin straps of the bag.

"I'll take coffee, if it's not too old," Tony replied.

"You're in luck," she replied. Walking off, she dropped the bag on the dining room table, intending to give the gift to someone who needed it. Continuing toward the kitchen, she called back to her brothers. "Where are Darlene and Andrea? Why didn't they come with you?" she asked disappearing behind the kitchen door.

"The wives went shopping with Mama," Tony replied, his voice carrying the distance.

"Tony!" Selinae heard Oscar, Jr. whisper in disgust as she reached to get a cup down from a cabinet overhead.

"What?" Tony replied innocently.

Then hot whispered muttering penetrated the walls to her ears.

"Selinae didn't want to go shopping," she heard Tony reply defensively.

"Keep your voice down!" Oscar, Jr. commanded, his harsh whisper carrying back to her.

Left out again, Selinae thought. Her brothers' wives saw her mother more than she did. As determined as she was not to let the exclusion bother her, she couldn't help but feel hurt as she filled a cup with coffee from the coffee maker.

Tony was right—she had plenty to do at home, rather than blowing her budget, spending money on things she didn't need. But that wasn't the point. She wasn't even given the opportunity to refuse. Who knows? It's possible she would have joined them if asked. She didn't have to buy anything.

She dropped a tablespoon of sugar in the cup, then stirred it before returning to the living room, her feelings masked from review under a blank expression. Oscar, Jr. wore a peeved frown, while indifference shone on Tony's face as he accepted the mug from her.

"Thank you," he said.

Oscar, Jr. put the baby down. The boy immediately began crawling around, heading straight for the coffee table.

"What's on your agenda for the day?" she asked.

"Nothing much," Tony replied. "Still belong to the gym?"

"No, I let my membership go," she replied.

"Too bad," Tony shrugged. To Oscar, Jr. he said, "We can probably find a pickup game at the park."

"What are you going to do about Andrew?" she asked, grabbing for the toddler's hand as he tried to eat a porcelain elephant. Oscar, Jr. reached him first, handed the figurine to Selinae, then settled back on the love seat with Andrew in his lap. The baby started to whine.

"Tony, look in the bag and get me a bottle, will you?" Oscar, Jr. instructed.

"You haven't spent any time with your nephew," Tony said, rifling through the baby bag. He pulled out a bottle, then tossed it across the room to Oscar, who stuck the nipple in his son's mouth. "We figured you'd like to baby-sit."

Selinae burst out laughing. Andrew stopped feeding to turn his head toward her, a curious look on his face. "I should have known this was not a social call," she said.

"You're about as tactful as a cactus," Oscar, Jr. chided his brother.

"I'm just doing my part to help move things along," Tony said. Oscar, Jr. snarled at him. "All right, all right," he said. Setting his mug on the coffee table, he sidled up next to Selinae and draped his arms around her shoulders. "My dearest, most favorite sister in the whole world—"

"I'm your *only* sister," she interrupted. "And no, I'm not going to baby-sit while you two run off and have fun."

"Come on, big sis," Tony cajoled, smothering her with kisses.

"Get away from me," she replied, laughing.

"Come on, little man," Oscar, Jr. said, joining them on the couch. He held Andrew close to Selinae. "Wouldn't you like to spend some time with your auntie?"

Tony playfully wrestled her to the floor, and Oscar, Jr. set the baby in her arms. They were all laughing uncontrollably.

Gosh, it felt good being with her brothers like this, Selinae thought. They hadn't laughed together in so long, she'd almost forgotten what it was like.

Finally, laughed out and exhausted, Selinae sat on the floor, her back against the couch, her nephew in her lap. She rubbed foreheads with the baby and giggled as he blew spit bubbles in a sign of glee.

"So, how you been doing?" Oscar, Jr. asked, his tone suddenly serious.

"Good," she replied.

"How's your career coming along?"

"Fine," she replied, a hint of wariness in her tone. "Why do you ask?"

"Can't we make a polite inquiry without falling under suspicion?" Tony replied. "We hardly get a chance to talk to you. You're always so busy, looking for a story."

"Before you got famous, you used to let us know when you had a piece published," Oscar, Jr. said. "I just happened to pick up a copy of *Ebony* this past summer and saw your name on an article."

He was exaggerating; she wasn't famous. When acceptance of her work was scarce, she recalled, they'd never really seemed interested. They'd make subtle hints that she'd made a mistake quitting her newspaper job. After several offers to help her find an eight-to-five job, she stopped talking about her work to them.

"What have you been working on?"

"*American Visions* bought the piece I did on the Creoles in Houston's Frenchtown. It'll come out in the upcoming spring issue," she said. "And I'm working on a documentary script for a production of it by the local PBS station. All the details haven't been worked out yet, so it's still tentative."

"Good," Oscar, Jr. said. "I'm glad to hear things are going so well."

In the ensuing silence, Selinae occupied herself playing patty-cake with her nephew. She didn't notice the somber looks her brothers exchanged over her head.

"You know," Oscar, Jr. said, as if feeling his way, "the folks are getting older. As much as they'd like us to believe they can do everything they used to, the truth is they're slowing down."

Staring at him curiously, Selinae felt her insides begin to quiver. She'd always thought her parents as healthy and would be around for many years to come. Her mother was fifty-two, worked out regularly, counted fat and calories constantly and looked 20 years younger for her efforts. Her father was another story, but he was still relatively young at fifty-five. Maybe Oscar, Jr. and Tony knew something she didn't know. It seemed they had a motive for visiting more profound than baby-sitting after all.

"The house is getting to be too much for them," he continued. "They're talking about selling it and moving into a retirement complex."

Selinae began to relax; she had been thinking the worst, that some deadly ailment had claimed her parent's bodies. "That seems like a good decision for them," she said matter-of-factly. "More coffee, Tony?" she asked, passing Andrew to his father.

"No, I'm fine, thanks," Tony replied.

"It would be a shame for them to sell that house after all the work they put into it," Oscar, Jr. said.

"Yeah," Tony added, "it sure would be. Not to mention what moving is going to do to their income."

"Why are you telling me all this?" Selinae asked, glaring from one brother to the other.

"Well, it doesn't make sense for the three of you to live in the same town, maintaining two separate households, when if you—"

Selinae cut Oscar, Jr. off. "Hold it right there," she said tersely.

"Just listen a second, Sel," Tony said.

"Stop," she said, holding up both hands. "I don't know what your motivation is for even bringing up the matter, and I don't want to know. But save your arguments for willing ears."

"But Sell," Tony countered.

"If you want a baby-sitter for them," she said in a chilly voice, "hire a nurse. If you like that house so much, buy it. If you're that concerned about their income, let them move in with you. But keep me out of your plans. I have no intention whatsoever of moving in with them," she vowed stringently. "Not that they'd go for it anyway."

"We talked to Mama about it," Tony said. "In fact, she was the one to bring it up."

"Well, as you mentioned, she's getting older. It's making her delusional. You saw us together the other night. Nothing's changed in fifteen years."

Feeling embittered emotions rising, Selinae reigned in her temper and clamped her mouth shut. It was useless getting angry with her brothers, she reasoned. They were not the root of the problem.

"Now, Selinae, don't go getting all upset," Oscar, Jr. said.

"What brought this on?" she asked, curiosity overriding her declaration of disinterest. She noticed that both of her brothers lowered their gazes, guilt and shame clouding their faces. "It can't be that bad," she said, forcing humor to her voice in order to draw laughter from them.

"The old man pulled out the will last night," Tony said somberly.

A tense silence filled the room. Selinae looked questioningly from one brother to the other.

"He cut you out of it," Tony said at last.

Selinae just then realized she had been holding her breath. With her brother's statement, she let it out in a rush. Her father hadn't merely cut her from a piece of paper she could care less about, she thought, his gesture symbolized cutting her out of the family. She never would have believed that his disappointment in her was so great as to lead to disclaiming her existence.

"Well," she said. She didn't know what else to say. She shrugged her shoulders and took another deep breath. She felt numb. "Why am I not surprised?" she said with rhetorical, calm indifference.

"Selinae," Oscar, Jr. said ruefully, "that's why we thought if we could get you together in the same space, you'd be able to work this thing out. I think you'll agree, it's gone on too long."

"I do agree, Oscar," she replied, dropping wearily onto the couch, "but we're not your clients. You can't intermediate for parties who are not willing to sit at the same table. It was quite evident at dinner the other night that we can't."

"We just thought we'd put some sort of solution on the table," Tony said. "Christmas dinner was a bust," he said with a disgusted snort. "The two of you snarling across the table at each other."

"We never said a word to each other," she corrected.

"You didn't have to. You shot enough daggers at each other to qualify," he said with dry sarcasm. "I was starting to feel like a soldier in Custer's army."

"I'm sorry about that," she said.

"That's not good enough," Tony exclaimed contentiously. "We're supposed to be a family. You and Dad are forgetting that. What do you think this is doing to Mama? What about us?" he demanded.

Before today, she hadn't given much thought to the effect the rift with her father was having on Oscar, Jr. and Tony. But now it seemed clear that they had been more than mere witnesses to her shaming. She had destroyed their childhood, taken it from them the night they were forced to watch her humiliation.

So engrossed in her own sense of victimization, she couldn't comfort them, and they had been too young to know how to comfort her. Then, for a long time, neither of them could bear to look the other in the eye.

As she looked at her baby brother, abject defeat in his posture, she wished that she could give him what he wanted. But too much time had passed in refusal and denial. It was just too late.

"Selinae," Oscar, Jr. said, "Tony's right. It's not fair for us to be caught in the middle like this."

"I've done my part," she said quietly, taking them both in her gaze. "I'm tired of beating my head against a wall. I'm not going to do it anymore. I'm getting on with my life."

She felt a strange sense of resignation come over her. Her sadness was tinged with relief. It was as if saying the words aloud somehow made it easier to accept the truth of what she had known deep down inside all along.

"You can't give up," Oscar, Jr. said desperately.

"I'm through," she said softly, with finality.

"But Selinae—" Oscar, Jr. protested.

With a finger at her lips, she shushed him. Taking both of her brothers in her sights, she looked at them with a half-smile of knowing on her face. "Tell Mama you tried," she said.

She was eager to escape before the build-up of tears in her eyes fell and intensify her brothers' discomfort. Though they never said it, she was the cause of the rift that tore their family apart, she thought, feeling the burdensome weight of blame. They would never let her forget it.

She walked out, ducking down the hall to her bedroom at the back of the house. Leaning against the bedroom door, she let the tears fall freely down her face.

Meandering about the room, she picked up a store bought frame with a picture of a girl smiling up into a man's face. The girl, long-legged and long-haired, wore a track club uniform and was holding out two gold medals that hung from red, white, and blue ribbons around her neck. The man was touching them, pride beaming in his expression.

Selinae nearly choked on a bitter sob as she set the picture facedown on the dresser. She tried to stop the flow of tears, pressing her fingers under her eyes. But they kept coming. They were tears of mourning. For a family; for a young girl's soul.

"Selinae! Selinae! are you all right?"

With a jerk of her head, Selinae snapped to attention at the sound of the distinctive voice, echoing down the hallway. She would recognize it anywhere, regardless of the tone. Sterling's voice. She felt a lurch of excitement within her.

"Selinae!"

Frantically, she wiped the tears from her eyes, using the back and front of her hands. What was he doing here? she wondered, opening the door to hurry down the hall. She wasn't in the mood for company. She even wished her brothers would leave.

Rounding the hallway corner into the living room, she froze, startled and confused by the picture that greeted her. Tony and Oscar, Jr. stood side by side like a couple of defensive tackles, while Sterling looked poised to rush.

A loud noise drowned out the thudding of her heart. Andrew was slamming a porcelain animal on the coffee table. She went around her brothers to rescue the tiny giraffe from the baby's clutches.

"What's going on?" she asked, picking up Andrew, who started to cry.

"Are you all right?" Sterling asked.

Her gaze met his and locked. Filled with a sudden longing, her breath suspended in her throat as he approached her, but he hadn't gotten very far when both her brothers stepped in his path.

"We told this guy you weren't seeing anybody," Oscar, Jr. said.

In that instant, Oscar looked and sounded just like their father, Selinae thought, her head snapping as she stared at him as if for the first time. She could almost see a red aura of hostility encircling him.

"Yeah, we told him to come back another time, but he refused to leave," Tony said, parroting Oscar, Jr. in tone and demeanor. "Common courtesy dictates that you call before showing up at somebody's house, anyway," he said to Sterling.

Selinae's eyes narrowed in annoyance. Where did they get off, trying to run her life?

"How do you know that he *didn't* call?" she replied, her tone challenging. She returned her brothers' shocked gazes as she placed Andrew in Oscar, Jr.'s arms.

"W-Well," Oscar, Jr. stammered lamely, "we were having a family meeting."

"The meeting was over," she said.

"Selinae," Tony said in a patronizing tone.

Selinae stuck out her chin. "I said it was over," she repeated tightly.

The instant Selinae walked into the room, Sterling felt a curious swooping pull at his innards. Except for a nod in passing, her attention was focused fiercely on the two men who tried to prevent him from seeing her. She looked like a warrior queen, ready for battle. It was a definite turn on.

He hadn't noticed the family resemblance between Selinae and the two men until she walked into the room. Had either one of the men offered an explanation of their presence in her home before, he thought, slightly miffed, he would have turned around and left. Instead, they acted like rogues, causing him to fear for Selinae's safety.

But no introduction seemed forthcoming, and he wasn't about to press the issue. Selinae must have her reasons, he thought. Witnessing a war of gazes—two sulky pairs versus her steely one—he felt suddenly uncomfortable.

"Well, we'll just get our things together and leave you to your company," said the bigger of the two men.

"That's a good idea," she replied.

Sterling noticed her tone had thawed somewhat, though she didn't give up any ground. He couldn't take his eyes off her as her brothers made fast work of leaving. From the periphery of his gaze, he saw them scampering about, righting items the baby had upended or rushing off to dispose a soiled diaper.

With his eyes riveted on her face, he noticed a slight puffiness just beneath the long elegant black lashes encircling her beautifully white eyes. She'd been crying.

His emotions split between anger and arousal. He wanted to wring her brothers' necks and take her in his arms and comfort her.

But he didn't move, other than clench and unclench his hands at his sides, immobilized by her impenetrable expression. Only her posture revealed her mood. She said nothing to him; nor did she look his way. He felt safe from her wrath. For now.

She was standing by the wooden head statue, arms folded across her middle like a belt, cinching her top to reveal firm, full breasts and a small waist. One long fine leg crossed over the other in black pants that fit her fine hips and shapely thighs like a second skin. She was the picture of regal assurance.

She hadn't called as she promised, and fearing losing her, Sterling had come to force the issue. He was driven by something about her that connected to a sensual, persuasive feeling within him. He didn't know whether it was real, imagined, or plain lust, but he had no intention of dropping it until he knew for sure.

He didn't have her consent, but hoped he would be able to talk her into going with him. There were three cameras in his car, fully loaded with both black-and-white and color film. One was for her to use.

He wanted them to share a fun outing, taking pictures. No private places, but public, in a crowd of people, so she'd feel safe in his company. It was a safety measure for himself, as well, he mused, wishing her brothers would hurry.

"Maybe we can get together again tomorrow?"

The brother with the baby spoke. Standing at the door with the infant in one arm and a diaper bag in the other, he'd gone from big bad bully to meek, mild lamb, Sterling thought.

"Call first," she said. "And thanks for stopping by." She smiled at them, and flicked the baby's cheek affectionately with her thumb.

He nodded meekly, then turned and walked off. The other brother leaned to kiss her on the cheek. He, too, had become docile.

"Bye, Sel," he said. "Sorry if we overreacted, okay?"

"Okay," she said with forgiveness in her tone.

* * *

Locking the door, Selinae's hand lingered on the knob. She lowered her head and wondered what she was going to say to Sterling. She had enough changes in her life to contend with, she mused. Severing one relationship was about all she could handle at a time.

She decided to thank him again for his timely appearance, then send him on his way. Pivoting, her lips parted to speak, she came to a sudden stop. She stood riveted, facing him. Her voice failed her.

She couldn't say what it was that affected her so, but coherent thoughts scattered like a crowd disbursing under the threat of gunfire. Maybe it was the pose he'd struck, as if he'd staked a claim on some significant discovery. Or, it could have been the fit of the burgundy knit shirt and freshly starched jeans he wore, refreshing her memory of his lean, sinewy body. Or just maybe it was the look in his eyes, piercing dark brown nuggets that were full of unspoken promises. Whatever it was quickened her pulse.

"Habari gani," he said.

Selinae shuddered inwardly as his deep, dolce voice, like a sweet rondo passage on a harp, went through her. She noted his Swahili greeting, the English translation of "what's the word?" She swallowed the lump in her throat before she replied with the traditional response. *"Kujichagulia."*

They fell silent. The atmosphere took on a dreamlike quality, hypnotic, lulling. Then Sterling moved toward Selinae, closing the short distance between them.

"You've been crying," he said, reaching out a hand to touch her.

"Yes," she said quietly, finding she couldn't lie to him. "But I'm okay now," she said against the hand that rested on her cheek.

With the warmth of his hand on the side of her face, she felt a yearning that was puzzling in its depth. Her heart was pounding; she didn't know how she steadied herself; her legs felt as if they had turned to jelly. He took her hands and pulled her against the wall of his chest. She leaned into him and rested her weight against his strength.

"You should have called me," he said, stroking her back tenderly.

"There was no need," she whispered raggedly.

But the need was within her and building. The heat that started on her face stole down her body. She breathed in his warmth, reveled in the faint smell of his skin, and when he tilted up her chin, she didn't resist. Everything that had happened to her that morning suddenly seemed unimportant, and she succumbed to his kiss. His mouth was firm, his kiss persuasive in a way that reminded her of his voice. Draping her arms around his waist, she kissed him back.

When he finally pulled away, her lips tingled from his brandishing, and she was breathless and dazed with wonder. She placed her hands on him for support and took hard, short breaths, noticing his breathing was as arrhythmic as hers, skipping across his chest as he drew new air into his lungs.

"Have you had breakfast?" he asked, then looked at his watch. "Maybe we better make that lunch."

Selinae's head was still spinning; it took her a while to catch up with this speedy change of direction he'd tossed at her. "Uh, no. Uh, what time is it?"

"Eleven-forty-five," he replied. "Why don't you change and we'll run out for a bite, then—"

"Wait a minute," she said with nervous laughter in her voice, hands over her bosom, "slow down." Her breathing still hadn't returned to normal.

"Uh-uh," he said, shaking his head from side to side, "we're getting out of here as fast as we can."

Propping her hands on her hips, she stared at him in defiance and disbelief. She didn't need a keeper to replace the two she'd just kicked out, she thought.

Sterling arched a brow, fixed her with a

knowing look. "Otherwise, we won't leave at all," he explained patiently. "And while that's not a bad idea," he said, his gaze roving over her seductively, "I have a feeling you'd regret it in a couple of hours."

Selinae flushed, realizing there was more than a grain of truth in his caustic words. Her resolve to send him away had flown out the window in his arms. A few more minutes cloaked in the warm blanket of desire and they would have been right where her body wanted to go, she thought disconcertedly. With the fight for her independence deflated, she nodded her head in agreement.

"Now hurry," he said.

Wordlessly, Selinae backed from the room and vanished down the hallway.

Despite the chill in the air, a warm sun brought out families looking for an inexpensive, fun outing within the Hermann Park complex. From their hillside view, Sterling and Selinae could see people spilling out of cars, heading toward the Burke Baker Planetarium.

They were sitting on a blanket spread over the low-cut rye grass that maintained its greenery even during the winter months. Selinae was eating a chicken leg, while Sterling was adjusting the ASA on one of his cameras.

They didn't stop to lunch upon leaving her house four hours ago. Sterling had started babbling excitedly about wanting to capture the halcyon spirit that he saw on the faces of the people who attended Kwanzaa the previous night. She had agreed to postpone lunch. At the time she was more than willing to become involved in an activity that would take her mind off her hunger. She got caught up in his enthusiasm, having felt a similar emotion numerous times when she was working on a story that was as exciting as it was challenging.

He'd looked for it in several places—the Galleria, a couple of museums, and finally, the nearby zoo. Though he'd taken dozens of pictures, he wasn't hopeful. An hour ago, he called it quits for the day, and they stopped to fill up the picnic basket he'd brought.

Stealing a glance at his arresting profile, an unconscious smile settled across her expression and a warm feeling of tenderness spread through her. Her first impressions of him held true in their second meeting, she mused. He was a take-charge man, fearless of the consequences, whatever they might be.

His home and his urbane manner spoke of a man who enjoyed a comfortable life. Yet, today he seemed like a man on a serendipitous mission. One of his missions seemed to be rescuing her, she thought, folding the chicken bone in a napkin to toss in the designated trash bag in the basket.

A burst of youthful laughter caught her attention. She looked in the direction from where the sound originated and spotted three young children playing tag with a man and woman, most likely their parents, as home base. A family, she thought, feeling a little happy, a little sad, a little envious.

"A penny for your thoughts," Sterling said.

Selinae looked at him abruptly, and his root beer eyes held her still. She was amazed by the tender gleam in their depths. She had to remind herself to breathe.

"I haven't had a lazy day like this in a while," she said, a smile spreading slowly across her face. For the first time in a long time, she felt a surge of the teenage exuberance that had made her popular in school among students and teachers alike. The cause of her happiness was literally right in front of her, though she couldn't believe that one man could so quickly change her entire world. Well, almost her entire world. "Thank you," she said.

"You're more than welcome," he replied. "Tomorrow I want to get an earlier start. Now that I know what I have to do to get you out of the house in a hurry." His look traveled the length of her body.

Selinae blushed, and Sterling's rich laughter filled the air.

"I'm sorry," he said, capturing one of her hands between his. "I didn't mean to tease you."

Her hand tingled in his touch. She smiled. "Yes, you did," she pouted, feigning hurt feelings as she pulled her hand from his.

Suddenly, he sat back on his legs and trained the camera on her. "I want to take your picture."

"No," she protested, turning her head away from the camera's lens. "I don't photograph well."

"Believe me," he said with confident assurance, "it had nothing to do with you; it was the photographer. He didn't know what he was doing."

Shaking her head, she affirmed, "No. Please, don't."

With a slight tilt of his head and an admiring look in his eyes, Sterling said, "You're beautiful . . . you know that."

Selinae studied him back, his words lingering in the air between them.

"I'll put it away if you insist," he said.

"Let me think about it," she replied after a while.

Sterling set the camera next to the others, then lay on the blanket facing the sun. A flock of white winged birds sailed across the clear windy skies.

"Tell me about your family," he said.

She started to say "I don't have one," but knew that reply would only result in questions that would be even more difficult to answer. "It's a pretty typical, dysfunctional family," she said, trying to keep her tone light.

"Your brothers seemed quite protective," he replied.

"Presumptuous," she corrected. "Actually, they came to do a patch job, so to speak."

"Ah," he said. "Who have you upset, your mama or your daddy?"

"My dad," she replied. "But that's nothing new. This time, he cut me out of his will."

"He'll get over it," Sterling replied, adjusting his hands beneath his head.

"He hasn't gotten over it in fifteen years," she said.

Sterling whistled. "Sometimes our expectations of the people we love are just too darn high," he said.

"Sounds like you know a lot about it," she replied.

"Firsthand," he replied. "Only, in my case, I was the one with the unrealistic expectations. It took me a while to get over it, but I did." He sat up and rested his elbows on his bent knees, staring absently across the park.

"What happened, if you don't mind my asking?"

"Oh, my mother did something that was unforgivable. At least, when I was nineteen, it was unforgivable. It involved a man, not my father. My father had been dead for quite some time. I was in my first year at Texas Southern University. I was a photography major, but awed by Dr. John Biggers, the art professor. I decided I wanted my photographs to resemble his art."

"I love his work," she said. "It's so soulful."

"I know what you mean," he said wistfully. "That's what I want to do with the camera, create images that go beyond the merely visual." He fell quiet for a moment, then cleared his throat. "Anyway, all during high school I was going about my business, not paying attention to practical matters. You know, the usual self-absorbed teenage mentality. We weren't rich. When my father died, my mother didn't know how to do anything except clean other people's houses, so that's what she did. I hated it, but we had to survive. She had worked about four years for this family when they hired her to manage one of their rental properties. By that time, I had started college. She got to live in one of the apartments rent-free. But there were other benefits, too," he said pensively. "She got a car, we had food on the table all the time, I got new clothes. We seemed to have money. I never thought anything about it, particularly when she gave me cash for tuition and books. I never questioned where our newfound wealth came from. Then one day . . . It was during the Thanksgiving break. I finished my exams and went home. He was there. I was crushed. My mama was sleeping with the boss's son. We argued and that's when I learned where the money for my education was coming from. I dropped out of school, left home, wanting no part of her. I left the city and went to Chicago. It took me a while to figure out I was punishing myself."

"What's 'a while'?" she asked.

"A little over five years," he replied softly.

As Sterling related his tale, Selinae had feared she was enthralled by a man who was just like her father. Hearing him admit his capacity to forgive, among other things, infused her with a wonderful sense of relief. She noticed his thoughts taking a turn, censoring memories as he continued.

"I was a stubborn young punk," he said derisively. "I had to learn the hard way. I was determined not to sell out professionally. I wanted to be an *artiste,"* he said, raising his hand and pinching his fingertips together. "But having to make a choice between a roof over my head and food on the table made for a painful, but valuable lesson. In the final analysis, I opted for eating and paying the bills."

"Is she still with that man?"

"Yes," Sterling said, glancing at her with a smile. "The social climate changed enough for them to come out of the closet. "They got married six years ago."

"And how do you feel about that now?"

"I'm jealous," he replied. "Not of him," he added hastily, "but of what they have together. I've never seen her so happy before. I want what she has. And I regret the time I've wasted, now that I know it never had to be that way."

"I guess we each come into our own when we're ready," she said musingly.

"Yeah," he said. "What about you? Are you ready?"

With the night of Kujichagulia fading, Selinae reveled in her good feelings and likewise, in the man whose arms were guiding her so assuredly and gracefully across the dancefloor. The music, the wine, and the gaiety surrounding them made her feel light-headed and giddy, as if all were right with the world.

It was in her world, Selinae mused, her head resting against Sterling's strong shoulder.

After leaving the park, they returned to her home with plans of attending the evening's Kwanzaa celebration to be followed by dinner out. An invitation, which was really a command from her Aunt Rae, to a house party, came unexpectedly. Presented with an opportunity to extend their time together, they added it to their list of things to do.

They arrived at a home bursting with a holiday-spirited crowd. Young children were scampering back and forth, replenishing plates of food, while teenagers manned the small living room, ranking on each other playfully. The bravura challenges of bid whist and domino players could be heard occasionally drifting down the open stairs to compete with the festive din of the conversationalists crowding the dining room and kitchen. None of it intruded on the mood set in the family room of the thirty-something generation.

Under low ceiling lights, several couples danced, wedded to the music and each other. Even before Sterling and Selinae walked in, the mood had been established, and it extended to embrace them in its romantic arms.

Rachelle Ferrell's "Waiting" was drawing to a close. Selinae softly hummed the words to the song. It was one of several old songs that had been taped for tonight's occasion, and it was one of her favorites.

With the phrase "patiently waiting" echoing in her head, her thoughts turned melancholy. She felt the refrain applied to her. It was what she had been doing, waiting patiently for her father to come around and accept her, shortcomings and all.

The song segued into another oldie, "I Try," interpreted by Will Downing.

Selinae felt the pressure of Sterling's arms tighten gently around her waist. Held so close to him, she wondered why she was ruining her evening with unpleasant memories. Particularly when new ones, happier ones, were even then being made.

She concentrated on savoring the moment, the music, the man next to her. They swayed, easy and slow, in tempo with the tender ballad, enraptured by its melody.

Selinae felt herself pulled even closer, Sterling's essence surrounding her, overwhelming her senses. Pressing his chin against the side of her head, his hands explored the hollows of her back, touching her with tender strokes that transmitted a sensual message up and down her spine. Her head lost the battle of restraint to her traitorous body. She snuggled into his all-male, all bracing nearness.

From the very beginning, an undeniable magnetism had existed between them, she thought. Even as she tried to deny it, then rationalize it away by giving it another name, it refused uprooting. And he, like a farmer tending his prize crop, never failed to water the seeds of attraction.

At the song's end, they sauntered to one of

the love seats pushed against the wall in the room. Other couples sat along the curtain of the brick fireplace, while others remained on the floor as the next song, a jazz instrumental, started up.

Feeling betrayed by her own thoughts, Selinae fanned herself with her hand. She couldn't look Sterling in the eye, wondering if he had felt the swell of her breasts, still tingling against the fabric of her dress.

"Want something to drink?" she asked.

"No, thank you," he said. "I just want to sit here awhile and catch my breath." He took her hand in his.

"Haven't gone dancing in a while," she teased. "You're out of shape."

"The dancing part is true, but my being out of breath is mostly your fault," he said.

"If you don't stop talking to me like that, we won't be planting that garden you wanted to get started on tomorrow," she said.

With a gentle, teasing laugh, Sterling pulled her closer and his breath tickled her ear, sending a tingle down her spine.

"Am I finally getting to meet the real Selinae?" he asked. "Or is the wine going to her head?"

Something had gone to her head, Selinae mused, but she didn't believe the wine deserved the credit. Shaking her head, she chuckled softly. "You're making me say crazy things."

"Good," he replied, "then that makes us even."

A mischievous look glinted in his eyes, an easy smile played around the corners of his mouth as he raised her hand to his lips and planted a kiss on her palm.

"Sterling," she breathed as a shudder passed through her.

"What?" he drawled innocently. "I merely asked a simple question. Which you have yet to answer."

"You ask too many questions for a photographer," she quipped, knowing he meant the question he asked earlier that day. "Asking questions is *my* job." She poked a finger to her chest.

"Then ask away," he replied, crossing his legs at the knee.

All of her questions were self-directed, she thought, now forced to come up with some innocuous inquiry. "What's your middle name?"

"Neal," he replied. "Yours?"

"I'm asking the questions here," she said laughingly.

With a strange, faintly eager look flashing in his eyes, he replied, "Tit for tat, lady. I'll accept nothing short of sharing."

Selinae could tell by the tone in his mellow baritone voice, it was a point he would not concede, no arguments, no compromises. She felt on the precipice of exotic ground, afraid of taking that step forward and afraid not to. She swallowed the lump in her throat. "Antoinette."

"Selinae Antoinette Rogers." Sterling savored the name on his tongue as if it were a fine delicacy. "Okay, what's next?"

Selinae wrinkled up her face in quick pondering. He was a man who knew his mind, she thought, while she could barely think past the desire smoldering in her. "No more questions," she replied at last.

"What?" he asked, somewhat amazed. "There's nothing else you want to know about me?"

"See how easy I am to please?" she asked, then realized the implications behind the innocent question.

"No you're not, lady," he replied, shaking his head from side to side. "You're complicated, and you scare the dickens out of me."

If he were scared, Selinae mused, she wondered where she fell on the Richter scale. She had a feeling the day of reckoning was fast approaching and could only hope she had answers by then. "Why don't you grow horns or something," she moaned.

"Why don't you just admit you want me as much as I want you?" he retorted.

At his brash declaration, her eyes blinked

rapidly in stunned succession before they settled on his face to study him silently. He studied her back; the look in his eyes contained a sensuous flame.

"I know what you've been thinking," he said. "Is he only interested in getting me into bed? Does he want a short fling or a long-term relationship? Can I trust him not to hurt me?" He looked at her pensively, then glanced down at her hand in his possession. "I can give you an answer to each and every one, but I can't answer for you." He looked up straight in her eyes; his were masked by some indefinable emotion.

It seemed everything Sterling said made sense, Selinae thought; everything he did was right. She didn't know if she could cope with his perfection, fearing she couldn't live up to it. She swallowed hard before she spoke.

"I find it hard to believe that you're afraid of anything," she replied in a barely audible voice.

"I'm afraid of making a mistake with you," he said. "I'd like nothing better than to take you to my bed and love you senseless. But I know you're not sure about me and I don't know how long I can wait for you to get all the answers you need. I'd like to think my patience is unlimited, but my . . ." He fell silent, a sheepish half-grin on his face, before continuing. "Well, I'm not so sure anymore."

With a somewhat self-derisive chuckle he held up her hand. "See? I can't even sit here without touching you. I've been wanting to do it all day, but I held back because you held back. I asked you early today whether you were ready. What I should have asked was . . . are you willing to take a chance on me?"

By the time they returned to her home, Selinae felt as if her emotions and thoughts were in dreamland. All evening Sterling had lulled her with his sagacious rhetoric and mellifluous voice, breaking down barriers of confusion and draining away her doubts.

Now she stood in her living room as he had commanded while he conducted a safety precaution search of her home.

If those horns haven't come out yet, she told herself, they never will. She had been searching for an excuse to say no to any combination of questions in her head, while every bone, cell, and nerve strand in her body said yes. Jubilantly and definitively so. He had answered all her unasked questions, and it was as he'd stated: The rest was up to her.

She supposed her skepticism was much like that of the millions of African Americans when first introduced to Kwanzaa. They questioned its value and relevance. Now, that same million and more embraced the celebration annually. They were asked to take a chance, and in doing so, found something that was essentially part of them—a missing link they couldn't do without. The parallel stuck in her mind.

"Everything checks out okay," Sterling said.

Selinae tracked his approach from the dining room with her inflamed heart in her eyes. She felt it beating in time to the echo in her head. *Take a chance. Take a chance. Take a chance.*

Stopping inches from Selinae, Sterling saw the confusion and desire in her amber eyes, a hint of vulnerability in their jeweled depths. He returned her gaze with his photographer's eyes, assessing the conflicting emotions he read in them.

It was no joke that he was afraid . . . afraid of losing her even before he could make her his. She was such an enigma to him. Never had he met a woman who radiated such warmth, yet guarded her life so vigilantly.

She seemed to respect his privacy almost too much, he mused. He found that irregular behavior for a journalist. He wondered if her lack of curiosity about him was self-protective. Although it presented an exciting challenge to the courtship, their lack of knowledge about each other made their relationship like walking through a mine field. He'd done that once before and swore he'd never do it again, he recalled, but his attraction to her had made a liar out of him. It was strong, had been from the beginning, and continued to grow more powerful by the second in her company.

Then again, there were instances when reminders of the first time he saw her at the park seemed like an ancient memory. He felt as though he'd known her for a long time. Her calming influence made him feel like he was home. He'd begun to suspect that his preconceived notion about settling down was somewhat outdated. A physical structure wasn't needed, he told himself, a physical sensation was. And one was swelling right then in the center of his groin.

Taking her hands in his, he said, *"Habari gani?"*

"Ujima," she replied softly.

He saw the breath tremble in her bosom and felt an uncanny urgency erupt in his gut. He wanted to protect her from the demon troubling her soul . . . to win her trust in him . . . to make her want him as much as he wanted her. He lowered his head to kiss her temple and waited. She stared up at him with a sweet expectant smile curled on her soft lips, pure desire now settled in her beautiful eyes, on her arresting face.

As if in slow motion, his head lowered to kiss her eye, on to the slightly rounded tip of her nose, then to her cheek. Guided by age-old instincts, his mouth wandered to the moist hollow of her throat, lingering there to enjoy the enticing fragrance of her skin. He could hear his own breathing roar in his ears, a tidal wave crashing against the walls of his chest.

A tiny mewl seeped past her lips, a tantalizing invitation for more, and he captured her mouth in a kiss full of passion and need.

In the bright lights of the living room, under the blessed symbols of Kwanzaa on the coffee table, he made love to her mouth, spoke to her soul with his lips, both gentle and demanding on hers. With their arms draped around each other, their bodies pressed together in arousal, their tongues sought each other's out. In the inner recesses of wanting mouths, a libation was offered, paying homage to the communion of man and woman, the building ground of family.

Sterling tore his mouth from Selinae's and stilled her wanton, wandering hands, holding them behind her back as he rested his forehead against hers. Seeking his breath, he said with an uncharacteristic falter in his voice, "Selinae . . . if we don't stop now, I'll—"

It was as far as he got, for she silenced him. In one fluid motion, she took his restraining hands and placed them around her waist. She stood on tiptoes, lifting her head as her lips brushed his. The whisper-light contact slew his thoughts of retreat. Lowering the white flag, he surrendered to her irresistible pull and reveled in the punishing sweetness of her kiss.

Touching became an art form. Neither body suffered a second's want for it as hands and fingers, driven by the urgency of mounting excitement, went to work. The purple, white, and yellow headwrap she wore fell first. The black, high-neck collared shirt next. Shoes made a trail to the bedroom.

Under the soft light of the bedside lamp, Selinae and Sterling paused to feast hungry gazes on each other. He was all honey and firm from his sculpted strong face, lightly pecked by a warm sun, down to his wide-shouldered, well-toned body. She was sienna and slim with firm, high-perched breasts and a tiny waist that widened into agilely rounded hips.

"You're beautiful," she said almost reverently.

"I've never known the meaning of the word before now," he replied, trailing a hand from the side of her face down to her breast, the tip dark and pebble-hard. He felt the tremulous breath she exhaled and sucked it into his lungs.

Selinae moved to her bed and waited for him to join her there. He did so without hesitation, stretching his strong body atop her soft one. Like a crofter, he began cultivating her aroused senses anew. She was an arable entity, her body and mind a fertile pasture to his sensuous tilling.

Her skin tingled when he touched her, and everywhere he touched her brought a gasp of wonder from her throat, traveling all the way up from her center. Twisting under his weight, arching her body as if to immerse her essence with his, she reaped as good as she sowed, and it was the best tending he had ever experienced. Her hands were magic tools, and he felt like a sapling under her ministrations.

She let him kiss her greedily and satisfied her own needy appetite from his lips. Then he moved, leaving her mouth burning with fire as his lips seared a path down her neck, her shoulders, and the satin plane of warm flesh beyond.

The old house came alive with Selinae and Sterling's harvesting, as if it had been waiting for such vibrancy to return to it ever since its past owners had left. Up until now, it had gone unfulfilled by its new mistress. Up until now . . .

When Sterling moved into Selinae, he gasped at the tightness of her sacred center. He attempted to restrain his thrusts, but her body insisted on the full strength of him, coiling tightly around his hardness. The breath rushed from him again in a wild gasp of pleasure.

He had to fight off the dizzying current

racing through him as he followed her lead, matched her seductive overtures into him stroke for stroke. With each possession, she arched up to receive him, propelling him to return for more. Their bodies made music and danced to it, as awe and passion-inspired sighs and groans filled the air.

Sighing praises to his name, Selinae felt herself infused with liquid fire. A fleeting thought, a wish for this ecstasy-ache to last forever, descended all too soon. Gasping in sweet agony, she shattered into a million glowing stars and her soul climbed to a heavenly place. Sterling joined her there shortly, his voice a rough moan of erotic surrender as he filled her with his love.

"Selinae," he said in a prayer-like whisper as his lips captured hers in a kiss that caressed her spirit. Then, windless, exhausted, divinely satiated, he collapsed atop her to hear her low, ecstatic laughter in his ear. With his head buried in her neck, he said in a muffled voice, *"Habari gani."*

"Kwanzaa yenu iwe na heri," she replied. With her arms wrapped loosely around him, she placed a gentle kiss on the side of his head and sighed with supreme contentment.

Too tired to move anything but his mouth, he said, "Translation, please."

"May y'alls Kwanzaa be with happiness," she said, and smiled.

* * *

Later, in the dark of the room, silent tears of joy slid down Selinae's face. With Sterling's sleeping form beside her, she could not stop pondering what had happened to her. She felt suffused with reverent sensations, a mixture of wonder, fear, and love.

The passion they'd shared, the reality and depth of it, was shocking. She couldn't help wondering if the way her body responded to him was a fluke as she glanced at Sterling, enraptured.

She also wondered what was next. Recalling his confident assertions, she knew he had an answer, but could he have anticipated one whose question had yet to be born?

Looming pervasively was the all-embracing affection she felt, the one that put rhyme before reason, feeling before thought, the one named love. Yes, love, she thought, even as she pondered how it was possible, or when it had happened, or whether she was confusing it with sex.

Yet, she knew deep down inside that no other word could describe what she felt. It was the most honest emotion she'd had in a long time, and she felt guilty for soiling it with questions and ruminations.

It had been too long, she mused. Much, much too long. Not since David, her very first lover, had she been able to complete the act of making love. They had both been young. Quite a bit of bumbling and fumbling had taken place. Though it hadn't been a totally unpleasant experience, it could never compare with her dreams and now with her indisputable proof of how utterly fulfilling sex could be with the right person.

A second attempt with a different partner while in college never progressed to consummation, she recalled somewhat sadly. Verbally abusive taunts from her past had crowded her memory and stole the moment. She had cried so hard, the poor young man she was with had been too startled to get angry with her.

A small cry escaped her throat unexpectedly, and Sterling was immediately awake. He saw her wet eyes, the tracks of tears on her face, and sat up to pull her into his arms.

"Ah, Selinae," he crooned gently. "Tell me," he pleaded.

Shaking her head, Selinae dried her eyes with her hands. "It's nothing." She let out a small laugh. "I'm just being silly, that's all."

"No, that's not all," he said with concern. "Damn. I knew it. I knew this would happen."

"No, no," she said, shushing him, her hand covering his mouth. "It's not what you think. I'm not sorry, and I have no regrets. It was the most wonderful thing that ever happened to me."

He kissed her on the temple before he spoke. "I detect a 'but' in that confession," he said. "It's been a long time for you, hasn't it?"

She smiled against his warm flesh. "A very long time."

"While it wouldn't have made any difference had it not been," he said, "I'm glad." He felt her smile widen. "Yes, I got some of the homies in me, too," he said, laughing at himself with her. Suddenly silent, he lay his head on hers. "Please . . . tell me what you're thinking."

Selinae sighed. Where to begin, how much to tell? Was she ready for disclosure, could he handle the truth? Her memory dipped into the past, dangerous territory.

"Selinae," he prodded gently, squeezing her body.

She pushed herself up, propping a pillow at her back and pulling the covers up to her chest. She drew a deep breath before she spoke. "I got pregnant when I was fifteen." She stared sidelong at Sterling, assessing his reaction. His face remained blank. "You're not . . ." she began, then fell silent, picking absently at the spread.

"What?" he asked. "Shocked? Disappointed? No, baby," he said, shaking his head. "We all have histories, Selinae. What happened? Did the boy desert you to the wolves?"

She detected a hint of anger in his voice when he said this last. "No," she said, a small smile tilting up the corners of her mouth. "He was very supportive and ready to assume his responsibility."

"Okay," Sterling said. "What happened?"

"We thought we were in love," she said, her thoughts filtering back to happy times. "He was a junior, vice-president of the student government, star basketball guard, honor roll. You know, the perfect guy."

"The kind daddies like to see their little girls date," Sterling said.

"His name was David," she said, then drew a tremulous sigh. "He wanted to be with me when I told my parents, but I wasn't so sure about their reaction. I had believed we were the kind of family where we could always go to each other, but this was different. My mother and I were never really close, but I knew my daddy would be disappointed. I knew what his expectations were for me. I had had a lot of success up to then as a runner. Our track team had made it to the nationals that year, and I had placed first in two events. There was a lot at stake, college scholarships, maybe even the Olympics. My father loved to go to the meets. He loved to help me train. He had everything set in his mind about how it was going to be. I knew the pregnancy would change things between us, but I had no idea how much. I thought it would be better if I told them alone. David let me have my way on this and my way turned out to be all wrong."

She shook her head slowly from side to side. "Never in all my life could I have dreamed a worse nightmare. My father went ballistic." She swallowed the lump that had lodged in her throat. "I didn't recognize him," she said in a soft, barely audible voice. "He was . . . a monster. It wasn't my daddy. It wasn't my daddy. It was some stranger . . . shouting and screaming, calling me horrible names, threatening violence. I almost believe he would have killed me if there had been no one there to intervene. My mother was screaming for him to calm down. My brothers were crying and trying to pull him away from me. Everything was loud and chaotic . . . all the crying and shouting, Daddy's angry threats. I tried to get away. He stopped me just as I reached that first step. I don't think it was deliberate. He just didn't realize his strength. His hand was on my arm and . . . I fell. All the way down to the bottom." She exhaled slowly, as if the action itself caused her pain.

Sterling suppressed his shock and dismay, envisioning the scene. A deep anger rose in him; he wanted to lash out, wanted to turn the violence she'd been subjected to back on her tormentor.

She held herself under tight control, her

expression vacant, almost as if she were talking about someone else. She told her story like a journalist, he thought, matter-of-factly, a straight reporting of events. He gently touched her cheek.

She continued. "My mama called Aunt Rae and Uncle Lou, who rushed over to the house. My daddy was throwing my clothes down over the banister, yelling at me to get out. They took me home with them. Later that night, they rushed me to the hospital. There was so much blood. So much blood. I lost the baby."

Tears fell in earnest, blinding her eyes and choking off her voice. Sterling pulled her into his arms and crushed her to him. "It's all right," he whispered as he stroked her back gently. "It's all right now."

"I didn't see him again until I was released from the hospital. He didn't come to see me. My mama took me home, but it was over between us, my daddy and me," she said, sniffing, wiping her running nose. "We didn't speak to each other for months. We were like two zombies. Then one day, he told me to get my shoes, but I wouldn't. I couldn't run for him anymore," she said, looking up at Sterling, as if pleading for him to understand.

"He'd lost respect for me as his daughter. And when I refused to run, he had no use for me at all. He told me to get out. I moved in with my aunt and uncle." She sought the warmth and comfort of Sterling's nearness, wrapping her arms around his waist, laying her head on his chest.

"I'm sorry. So sorry," he said over and over as he continued to hold her, trying to stroke the pain from her body.

"I thought I was special to him because I was his firstborn and only daughter," she said in a young girl's voice, then self-derision marred her tone. "I used to think that, you know? But what it boiled down to was that I was his star runner. The one who was going to get him to the Olympics." She snorted bitterly. "Now you know all my dirty little secrets," she said lightly. "I'm the rotten seed in the Rogers' family. And all you can do with a rotten seed is throw it away."

"Stop that," he commanded, his anger slipping into his tone.

"This Christmas was the first time we've spent more than thirty minutes together in the same place," she said as if speaking to herself. "But there's nothing there anymore. If there ever was any truth in our relationship, it's been dead a long time. I just never wanted to admit it. Now I can," she said in an emotionless tone.

Sterling didn't believe her for a minute. He took the declaration for what it was—a form of denial, a painkiller to deaden the deep wound.

This woman, his woman, he thought, was

much too caring and sensitive. She felt too deeply. After all, it was her warm and enchanting nature that had attracted him to her in the first place.

While it was good for him, the trait worked against her as far as her family was concerned. He'd seen glimpses of her vulnerability, recalling the confrontation he'd witnessed with her brothers, although she tried to hide it under a strong, impassive facade.

Still, he thought, never in a million years would he have guessed the shadows on her soul had been cast by her father. He'd like to beat the hell out of Mr. Rogers, but he knew Selinae would rush to the bastard's side like a mother hen in a second.

Recalling his lament of ever getting next to her, he had no complaints about her response to him in bed, he thought. He recognized the oblation of her flesh to him and was all the more determined to cherish it like the priceless gift it was. She was more woman than he expected, more than he could have ever hoped for. But he wanted all of her: *both in and out of bed.*

And he thought he had all the answers, he chided himself. But he had no answer for this. At least, not one Selinae would entertain.

Even as he feared he was no match for her enemy, he knew words of comfort alone were not enough for his woman. He was going to have to show her she no longer had to suffer in silence.

It was going to be a painstaking lesson, he thought, knowing that family fights were far more harmful than a gang of homies. The scars ran deeper; the healing took longer.

Wondering whether he was up to the task, Sterling prayed for the guidance and strength from the Creator.

Selinae finally drifted off. Sterling contented himself with just holding her in his arms until he too joined her in the liberating state of dreams.

But bright and early the next morning, reality came calling once again with the ringing of the doorbell. The sound roused them both out of sleep. Both hoped it would subside; neither wanted to leave the haven of the other's warmth.

"Maybe they'll go away," Sterling said, pulling her closer to him. He nuzzled the side of her neck, crushing her to him. "Hmm," he sighed at length. "I could get used to waking up next to you."

Feeling the stirring of desire awakening in her, she arched her body into his. "I know what you mean," she said. He drew a sensuous moan from her throat as his mouth devoured the softness of hers.

The ringing of the doorbell persisted.

Lifting his mouth from hers reluctantly, he asked, "Want me to send them away?"

"It's probably my brothers, who will positively drop dead at my front door if you answer," she quipped laughingly.

"I'm not afraid of your brothers, Selinae," he said in a plain, serious voice.

Selinae stared into his face; a savage inner fire glowed in his chocolate eyes, bold lights of confidence and determination in their depths. The look strengthened her resolve to take a chance, shored up her still distant goal of liberation. Wanting to feel only the protective weight of his arms around her, she said softly, "Then go . . . send them away and come back to me."

"Where's Selinae?"

The question, more like a demand, hung in the air as if supported by an invisible string of thread. Sterling merely stared in stunned amazement at the two women at the door.

The speaker was bedecked in a teal designer suit that complimented her slender frame and caramel complexion to perfection. Long, thick black hair fell in luscious curls around her shoulders; her makeup was expertly applied. The features of her oval face were delicately carved, but her expression was austere, her manner haughty. Sterling realized at once that he was facing a mother's wrath.

His heart began to pound like a kettledrum in his chest. What a state he was in—shoeless, shirtless, clothes discarded the previous night folded over his arm, his plan to shock Selinae's brothers ridiculously backfired. With an insipid smile spreading across his face, he opened his mouth to speak.

"Where's my daughter, young man?"

"I told you we should have called first," her companion chided.

Sterling flashed a weak smile at Mrs. Roger's companion, Selinae's Aunt Rae, whom he'd met the night before. Finding his voice, he said, "Good morning. Won't you come in? I'll get Selinae for you."

Aunt Rae winked at Sterling as she trailed Cora Rogers into the living room.

After locking the door, Sterling was eager to escape. Reaching the hallway door, he bumped into Selinae. He flashed her an "uh-oh" grimace. She gave him a seductive smile and patted him on the arm, then winked in response to his mildly scolding look that told her to behave.

Walking around Sterling into the living room, Selinae tightened the belt of the robe she'd put on. "Good morning, Mama, Aunt Rae. What are you two doing up so early?"

"It's almost eleven," Cora Rogers replied,

staring pointedly at Selinae before turning her gaze on Sterling.

Pointing a thumb at the woman by her side, Aunt Rae said, "I couldn't stop her from coming, so I figured I might as well come along. Good morning, Sterling." She flashed him a broad, winking grin.

"Good morning, Rae," Sterling replied. Absently, he rubbed the side of his neck. He hadn't been this nervous since his first date in high school.

Pulling Sterling alongside her, Selinae said, "Sterling, I'd like you to meet my mother, Cora Rogers. Mama, this is Sterling Washington."

"Sterling," Cora said flatly.

"How do you do, Mrs. Rogers?" Sterling replied. Regaining his wits, he extended a hand to her, his most charming smile intact. "It's a pleasure to meet you."

Unimpressed, Cora shook his hand weakly as if afraid of catching something.

"Uh, why don't I put on a pot of coffee," he said, backing from the room, clutching the armload of clothes.

"That's a good idea," Aunt Rae said as she situated herself on the couch.

"I keep the coffee in—" Selinae started.

"I'll find it," Sterling said, cutting her off as he vanished behind the kitchen door.

Silence reigned until Sterling was no longer

visible, then conversation levels dropped to a soft decibel.

"When your brothers told me you kicked them out—" Cora began in an incensed whisper.

"How are you doing, Mama?" Selinae said, kissing her mother on the cheek. "You look wonderful, as usual."

For a second, Cora was flabbergasted. "I'm fine, Selinae. How are you?" Before Selinae could answer, Cora pointed toward the kitchen. "I suppose that's evident."

"I want details," Aunt Rae said, clapping her hands together in a sign of eager excitement. She smiled at Selinae with anticipation, undaunted by the glower on her sister's face.

"Will you behave yourself, Rae?" her sister snapped. "Selinae, what do you know about this man?" she asked, setting her expensive handbag on the coffee table.

Pulling up her caftan and resting her leg on the couch, Aunt Rae replied in a bored tone, "I thought we'd covered that ground."

"I don't want to hear any more of your nonsense," Cora returned, then faced Selinae headlong, her arms folded across her bosom.

It never ceased to amaze her that her mother, Cora Shaw-Rogers, and her aunt, Rae Marie Shaw-Willis, were of the same blood. Aunt Rae was a practical, earthy woman who embraced life heartily and without fear. She was usually robed in African attire. Her mother, on the other hand, clung to some outdated etiquette code that had never applied to black women in the first place. Though she was stronger than she looked, she lived the stereotype of the gentile, southern woman. They had been at odds from the moment Selinae graced this earth. A tomboy, she had always been daddy's girl. At least, until . . .

"Selinae," Cora said impatiently. "Are you going to answer me?"

Sliding onto the love seat, Selinae crossed her legs at the knee, careful to close the folds of her robe. "It's always good to see you, Mama, but I'm curious as to what precipitated this visit. Does your husband know you're here?"

"That's your father you're talking about," she scolded harshly, "and I don't need anybody's permission to visit my daughter."

"She never said or implied that you did," Aunt Rae said, coming to her niece's defense.

"Selinae," her mother said, her eyes trained on her daughter, "what do you know about this man? Your brothers said you didn't even introduce them yesterday, and last night at Rae's house you barely said a word to them."

Selinae smiled to herself. She and Sterling were leaving the party as her brothers had driven up, she recalled. She had called out a greeting and then continued on her way. She didn't want another interrogation, not when she had been having such a blissful evening.

"You just met him, Mama," Selinae said. "His name is Sterling Neal Washington."

"That's a name that means absolutely nothing to me," her mother said.

"I already told you, he's got a good income, he's single and he doesn't have any venereal diseases," Aunt Rae interjected, finishing with an impatient tsk.

Selinae hid a smile behind her hand. Sterling was going to get an earful today, she thought.

"Rae Marie Shaw-Willis, shame on you," Cora chided, outraged. "And how do you know that, anyway?"

"I asked," Aunt Rae replied. "I get all the pertinent information up front," she boasted proudly. "What more do you want to know?"

"I sure don't want to know any more from you. Selinae, you never mentioned this man when you came over for dinner the other night."

"The subject never came up," Selinae replied. She didn't dare tell her mother *when* she'd met Sterling. Not after he had answered the door in such a state. "We've been seeing quite a bit of each other. He's a photographer. Maybe you've seen his work."

"Who does he work for?"

"The question is who *doesn't* he work for,"

she replied. "He's taken pictures for the *Smithsonian, National Geographic,* and lots of other publications, as well as for individuals and corporations. He's from Houston, attended TSU, just recently moved into a new house right across the street from MacGregor Park." Watching the interested gleam come to her mother's eyes, she knew she'd put Sterling's assets in the proper order.

"Well, that's a blessing," Cora said with a hearty sigh of relief. "At least he's not a bum." She sat on the opposite end of the couch from her sister, closest to Selinae.

"I've never dated bums," Selinae replied softly.

"You know what I mean," her mother said, waving her hand dismissively. "Is it serious between the two of you?"

"I'm not sure I understand your question," Selinae replied, stalling.

"Yes, you do," Cora said. "I didn't raise no dummies."

"If you're so sure about that, then why are you here?" Selinae replied, giving her mother a sidelong glance. She had a sinking feeling the visit was going to duplicate the one she'd had with her brothers the day before.

"We're concerned about you," Cora replied. "There's no need to be flippant. Maybe he'd like to come with you New Year's Eve. We're all going to church together. In fact, that's one of the reasons I came by. I want to take you shopping."

"It's too late," Selinae said under her breath.

"What was that?" Cora demanded.

"I said Sterling and I have other plans for New Year's Eve," Selinae replied.

"What's more important than spending time with your family?" Cora shot back at her.

"You want a list?" Selinae said, losing patience.

"What's that supposed to mean?" Cora asked.

"You know damn well—" Selinae started, then caught herself.

Wagging a finger at Selinae, Cora said, "Listen, young lady, I'm your mother. You don't use that kind of language in my presence."

"I'm sorry," Selinae said, suddenly contrite. "You're right, of course, but that still doesn't change anything. I'm sure Tony and Oscar junior told you how I feel. I don't feel up to repeating myself."

"Two wrongs don't make a right, Selinae," Cora said. "I thought you were mature enough to realize that."

"Oh right, make *me* the villain here," she snapped. "I guess I do have to repeat myself and I promise this is the last time I'm going to say it. I've had enough," she stressed emphatically. "I'm not going through it anymore with your husband. My hoop-jumping days are over."

"So what does that mean, that you've cut all of us out of your life? You disavow us as a family. Is that it?" Cora inquired hotly, her voice rising.

Was that what she had done . . . mentally severed ties with her family? Selinae asked herself, her bottom lip folded in her mouth. She answered with a shake of her head. No, she thought, she didn't believe that. She wasn't that vindictive. She was merely determined to pull the pieces of her life together the only way she knew how. Running home again at the promise of mending the bond that had long ago been severed was destructive to her. She couldn't let herself be fooled again, to hope where there was no hope.

"Selinae . . . ?"

She looked up to see Sterling completely dressed, smiling down at her, and felt renewed strength. This was the direction she wanted to move in. Toward life. Toward love.

"Where should I set this?" he asked, indicating the wooden serving tray with service for four in his hands.

Sterling had hoped that some vigorous yard work would help him pass the time. The euphoria he'd felt after having charmed Mrs.

Rogers had worn off. Now he was playing a solitaire guessing game of "she's coming, she's not coming" with himself as he tilled a square plot of land in his backyard under the bored gaze of his dog.

The garden was in the far back left-hand corner of the spacious yard. It faced his neighbor's, separated by a fence that was covered with clinging vines. A roll of chicken wire and empty bags of compost and fertilizer lay on the ground nearby.

His fat puppy Hannibal was stretched out on the patio floor near a kidney-shaped pool in the center of the yard. The pool held dead leaves and streaks of dirt instead of water.

It was early evening, between five and six. The air smelled clean and fresh, with a faint odor of pecan wood burning in a nearby fireplace. The weather was clear but nippy; the air current was rising with the promise of a winter's cold.

Sterling felt only frustration as he worked up a sweat.

Wondering how long it could possibly take to buy a dress, he squatted to untangle a piece of plastic debris from the moist black dirt imbedded in the iron spikes of the tiller. He tossed it aside and remained squatting, absently massaging a handful of soil, resting his head along the wooden handle of the tiller.

She should be here with me, he thought fiercely.

He'd made a mistake, he chided himself. He shouldn't have encouraged Selinae to go off with her mother and aunt. He should have insisted on keeping to their plans of starting the garden together, he told himself, gripping the handle of the tiller.

He ran the risk of not seeing her again, he thought fearfully, vigorously mixing the soil in the bed. Or of her losing her newfound faith in him at the hands of her family.

Sterling stilled. Leaning against the tiller handle, the memory of the previous night closed around him, blacked out the present and filled him with a keen yearning. With the indelible sensations of one night in her loving arms running freely through him, Sterling felt confirmed in what he'd up till then only suspected. He could strike out lust, he decided; what he felt was no temporary diversion. Selinae set his heart into motion: He'd only been surviving before he met her.

He was fragile as far as Selinae was concerned, he thought uneasily. She could easily scorch him.

He wiped his sweaty palms on his pants and resumed his task. There wasn't a thing he could do about his present situation except try not to think about it, he told himself, and yet his thoughts continued to drift back to the obstacles between them.

The distance between her and her father

could conceivably work to his advantage, he mused with a slight sense of relief. But for all her dainty, ultrafeminine ways, Cora Rogers he pegged as a viper.

That left him in a precarious situation. He didn't know if Selinae's trust in him was up to the test if it came down to a contest of wills between him and her family.

He couldn't recall ever being so afraid of losing anything in all his life. And even *that* had been on the line before, he mused, recalling the week he'd spent in Johannesburg photographing the first elections open to black South Africans.

Just then, he heard what he thought was a car engine shutting down out front. His suspicions were confirmed by Hannibal. The short-haired, black and tan dog lifted his big head, his snub nose pointed alertly. Tossing the handle of the tiller aside, Sterling hurried into the house, Hannibal on his heels. He ran through the kitchen, bypassing the family room, and down the short corridor to the foyer, his heart racing ahead of him. Reaching the door, he drew a deep, calming breath, but was too impatient to compose himself further. He opened the door with a flourish.

"Did I come at a bad time?"

The dog wagged its tail jubilantly, while animation fled from Sterling's expression. He managed a slight smile as he looked into a face that was a female version of his, the features softer, smaller, and older. "No Mama," he said, "come on in." He tried not to sound too disappointed.

"Hi, baby," she said, patting Hannibal. To Sterling, she said, "I got some stuff in the car." Backing from the door, with Hannibal running playfully around her legs, she said, "Come help me."

Dutifully, Sterling followed her to the luxury blue car, trying to summon some enthusiasm. His mother pulled out a large roasting pan from the backseat and put it in his hands, then grabbed two large bags. The smells wafting from the containers didn't go unnoticed.

"Boudain?" he asked with a slightly raised brow, a grin starting to spread across his face.

"And lemon meringue pie and praline cheesecake," she replied. "All your favorites."

Suddenly suspicious as to the nature of her visit, he asked, "Mama, where's Guy?"

"Oh, he went to see about his sister," his mother replied, heading back to the house. Hannibal led the way.

Reaching the door, Sterling hesitated. What if Selinae came by and saw his mother's car parked outside? If she thought he was entertaining another woman, she would surely drive off without coming in.

"Mama, let me put your car in the garage,"

he said, setting the pan on the floor inside the foyer.

"I'm not going to be here that long," she replied.

"Mama, just give me the keys," he instructed, his hand held out to her.

Moments later, with his mother's car safely tucked in the garage and the door pulled down, Sterling strolled into the kitchen. His mother had already laid out a plate of food on the bar counter and was putting more away in the refrigerator. He saw Hannibal sneaking out the back door, his massive jaws clinging to a long boudain sausage.

"Mama, he shouldn't be eating that," Sterling scolded mildly.

"It ain't gonna kill him," his mother replied.

Sitting at the bar on the kitchen side, he picked up one long sausage and took a big bite. "When he starts complaining about his dog food, I'll send him to your house," he said, chewing.

"I put some smoked turkey, dirty rice, and cornbread dressing in the box," she said. "Your grandma sent you some étouffée. It's in the freezer." She grimaced as she turned around to face him. "You could have washed your hands. I at least taught you that much."

"Tastes better this way," he said with a mouthful.

She merely shook her head. He smiled, continuing to eat with his fingers. His Mama wasn't an educated woman–she had never graduated from high school–but she was smarter than a lot of people he knew. A dark-skinned Creole woman, bronze complexioned like he was, she retained her Louisiana accent even though she'd been in Houston for nearly forty years. Neither fat nor muscular, she had a hefty bosom and ample hips. Hair that fell to her waist was peppered with gray strands at the temple. It was customarily plaited and twisted into a ball at the back of her head. Though she could cuss and fuss with the best of them when in a temper, it had been her warm, caring nature and good cooking that had attracted Guy Ladd to his mama.

Staring across at her profile, Sterling felt a certain tension in the air. His mother looked worried, he suddenly noticed. Immediately, he grew concerned.

She trained her large, expressive brown eyes on him; a smile faltered on her wide lips. Sterling stopped chewing. He gulped down the chunk of food in his mouth, wondering if she and Guy had had a fight. Licking his fingers clean, he got up to go to her.

"Mama, what's the matter? Are you and Guy getting along okay?"

"We're getting along fine," she said.

"Then what's wrong?"

She walked away from him, into the family room. He followed, watching as she scanned the contents of the room: four large packing boxes, a floor lamp, and a red beanbag chair.

"When are you going to fix up this place? Ain't nowhere for a person to sit," she fussed, propping her hands on her hips.

She spun around and bumped into Sterling. He put his hands on her shoulders and stared down into her face with a stern look. "Patricia Thibodeaux-Ladd, talk."

"You just like your father," she said huffily. "Think you know everything . . . always trying to drag stuff out of people. That's why ain't no woman here now. You probably scare them off."

"I'm too old to bait, Mama," he said, a hint of a smile in his expression.

"Ain't nothing to talk about," she scoffed. "I told you ain't nothing wrong."

"I don't believe you," he said, holding her still when she tried to squirm out of his gentle possession. "Here," he said, leading her to a stool at the counter, "sit down right here and tell me what's going on."

She obeyed, situating herself comfortably on the high stool. She set her hands primly in her lap, but couldn't keep them still. "I guess I might as well get over it, huh?" She looked up at him, biting down on her lip.

"I'm pregnant," she said, a bittersweet expression on her face.

"Pregnant," Sterling whispered absently. A sudden panic that had nothing to do with his mother's announcement assailed him. Selinae's image filled his wide-eyed, faraway gaze.

"I'm not that old," his mother said. "I was sixteen when I had you. I am older than the average mother, but the doctor said I'm in good health and he don't anticipate any problems."

He barely heard her, his mind elsewhere. Selinae! He hadn't used anything to protect Selinae, Sterling thought with a shiver of vivid recollection. And with everything he knew about her previous encounter . . . ! He clutched the sides of his head and bit off a curse.

"I knew you'd be upset," Patricia said, resigned.

Sterling felt split in two as he took in his mother's woebegone expression. "No, Mama," he said, eager to make her understand. "I'm not upset with you." With a hollow chuckle, he said, "Hell, it's none of my business." He gave her a broad grin and kissed her on the cheek. "Congratulations. I think it's great news. How does Guy feel about it?"

"Guy can't contain himself," she replied laughingly, wiping at her misty eyes. "Are you sure you not mad at me? I mean, you still my baby, you know." She smiled at him shyly.

"Mama, I'm thirty-six years old," he said, laughing at her. "I'll still be your baby if you want, but I'm a little old to be jealous, don't you think?"

"You're right. You need to be having your own babies," she scolded teasingly. "If you had been supplying me with grandbabies . . ."

"Oh no, you can't blame this one on me, old lady," he replied, draping his arms around her in an affectionate hug.

"I'm not old," she retorted.

"No, you're not," he said. "I'm really glad for you and Guy."

"Now, where's that woman?"

"What woman?" he asked.

"The one you were expecting when you opened the door to me," she said, grinning at him slyly.

Sterling felt his face grow warm with embarrassment. When the doorbell rang his blush doubled in intensity. "I'll be right back," he said with a quick snap of his shoulders as he hurried from the room.

Nearing the door, he braced himself and schooled his expression. Filled with anticipation, he opened the door.

Selinae was staring up at him with an admiring gleam in her gaze, a hint of erotic memories in her bright eyes. Though she was chicly dressed in a black and white mesh wool blazer with a single button over a white blouse, starched jeans hugging her fine hips, and black boots, he saw her naked, her slender brown body glowing with desire and passion.

A thrill of excitement coursed through him. He thought he'd explode with joy at seeing her.

"I was afraid you wouldn't come back," he said, his eyes raking her possessively.

"Don't make me do that again," she replied, crossing the threshold to step into his waiting arms.

As she draped them around his waist, he heard the thud of her handbag and all-weather coat as they hit the floor. He laughed: it was partly nervousness, but mostly just because it felt good to do so as he crushed her to him.

"Was it that bad?" he asked, his lips on her hair.

"No. Not at all, really," she replied, her head resting against his shoulder. "Tiring. It was different. I don't know. I—"

She stopped talking suddenly, perhaps fearing she'd disclose more than she intended to. Sterling wasn't sure how to interpret her mood, wanted to question her about the time she'd spent with her mother, but Cora Rogers didn't seem too important right now. Selinae was here in his arms, and all his dread vanished.

"I missed you," he said, kissing the side of her face.

"I missed you, too," she replied. She looked up at him and tweaked her nose. "You obviously started without me."

He threw back his head and let loose a peal of laughter, then squeezed her to him for a quick hug. "I need a shower, I know."

"Is it big enough for the both of us?" she asked.

"Sterling . . . ?"

Selinae's head jerked up and she backed out of Sterling's embrace, staring at the woman approaching them from the back of the house.

"I think I'll run along and let you entertain your company," Patricia said.

Looping an arm around Selinae's waist, Sterling spun around to face his mother. "You just couldn't wait for me to bring her back to meet you, could you?" he said with a teasing grin.

"I heard the mention of a shower and figured I'd make tracks," Patricia said. "I didn't expect you to be standing in the door."

"Well, it's all right, Mama, and you don't have to leave," he said. "Meet Selinae Rogers. Selinae, this is my mother, Patricia Ladd."

"I'm so glad to meet you, child," Patricia said, taking Selinae's hands between hers.

"It's nice meeting you, too, Mrs. Ladd," Selinae replied shyly.

Noticing the blush on her face, Sterling smiled down at her with a conspiratorial look in his eyes. "It's been sort of a mothers' day, hasn't it?" he said.

As eager as she had been to get back to him, Selinae didn't mind sharing Sterling with his mother. She was introduced to Hannibal, who enjoyed her attention and stayed at her side during a tour of the house, and then when they all adjourned to the kitchen.

"You hungry, child?" Patricia asked. "I brought some good old turkey and dressing and—"

"Mama," Sterling interrupted, "Selinae doesn't eat meat."

"Oh, you one of them vegetarians, huh?" Patricia said. "What about shrimp? You eat shrimp?"

"Does she ever," Sterling said. "I took her out to dinner the other night, and she ate a whole plate all by herself."

"That's not true," Selinae said. She feigned an outraged look at him, then slapped him on the shoulder playfully.

"Ouch," he said, rubbing the spot.

Without further instructions, Patricia set out to prepare a feast. Within minutes, the counter was laden with plates of food and dessert, and a bowl of étouffée for Selinae.

"Give me that back," Sterling said, chasing Hannibal, who was clutching a large turkey drumstick Patricia had given him. Hannibal scooted out the back door, his jaws firmly around his meal. "Mama, I've told you already about giving my puppy table food," Sterling said.

"It ain't—"

Sterling cut her off. "I know, it ain't gonna kill him," he said in the familiar Louisiana accent, sitting on the stool next to Selinae. "Are you going to eat some of this, too?" he asked Patricia, indicating a plate laden with food—turkey, dressing, two large slices of two different pies—on the counter before him.

"No, that's yours," she replied, taking a bite of her own slice of pie.

"Goodness, Mama, you must think I'm a growing boy," he replied, shaking his head as he picked up his fork.

"Eat what you can and put the rest back," she advised reasonably.

"It would have been a lot simpler if you hadn't warmed up so much," he said.

"Selinae, is he always fussing about something around you, too?" Patricia asked.

"Let's just say," Selinae replied diplomatically, "he has something to say about everything."

"That's him. Always been that way," Patricia said. "That's why I was so happy when he got his first camera. He stopped talking when he got behind it."

"I'm thirsty," Sterling said, rising. "How about you? I got Diet Coke."

"That'll be fine," Selinae replied.

"I'll get it," Patricia said.

"No, you sit down," Sterling commanded, sauntering to the refrigerator. He popped the tops of three cans of soda, then filled three glasses and passed them around.

"Is that hot enough for you, Selinae?" Patricia asked, indicating the bowl of shrimp stew.

"It's incredible, Mrs. Ladd, thanks," Selinae said. "You're a wonderful cook."

"You gave her enough to feed a hundred people," Sterling grumbled good-naturedly as he forked a piece of pie.

"Don't talk with your mouth full," Patricia replied.

Selinae felt content to sit quietly eating, as the talk evolved to entertaining stories about Patricia's Creole relatives, who'd refused to embrace the twentieth century. Occasionally, Patricia would slip into her patois and Sterling would admonish her to speak English.

"I don't want Selinae to think we're talking about her," he explained.

Selinae felt cherished. Sterling gave completely of himself to both of them. He was respectful and wonderfully patient with his mother, and attentive to her. With each passing second of this day, she mused, she had a new blessing to count.

Witnessing the loving exchange between Sterling and Patricia, Selinae thought about her own relationship with her mother. She was still somewhat surprised by the conversation they had had that day. Aunt Rae, for the most part, had been a silent buffer. She had come to act as referee. As it turned out, she wasn't needed in that role.

Her mother had surprised her by not talking further about Sterling. That was not to say he hadn't been in her thoughts, Selinae mused, a smile spreading across her face. She had a feeling that the outraged performance Cora Rogers had put on at her house was just for show, an act for Sterling's benefit.

They had gone to Cora Rogers' favorite shopping center, the Galleria Mall, she recalled, taking a sip of her drink. Though she had no intentions of letting her mother buy her anything, she indulged her by trying on some of the high-priced, designer clothes her mother picked out. Modeling an elegant knit pantsuit, bespeckled with hand-sewn pearls, she knew the outfit looked gorgeous on her. It didn't take too much encouragement from her mother and Aunt Rae for her to buy it. It was going to set her budget back for six months, but it would be appreciated, she thought, stealing a glance at Sterling.

Switching his attention from his mother to her, he caught her staring at him, and tenderly his eyes melted into hers. She felt an electric current travel the length of her spine as an unspoken communication passed between them.

"I'm sorry, Mama, what did you say?" Sterling asked after a moment.

Freed from his enraptured gaze, Selinae wetted her suddenly parched throat by taking a drink. As Patricia Ladd launched into another tale, Selinae couldn't help believing that her feelings for Sterling had opened up a new world to her, as her thoughts returned to her mother.

After spending two hours in the ritzy store, they'd strolled through the mall, window-shopping. With her box clutched in her hand, she was afraid to look at another item for fear she would cave in to a call-to-purchase.

They stopped at a café overlooking the mall skating rink for coffee and dessert. The better part of their time together was spent there, absently watching the skaters and talking.

No, she amended silently, they did more than talk. They *communicated.* Though her mother had given her quite an earful, one thing in particular stayed with her.

"The reason you and your father used to get along so well was because you're so much alike," Cora had said. "Then when you became a woman, an independent thinker, he simply couldn't take that his little girl was growing up and away from him. He thought he could be everything for you. Despite repeated warnings," she added, laughing softly before a pensive silence fell across the table.

She had noticed Aunt Rae take her mother's hand as if to pass her strength into her. Another surprise. She had no idea the two sisters were so close.

"That's why," Cora had continued softly, a tenuous smile wavering on her lips, "he was so hurt when you got pregnant. To him, it meant you had cut him out of your life. He simply couldn't handle what he perceived as your rejection of his love."

"But I tried since then to show him that wasn't true," Selinae protested, unable to keep the hurt from her voice. "You know I tried."

"Yes, you did," her mother said, covering her hand affectionately.

She had snatched her hand away. It wasn't in offense at her mother's touch, Selinae mused, but because she feared the gesture would make her lose it. She hadn't wanted to cry.

"See, that's what I'm talking about," Cora had said. "You've always done that to me, Selinae. Your father is the same way. After all these years of marriage to him, there is still an area of his life that he won't share with me. As if he expects *me* to compound his hurt. I don't know what to do about you two anymore."

It had taken her a while, Selinae recalled, a second glance at the sad gaze in her mother's eyes to realize what her own pride had wrought. Without saying a word, she took her mother's hand between hers. The simple gesture seemed to alter their relationship, elevate it. At least her view of it. All these years she felt her mother had abandoned her when she'd needed her the most, when now she had to consider the possibility that she had been the one to push her mother away.

"It's getting late," Patricia was saying, bringing Selinae out of her reverie.

Embarrassed to have been caught woolgathering, Selinae smiled politely as she rose to walk around the bar to the kitchen. Sterling was helping his mother into her coat.

"It was nice meeting you, Mrs. Ladd," Selinae said.

"I hope I see you again," Patricia said. "If this boy of mine gives you a hard time, you just call me."

"And what you gonna do?" Sterling said playfully in a gruff voice.

"Go upside your head," Patricia replied, knuckling his temple.

"I'm going to have to hire a bodyguard to protect me from you two," Sterling said as he pulled Selinae next to him, his arm around her waist.

"It's been a good day," Patricia remarked as she led the way to the front door.

"Yes, it has," Sterling echoed, smiling down at Selinae.

After seeing Mrs. Ladd off, they returned to the bright warmth inside the house. Selinae felt a bottomless peace and satisfaction as they stood in the foyer. Sterling was looking at her with an entranced gaze, his hand still on the knob of the door.

"Stay with me tonight."

It was part question, part declaration. Selinae didn't hesitate in reply.

"My overnight case is in the backseat."

"I'll be right back," he said as he vanished into the cold night.

Finally, she thought, the spirit of the holidays had seeped into her soul. Wishing she could bottle it up for safekeeping year-round, she strolled into the study and clicked on the light. She had noticed earlier the kinara and mishumaa saba already set up on the coffee table and wanted to light the next candle. It was still the day of Ujima, the fourth day.

Had it really been only four days ago that Sterling had come into her life? she asked herself, amazed. Sterling peeked into the room and caught her looking through the desk drawer.

"If you're looking for a light," he said, "it's in the bottom drawer. I'll run and get the wine."

When he returned shortly with a brass wine goblet, Selinae was already on her knees before the coffee table. He joined her, setting the goblet on the corner of the table.

"Can we amend this as we go along?" he asked, tugging at his shirt. "I'm still in dire need of a shower."

Selinae chuckled. "Me, too."

He grabbed her around the waist and growled into her neck playfully. She laughed before he stilled, staring at her with an intent look in his eyes. She felt at once tongue-tied and full of words as she caressed the sides of his face, her eyes bright.

"I've never felt this way before," she said in a soft voice. "It's a little scary, you know. We've only known each other a short time, but I feel as if I've known you forever."

Sterling took her hand in his and clasped it next to his mouth, his adoring gaze never leaving her face. "Thank you," he whispered in her palm before he kissed it and held it reverently next to his cheek. "You've given me so much, and the more you give, the more I want. I went crazy today without you. I don't think I'll ever get enough of you."

Selinae stared at him, almost unable to believe that he cared as deeply as she.

"My mother," he said in an affected voice, "came by to tell me she's pregnant."

Selinae's eyes widened. "Is that good?" she asked tentatively.

"Yes," he replied. "I believe Guy has always wanted a child, but she's always refused. She was afraid to tell me," he said with a soft chuckle.

When one was happy, she wished happiness for the world. "Good for them," she said sincerely.

Sterling swallowed, then breathed in deeply.

"What's the matter?" she asked, alert to the sudden change in his expression, the unfamiliar hesitancy about him.

"I didn't do anything to protect you when we made love. I've been thinking about it ever since my Mama told me her news. I'm sorry, Selinae." His eyes narrowed with regret.

"I'm not," she said in a barely audible voice.

"What? What did you say?"

"I said I'm not sorry," she repeated in a stronger voice. "Admittedly, getting pregnant was the last thing on my mind for a while there," she said in a sensual, teasing way.

"Selinae, how can you say that? I mean, what if you're pregnant?"

Selinae shrugged dismissively.

"You can't possibly want to put yourself through that again," he said. "Things would go from bad to worse."

"Sterling, what are you talking about?"

"I'm talking about you and your father, that's what I'm talking about."

"I don't have a father," she said, a hint of annoyance in her voice. "And so what?" she asked, flicking a light over a candle. "This is my body. I do with it what I want, father or not."

Halting her, Sterling said in a stern voice, "Not in this." He took the lighter from her and flung it on the table.

Selinae sat back to stare at him wordlessly, her heart pounding, a puzzled frown on her face. She was momentarily transported back in time. She felt she was looking at a stranger, the same way she had felt about her father all those years ago . . . Sterling's expression made it obvious that she had made a mistake, she thought. *Again.*

Even as she prayed it wasn't true, she mused morosely that Sterling wasn't the man she thought he was. She felt his gaze on her, but she couldn't return his look, fastened hers on the candles. Both sets, the three red ones on the left and the three green ones on the right blurred into the black candle in the center of the kinara under the threat of her stinging tears. She pinched the corners of her eyes with her fingers.

Spacing out the words evenly, she said in as strong a voice as she could muster, "Oh, you don't have a thing to worry about, Mr. Washington. If by chance I do get pregnant, I won't hold you responsible. I'll swear it on a stack of black bibles." Raising a hand as if taking an oath, she said, "I, Selinae Rogers, hereby promise not to—"

"Stop it!" he said, grabbing her hand from the air and holding it tight. "You're talking nonsense. You think I'd abandon my own child? How could you think so little of me?"

He forced her to look into his face, his dark eyes. They matched hers, showing the tortured dullness of disbelief.

"I don't even know why we're having this stupid argument," she said with frustrated contriteness. Drawing a deep breath, she picked up the lighter and lit one of the green candles. "There is no child."

She stared at the light, trying to make it take hold on the short cord protruding from the top of the candle. She found herself wishing desperately for the light to hold. But she hadn't left the fire on the wick long enough, and the flame was extinguished.

"Does the possibility exist?" Sterling asked.

Staring absently at the candle she had tried to light, Selinae reasoned that she had been presumptuous. She had felt one-hundred-percent positive that her disclosure would prove to Sterling that she really was ready for a commitment. She now saw that it took a long time for the fires of commitment to take hold. She placed the lighter back on the table, then sat back, her hands folded in her lap.

"Does it?" he demanded.

Selinae swallowed as she nodded her head affirmatively.

"You used me, didn't you?" he asked.

Her head jerked up to stare at him. "I *used* you? What is that supposed to mean?"

"You knew I couldn't resist you," he said. "You led me by the nose right to your bed, knowing all along the chance we were taking. And stupid me did all my thinking below the waist."

"That's right, blame me," Selinae spat out, getting to her feet. "You're no different from the rest of my family."

"You used me to get back at your father," he said, following her into the foyer.

Selinae spotted her overnight case on the bottom step and grabbed it. "Getting pregnant would be the perfect plot of revenge against him for cutting you out of his will," Sterling continued.

Opening the hall closet door, Selinae got her coat and purse.

"Well, let me tell you, it's juvenile, a teenage girl's twisted logic. Where are you going?" he demanded as she opened the front door.

"Someplace where I don't have to listen to *you,*" she tossed over her shoulder.

"That's right, run away," he retorted, following her outside. "I thought you didn't want to run anymore, that you'd hung up your running shoes."

As she got into her car, she said, "I'm walking, then. How's that?"

With tears rolling profusely from her eyes, Selinae argued both sides of their disagreement on her drive home.

Maybe she'd expected too much from him. He'd been so strong and secure within himself, she had failed to assign a very human trait to him. Fear.

She had spoken from the heart at the moment with no serious consideration as to what she was saying. Though it was true that she would love to have Sterling's child, she realized how selfish her thinking was, even immature. A child was a major responsibility. But she had felt so strongly about Sterling, so . . . right. Revenge against her father was the last thing on her mind.

Arriving home, Selinae changed her clothes, then ambled about the house. She went into her study and turned on the light. The red glow on the answering machine informed her of messages. She pressed the button, then waited as the tape rewound.

"This message is for Selinae Rogers." She

stood alert, instantly recognizing the stentorian voice on the machine. Her father's voice. "If you want this box of medals and trophies, you better have someone pick them up. Otherwise, I'm throwing them out."

The machine clicked to a halt. In the dead silence, Selinae stood as if pinned to a wall. Fresh tears streamed down her face.

Moving with efficiency and purpose, Selinae began collecting the tools of her trade from the desk drawer in her study as the printer droned softly in the background.

Tape recorder. Pens. Notebook. Beeper. She put them all in a black leather bag that was on the floor, propped against the desk.

When the print job was completed, she set the bag on the desk, then removed the page from the tray. She scanned it thoroughly. Satisfied, she placed the sheet in a manila folder and lay it on the desk.

She reviewed the notes she'd scribbled when she got the call at seven that morning from Marcia Matthews, an old friend who was the managing editor of the *Houston Triumph*. a local black newspaper that came out bi-weekly, on Saturdays and Wednesdays.

It was the kind of story she no longer wrote, the kind that had contributed to her burnout as a crime-beat reporter. But because Marcia was a close friend and caught in a pinch—all of her reporters were either on vacation, sick with the flu, or on an out-of-town assignment—she agreed to cover it.

The paper was put to bed on Friday and Tuesday evenings. It was now after nine: she had until three today to pull all the pieces together.

Crime didn't take holidays, she mused, as she shut down her computer and printer. A teenage girl had disappeared from the Galleria skating rink. The incident had occurred the previous night, and the police had no leads. Though the father was not yet a suspect, the police investigator whom she'd interviewed over the phone was ruling nothing out.

It was not her job to pass judgment, Selinae reminded herself. Just report the facts. She was on her way to interview the father who'd reported the girl missing.

No photographer had been lined up, she noted, as she grabbed her bag and left the room, darkening it behind her. She hoped the family had a decent picture of the girl.

In the living room, she picked up her coat from the couch at the door. She wondered if she should feel guilty for the sense of purpose she felt. While the assignment was taking her mind off her own troubles, it came at the expense of someone else's misery.

After a night of tossing and turning in her

bed, which seemed ominously big and empty, she decided the turmoil she felt over Sterling was just not worth it. She had enough conflict in her life and needed less of it, not more. She would get over him. It would just take a little time.

As she adjusted the coat over her knit pantsuit in saddle and white, his image flashed briefly through her mind. She held the folds of the coat in tightly clenched hands. The purposeful light in her eyes dimmed.

It was as she had feared, she thought: she'd imagined Sterling to be something he wasn't. He had been unable to distinguish her feelings for him from those for her family. He thought he knew what was best for her better than she herself did. He was indeed very much like her father. A disheartened sigh escaped her lips.

Reminding herself that she had a job to do, Selinae gathered her things, opened the door, and walked out into the cold, bright morning. The promise of winter had long last come. It was a pretty day, with the sun perched high in the clear blue windy skies. Several kids were outside, bundled in coats and knit caps, giving their Christmas toys a workout. Selinae locked her front door and headed for her car, which was parked in the narrow driveway.

When the dark green Jeep Cherokee rolled to a stop on the street in front of her house, she came to an abrupt stop, her heartbeat accelerating. Sterling got out of the vehicle, and Selinae swallowed the lump that had suddenly lodged itself in her throat.

Feasting on him with her gaze, she felt her resolve crumble. He was dressed in a sleeveless sheepskin jacket over a gold plaid shirt tucked into starched black jeans at his narrow waist. Boots completed the ensemble.

The tentative, unsure quality of his movements surprised her. She guessed that he was trying to assess her reaction to his unexpected appearance. It was the most vulnerable she'd ever seen him, and it softened her hard-sought determination to put him out of her mind.

Then he seemed to change. With the customary grace of one who was in total control, he became imbued with purpose. Like a modern-day avenger, she thought, ready to take the weight of the world on his broad shoulders.

Nearing her, Sterling said, "Good morning."

Selinae attempted to banish her desire to embrace him. "Do you have your equipment with you?" she asked, fighting to keep her tone professional.

Caught off guard by the query, Sterling slowed his pace to a halt. Staring at her warily, his eyes were sharp and assessing. The glare from the sun caught the curious hue in their sassafras depths. He glanced over his shoulder at his vehicle, then back at her.

The impulsive question now out, Selinae wondered what she was doing, inviting the enemy into her camp. Trying to prevent the inevitable, she answered herself with chiding. It was much like the game she'd played with her family, allowing them to toy with her emotions, even knowing it was useless. When would she ever learn?

"It's in the truck," he said.

Committed, she couldn't back out. "I need a photographer for an assignment I'm on," she said.

"Your car or mine?" he asked without hesitation.

"I'll drive," she replied.

Backing away, he said, "Let me get my stuff."

It took several tries before she could get the key in the car door to unlock it. With a mixture of hope and dread creating havoc within her, she rationalized that she'd made a sound, professional decision. A photo of a distraught father, she told herself, would go a long way to creating a heightened interest in the story. After all, a young girl's life was at stake.

Within seconds, Sterling was tossing his camera bag in the backseat, then he opened the front passenger door and got in. Wordlessly, she backed out the drive and drove off for the Southpark residence in the southeast section of town.

"Mr. Simpson, I'm Selinae Rogers, the reporter from the *Triumph,* and this is Sterling Washington, a photographer," Selinae said, introducing them to the Simpson family, a father and two daughters, who opened the door to them.

"Yes, please come in," Mr. Simpson replied, ushering them inside. "This is my oldest daughter, Charlotte and my baby, Jackie," he said, pointing from one to the other daughter. With acknowledgments exchanged between them, he led the way to the back of the house.

The house was of the same one-story design as the others on the block, in a neighborhood that was borderline middle-class, Sterling noticed. Hardworking people struggling to make ends meet. But the sense of a close family permeated the neat, clean interior, with its furnishing outdated and worn. The smell of coffee and nicotine permeated the den, a homey, midsize room bursting with items collected over the years.

"Please have a seat," Mr. Simpson said, gesturing around the room.

While Selinae settled in a tattered floral-print armchair, Sterling unpacked his camera bag. The three Simpsons took the couch. Sterling checked the light against his portable light meter.

"May I open this?" he asked.

Receiving a wordless nod, he strolled across the room to the picture window on the east wall to open the curtains to the morning's bright sun. Again checking the meter against the extra natural light, he nodded, satisfied. He would have to push the film a little, but he could make the adjustments in his darkroom during the developing process, he told himself confidently.

As Selinae performed her reporter's preliminary introduction, Sterling double-checked the cameras, then stood unobtrusively at her back, with an uninhibited view of the family.

They were all of a berry-brown complexion, with the same piercing dark brown eyes and long, arched brows. He wondered with mild curiosity what the missing daughter looked like, as Selinae explained to the family why she used a tape recorder in addition to taking notes.

Recalling their cold, silent drive to the Simpson home, Sterling felt jealous of the warmth she extended them in her tone and manner. Still, he was impressed by her skill at putting the worried father at ease in his own house.

He had yet to figure out how to bridge the deliberate distance she put between them.

Shortly after backing out the driveway, she gave him all the details of the incident surrounding the missing girl, Tierney Simpson, as well as the possible angles she might pursue and the kind of shot she was looking for to accompany the article. It was all done with professional detachment, reporter to photographer.

Then she was silent, he recalled. She never took her eyes off the road. Her demeanor was stiff and reserved, prohibiting conversation. In the silence that engulfed them, he felt unnerved by the change in her, the unfamiliar, stoic face she wore.

But whatever she was feeling, he reminded himself, the invitation to accompany her was his good fortune.

"Would either of you like a cup of coffee?" Mr. Simpson asked.

"None for me, thank you," Selinae replied, setting her tape recorder on the coffee table.

Sterling echoed her reply. With a camera hanging around his neck and another in his hands, he remained at the ready. As the eldest daughter went to fill her father's cup, he said, "I'm going to take a lot of pictures, and I'd like to get one of Tierney before we leave." To Selinae, he explained, "I'm going to shoot both black and white and color."

Selinae turned her gaze on him. "We already went over what I need," she said with a significant lifting of her brows.

He got the message; he could shoot whatever he wanted as long as she got the picture she requested. His jaws clenched tight in a sign of pique. It was an insulting comment.

He could ring her lovely neck, though it was buried under the collar of her knit top. Her outfit, though flattering to her complexion and figure, was like a suit of armor, he thought. Wondering if she covered up for herself or against him, a hint of amusement lit up his eyes. A brief memory of the ecstasy they found in each other's arms entered his mind.

"I know this is a painful time for you, Mr. Simpson," Selinae said in a soft, sympathetic voice, "but—"

"No, no, no, Ms. Rogers," Mr. Simpson replied. "I'll do whatever I have to do to get Tierney back."

The tone triggered Sterling's full attention to the job he had accepted. It was obvious that the fifty-something father had been up all night. His dark eyes were bloodshot. He was unshaven; his short beard was a stubble of knotty hairs on his troubled brown face. His big calloused hands shook as he accepted a cup of coffee from Charlotte, who rejoined the group, kneeling on the floor next to him. *Click.*

Mr. Simpson had been chain-smoking, he noticed. The ashtray on the coffee table, where the tape recorder was running, was full of butts. A crushed pack of cigarettes lay next to a newly opened one.

Rubbing his hands together nervously, Mr. Simpson said, "I don't know where to start."

"Wherever you want to," Selinae replied, her pen poised over the pad in her lap.

"Tierney likes to skate," Mr. Simpson began slowly, in a wavering voice. "She wanted to take up skating, but it's expensive, you know." He reached for the pack of cigarettes, then changed his mind. "She's on the school's track team. You ought to see her. Boy, can she eat up a track." He chuckled with a proud musing light twinkling in his dark eyes.

Sterling tried to read Selinae's reaction, but her expression was impenetrable; whatever she thought or felt did not show in her expression.

Damn! Sterling chided himself, he'd missed a shot.

"She tried to talk some of her friends into going with her, but she couldn't get anybody," Mr. Simpson continued. "I didn't want her to go alone, but Tierney . . . she's a determined one, that child. All of my girls are like that," he boasted proudly. "And every last one of them likes to do something different. Charlotte is into designing clothes, and my baby here"—he paused to squeeze Jackie's hand—"plays basketball. I like them to do things, you know, be involved in something constructive." He took a sip of coffee, then set the cup down and reached for the pack of cigarettes. Charlotte snatched the pack before he could reach it.

"You've been smoking like a train," she scolded mildly. "You're stinking up the place with these nasty old cigarettes."

Mr. Simpson chuckled halfheartedly. "They're always after me about these cigarettes. If Tierney was here, she woulda flushed them down the toilet. I waste more money buying cigarettes I don't get to smoke, you'd think I'd get the message." His eyes clouded, and his voice choked off. "I'm sorry."

"That's quite all right, Mr. Simpson," Selinae said soothingly. "Just take your time."

He sniffed, wiped at his teary eyes with his arms.

Click.

"I dropped Tierney off at the rink around two yesterday," he said. "I was supposed to pick her up at five, but I was running late. I got together with some friends of mine to watch the game at a buddy's house. We got to drinking and talking . . . well, you know how that is."

He looked headlong at Selinae with guilt in his eyes, glassy with tears. *Click.*

"The time got away from me. I didn't leave his house until almost a quarter to six. I called the house to see if she had called, but wasn't nobody here."

As the sorrowful voice of Mr. Simpson droned on, Sterling caught his mind wandering. He wanted to distance himself from the Simpson family's plight."

Oh yeah, he sympathized with them, but for the most part he felt immune from the horrible ordeal they were suffering. He took comfort in the fact that it was not happening to him. The perception went against the very nature of Kwanzaa, he reminded himself. It meant he hadn't internalized the principles celebrated for seven days to be practiced year-long, the sense of community it purported to instill in all African Americans to enhance appreciation for and recognition of the value each individual brought to the group.

But what if he were in Mr. Simpson's shoes? What if it were Selinae who was missing, who had been plucked right out of his life as if she never existed?

". . . but she wasn't where she told me to pick her up," Mr. Simpson was saying. "You know, by the movie theaters. I just knew she was going to fuss about my being late."

Disconcerted by the thought, Sterling recalled his fear of losing her in a battle between her parents. Now, staring at her lovely profile, he realized he could have lost her even more effectively all by himself.

". . . I went inside to look for her. I thought maybe she'd forgotten the time, too, and I'd find her out there on that ice, skating her little heart out . . ."

After she'd stormed out of his house, Sterling considered whether he'd overstepped his bounds. He believed initially that he had not just a duty, but a right to point out her immature thinking. Roaming about his house, alone and completely dissatisfied with himself, he was forced to reexamine his motives for the psychological diatribe he'd subjected her to. And he hadn't liked some of the answers he came up with on his own . . . without reminders of the anguish in her eyes that had haunted his sleep.

Dabbing at the tears filling his eyes, Mr. Simpson said, "I asked around, but nobody saw her. I didn't know what to do, what to think. I ran into one of the security guards and that's when we decided to call the police."

Sterling debated calling her to confess his doubts, but decided against it. He convinced himself that once Selinae analyzed the situation, she would see that he was right. He'd held fast to that belief until now.

In blurting out his suspicion of her plot to

exact revenge on her father, he'd overlooked a painful element of his own personality. He never had considered himself a coward, but this time he had been a victim of fear. His feelings for Selinae were so intense, subconsciously, he felt in grave danger of losing himself. To deal with his own fearful emotions, he'd turned his anxiety on her.

Unconsciously, Sterling lifted the camera gingerly between his hands and peered through the small aperture. Sitting serene and attentive, Selinae's alluring profile filled the viewfinder. His chocolate darling, he mused with a soft smile. *Click.*

She nodded her head, the pen held to the side of her mouth. *Click.* She scribbled away on her pad as the corners of her mouth tightened. The camera caught the agitation that flickered across her eyes. She was obviously disturbed by the story. *Click.*

Assailed by a flurry of disconnected thoughts, Sterling recalled the young toughs in the park, cloaked in macho myths of what constituted a man. Switching cameras, he photographed the tears flooding Mr. Simpson's eyes, and felt ashamed of himself. He knew better than the homies, he chided himself, but had behaved no better than they.

"If I'd been on time, instead of off somewhere drinking," Mr. Simpson exclaimed with grief and guilt, "this wouldna' happened. My

Tierney would be home now. God, please take care of my baby," he cried, breaking down.

Click. Photographing the father's wretchedness, Sterling recalled fathoming himself as wise as Solomon on the subject of love. Experiencing it for the first time, however, he now knew his contentions were nothing more than intellectual sophistry.

"I'm sorry, Miss Rogers," Mr. Simpson said, rising. "Excuse me."

"Take your time, Mr. Simpson," Selinae said in a quivering voice.

Click. The camera captured Selinae touching the corners of her eyes, as she pressed away droplets of tears.

He loved Selinae, he thought, lowering the camera. That was the truth, plain and simple. The acceptance of it was freeing. He felt a warm sensation, like a soft cloud floating through his body, a halo settling over the spot that was his heart. He wondered why he'd ever fought the feeling.

Selinae poured her third cup of coffee. With the fatigue of the previous day oozing from her every pore, she felt as sluggish now as when she awakened that morning. The Tierney Simpson piece had taken a lot out of her. She was an easy target for the despair that lay dormant in her, now that the story was behind her.

Steaming mug in her hand, she sauntered to her study and sat down feebly on the day-bed. The phone rang as it had been doing ever since she got up an hour ago: It was what had awakened her in the first place, and she had yet to take a call personally.

"Selinae, this is Holly. I was reading my *Triumph* this morning and lo and behold, there's your name on a front-page story. I just wanted to say what a good job you did. Talk to you later, girlfriend."

Recording the message for later playback, the tape on the answering machine rolled to a stop. Just as it reset, the phone rang again.

"Selinae, this is your mother. I know you're probably not at home . . ."

Selinae chuckled sarcastically at the implication in her mother's voice, before sadness settled over her expression like a gray cloud. She wished against her better judgment that she *were* with Sterling, as her mother no doubt assumed.

". . . Anyway, we saw on the news last night about that missing girl and your brother went out and got a copy of the *Triumph* this morning. I read your article," she said, with pride in her voice. "I'm sure I don't have to tell you, but I found it quite moving. And the pictures taken by your Sterling Washington were absolutely wonderful. Call me when you get in."

"He's not my Sterling, Mama," Selinae whispered tormented.

As the machine clicked off to reset, silently, she conceded that she and Sterling did work well together. He was an attentive photographer, capturing the spirit of the quotes she'd selected to use. Even without the story, she would have been inspired by his photographs.

But of course, that was to be expected: She needn't read anything more into it than a harmonious professional rapport between them, she told herself. Marcia had been so impressed with the quality of the pictures that she decided to give the story more space and run all of the photos he'd submitted.

And to his magnanimous credit, damn him, he didn't charge the paper a dime, she recalled. He told Marcia to call it his "contribution to the community."

Just as she was convinced he wasn't the man she thought or had hoped he was, Selinae thought, he did something to highlight the error of her belief.

His largesse to the community, however, didn't extend to her, she thought, recalling his accusation. In a way he'd been right; she had used him. She'd been so determined to make changes in her life, she hadn't stopped to analyze her choice.

With the mug to her lips, she stared absently across the room. The object in her gaze was but a black space, a nondescript emptiness. It was her future looming over her. She knew what she had to do. With pain glittering in her eyes, she took a deep breath.

There were several story ideas already outlined and ready for her undivided attention. Work—researching, interviewing, writing—had never failed her. It would be her manna again.

The peel of the doorbell broke into her thoughts. Guessing the identity of the unexpected caller, she sat frozen as if the lack of movement would make her invisible. "Go away," she pleaded softly. "Please, just go away."

When the doorbell stopped, pounding followed. "Selinae, I know you're in there." It was Sterling, as she'd guessed. "Come on, Selinae, open up," he called out persistently.

She couldn't prolong the inevitable forever, she told herself. The sooner she got it over with, the sooner she could begin to heal.

Opening the door, her eyes took in his powerful presence, drank in the sensuality of his physique. Looking down at her with a light of desire illuminating his mellow brown eyes, she felt an eager tension emanating from him. Instantly and automatically, her traitorous body made a mockery of her vow—at the base of her throat a pulse beat and swelled as though her heart had risen from its usual place.

He wore a bulky navy sweater with geometric designs patched in leather across the front, blue slacks, and stylish boots. How was it that he seemed to grow more virile and infinitely more desirable each time she saw him?

"Habari gani," he said.

She debated replying . . . to the greeting that had become a ritual between them . . . to the intimate tone in his voice . . . to the look in his eyes bathing her in approval.

"Kuumba," she spoke at last.

He leaned toward her, and unconsciously she felt herself gravitating toward him. But at the last second she caught herself and pulled back. The kiss that would have touched her forehead instead grazed her eye.

Visibly undaunted, he crossed the threshold into the living room. "Can I get a cup of coffee?" he asked.

"Suit yourself."

Taking the cup from her hands, he said, "I'll warm yours up while I'm there."

As she turned to walk off, eager to escape the warmth of his expression, he pulled a rolled-up newspaper from his back pocket and slapped it in her hand. With a shuddering sigh, she watched him stride off to the kitchen.

She tried to muster a shred of anger at her vulnerability to him, but the hot emotion coursing through her was desire, plain and simple. Settling for self-disgust, she marched off to her study, the newspaper in her grip.

She spread the paper out on the desk and smoothed it flat with her hands, trying to calm the erratic beat of her heart. Staring down at the paper, she blinked several times to clear her eyes, and forced herself to focus.

The layout was impressive. The name TIERNEY SIMPSON appeared in bold black letters and graced the top of the color photo on the top fold of the newspaper. Below it were the words HAVE YOU SEEN HER?

Selinae reread the quote from Mr. Simpson she had chosen to set off in italics.

"I don't understand what's becoming of this society. Females are treated like expendable items, not the bearers of the future we claim to be so concerned about."

A three-column article followed the quote, with a sidebar of Tierney's physical description, as well as the photos taken of her room in which posters of famous black runners donned her walls. But it was the quote that stuck in Selinae's mind.

As before when Mr. Simpson had uttered the words, she felt envious of the love this father had for his daughters, his reverence for women in general. Absently drumming her fingers on the paper, she couldn't help thinking that her father felt just the opposite about her. Why was she so hard to love? she asked herself.

If her own father didn't love her, how could she believe that any other man would?

She'd made a big enough fool of herself once, she thought, recalling all the overtures she'd made to her father. She simply couldn't put herself through that again. It was too hard on the mind. Her heart simply couldn't take any more abuse from the people she cared about. Even the man she loved.

Suddenly, she felt Sterling's presence. The sexual magnetism he emitted telegraphed his entrance into the room before he spoke. Even the air around her took on a different feel.

"You see the article?" he asked conversationally, striding toward her with two cups of coffee.

"Yes," she said, accepting the mug from him. Standing so close to him, she felt overpowered by his scent. It worked like an aphrodisiac on her senses, precipitating an unwelcome surge of excitement in her. He was so disturbing to her in every way, she feared succumbing to a perilous fate. She sauntered to the other side of the room and sat on the daybed, deliberately taking up the entire couch.

"We do good stuff together," he said, glancing proudly at the paper. He leaned with his hip on the desk, looking at her. "Just think what we could do with prep time. We'd be seriously in demand."

That day would never come, Selinae thought. She would see to it. But she held her tongue.

"What else are you working on?" he asked.

"Nothing," she lied, taking a sip of coffee.

She heard the frustrated sigh that escaped his throat, then looked up into his face. His brown eyes were a mixture of humble pleading and unquenchable warmth, and the combination sent her mind swimming through a haze of feelings and desires. She wondered for a fleeting wistful second whether her decision was too hasty, before reminding herself to stay on course, regardless of what he said or did. Regardless of the gaping hole widening in her heart.

"I'm so sorry about the other night," Sterling said, abject guilt in his expression and voice. "I was out of line. I can imagine what you thought of me, and every time I think about what a coward I was . . ." He fell silent, his expression grim. He drew a deep breath before he spoke again. "Will you forgive me?"

She stared at him, momentarily speechless in her surprise at his apology. She was finding him to be an ever-changing mystery; he was bigger than she thought. But no apology was needed, she mused, scooting closer to the back of the bed, quiet and withdrawn.

"How about we get out of here and see

what kind of trouble we can get into?" he suggested hopefully.

"I don't think so," she replied.

"Well," he said, rubbing his hands together with relish, "we could get breakfast. Have you had breakfast? I haven't."

"No," she said, shaking her head from side to side. Forcing conviction into her voice, she said, "Nothing. We can't do anything together anymore."

Staring into his face, she watched the light extinguish from his eyes as his jaws clamped together, his expression questioning. Unable to hold his eyes, she lowered her gaze into her cup.

"Selinae, I don't get it. What's going on?"

"We're different, you and I," she said, her heart pumping against her rib cage.

He raised the mug to his lips as if to drink, then set it down carefully on the desk. "From where I sit, that's good."

"Don't be cute," she said sharply. "You know what I mean."

"All I hear, or think I hear, is you trying to tell me that it's over between us," he said. "When the truth points to just the opposite."

"I don't know what arrow you're looking at because I don't see it that way," she said. "It was nice, but it wasn't meant to be. I admit I'm at fault for letting things get out of hand, but there's no way to go back and undo what's been done."

"So let's pack it in right now and cut our losses, huh?" he said sarcastically, his arms folded across his chest. "Is that what you're saying?" His steady gaze bored into her.

Selinae winced slightly. "Yeah," she replied slowly. "That's it." With the cup raised to her lips, she said mirthlessly, "You have a way with words. Maybe you ought to consider adding writing to your career."

"Uh-huh," he muttered mockingly. "Well, try these words on, Ms. Rogers. In the short amount of time that I've known you, I know that I care for you more than any woman." He paused to clear his throat. "I–"

The phone rang, and he turned toward the intrusion with a grimace. It rang a second time. "Are you going to answer that?" he asked.

The answering machine clicked into action. Within seconds, a male voice resonated clearly through the connection. "Selinae, I heard about the story you wrote, so I guess that's why you didn't respond to my previous message. I'll keep your medals and trophies until tomorrow night. If you haven't collected the box by then, I'm taking it to the dump site first thing Monday morning."

Selinae felt as if she were starting to disappear from the world. As the haughty voice rang in her ears, her mind was blank. She absently noted the angry mask that was Sterling's expression, the fury glowing in his eyes.

"Selinae."

Reaching for her, his quiet voice of concern nudged her out of her musings, a consciousness of cessation, a strange emptiness.

"Get out," she said softly, her expression void of emotion.

"Selinae," he crooned, pulling her into his arms. She stiffened in his embrace. "Please, let me—"

"I said get out."

Sterling stood at the front door of a desirable address in an upper-middle-class, racially mixed neighborhood in Missouri City, a scant twenty-minute ride from Houston. The temperature had dropped significantly. It was freezing; the sun had hidden its face.

Warmed by his residual anger, Sterling was oblivious to the cold. He recalled leaving Selinae's, feeling helpless, without an idea of what to do. He only knew his feelings for her wouldn't allow him to sit on his hands and let her father destroy her with his cruelty.

She probably wouldn't appreciate his interference, he thought, but it was not in his nature to do nothing. Besides, he didn't have anything to lose. Selinae had kicked him out of her house; he would not be thrown out of her life, as well.

He was prepared to beg if he had to, to accept any terms she set, as long as she didn't let his one mistake keep them apart. He may be a fool, but he believed with all his heart that they belonged together. And that meant eliminating the obstacles between them. He pressed the doorbell again.

Finally, a big, insolent-looking black man whose once well-toned body had gone soft with age and lax diet, opened the door. Sterling recognized him instantly. He had Selinae's mesmeric eyes and smooth, rich complexion. There was no mistaking the two of them were father and daughter.

"Yes?" Mr. Rogers inquired, instinctively on guard.

"Mr. Rogers," Sterling said, "my name is Sterling Washington."

"Ah," Mr. Rogers replied, his face full of mocking. "The man who is sleeping with Selinae, who got my wife and sons all in a tizzy."

"No," Sterling corrected, "I'm the man who's going to *marry* Selinae." He was trembling with rage, but he suppressed it. He didn't know what this visit would accomplish; it might blow up in his face. But it couldn't make matters any worse.

"Well, Mr. Washington, I don't know why you've come to see me. If it's to ask my permission to marry her, let me tell you, you don't need it. I could not care less who she's sleeping with."

"I didn't come for your permission. I just want you to keep your wife and sons away from Selinae," Sterling said. He was pleased by the surprise that crossed Oscar Rogers's face. "They only upset her with what I can see for myself are nothing more than false promises of reuniting the two of you."

"There will be no reunion," he said sternly. "There's no one for me to reunite with."

"Good," Sterling replied, smiling coldly. "Now if you'll just give me Selinae's things and keep the rest of your family out of our lives, everything will be just dandy."

The center was buzzing with excitement; the program was well under way when Selinae arrived. Though she wasn't in the mood for the dual festivities, the celebration of Kuumba and the karamu that followed, she wanted to get her mind off Sterling. She came to glean enjoyment from the young, as part of this night's events was given over to the children.

The children's program was dedicated to Tierney Simpson. The missing girl's picture graced thousands of brightly colored flyers offering a reward for information leading to her return. Everyone who entered the center was asked by a young host or hostess to contribute to the fund.

With a flyer in her hand, Selinae made her way into the center of activity. A plethora of delightful aromas met her at the door. The room was packed, not an empty seat visible on first glance. The works of young artists, murals depicting the cultural life of Africans and African Americans were tacked high for viewing. Red, green, and black streamers hung from the ceiling. Tables laden with food in covered dishes were set up around the outer isles; chairs were placed in a semicircle; the Kwanzaa setting occupied the center atop a large mkeka.

Selinae deposited her offering—several loaves of banana bread—in a colorful hand-woven basket, then searched for a seat among the crowd. As a troupe of youngsters demonstrated various martial arts skills, she located a spot nestled between a couple of tables midroom.

Remembering the first night of Kwanzaa—Sterling literally at her side, pressing into her with all his warmth—Selinae felt a bittersweet regret. The tender emotions for him were still there, though slightly impaired by her decision to rid her life of him. All day she had pondered how to erase him from her memory when he had fit into her life with such frightening ease, and all day she had drawn blanks; no answers, only despair.

Applause jolted Selinae back to the present. The emcee, an experienced teenage celebrant of Kwanzaa, walked up to the microphone. He led the audience in another round of applause for the performers, then announced the next offering. A kindergarten-age group of youngsters from the Freedom School assembled on stage.

All were clad in African attire, the boys separated from the girls. The adult leader stood off to the side of the platform stage to orchestrate their performance. A young girl stepped out from the choir of children to the lowered mike. She stood patiently poised, awaiting the cue from her teacher before she spoke.

Unconsciously, Selinae pressed her hand across her stomach. To have a child, a little girl like that, with Sterling. To be a family. She chided herself for the thought. She had to stop thinking about him.

"We are African Americans," the youngster began, loud and clear. "And proud females to boot; we were born into a legacy of greatness; of which no man dares dispute. We don't deny the grandeur of others; but hold our own in high regard; tonight we bring praises to our mothers; whose faith has brought us this far. The seeds of our knowledge are centuries old; and of course, all our stories have yet to be told. . . ."

The audience was awed, and the proud parents of the girl beamed as the precocious child delivered forth the words like a wise old woman. Selinae was similarly impressed and lost herself in the child's speech.

"Running through my veins is the wisdom of Cleopatra the Seventh; the courage of Nzingha; the truth of Sojourner; and the creativity of Maya Angelou. The Goddess Ma'at sits on my shoulders, balancing truth and justice in my soul, filled with my mother's love.

"I am proud to proclaim my past. I am prepared for the challenges of the present. I shall be ready to meet my future. After all, ain't I a woman like Cleopatra, Nzingha, Sojourner, Maya, and Georgia Townsend, my mama?"

Applause like a giant roar resounded through the room. The young boys from the school took center stage next, but the young girl's words continued to ring in Selinae's ears. She wiped at the tears brimming in her eyes.

Many black women had overcome greater adversities than her own. She felt ashamed of herself for not following the examples of strength and courage and wisdom laid out before her so clearly. She had behaved as if she were a child, but without the benefit of the wisdom this special child spoke, she thought.

On the heels of the silent taunt was an equally damning one. If she indeed carried Sterling's baby, then she had already failed the test passed by many mothers before her.

Selinae didn't stay for the closing celebration. The seeds of thought planted in her mind by the children, she left before the karamu began, missing the tamshi la tutaonana, the farewell statement given to close out the karamu and end the year. Her mind had yet to close out the present one.

A chorus of percussionists played a lively beat to accompany the festive gathering for the karamu. Even as his mind told him he'd never find Selinae in the crowd, Sterling forged ahead, gripping his camera next to his chest. With a sheen of purpose in his eyes, he scrutinized female faces, looking for a chocolate-coated, ethereal one with enchanting, sensitive eyes.

He spotted her once in the crowd, catching a mere glimpse of her before losing her again. She sported a new hairstyle; small curls of her dark hair were entwined with red and gold beads, forming a crown on her head. She looked like a goddess.

Cutting through a line, he made his apologies and left the hub of activity to check the offices on the other side of the dividing wall. He even paid a girl a dollar to check the ladies' room. Still no Selinae. He returned to the main room, where the food lines had thinned while the myriad of sounds—voices, music, merrymaking—had increased.

He believed he'd captured the look he'd been searching for and could hardly wait to develop the rolls of film he had shot tonight. Particularly those of the children. Watching them perform, he felt as proud as their parents must have been. He couldn't help but wonder what it would be like to have a child with Selinae.

Oh, he knew it was irresponsible, but the night's celebration created a strange feeling in him. The children were so eager to embrace the harvests of life. So unafraid.

Sterling stopped to rub his lids, his eyes aching from his intense search. He'd give anything to have Selinae come to him. But that wasn't going to happen, he chided himself.

After making so many overtures to her father, she was not about to put herself in a position to be rejected again. Not unless she was absolutely certain of her welcome.

Uttering a heavy, weary sigh, Sterling wondered what it would take, how far he was willing to go to get the woman he loved.

But he already knew the answer. There were no limits where she was concerned. Making his way through a line to leave the center, he wondered what kind of father he would be.

* * *

On New Year's Eve, the sixth night of Kwanzaa, with no place to go, Selinae chided herself for sitting in the car, idling in the driveway of her home.

"Wasting gas," she mumbled.

The heater was blowing at full blast; its muffled sound competed with the announcer on the radio, playing a countdown of the top recordings of 1994.

Despite the lights shining brilliantly around her little house, it appeared big and ominous and sinister. She debated going inside, fearing the empty silence would haunt her.

There was a place she *could* go, she mused. Sterling's. Whether he would let her in was another matter. She had kicked him out, told him nothing he could say would change anything between them, she recalled. But now she questioned her decision to be rid of a man who made her feel whole.

In spite of the doubts and reservations she had, she wanted him. High-handed assumptions and all. After all, there could be no conditions on love.

The solution was simple, she told herself, her hand moving to the gear stick as if with a volition of its own. He lived nearby; she could be there within ten minutes. All she had to do was drive over, ring the doorbell, and see for herself how he truly felt. How he interpreted his claim of *caring for her more than any other woman.*

But her fear returned. Could she accept his answer if it weren't the one she wanted to hear?

Selinae felt bewildered all over again. But one thing was absolutely clear. She loved Sterling Washington. Love wasn't a cure-all for the aches and pains that had plagued her life, but it was the only truth in her world of shifting realities. She had but one two-part question to answer, she told herself.

Was she an inheritor of the legacy of strength, wisdom, and courage of her ancestors? If yes, then, was she prepared to risk harvesting the fruits of love?

Selinae backed out of the driveway and drove off.

Driving home on deserted streets, Sterling envied the revelers inside warm houses celebrating as the New Year rang in. He was exhausted and cold from sitting for hours parked in front of Selinae's home waiting for her to return.

Pondering where she could be, he guessed she was hiding from him. And from her family as well, no doubt. He was disgusted with all of them for creating an environment that had sent her running off to be alone. They were all guilty of imposing their wishes on her, never stopping to consider her feelings.

Good intentions, he mused sarcastically, braking at the red light.

From the traffic signal, he could see the floodlights surrounding the exterior of his house. As the light turned green, he was filled with abhorrence about returning home. Sleep was out of the question. Maybe developing the pictures he'd shot tonight would help the time pass tolerably, he thought.

As he turned into his driveway, he did a double take, seeing Selinae's car in front of one of the closed garage doors. His heart began to beat as if a pack of wild horses were stampeding through his chest. He braked to a jolting stop and hopped out of his vehicle to run to her car.

Her head rested against the headrest, her eyes closed. Alarmed, he rapped on the window.

Selinae sat up with a jolt, her gaze disoriented as she looked out the window. He noticed her sag with relief in her seat, then he heard the locks pop up on the doors.

He opened hers and stared transfixed, as if she were sage words on a page to remember forever. She offered him a small, shy smile that sent shivers down his spine.

"It's freezing out here," he said at last. "Why don't you come inside?"

"Are you sure?"

Sterling was awed by her hesitancy, her voice as soft and tentative as the expression on her face. He had to curtail his eager excitement. Don't blow it, he cautioned himself.

"I went to your house."

"I wasn't there."

"I know. I left the karamu when I couldn't find you."

"You were there . . . at the celebration tonight?"

"Yes," he replied to the flicker of surprise in her eyes. "I spotted you once, but by the time I made my way through the crowd, you were gone."

He watched as her lids came over her eyes, noted the familiar serene persona she donned.

"I didn't stay for the karamu. I had too much thinking to do to celebrate."

The thoughtful quality in her voice and the reality of her presence bore witness to the truth, he thought, nodding with understanding. He wondered what finally had convinced her to come.

"I parked in front of your house and fell asleep behind the wheel, waiting for you to come home."

"I'm sorry," she said, her eyes leaving his face for the briefest of moments.

"Don't apologize. This is better," he said insistently. "I'm just glad you're here . . .

safe . . . with me. You are staying, aren't you? I mean, at least for tonight. You don't have to, I just thought . . . Goodness," he said, laughing, "I'm babbling like an idiot."

"If that's what you want," she replied.

Sterling felt a shudder course through him. She had no idea how sensuous her voice sounded, the utter delight he felt hearing her promising words. So affected by her presence, he had to clear his voice before he spoke. "Yes. It's what I want more than anything."

"Then I'll stay . . . at least for tonight."

He was willing to accept any condition—one night or forever. He extended a hand to help her from the car. "Did you bring your case?"

"No," she said, pulling her coat around her tightly. "Just me."

Closing the car door, he took her hand in his and led the way inside the house. Hannibal greeted them at the door, barking noisily.

"It's just me, boy," Sterling said, clicking on the lights in the foyer. Hannibal's vigilance turned into happy yelps as he sought Selinae's attention for a rub behind the ears.

"Hi, boy; hi, Hannibal," she said accommodatingly.

"Let me take your coat."

With her coat and purse in his grip, Sterling stared at Selinae. He couldn't be jealous of a dog, he told himself, but he would much rather it were him that was the object of her affection.

"Go to your room," he commanded to Hannibal as he hung the coat and purse in the hall closet. The dog whimpered, displeased, but obeyed his master.

Selinae stood, her hands crossed loosely in front of her. Apprehension still lurked in her eyes. Coveting her with his gaze, his eyes roamed the length of her, the warmth of her shapely throat, the suggestion of nubile curves beneath the simple, long sleeved black dress with its dropped waist and pleated skirt, her ankles sheathed in black velvet boots. She looked like a young princess, exquisite and fragile, unaware of her powers over him. Feeling his pulse beat in his throat, he swallowed hard.

"Would you care for something to drink? Some food? Have you eaten?"

"No. Nothing, thank you," she replied.

She moved lightly but with enough sway to pull the skirt of her dress in alternative directions as she backed away and sauntered off to the study. He followed, and stood in the doorway to see her staring at the box on his desk. It overflowed with trophies, ribbons, and medals. He felt a moment's panic and rushed forward, an explanation tripping off his tongue.

"I, uh, went by your parents. Well, I guess

you can see that . . . uh, I thought maybe . . ." He couldn't decipher her look; she was so still, he feared her response.

"Turn off the lights."

Puzzled, he watched as she dropped to her knees in front of the coffee table and began lighting the mishumaa. After lighting the sixth candle, she looked up at him with a significant lifting of her brows.

Goaded into action, he turned off the overhead light and paused near the door, letting his eyes adjust to the new light. The candles flickered and danced in the dark; casting her in silhouette. She sat Indian-style on the floor, the skirt of her dress bunched primly around her legs.

He kneeled next to her and fixed his eyes straight ahead at the candles, as she did. "There's so much I want to say to you."

"Then tell me; I'll listen," she replied softly.

"I know; you always do," he replied ruefully. "Maybe I should shut up and listen to you for a change."Imploring her with his gaze, he said, "Tell me, Selinae. Tell me what you want, what you need."

She raised her legs and clasped her hands around her ankles, her chin resting on her knees before she spoke. "It's not that easy," she began slowly, as if feeling her way. She stopped suddenly and smiled in exasperation.

"It's why I prefer writing. I can get my point across better."

"Take your time," he said gently. "Get it right . . . the way you want it."

"I think I told you before that I'm not hard to please."

"Every time you give me a headline answer," he said, "I put words in your mouth."

"I have simple wants, simple needs," she continued softly, her eyes open, frank. "I want to be needed and I need to be wanted."

As her voice faded to a hush stillness, Sterling felt a cascade of warm sensations rush through his body. Even as he cautioned himself not to assume she expected those things from him, he couldn't suppress the sense of sublime appeasement he felt.

There. She'd said it . . . as plain and simple as she knew how. Watching Sterling's expression, she knew that the specifics weren't important. There was no mapping out love. One could not plan it like a crop, with dimensions and seasons. It grew, and those imbued with its powers flourished and died, leaving its legacy for others to consume. It was the natural course of life.

"I'd forgot some valuable lessons . . . fundamental to living, in fact," she continued. "Some came from observing other people's pains and victories; some I experienced first-hand. There are different kinds of love. The highest, the supreme kind, of course, is seldom attained by man . . . especially those of us who aren't attentive, or attuned to and respectful of self and nature." She lifted her shoulders in a sigh. "They are defined by the particular sender and object of affection . . . you know, brother-to-brother, sister-to-mother, daughter-to-father, woman-to-man."

Wondering if comprehension reached him, she lifted her gaze to his. He was still watching her with gentle eyes, patience and understanding. She continued.

"It's all love, the feeling between these partners . . . but it's different. Humans are greedy. We want it all and we want to control it. Then it's no longer love; it's something else. To limit or temper the depth of love is sacrilegious, regardless of the reason. But you and I both know it happens so much, we chalk it up to human shortcomings—if we bother to examine it at all. Nevertheless, it does not mean that we should stop striving to attain perfection or even disclaim the potential for love from another source just because one seems missing." She folded her bottom lip in her mouth, looking at him with a profoundly contrite expression. "It's what I did to you, and I'm sorry. I convinced myself that I couldn't accept your affection and was willing to throw it away, just because I didn't have my father's love. And that's not true. *I'm* bigger than that; my capacity to grow, to love and accept love is limited only by small-minded thinking." With a sheepish half-grin on her face, she said, "I like to think I'm a fairly intelligent person . . . most of the time."

"I love you," Sterling said.

Selinae felt doubts and fears flee her soul, replaced by a new sensation. A sense of rejuvenation coursed through her, gathering her emotions together in righteous harmony. She looked at Sterling with a smile that transformed her face into pure delight, her brilliant eyes lit from within. "No questions?" she asked softly.

Sterling shook his head from side to side. "I have all the answers I need or want," he replied, his voice simmering with emotion.

Reading his thoughts through his eyes, the sparkle of untethered desire in their depths, Selinae finally followed her heart. She wrapped her arms around his neck; his automatically curled around her waist.

They both it seemed, had been waiting for each other forever. The struggle they had gone through to reach the present only enhanced the pleasure they felt now. Tingling from the inside, she lifted her head to meet his mouth halfway. Their lips touched in a series of slow, revelatory kisses.

"Stay," he said, his lips touching hers like a whisper.

Quivering, she replied, "Forever."

"Yes. Forever," he echoed, and their mouths sealed in earnest for a lingering kiss that sent currents of desire through them both.

The kiss recovered stolen moments and restored memories that had been placed aside in order to build a stronger foundation of unity. His tongue delved past her lips, forging a special truth in the inner recesses of her mouth. She answered with a moan, accepting his tongue to define their partnership as equals. In passionate solidarity, both were consumed by the commitment inherent in the kiss, its sweetness and its depth.

It was late, or rather, very early in the new year, when the telephone rang in Sterling's sleep. Dreaming of passions spent, he smiled unconsciously, and tightened his possessive grip on the soft, warm body curled next to his.

The phone rang again, and he frowned; he mumbled unintelligibly. It was echoed by an equally muddled, female sound of protest.

The telephone rang a third time, rousing him awake. Clearing his throat, he reached for the phone on the bedside table.

"Hello," he said in a groggy voice, his lids still closed over his eyes. "Yes it is; who's calling?" Opening one eye, he peeked at Selinae, her head on his chest. "Yes, she's here, Mrs. Rogers. But she's asleep and I'm not going to wake her up. I'll have her call you at a reasonable hour," he said sourly. "Emergency? All right, what's the emergency? . . . Oh," he said, "in that case . . ." Pulling the base of the phone to the bed, he said, "Selinae, wake up, it's your mother."

"Tell her Happy New Year and I'll call her later," Selinae mumbled, otherwise not moving a muscle.

"It's about your dad," he said.

"What else is new?" she quipped, sleepy-voiced.

"He had a heart attack, babe," he said somberly, "he's in the hospital."

From high in the endless blue skies, the mild sun shone down on the fabulous array of colors in the stands and on the field of the high school stadium. It was the second Saturday in April; the first meet of the youth track and field season; the year, 2002. A picnic kind of day, it was perfect for the athletes: no wind, no hot sun.

The stands were packed with spectators; the center of the field was just as full with long jumpers, pole vaulters, discus throwers, and runners warming up. Coaches who were not allowed on the fields sat anxiously, hoping their young athletes would remember their training. Parents watched eagerly.

Sitting up high on the wooden bleachers amid a cluster of fans, Oscar, Senior felt perfectly content. He was acting on doctor's orders to eliminate stress in his life, and had adopted the axiom *what will be will be.* Having survived a major heart attack, he was just grateful to be around to witness this magnificent event. Like many others, he held a pair of binoculars in one hand, a stopwatch in the other.

The first heat of the primary girls race was about to start. Four teams of girls between the ages of six and eight spaced themselves one-hundred meters apart on the synthetic, all-weather track for the relay. Poised attentively, he raised the binoculars to focus on one runner in a navy and white uniform. His heart filled with pride and love.

Bronze-brown with liquid amber eyes, the young runner was already well-toned at six years and seven months old. Long dark braids were clasped together at the back of her head with a rubber band.

She was Imani, the new light in his old life. Her name meant *faith,* and thanks to the faith her mother Selinae, possessed, he had been granted the honor of knowing his granddaughter.

He glanced at Selinae, sitting beside him, hand in hand with Sterling. His beautiful daughter glowed from within and again his mended heart felt a pang as regret raced through him. He had hurt his daughter so much that no apology could properly absolve him. Oscar smiled as he remembered the depth of her forgiveness.

It had not been easy for Oscar Rogers, Senior to admit his faults to his daughter or himself. He had seen Selinae's struggle during their first shaky steps towards reconciliation. But her husband Sterling had much to do with her strength and healing, and he felt that he could never find the right words to give his thanks.

He looked at Imani again, her name the last feast day in the Kwanzaa celebration. The last day of the holiday changed all their lives, he recalled. Being so close to death changed his view on life. Selinae found the impetus to enter the family again, and even the missing girl Tierney Simpson was found, safe and unharmed. It was a new beginning for all.

The starter on the field raised his pistol in the air, and the runners took their starting positions: some stood upright, some crouched, and some assumed three-point stances like football players. The gun fired, and simultaneously Oscar, Senior pressed the starting button on the stopwatch. His gaze was riveted on the team's lead-off runner as she sped around the track, the blue aluminum baton a blur with the pumping motion of her arms.

Watching her run forward in full speed, his thoughts sped back to over twenty years ago. He'd been a fool for many of them, he recalled. He'd been granted a reprieve by the Creator and Selinae to enjoy what was left of his life.

And if he didn't want to miss the rest of this race, he told himself, he'd better pay attention.

The tempo of his pulse picked up as the second runner handed off to the third, who kept running. Coming up the curve toward the final leg, he stood, a coach's prayer echoing in his mind. He stared enthralled and amazed at the poise of Imani. She didn't break a stride as she took the baton, heading for the finish line. He wanted to boast loudly, "That's my grandbaby."

"Good handoff," he exclaimed instead above the roaring din of cheers. His heart pounded in sync with her lightning-quick strides as her little feet in brand-new spikes ate up the track, leaving a trail of imaginary dust in her opponents' faces.

"Go, Imani, go!" he shouted, his encouragement louder than even his daughter's. "Move them arms . . . run, baby, run . . . that's it. All the way . . . all the way! That's my girl," he said.

Imani crossed the finish line first, and his hand jerked as he depressed the timing button on the watch. He didn't bother to look at the time; it wasn't important. The victory was in running a good race, he thought. He wouldn't have cared if she came in last.

"I almost missed this," he whispered tearfully, a proud smile on his lips.

"We'll make regionals this year for sure!" someone yelled amid the cheers erupting in the stands. A fellow parent seated three rows below called up to Oscar, Senior.

"Whadda ya say, Oscar . . . think you got a future Olympian on your hands?"

Oscar Senior smiled proudly. "Only if she wants it," he replied, pinching back the tears in his eyes.

Sarah's Miracle

by
Francis Ray

This is the saddest day of my life.

Sarah Marshall listened absently to the lunchtime chatter of the three women around her. They were talking about the Christmas holidays. Yet her mind was on one thing—rather one person. Blake Williams. She hated more than anything in the world to leave him, but she had no choice.

But she had learned early on as his executive secretary, Blake had little respect for people who didn't stand up for themselves. Well, she was standing up for herself now. She just wished it didn't hurt so much.

"Sarah. Sarah! You better stop daydreaming, girl, you've got trouble coming your way," Lynette whispered.

Sarah focused her attention on the rich mahogany face of the young woman speaking, then turned in the direction of Lynette's gaze. Sarah sucked in her breath. Despite the tailor-made charcoal suit Blake wore, the barely concealed anger in his handsome face made her think of a Moorish king leading his tribesmen into battle.

Instead of a sword in his hand, however, Blake clenched a sheet of paper. However everyone in the office knew that his tongue could be as lethal as any blade. Now, he was walking directly to her.

Chairs scraped around her and Sarah knew the other women were making a run for it. She'd run, too, but eventually she'd have to face him. She just wished she wasn't in the cafeteria of Williams & Williams, and Blake wasn't the CEO.

Most of all, she wished she didn't love him.

"What is the meaning of this?" Blake asked, shoving the white sheet of paper within an inch of Sarah's face.

Despite her trembling legs, Sarah stood and picked up her lunch tray. "Perhaps we should discuss it in your office."

"Let's go then," he said through clenched teeth.

"I have to put the tray up," she argued weakly.

Rapier-sharp black eyes cut to the tray, then shot back up to her face. For a moment he looked as if he might snatch the tray out of her hands. "You have exactly one minute to meet me at the elevator," he said instead.

He was gone before Sarah could say a word. Looking straight ahead, she put the tray on the conveyor and walked swiftly from the lunchroom. She didn't have to look around to know that every person followed her with their eyes and was glad it was her being summoned and not them. Blake, like some Moorish kings, was not known for taking prisoners.

He was waiting at the open elevator. Head high, she stepped on. He silently flicked off the stop switch and jabbed the button for the eighth floor where the executive suites were located. The elevator stopped on the fifth floor. Two chattering women were waiting and started to get on. They looked at Blake's forbidding face and froze like rabbits caught in the light beams of a car. The door slid closed without them entering the elevator.

Sarah stepped off at the eighth floor, walked through her office into Blake's, and took a seat in front of his massive, hand-carved teak desk. She'd seen the desk at an antique store and immediately thought of Blake. Both man and desk had similar coloring, both were coveted for their richness, both had an ageless beauty. She'd known he needed to replace his styleless desk and mentioned the teak one. He had purchased it the same day.

"I'm asking you again, Ms. Marshall. What is the meaning of this?" Blake snapped once the door was closed.

Crossing her legs at the ankle, Sarah folded her shaking hands in her lap. "It's my resignation."

"I can read!" he thundered. "What I want to know is why?"

Sarah's heart lurched. In her wildest dreams, this was the moment Blake confessed his love for her and begged her not to leave.

"You're the best secretary I've ever had," Blake continued, putting a swift end to her imaginings. "You can't do this to me. You know we just completed the takeover of Reynolds Manufacturing. After the first of the year, I'll be in Savannah more than I'm here in Atlanta. No one can run my office like you can."

With a sigh she allowed her shoulders to droop slightly. She might have known. After all, if he hadn't noticed her in five years, another five wasn't going to matter. The only time he really looked at her was if something went wrong. Then his look was enough to send most people scurrying from the room. All Blake Williams wanted was the business to continue in an orderly fashion. He might be yoked at the neck to his and his father's company, but she wasn't. "I'm sorry, Mr. Williams, my mind is made up."

"I'll raise your salary."

"It's not the money."

"You need more help?"

"Janet and Gloria are fine," she said, referring to her two assistants.

"Then what is it?" he asked, coming over

to grasp the padded arms of her chair, his dark, handsome face inches from hers. "This isn't like you. You plan everything months in advance. Why this sudden urge to leave?"

Sarah felt heat pool in her cinnamon-hued cheeks. From the way Blake's eye narrowed, she knew he had noticed.

He straightened abruptly. "The kiss," he exclaimed triumphantly. "You're leaving because of one measly kiss."

His "measly kiss" to her had been a little bit of heaven. But it hadn't taken long for it to turn into hellish torture. "That's not the reason."

"I apologized, didn't I?" Blake paced in front of the narrow space between her and the desk. "I was just so happy you were back at work." He stopped, then quickly continued. "The three days you were out with the flu were the most hectic I've ever had. The nut they sent to replace you didn't know spit about a corporate office."

Slowly, she raised her head. "I plan to personally train my replacement as soon as you hire one."

"I want you," Blake repeated.

"You can't have me," Sarah said, then flushed again at her phrasing. Blake was razor-sharp. She didn't put it past him in his present mood to come back with a rejoinder that would sting her ears.

Blake stopped and spun on his heels to face her. For a long moment, he simply watched her. Sarah forced herself not to fidget and returned his gaze. Finally, he sighed and leaned back against his desk. "At least tell me why."

"I'd like to travel and see a little of the world before I'm too old to enjoy it," she said, glad she had rehearsed her excuse.

"Come on. You can't be older than thirty-two or thirty-three," Blake scoffed.

"I will be thirty on New Year's Eve," Sarah said through clenched teeth.

"Well, there you are then," Blake said, seemingly oblivious to her wounded tone. "You're nine years younger than I am and you don't see me retiring."

"Your father owns the company and you're a full partner. There is no way you can compare us." She stood. "If there is nothing further, I need to alert the switchboard I'm back from lunch."

"We haven't finished talking."

"Nothing will change my mind. I should get back to my desk and the phones. Remember, you sent out a stern memo about the phones being answered promptly and routed correctly," Sarah said, scooting around the chair. "I'd hate to get fired before I quit, especially with Christmas so close."

"You could have given me more than two weeks' notice."

Sarah shook her head. "My last day has to be on New Year's Eve because my cruise leaves January first. Two weeks was all the notice I could give."

Her hand was on the brass doorknob when his voice stopped her. "Ms. Marshall."

A shiver ran down her spine. Something about the tone of his voice made her think of long rainy nights and warm silk sheets.

She glanced over her shoulder. "Yes?"

"Are you sure it wasn't the kiss?"

Her hand clenched on the knob. "Yes, sir, I am," she said, then escaped through the door.

Well, you messed up this time.

Folding his arms, Blake stared at the closed door. The first impulsive action he could ever remember committing had cost him the best secretary in Georgia.

Seeing her back at her desk when he came to work early that morning, he had been so overwhelmed with joy that he had dropped his attaché case, pulled her to her feet, and kissed her full on the lips.

Somehow, the intended brief gesture of thankful welcome had lengthened as she seemed to soften and melt against him. His tongue had slipped past her lips. He'd almost gone down for the count when her tongue, as shy and darting as a hummingbird, touched his.

It had taken all of his considerable power to set her away from him. By the time his haze of desire had cleared, she was standing there trembling, her eyes glassy, her face flushed.

She had looked like she needed to be in bed with a cup of hot tea or soup. Instead she was at her computer, and he was kissing her for all he was worth. He had apologized and explained the reason behind his exuberance. She had nodded and gone back to the computer, her usually straight shoulders hunched, her agile fingers fumbling on the keys. She looked as if she needed a hug. When he had gone out for lunch, he had bought her a gray, furry koala bear instead.

Sarah's brown eyes had widened as much as the animal's button brown ones when he gave it to her. She had looked so pleased when he told her he had seen it while passing a shop in the mall. Then he had beat a fast retreat into his office.

Now look where his impulsiveness had gotten him.

The red light of his intercom flashed. "Yes?"

"Your meeting with the Kendrix group is

in thirty minutes," Sarah said, then the line went dead.

Blake picked up his attaché case and headed toward the door. Where was he going to find a secretary who could organize his life like Sarah did? Just as he was doing now, he had a tendency to focus on one problem and shut everything else out. Sarah knew that, and kept him on his toes. She also didn't have any trouble following his rapid transition of thought when he was really into an idea.

She was intelligent, efficient, trustworthy. If she said something was done or couldn't be done, that was that. He depended on her broad base of knowledge, her ability to smooth ruffled feathers. More than once she had averted a disaster with an employee or with one of his clients while he had been out of town.

She didn't quiver in her shoes if there had to be an immediate decision and he was incommunicado. She always did what he would have done. She put the customers, who helped make Williams & Williams one of the state's top manufacturers of electrical supplies, first.

Why did she have to let a little kiss end a perfect working relationship? Because no matter what she said, Blake had a strong suspicion the kiss was responsible for the mess he was in now.

As he passed his desk, Sarah asked, "Mr.

Williams, will tomorrow afternoon be all right for you to start interviewing my replacement? You're open from two until three."

As she stared up at him with cool, brown eyes, every strand of her black hair in place, her prim navy blue suit jacket buttoned to her throat, Blake had to wonder if he'd merely imagined the fire in their kiss.

"Mr. Williams?" she prompted.

"That will be fine," he said, and left the office. If Sarah wanted to resign, he couldn't stop her. He would train a replacement to be just as efficient, he vowed.

Blake believed his vow until a Kendrix representative asked him for some analysis figures he neglected to bring to the meeting. He called Sarah, and in less than a minute she had the information to him and was standing by her computer ready to give him any other data he needed. He walked away from the meeting with a handshake and a commitment from the Kendrix representative to come by the next day and sign on the dotted line.

Thoughts of Sarah played in Blake's mind as he opened the heavily carved door to his house. His sanctuary. When he went home he needed a place to relax, throw something on the grill if he chose, and on those rare occasions, relax in the pool in peace. Thanks to

Sarah, for the past two years he had had that sanctuary.

Crossing the marble foyer, he glanced around the comfortable den, decorated in his favorite color, green, with splashes of red and yellow medallion accents. He hadn't been crazy about the idea of red or yellow, but Sarah had a decorator do a mock-up with miniature furniture, and he had liked it on sight.

Every room that Blake enjoyed spending time in, she had been responsible for. One of the few times he had seen Sarah grinning like a kid was the day he told her he had signed the papers to his house and the day she arranged for the movers to settle him in.

He had been delightfully surprised to find Sarah was waiting for him with the house keys and a bottle of champagne. His lady friend at the time had dropped by unexpectantly and Sarah had hurriedly left. He frowned as he remembered he still had that unopened bottle of champagne.

Going into the kitchen, he placed his case on the bright yellow counter. In the oven he found his dinner, stuffed pork and broccoli. Taking it out, he turned on the oven and set a pan of rolls inside. Sarah again.

She had found Mabel Johnson, who was as meticulous about cleanliness as he was, and cooked like a French chef. Mabel didn't mind his erratic schedule and always had dinner ready for him if he was going to be home.

Blake ate to the company of a jazz station, cleaned up the kitchen, then went into his office. Sticking out of his fax machine was his revised schedule, which included three interviews. Sarah again.

After five years, how could she walk out on him, especially when the company was experiencing its best growth spurt in years? The profit margin had risen 12 percent in the last quarter. Still, Blake didn't want to be overconfident. He realized things could turn sour just as quickly. That's why he liked his personal life to be calm and consistent. Fax in hand, he plopped down in his desk chair.

He had grown up with too much inconsistency. He loved his parents, but they were into the corporate structure to the hilt. He had often joked with his brother and sister about when their parents could possibly have found enough time to have them.

That fast-paced lifestyle was one of the main reasons Blake resisted his mother's constant badgering about his getting married again. His first marriage hadn't lasted a year. On returning from one of the many trips he had taken seven years ago, he had come back to their apartment to find Clarissa packed.

With tears streaming down her cheeks, his wife had told him that he loved his job more than her. She had been wrong. He loved winning. He could not abide failing whether it be business or love. He would not fail with another woman. He would not give himself the chance.

Since his father retired last year, Williams & Williams took most of Blake's time. And dammit, the small amount of time he spent away from business he wanted to be calm. Sarah assured him of that calmness. Sarah couldn't leave. She was as much a part of his business as his personal life. And he wasn't willing to do without her.

Blake rocked forward in his seat, a smile replacing the frown. He had his answer. Approach her like a business deal. Find her weakness. Everyone and every company had one. Find the weakness and use it to your advantage.

"I hope you bought cruise insurance because I'm coming after you, Sarah Marshall."

Sarah stared at her reflection in the bathroom mirror and tried to be objective. She wasn't beautiful, she admitted, but she wouldn't turn anyone to stone, either. Her thick eyebrows had a natural arch. She thought her nose seemed the appropriate size. Her high cheekbones were a gift from her half-Cheyenne/half African-American paternal great-grandmother.

Sarah had always thought her lower lip a bit too full, but Cynthia, her oldest sister, had always disagreed. She was constantly after Sarah to wear a bolder lipstick or blush to bring out her assets.

She wasn't comfortable with anything more than a hint of color. The only thing worse than not being noticed by Blake was his knowing she was trying to attract his attention. Her two index fingers traced a line from her ears to her chin. Another gift, this time from an unknown ancestor. All the Marshall women had heart-shaped faces.

All of them had gotten their man, too. Why couldn't she? The only man she had ever loved thought she looked years older than she was. Turning off the light, she went into the living room of her apartment to gaze at the Christmas tree lights. In spite of the depressing day, just looking at the tree made her heart feel lighter.

Decorated with handmade angels dressed in white satin and gold lace, and the various ornaments she had received over the years from friends and family, the tree was a symbol of love and sharing. The tip of the fat, blue spruce almost touched her ten-foot ceiling. Her brother and cousin had grumbled all the way from the tree lot to her apartment. She had appeased them with her special home-made pecan pie and coffee.

For her, the Christmas season was the happiest of them all. Even confirmed grouches found a smile or two to share with others.

Blake tended to loosen up, too. But he had never loosened up enough to notice her—except for the "measly kiss." Instead she had to stand by and watch an endless parade of long-legged, bosomy women in short skirts go in and out of his office and his life. She had flirted with the idea of wearing spandex to work but knew it would be not only unprofessional, but obvious. She had breathed a sigh of relief when each relationship failed, then sent flowers to the next woman.

She watched a slim finger trace the brown face of one of the Christmas angels. Blake simply didn't see her as a woman. To him she was a walking, talking, thinking datebook. She glanced down at her fuzzy slippers and long flannel gown. There was no way she could compete with the women who caught Blake's attention.

To do that, she'd need a miracle.

Sarah awoke the next morning to the ringing of her telephone. One lid fluttered upward. She eyed the clock: 6:52. Eight minutes before her alarm was due to go off. Wondering who could be calling her at such an early hour, she picked up the receiver. "Hello?"

"Sarah, why are you quitting your job?" her mother asked worriedly. "Are you all right? What's going on?"

All thoughts of further sleep fled. She didn't have to ask who the blabbermouth was. "Mr. Williams had no right to tell you. I had planned on telling everyone when we were all together for Christmas dinner."

"But why would you quit? You've worked there for years," Venora Marshall reminded her youngest child.

"All the more reason for a change. I'll be thirty in less than two weeks. I plan to start my new decade and the new year off right." Too agitated at Blake to remain in bed, Sarah threw back the covers and got up. It was a good thing he didn't know *where* she planned to start her new year. Who knew what kind of mischief he would cause then?

"How will you pay your bills? What about health insurance, your car payments, credit cards?" asked the practical Venora.

"For a little higher payments I can take my health insurance with me, my car will be paid for in two months, and you know I pay cash for most of my purchases anyway," Sarah reassured her. "Mother, I'm old enough to take care of myself."

"Oh, honey, I know you can take care of

yourself. Heaven knows, you're the most sensible of any of my five children. It's just that this isn't like you. Mr. Williams is as puzzled by your resignation as I am."

"Mr. Williams has a big mouth and I plan to tell him so," Sarah shot back.

"Sarah, you stop talking like that," her mother told her. No matter the age, her mother still chastised all of her children when she thought they needed it. "You should be grateful your boss thinks enough of your abilities to want to keep you."

"What he wants is someone to run his office and his life while he runs Williams and Williams," Sarah said tightly. "Well, I have a few wants of my own and one of them is to travel and see a little of the world."

"By yourself?"

"If I desire. My first trip will be on a cruise."

"Aren't they dangerous?" A tinge of worry crept into her mother's voice. "I don't think you should go by yourself."

"Mama, I thought you just said I was sensible. I know how to take care of myself. Besides, I may be as lucky as one of the women at work. She met her husband last summer on her cruise to the Bahamas. We had a baby shower for her a couple of weeks ago," Sarah said, knowing the mention of marriage and a family would win her mother's support more than anything.

"Really?" Venora sounded intrigued. "Where are you going on your cruise?"

"The Bahamas." Sarah left out she had no intention of looking for a husband. Besides, how often did women find husbands on cruises? "Goodbye, Mama. I have to get ready for work."

Angry at Blake for trying to pump her mother for information, Sarah stalked into the bathroom. He had overstepped the line of professionalism, and to take a quote from her grandmother, Sarah was going to tell the high-handed rat "how the cow ate the cabbage."

An hour later, Sarah entered Blake's office and stopped in her tracks. Blake was serving coffee to her two assistants, Janet and Gloria. They were sitting at a round table laden with fresh fruit and pastries. When they saw her, both women hastily put a beignet back on a china plate and blotted their mouths with white linen napkins taken from their laps.

Sarah was seething. Any imbecile could see that Blake, having failed to get any information from her mother, had moved on to her two assistants. Both women held Blake in awe and to have him personally serve them, and have his attention focused exclusively on them, was probably a fantasy come true. It was a good thing they didn't know what Sarah's own personal fantasy was.

"How dare you interrogate my mother and my assistants. If I hadn't already handed in my resignation, I would after this," Sarah said heatedly.

Blake calmly placed the coffeepot back on the silver tray. His black eyes were piercing. "Careful, Ms. Marshall. I'll only take so much, even from you."

"So fire me."

"Sarah, please," Janet said, rising to her feet and coming to her. "Mr. Williams wasn't interrogating us. We were trying to think of a going-away gift for you."

Sarah's accusing gaze swung to Blake.

"I could hardly ask your mother's opinion about a going-away gift without telling the reason why could I?" Blake said smoothly.

Gloria joined Janet and Sarah. "It was supposed to be a surprise. You weren't due for another ten minutes."

He didn't fool her for one second. He was up to something. "*If* I jumped to conclusions, I'm sorry," she said tightly.

Blake's dark eyebrow lifted in annoyance. Gloria and Janet may not have understood her meaning, but he had. "As Gloria said, we weren't expecting you so early, but since you're here, why don't you alert the switchboard operator. You know how I feel about calls."

Gritting her teeth, Sarah left the office. He was paying her back for yesterday. Picking up the phone, she called the operator. Once she hung up, she glared at Blake's door. He could snoop all he liked, but he wouldn't find out anything.

"I-I think Ms. Marshall is in love."

"What!" Blake bellowed.

The young woman standing in front of his desk jumped. Her arms clutched a bulging manila folder tighter to her chest. Her startled eyes on Blake, she started backing up.

Blake came out of his chair and clasped the fleeing woman by the arm before she could back up any further. "Janet, forgive me for yelling. I was just taken by surprise," he said, a reassuring smile on his face. "I guess I never thought of Ms. Marshall having a social life."

Janet stared into Blake's face with rapt fascination. Blake gently guided her to the chair in front of his desk, then retook his seat. "Please, continue."

The woman continued to stare at him.

"Janet?"

She started, then swallowed. Her arms still clutched the folder.

Blake fought back his irritation. Janet might know the reason behind Sarah's resignation. The breakfast he had held to gain information from her assistants had failed miserably. He kept trying to lead the conversation to the reason behind her leaving and his desire for her to stay, but initially both women had been too nervous to say a word. Just when they'd begun to loosen up, Sarah had showed up.

After she left, they were so concerned that she thought they were being disloyal, they overcompensated. Neither could stop talking about what a wonderful person she was and how sensitive and romantic she could be.

Blake learned that she cried at every wedding and baby shower, loved walks in the rain, and only read books she was assured had a happy ending. With a smile, he had thanked them for coming and asked them to take the food with them. Blake enjoyed the new information he received about his secretary. Sarah was quite a woman—a woman who still had many surprises within her. He wanted to know them all.

Janet had called him fifteen minutes later asking to speak with him privately during lunch. Only now, she wasn't doing very much of anything except staring at him.

"Janet, I hate to rush you, but Ms. Marshall will be back from lunch soon," Blake prompted. "What was it you started to say a minute ago?"

Moistening her lips, Janet straightened. "I said I think she's in love. I didn't mention it in front of Gloria because I didn't want to be disloyal to Ms. Marshall." The folder crinkled.

"The only reason I'm saying anything now is because I don't think she wants to go."

"Neither do I, Janet. So if there's a way to get her to stay, I'd like to know about it," Blake said with more patience than he felt.

Janet nodded and her fat, gold-tipped braids bobbed up and down. "It was the day she became sick with the flu. She had been taking medicine all day to stay at work because the department heads were giving their monthly reports to you. By the end of the day she was wiped out."

Janet's ebony-hued faced looked thoughtful as she leaned forward in her chair. "You had gone for the day and I came in to give her some copies she asked me to run off. Her head was on her desk and she was . . . crying."

Blake found himself leaning forward. Something stirred inside him. He didn't like the idea of Sarah in tears.

"When I asked her what was the matter, she said, 'I love him. But I don't know if I can take him looking through me like he did today much longer.' Then she excused herself to the ladies' room."

Janet bit her lower lip again. "She's never mentioned it again. I don't think she would have said anything if she hadn't been ill and taking all those antihistamines and decongestants. To this day, I don't think she remembers telling me." Janet shook her head. "She's leaving because one of your department heads won't give her the time of day. I don't know if it's because he doesn't like her or he's afraid of the rule against fraternization here."

"It's a necessary company policy," Blake responded sympathetically. "I don't want anyone in management dating people under them. There is too great a chance of someone getting the wrong idea and yelling harassment. However, I don't see why this would have presented a problem to this mystery man. Ms. Marshall is answerable only to me." Blake rose and showed the young woman to the door. "Thank you for coming. I'll take it from here."

"My baby has Sickle-Cell Anemia and Ms. Marshall never minds if I have to take off. All she says it, 'Your son is your first priority.'" Janet looked at Blake with steadfast eyes. "Although Jamaal is sick sometimes, I wouldn't trade him for a hundred healthy babies. The only reason I told you Ms. Marshall's secret is that I've seen her look at Jamaal and other babies. She wants a family of her own. I figured if anyone could help her, it would be you."

Blake was touched by the young woman's devotion to her child and to Sarah. "If Jamaal ever needs anything, you let me know."

Janet's eyes widened and she shook her head. "I didn't tell you be—"

"I know, and that's why I'm offering." He grasped the doorknob. "Goodbye, Janet, and thanks."

Blake returned to his seat deep in thought. Sarah was in love. Who could it be?

He reared back in his chair and tried to visualize his Sarah looking up at a man in passion. He couldn't. He could only see her face, dazed and flushed, after he kissed her hello. No matter, he had to find out who she was interested in.

He rocked forward and placed his arms on his desk. Twelve single men was a lot to go through. He didn't imagine for a second Sarah was foolish enough to let herself fall in love with a married man. Most women could be seduced into believing a man's lies were truths, but according to Janet the man Sarah loved didn't know she existed. That meant she had been seduced by her own fanciful imaginings.

Getting up, Blake looked out the window at the towering gold and glass buildings. Arms crossed, he leaned against the window. Since he couldn't very well parade the possible candidates though his office, it stood to reason he had to take Sarah to them. Once he found out the man's identity, Blake would send him to Savannah. After he was gone, Sarah would have no reason to leave. No man was forcing Sarah to leave him.

Checking his watch, Blake knew Sarah would be back from lunch. She was as punctual as she was efficient. He punched in her intercom.

"Yes, Mr. Williams?"

The cool crispness of her voice annoyed him. He had heard her use that tone with difficult people, but never to him. He was trying to help her and she was getting an attitude. "Ms. Marshall, could you please ask the head of each department and their assistant to meet me in one hour in the conference room. You'll attend also."

"Some of them may not be available on such short notice," she said.

"This meeting is not elective," he said and hung up the phone. Blake reared back in his chair. He didn't have to worry about anyone missing the meeting. Sarah would make it clear to them he wanted them there.

Less than an hour later Blake stood at the head of the oblong conference table and watched his upper management people enter. Portfolio in hands, they sat in one of the padded seats around the gleaming oak table or in one of the extra chairs Sarah had had the maintenance department bring in.

As Blake anticipated, each department head

and his or her assistant was present. As he had also expected, the single men were clumped together in two groups, the married men in another, and the three women were scattered around the room. Men in executive positions tended to be more cliquish than their female counterparts, he noticed.

He glanced at his watch and the hushed voices immediately quieted. It was nearly two o'clock. The boardroom door opened and Sarah entered. Every head swung to watch her walk to the front and take a seat to his immediate right. From the furrowed brows and narrowed eyes, he could see the unspoken questions and suppositions forming in his employees' minds. Sarah seldom came to these meetings unless he wanted her to take notes so there could be no mistake of what was said. When he took names, he left no room for errors.

While everyone else in the room was looking at Sarah, she was looking at her notepad. The least she could do was give him a little help, he thought before turning to the waiting group of men and women.

"Good afternoon, and thank you for coming on such short notice. I've always thought of this team as an integral part of Williams and Williams' success. You take pride in what you do and that pride is reflected not only in increased profits, but job satisfaction . . . until now." He paused to let his words sink in. Chairs creaked as people sat up straighter. Their eyes were riveted on him. He wished he could say the same about Sarah.

"Come the new year, we will be one less." Heads turned as people in the room glanced around to see who might be leaving and if it was voluntary. Some were unable to keep the speculative looks from their face and the possibility of moving up. Blake noticed no one glanced at Sarah who wore a blank look upon her face. He wondered; was she praying the mystery man would ask her to stay?

"I won't keep you in suspense any longer except to say, the person leaving is a vital part of the company. Her dedication and hard work has made the job of each person in this room a little easier." Before the people in the room got whiplash from looking back and forth at the three stunned women executives, Blake stepped back and grasped Sarah by the arm. He was surprised by how stiff she felt.

"I consider Ms. Marshall irreplaceable and I hate like hell I couldn't talk her into staying." Stunned silence. That was the only way Blake could describe the sudden quiet that descended on the room. His gaze swept the single men, looking for some hint of sadness, disbelief, but all he saw in most of their faces was disappointment that there wasn't going to be a vacancy.

"I thought I'd give you fair warning that when Ms. Marshall leaves, you won't have a buffer. Forewarned is forearmed," Blake joked, trying to take the spotlight off Sarah.

It worked. One by one, then in twos and threes, people came forward until Sarah was surrounded by employees wishing her well, asking about her plans, or to jokingly request that she stay and protect them. Sarah smiled good-naturedly, and for a while, Blake thought he might have pulled it off, until she looked at him. The smile on her face was as stiff as her body had been.

Perceptive as Sarah was, Blake knew she had probably read the men as well as he had. They weren't as disappointed by her leaving as they were of not moving up in the company. It must have hurt to finally be faced with the man's callousness. Thank goodness the others didn't feel that way. He noted with mild dissatisfaction that only two of the single men made it to the front. The embrace they exchanged with Sarah was more brotherly than passionate.

His plan had failed. As Sarah lifted her sad, brown eyes to his, he couldn't help thinking that whoever the man was, after hurting Sarah, he didn't deserve her.

"Sarah?"

Sarah's head jerked upward, her eyes widening on seeing Blake less than a foot from her desk. Furiously, her hands swiped at her tear-stained face.

Another two steps and he was leaning over her. His darkly handsome face was lined with concern. "Are you all right?"

She sniffed one last time and tried to bring a halt to her crying. She didn't want to leave him. She didn't want to hear one day that he had married another woman who had borne his children. She had wanted to be that woman. Why did things have to turn out this way?

"Shall I call someone?" Blake asked softly.

"No," she said, brushing the last tear from her cheek. "I guess I'm not as ready to leave as I thought I was."

"You can always change your mind." Blake sat his attaché case on top of her desk. "You can even take your cruise."

"I can't stay." Fishing in her oversize purse, she located a tissue and dried her eyes. "I didn't expect you back this late. It's after six."

Blake accepted the discussion of her staying and her crying as closed. "I needed some papers."

"Well, good night." She stood and came around the circular desk. "I'll see you in the morning."

For some odd reason he didn't want to think of her going home alone to cry over some guy. "Would you like to go out to dinner?"

Her mouth dropped open as she turned her head. "Excuse me?"

He had done it again, acted on impulse with Sarah. He only hoped this time wasn't as disastrous as the first. "I'd like to talk with you about some ideas for the new company in Savannah. I planned to do it later, but for us there won't be a later. Besides," he added with a grin. "I'm hungry."

He saw another tear roll down her cheek and something stirred within him. "Sar—Ms. Marshall. I'd really appreciate your help. That is, if you don't have any other plans?"

Trembling fingers gripped her purse. "No. No, I don't."

Blake grinned. "Good, I'll get the papers and give you a chance to freshen up."

"All right," she said and watched Blake go into his office. Her bag clutched to her chest, she went down the hall into the ladies' room. Moist paper towels in hand, she bathed her red, puffy eyes.

She pulled the hairpins out of her thick, shoulder-length hair. Wetting her hands, she moistened, then combed her hair. The resulting soft waves framed her heart-shaped face and took the emphasis from her eyes. After a touch of wine-colored lip gloss, she went back to her office. Blake was waiting outside her door.

On seeing her, he looked rather startled.

"Is . . . is something wrong?" Sarah asked.

"No, I guess I've never seen you with your hair down before."

Immediately, Sarah began digging in her purse for her hairpins. She stopped on hearing him say, "You should wear it down more often. Ready?" His hand cupped her elbow.

"Yes." The casual touch sent tiny waves of pleasure through Sarah. Although they worked together, she could count the times on one hand that Blake had touched her. "I-I brought my car, so I'll follow you."

"I'd prefer following you." He released her arm to jab the elevator button. "Do you know where Jo Jo's Bar-b-que is?"

Panic sliced through her. "We're eating barbecue?"

A frown puckered Blake's forehead as he led her onto the elevator. "You don't like barbecue?"

"I do, but it's . . ."

"Messy?" he supplied for her and grinned. Her heart did a little flip-flop. "I've got a craving for ribs. Please don't disappoint me, Ms. Marshall."

Sarah looked into his teasing face and knew she'd risk the embarrassment of dropping sauce on her clothes and getting meat stuck in her teeth, if he'd just smile at her like that more often. Maybe, just maybe one day she could make him crave *her.*

Jo-Jo's was filled to capacity with the holiday crowd. Mouth-watering smells curled around the spacious restaurant, which was done in a Western theme. Christmas carols instead of the usual fifties blues tunes filled the room.

"Eat up, Ms. Marshall."

Sarah looked from the plate of barbecue ribs, coleslaw, and corn on the cob to Blake's smiling face. He had taken off his jacket, his tie was tucked out of harm's way inside his blue-striped shirt, and in his hands was a succulent rib, dripping with rich, dark sauce. Strong white teeth bit into the meat. He chewed with enjoyment. She smiled as she noticed not one speck of sauce dropped onto his shirt.

"Mr. Williams, all I wanted was a chopped beef sandwich," she said, hoping her stomach didn't begin growling again. She had eaten only a bowl of cereal for breakfast and it was past seven in the evening.

"You mean you are going to sit over there all clean and watch me make a pig of myself," Blake said, taking another healthy bite.

She smiled despite herself. He looked as

carefree as a little kid. "The thought had crossed my mind."

"All right, we'll send your plate back, order you a sandwich and while it's coming you can tell me about your plans once you return from your cruise," Blake said.

Another kind of panic assailed her. If she ordered a sandwich, she'd finish eating before Blake did and then she'd have to talk. There were a few things she didn't want him to know. "There's no need to bother the waitress again," she said. "This is fine."

"You better take off that jacket or you may get sauce on the sleeves," Blake said, picking up his corn.

Sarah nodded her head and unbuttoned her brown wool jacket. Always the gentleman, Blake was immediately behind her to take her jacket and drape it over her chair. "Thanks," she said over her shoulder.

He sat back down and picked up his corn. When he looked back up at her, he froze. Where the jacket was prim, the sheer, flirty white blouse she wore underneath showed a provocative swirl of lace over the rounded swell of her breasts. Very nice breasts, if he was any judge.

"What's the matter?" she asked in a breathy voice.

For an insane moment Blake wondered what she sounded like in the throes of passion. "I'm just wondering if I'll have to pay the cleaning bill."

She smiled. "I'm a great believer in wash-and-wear. Here goes." Finger and thumb of each hand picked up the smallest rib. She took a tiny bite.

Blake swallowed his corn after a couple of chews. It was that or choke. Watching his secretary's delicate pink tongue flick in and out of her mouth was too much of a reminder of the kiss they had shared, too much of a temptation to wonder what else that little tongue could do. He was about to drag his eyes away when she put one end of the rib between her lips and sucked. His corn dropped onto his plate.

"Bla—Mr.Williams, are you all right?"

"Yeah," he managed to say. "I'm just stuffed."

"We don't have to stay . . ." Sarah suggested.

"No, please finish." He picked up his fork carefully to keep his wandering gaze on his food. His six months of abstinence must be getting to him. "Have you thought about who I should keep as the key people at Reynolds?" Perhaps it would be best to talk about business.

"Not very much." Thankfully for Blake's sake, she put her rib down and cleaned her hands. "I know Mr. Larson who was in on the initial takeover feels there may be some disgruntled employees who will try to slow the transition down on purpose, and frankly, I can't blame them."

"I'm saving them," Blake told her. "Reynolds' son was more interested in gambling than taking care of his father's company. It would have gone bankrupt within the year."

"I know that and you know that, but how many of the employees know it?" Pushing her plate aside, she placed her elbows on the table, linked her hands together, and rested her chin on top. "Reynolds is family owned like Williams and Williams. A lot of those people probably started with Jack Reynolds' father. They're afraid of losing benefits, being forced into retirement, and they resent you. Larson is a great front man, but he has all the warmth of a rock."

Blake knew Sarah's reading of the situation was correct. He had always admired her judgment. "So what do you suggest?"

Sarah cocked her head to one side in a teasing gesture. "Just what you have probably already planned. Take Madison with you when you go. Besides smoothing all the feathers you're sure to ruffle, he can reassure the people regarding their benefits and job security. I'm sure you'll make it very clear that you'll only keep those employees who show complete loyalty. You care too much about people not to give them the chance to stay."

"It doesn't seem to be working with you," he said softly.

She stiffened. "I thought we were finished discussing that."

"Sorry," Blake said. "It just slipped out. I value you and your opinion and I hate to lose you."

"Sometimes we have no choice." She reached for her jacket and rose. Blake followed. "I'd like to wash my hands before we go."

Blake watched Sarah weave her way through the tables and was more determined than ever to keep her with him.

"Ms. Marshall, please come into my office."

"Yes, sir," Sarah said and stood. Two days had passed since they'd gone out to eat. Her face still felt hot when she remembered looking into the mirror of the restroom and seeing the blouse she wore that night. Sheer and revealing, it had been a gift from Cynthia. She never wore it at work without a jacket and she never removed her jacket. She had hardly been able to face Blake when she came back to the table. No wonder he had dropped his corn.

She brushed her hand over the chestnut-colored wool crepe suit before entering Blake's office. She had expected him to be behind his desk; instead he was in front of it, arms folded, legs crossed at the ankle. The late afternoon sun shown through the glass window at his back, silhouetting him. Sarah caught her breath.

"Yes, Mr. Williams?"

"Ms. Marshall, I seem to have a problem," he said. "I find I am without a date for tonight."

Sarah kept her face impassive. "The list of your past acquaintances is in your file under D, for dropped."

Blake's thick eyebrows climbed toward his short, curly black hair in obvious annoyance. He'd never liked the way she filed his old girlfriends by bills for flowers or dinners.

"I'm aware of where I can find their names. You cross-filed everything for me and put it in the computer." Blake unfolded his arms and came toward her in an effortless stride that made her think of a jungle cat on the prowl. "I've been thinking. Since you're leaving, why don't I take you to the dinner party."

"Me?" Her pen dropped soundlessly to the carpeted floor. Blake casually picked up the black and gold pen and handed it to her.

"Mrs. Atkinson is not going to be happy if I show up without a dinner companion. I don't want to upset one of the board members," Blake explained.

"Why me?" she asked, wanting to accompany him and terrified at the same time.

"I thought you might enjoy the evening,"

Blake said casually. "You'll know most of the people there and it will give everyone a chance to say goodbye to you. Mrs. Atkinson lives in a wonderful old thirty-one room mansion. It's a turn-of-the-century treasure trove. During Christmas, the house and the grounds are decorated with more than a million white lights."

Sarah knew the house. It was only partially visible from the street, but cars still crept past, trying to see the impressive array of glittering lights.

"If you come, I promise to ask Mrs. Atkinson to take you on a tour and, if she can't, I will," Blake said coaxingly, flashing his most irresistible smile. He'd give Sarah and her mystery man one last try. "Please help me out."

"Well . . . Okay," Sarah found herself saying. New Year's Eve was only eleven days away. After that, she'd never have to see Blake again.

"Great. I'll pick you up at eight. If you want to take off now to fix yourself up, it's okay with me."

Sarah stiffened. "I know I'm in my dotage, but even I don't need seven hours to get ready."

"I only meant you might want to get your hair . . ." Blake trailed off at the frosty look Sarah was sending him. "I'll pick you up at eight."

Without a word, Sarah returned to her desk. Sometimes she could strangle Blake. Just because she dressed conservatively and wore her hair pulled back was no reason to think she couldn't manage a little dinner party. If it was the last thing she did, she was going to make him notice her. Tonight he was going to drop more than his corn.

Blake blinked. "Sarah . . . Ms. Marshall."

Sarah's nervous smile on opening her apartment door blossomed. The awe in Blake's voice made her heart sing almost as much as hearing him say her name. After five years he was finally looking at her the way a man looks at a woman he'd like to know better. She sent a silent thanks to her oldest sister, Cynthia, who had helped in Sarah's transformation.

She had called her sister from work. It was Cynthia's bingo night and Sarah could hear the reluctance in her voice until she mentioned Blake's comments about her age, her hair, and "fixing herself up." After Cynthia made some remarks about Blake's parentage, she'd been more than willing to help.

From the way his gaze kept drifting to her cleavage, Cynthia had been right to insist Sarah wear the red sequined, strapless bustier instead of the deep amethyst jacket and mid-calf skirt she had planned. For some odd reason, she didn't feel any of the embarrassment she'd felt over him seeing her in the sheer blouse.

"Good evening, Mr. Williams. I'll get my coat." Stepping back, she invited Blake to enter, then closed the door. "Have a seat, I won't be but a moment."

Blake stood and watched her walk away. He was too stunned to take a seat. She was captivating. He couldn't imagine why he had never noticed her lush lips or the sparkle in her brown eyes or her wonderful cheekbones.

He heard the slight rustling of her floor-length red satin skirt before she emerged from the bedroom. He openly studied her as she made her way to him. He couldn't have been that blind. As she drew closer, he thought he had his answer.

She was wearing makeup. Subtly applied by the light stroke of a master, but there just the same. Automatically, he took the matching long red coat she held and helped her put it on. *And* caught a whiff of her perfume. Where the makeup was subtle, the perfume shouted seduction. It was as alluring as the woman staring up at him through a sweep of dark lashes.

"I have to tell you, I'm very excited about going to Mrs. Atkinson's house," Sarah said. "I've wanted to see the inside of it since I was a little girl."

"Then I'm doubly pleased about tonight."

Sarah frowned. "Doubly?"

"I have a beautiful dinner companion and I'm making one of her childhood dreams come true," Blake said softly, then almost grimaced. He had spoken on impulse again. Sarah was his employee—a trusted secretary. He had to remember that.

Sarah felt as if she was going to melt into a little puddle. "Th-Thank you."

"Thank *you,*" Blake said and lightly grasped her arm. "Ready?"

She nodded. Wait until she told Cynthia she was a modern-day fairy godmother.

"Did you plan to leave the lights on on the Christmas tree?" Blake asked.

"On, no. I forgot," Sarah said, then rushed to unplug the lights before Blake could see her flushed face and realize that he was the reason she was flustered.

"The tree is something," Blake said, his finger tracing the halo of a dark-skinned angel. "How did you get it up here?"

Sarah laughed. "By promising, bullying, and bribing my brother and cousin. It's a yearly ritual we go through since I've been on my own. I have to have a live Christmas tree every year. The bigger the better."

"I've not had a tree for years," Blake said matter-of-factly.

"How could you *not* have a Christmas tree?" Sarah looked horrified.

"Never had time or never got around to it, I guess," Blake said as he led her from the apartment.

"I admit they can be a bother, but once all the lights and ornaments are on, and you sit back in the dark room and enjoy the tree in all its glory, it's worth the effort," Sarah said.

Blake glanced at the dreamy expression on her face before they went down the two flights of stairs to his car. Sarah was being the romantic again. He couldn't help feeling enchanted by her.

"We have a little time before we're due at the Atkinson's," Blake said. "Would you like to drive around and see some other Christmas lights?" It wouldn't hurt to indulge her.

"Oh, yes, please."

"You got it," he said with a wink.

Blake smiled as Sarah oohed and aahed at another display of lights. He was glad she enjoyed it, but he hadn't been able to get into the spirit for years. Christmas was too commercialized. If merchants pushed their marketing plans any further, they would begin their pitches in July.

"The Atkinson's house is around the corner. Close your eyes, I want you to get the full effect," Blake told her.

Stopping across the street from the three-story Gothic mansion, Blake helped Sarah out of the car.

"Open your eyes and take a quick look. It's too cold outside to linger."

Sarah slowly opened her wide, dark eyes. "Oh, Blake," she said in a hushed whisper. "It's the second most magnificent thing I've ever seen." She started toward the life-size nativity scene on the edge of the south lawn.

"Sar—Ms. Marshall, it's too cold for you to wander around the yard."

"I'm not cold," she said and continued on.

Muttering under his breath, Blake followed.

Sarah stood in front of the manger scene on the lawn, her expression as solemn as that of the brown sculpted figures before her. "Do you believe in miracles, Mr. Williams?"

"Not especially," Blake said, his shoulders hunched in his cashmere coat.

"I do," Sarah said. "Love is a gift, but when it's returned, it's a miracle." Without another word, she went back to the car.

Blake followed. The jerk Sarah was in love with didn't know how lucky he was. Unlike Clarissa, Sarah wouldn't fall out of love because her man wasn't with her every night. She had a deeper understanding of love and more resilience. It would serve this mystery man right if some other guy took her from him. Blake stumbled on the curve when he thought of himself as possibly being that man. Shaking the notion away, he got in the car after helping Sarah in and drove to the front door, where a valet awaited them.

Sarah emerged from the car, her eyes sparkling as much as her gown. He never wanted to see that sparkle dim, the way Clarissa's had. He'd never do that to Sarah. Somehow Blake knew Sarah didn't say the word *love* casually. She'd mean the forever kind of love and expect her man to mean it the same way.

The longest Blake had remained in a relationship since his marriage had broken up was four months. He was being foolish; Sarah wasn't for him. The only reason he had brought her to the party was to help her snag the guy she was interested in.

Sarah dazzled all the guests, even the board members who usually were as stiff as pokers. She had a way of looking at a person when she was talking to them that let them know they had her total attention. It was unnerving as well as gratifying when she turned those big brown eyes on you. Although Blake watched the single men from his office closely, he couldn't tell if she paid one any more attention than she did the others.

But they were all paying a lot of attention to her. A couple of times, he wanted to grasp her sequined top and pull it up to cover her breasts, the way the men were ogling her. The idea of his fingers against her soft, yielding flesh had him gritting his teeth and stepping outside for a breath of fresh air.

Later that evening he stood looking at the wonder sweeping across Sarah's face as they toured Mrs. Atkinson's house together. To his annoyance, he was having a hard time remembering his policy on fraternization and his avowal that Sarah wasn't for him. He had never met a woman more open to life.

It was still difficult to match the woman who had charmed every person at dinner to the quiet, efficient woman at his office. This Sarah had an easy laugh and had even once giggled like a schoolgirl. The Sarah at the office rarely broke out of her businesslike demeanor.

With her arms outstretched and her head thrown back, Sarah turned slowly beneath a two-hundred-year-old chandelier. "What I wouldn't give to have danced here."

"May I?" Blake asked.

Sarah swayed. Strong fingers closed around her bare arms, steadying her. "Th-Thank you."

Slowly, gently, he pulled her into his arms. Her skirt rustled as he fitted her closer to him. The smoothness of her bare skin tempted him to see if she felt this good all over. He felt his body harden. Sarah sucked in her breath, but she didn't move away. She simply watched him with wary eyes. Smart woman, his Sarah. She knew he wasn't the staying kind and that was the only kind she wanted. Too bad for both of them.

He began to waltz her around the immense ballroom. They glided effortlessly on the polished hardwood floors. Their steps matched perfectly. Gilt-edged mirrors caught their reflections as they passed.

Unable to bare the burning intensity in Blake's eyes, afraid he'd see a matching one in hers, Sarah lay her head on his chest. Suddenly he stopped. She lifted her head and stared up at him, holding her breath, hoping, praying he'd kiss her. His dark head bent. Warm lips grazed her cheek.

"There. Now you've had your dance." Straightening, he stepped away and continued the tour.

Sarah fought back the tears. He might have noticed her, but he still didn't think of her as a desirable woman. She'd bet everything she owned that he hadn't kissed any of the women in his drop file on the cheek.

They stopped before a priceless collection of eighteenth-century paintings. Sarah tried to summon an ounce of some enthusiasm, but her heart wasn't in it.

"Tired?"

She studied the pleated front of his white shirt. "A little. Do you mind if we leave now?"

After saying goodbye to the hostess, he took her home. Sarah didn't say one word on the way back. She was afraid that if she did, she'd start crying. Blake unlocked the door for her and handed her back the key.

"Would you like me to check the apartment for you?"

She shook her head, sending tendrils of curls dancing around her face. Blake caught one of them and rubbed it between his finger and thumb.

"For some men, one kiss is not enough." He dropped her hair and stepped back. "Good night, Ms. Marshall."

Sarah went straight to her bedroom. Blake had given her hope again. He was definitely looking. She just had to make sure he didn't stop before New Year's Eve.

"Who would have thought Sarah was such a fox?" asked the appreciative male voice. "I couldn't believe it was her when you two walked in last night."

"Yeah," Blake said, barely able to keep the annoyance out of his voice. Andrew Fields was the head of accounting. He was also the third man in as many hours to drop by Blake's office and offer his unsolicited opinion on Sarah.

"She has some traffic-stopping legs," Andrew said, scooting forward in the leather chair in front of Blake's desk. "Never thought I was into knees very much, but Johnson pointed out this morning what a great pair Sarah has when we saw her at lunch."

Blake ground his teeth together and uttered another noncommittal "Yeah." Johnson was Fields's assistant and another guest at Mrs. Atkinson's dinner party. Blake had never liked the way some men discussed women as if the only thing about them that mattered was the way they were put together. He discovered very quickly that morning that he felt almost violent when the woman in question was Sarah.

The only reason he tolerated their comments at all was on the outside chance that one of the men was the one Sarah had her heart set on. The men were good looking enough, Blake supposed, but the more they talked, the more convinced Blake was he had yet to meet *The One*. His Sarah would choose someone more settled, more grounded, more interested in her as a person.

"Aren't you dating Marsha Anderson?" Blake asked. He was fast approaching his endurance limit.

Andrew laughed and winked his eye. "Dating, yeah, but she doesn't have any claim on me. If I see a pretty woman, I'm free to go after her."

"I see." Blake mentally crossed Andrew off the list of possibilities. Sarah would demand fidelity. "The report looks fine."

The well-built man in his early forties rose

to accept the dossier Blake handed him. Instead of leaving, he tapped the blue folder against the palm of his hand. "I wonder if she has a date for the company's Christmas party tomorrow night?"

"Since Marsha doesn't work here why would she need a date?" Blake inquired innocently.

"I meant Sarah."

"I don't know what *Ms. Marshall's* plans are," Blake said pointedly.

Andrew was a perceptive man and he liked his job. He got Blake's message. "I meant Ms. Marshall. Since she's leaving, it wouldn't be against policy to ask her out, would it?"

Blake's smile revealed the barest hint of teeth. "She hasn't left yet."

Andrew swallowed.

There was the briefest knock on the door before it opened and Sarah came in. Her long-sleeved, mid-calf dress looked demure until she moved. The center split ran five inches above the knees. With each step she revealed a flash of long leg.

Blake's grip on his pen tightened. Sarah was fast becoming a distraction. Except for the colorful beads around her neck and in her ears, she was all in pink. She reminded him of cotton candy, sugary sweet and good to the last, mouth-watering bite.

Earlier that morning she had come in to take a private letter. She had sat in her usual chair to his right and crossed her legs. The light wool dress she wore had slid back to mid-thigh. When her innocent brown eyes had met his across his desk, he had never been more thankful that he was sitting down.

"Excuse me, Mr. Williams, Mr. Fields, for interrupting, but we need Mr. Williams's decision on my replacement today and he is scheduled to be in meetings all afternoon."

"Think nothing of it," Andrew said, his gaze slowly running the length of her body. "I only wish it was under other circumstances. You'll be missed."

"Thank you, Mr. Fields," Sarah said and turned her attention back to Blake. "There are three final candidates. Choose one."

Out of the corner of his eye, Blake saw Andrew's brow furrow at Sarah's command. No one else in the company would dare issue him a direct order or enter his office without permission. But there was no one else like Sarah. She intuitively knew when to push, when to back down, when to retreat.

"If you'll excuse us, Andrew, Ms. Marshall and I have some work to do," Blake said, unable to keep a tiny smile off his face. Sarah had looked at Andrew with her usual cool efficiency. He'd known his Sarah had better taste.

As soon as the door closed, Sarah said, "Since you're in such a good mood, this shouldn't take long." Opening each folder, she placed them on Blake's desk in front of him. "You balked this morning."

"I want you to stay," he said and watched color bloom in her light brown cheeks. He wondered if she did the same when she was around *him*.

"This isn't easy for me, Mr. Williams," she told him quietly. "I have a lot of fond memories here, but it's time for me to move on."

"There's nothing I can say to make you change your mind?"

"No. I'm sorry," she said, her voice as sad as her eyes.

He picked up the first folder. "My heart's not in this, but I guess I have no choice. Come around here and tell me what you think of this applicant."

"Pardon?" Her large brown eyes widened.

"Help me choose which one," Blake requested. For some reason, he was beginning to like the idea that he could shake Sarah's calm when no one else could.

She came around the desk and leaned over Blake's shoulder.

He sucked in his breath. Once again he had made a mistake where Sarah was concerned. She was wearing that alluring perfume again. He twisted uncomfortably in his seat. If he kept acting like an undisciplined teenager, he'd walk bent over until New Year's Day.

Clearing his throat, he asked, "What do you think of this one?"

"She has very good skills and comes highly recommended by her present boss," Sarah said. "I might as well tell you that none of the three finalist's bosses are happy with either of us."

A dark brow rose. "Why?"

Sarah grinned impishly. "I'm leaving and you're going to replace me with their secretary."

"They're wrong about one thing."

"What's that?"

Blake caught her puzzled gaze. "I may hire a secretary, but there's no way to replace you."

Sarah's throat tightened. "I . . . thank you."

Blake caught a hint of the curve of her breast from the open lapel of her dress and leaned forward to lessen his discomfort. What the hell was wrong with him? "Would you consider a month's leave and then come back to work?"

"No," she said softly.

Blake picked up another folder. "She likes colors, doesn't she? I may not remember the other women, but I remember her. She had on the brightest shades of gold and purple I have ever seen."

Sarah's lips curved into a sad smile. "At least people will always notice her."

Blake caught the wistfulness in her voice.

"Some women shout, others whisper. I'll take the whisperers any day."

Warmth curled in Sarah's stomach. "Then, I think we should pass on this one."

"Whatever you say, Ms. Marshall," Blake said and picked up the next folder. "I'm in your hands."

Sarah had never been so nervous in her life. But it was too late to go home. Taking a deep breath, she rang Blake's lighted doorbell. No answer. She rang again.

"You did call and say we were coming, didn't you?"

Sarah ignored the agitated voice of her older brother, Randle. Blake was at home. He had told her he planned to be home all evening.

"What if he has a woman in there with him?" her cousin, Antoine asked, voicing her worst fear.

"He hasn't had a steady ladyfriend for over six months," Sarah said and pressed on the doorbell again.

Both men shook their heads. "You ever hear of one-night stands, little sister?" Randle asked.

She turned on her brother. "I'm not totally naive. Just because I don't sleep around is no rea—"

"Ms. Marshall, what are you doing here?"

Sarah wanted to sink through the concrete porch. Of all the embarrassing things for Blake to overhear her say, she couldn't think of anything worse.

Slowly she turned to face him. Once again she was struck by his dark, masculine beauty. A man had no right to look so good in something as simple as a black turtleneck sweater and jeans. Nor should he have such mesmerizing black eyes that made a woman want to curl up, preferably in his lap, and purr. Even though the temperature outside was in the low thirties, her body heated. Her wayward thoughts rattled her even further.

"Good evening, Mr. Williams. I, that is, we, stopped by to drop you off a Christmas tree. I started to ask if you wanted to go with me to pick one out because choosing a tree for another person can be a bit tricky. After all, some people like fat trees, some like skinny ones, some like them tall, others short . . . then there's the *type* of tree."

Blake opened his mouth to say something, but she continued on. "Then I decided you probably didn't care that much, so I decided to pick one out for you. Since you liked my tree, I decided to get you a similar one. I'm sorry it's after eight, but it took me longer than I thought to find just the exact one and then I had to wait on my brother with the truck. But if you don't like it, you don't have to take it."

"I'm sure I'll like the tree, Ms. Marshall," Blake muttered, flabbergasted.

"Well, if you don't, I understand. I mean, I'm your secretary, I know you have high stand–"

Warm hands settled on her shoulders, stopping Sarah's nervous flow of words. He couldn't believe she was so agitated about bringing him a Christmas tree, when she had handled every possible major disaster at his office with unruffled calm. Or was it the fact that he had overheard her comment about her love life, or rather lack thereof, that made her nervous? Sarah was becoming more interesting by the day.

"I'm sure the tree you picked out is perfect, Ms. Marshall," Blake said. "Come on in and get out of the cold."

"Thanks, man," Antoine said, "I didn't think she'd ever wind down."

Sarah shot her cousin a hard glare over her shoulder.

Antoine smiled. "Get out of the way, cuz, and show us where you want this thing."

"You heard the man, Ms. Marshall." Blake stepped past Sarah and introduced himself to both men. "I might have known she'd have her yearly helpers with her. Well, let's get this inside and see what it looks like."

Dismissed, Sarah went into the den and directed the men to place the tree in front of the floor-to-ceiling window looking out over the backyard.

"Sarah, next time try to pick out a smaller tree," Randle said, rubbing the small of his back.

Antoine nodded. "If it wasn't Saturday tomorrow, I'd have to take off work."

Sarah harrumphed. "What work? You two are partners in an advertising firm. You do most of your thinking sitting down," she accused. "You're just upset because I'm only going to make you one pecan pie each."

"Well, I don't have any pecan pie, but I do have a growing selection of cookies, candy, cakes, log rolls, and who knows what else in the kitchen from friends and business associates," Blake told the two men. "You're welcome to help yourself."

Randle and Antoine exchanged meaningful looks and grinned.

"You don't have to feed them. I already . . ." Sarah's voice trailed off. The men had already left the room. In a matter of minutes they returned. Her brother and cousin each had an Irish whiskey cake in their hands.

"Greedy," Sarah said, but she was smiling.

"For that, you don't get any." Randle sniffed his cake and let out a deep sigh. "I can't wait to take a bite out of this baby. Thanks, man."

He slung his arm around Sarah's slim shoulder. "Ready to go?"

"No."

"No."

Sarah and Blake both spoke at the same time.

Sarah nervously studied the snowflake pattern in her red and white sweater.

Blake looked undisturbed by the hard, reappraising stare her brother was giving him. "I'll be happy to take her home, after all the trouble she went through to get me a tree."

"She drove her car."

"Then, I'll follow her and make sure she gets home all right."

Sarah stepped from under her brother's arm. "I can see myself home."

"No."

"No."

This time the no's came from Randle and Blake.

"I really need help decorating this tree," Blake said. Then added, "I promise to have her home in a couple of hours."

"A lot can happen in a couple of hours," Randle mumbled.

"Randle, I'm not in high school any longer and if you don't stop embarrassing me, I'll never cook for you again," Sarah said.

Her brother smiled sheepishly. "Sorry. I keep forgetting the baby of the family grew up." He stuck out his hand to Blake. "Get her home before ten."

Sarah groaned. Blake smiled. "You have my word." He was still smiling when he came back from seeing Randle and Antoine off. His eyes lingered on Sarah, who was standing in front of the tree, both hands stuck in the back pockets of her jeans. "Thanks for the tree," Blake said gently.

"You're welcome." Her hands came out of her pockets to cross over her breasts. "Sorry about Randle."

"He was just doing what loving big brothers have done since the dawn of time," Blake said good-naturedly.

Sarah wrinkled her nose. "Spoken like a true big brother."

"Guilty as charged. Dianne purposely chose another college to get away from me and my brother, Carter. But she didn't know I had a friend watching over her at Fisk," Blake said, with a wink.

Sarah stepped closer to the tree and fiddled with a stray branch. "I've always been able to take care of myself no matter what my brother thought."

Blake studied the top of Sarah's dark head, but he wasn't fooled. She wasn't talking about the past, but the present. "Big brothers probably overcompensate because we know men can lie. We've heard their games run so many times to so many women we're determined our sisters aren't going to be any man's victim. Some men say 'I love you' with no more emotional commitment than 'pass the sugar.' Some women, like you and Dianne, grew up without lies and deceit and don't expect it in others. Randle and I know that, so we try to protect you."

"So, how did Dianne know when she met her husband that he was the right one?" Sarah asked, finally turning to face Blake.

"She told me she cried every time she had to leave him to go back to her dormitory," Blake remembered with a smile. "It was a good thing she was a senior when they met. The one thing my parents demanded was that all of us finish college."

"Sounds like my parents." She looked back at the bare branches. "So, how do you want to decorate your tree?"

Blake threw his arm over Sarah's shoulders in the brotherly way Randle had. "*Our* tree. I'm open to suggestions."

Sarah's knees went weak. "Most people have a theme. What is your favorite Christmas memory?"

"My junior year at college. Everyone was home. The airports were shut down and it forced all of us to cancel our plans to scatter with friends or for business and spend the holiday as a family. The time bought us closer together."

"Do you remember the tree?"

Blake thought a moment, then said. "It had a lot of gold ribbon, white lace, and crystal icicles."

"My mother is incredibly sentimental and never throws anything away," Sarah said thoughtfully. "Do you think your mother might still have the decorations?"

"There's only one way to find out." He grabbed her hand and started for the garage.

It took thirty minutes of searching Blake's parents' cluttered attic before the gold and white decorations were located. His mother was only too happy to have another box out of the way. The senior Williams' tree was decorated with gingerbread, in deference to their three-year-old only grandchild by their daughter.

During Blake and Sarah's visit, his parents dropped none-too-subtle hints that he was getting older and it was about time he remarried. Since they had seen Sarah with Blake at the Atkinson's party, they both kept giving her questioning looks.

Sarah had never seen him embarrassed before. On their drive back to his house, she pointed out that his parents' comments were probably payback for all the times he'd embarrassed his sister, Dianne. The single Randle always got hints from their mother on Christmas day.

In his den, Blake put the box of decorations down by the tree and braced his hands on his hips. "There's no way you can compare the two situations. We were trying to protect you and Dianne. My parents would marry me off to the first childbearing woman they could find."

"You're exaggerating," Sarah said, setting a smaller box beside Blake's. "They love you too much to saddle you with a woman you didn't love."

"Well, they're going to have to wait a long time because I'm not planning on falling in love with anyone."

Sarah hands paused only slightly on lifting a string of gold beads out of the box. "Sometimes love sneaks up on you when you least expect it."

"It's not sneaking up on *me*. I've seen what the corporate lifestyle can do to a marriage up close and personal, thank you. You're traveling most of the time and when you're not, you spend long hours at the office. It would take a very special love to withstand being apart so much." Blake shook his dark head. "You've been on a couple of business trips with me before. You know how men and women cheat on their spouses. At least Clarissa didn't cheat on me. I wouldn't have been responsible if she had."

"There are a lot of women who wouldn't dream of being unfaithful to their husbands," Sarah argued.

"I know that," Blake agreed. "My mother is a perfect example. I also remember her being gone most of the time. I see her more now than I did growing up. I'm not going to put a woman or a child through that."

"If people love each other enough, frequent separations don't have to be a problem," Sarah said, hoping she wasn't revealing too much.

Blake opened his box and took out a handful of snowflake-shaped Christmas lights. "Williams and Williams is the only wife I'll ever have."

"You sound so certain," Sarah whispered, disappointment lining her voice.

"I am," Blake said emphatically.

Sarah's hand shook as she pressed out a wide, gold bow. "Not me," she said with forced brightness. "I intend to have it all. I may be starting a little late, but that just means I'll have to work harder and faster."

Blake's thoughts hung on the words *harder and faster.* He doubted seriously if the picture his unruly mind conjured up of Sarah in bed with him pumping into her body harder and faster was what she meant. This plan of his wasn't working worth a damn. "Leave that. It's almost ten."

"I thought we decided to ignore Randle." She picked up another bow.

"We did. But tomorrow night is the Christmas party and you don't want to be too tired to enjoy it," Blake said, purposely holding the bunched lights in front of his suddenly uncomfortable jeans.

Sarah's thumb slid back and forth over a string of gold beads. "I can stay and help with the tree. I'm not even sure I'm going." Given a choice between Blake and a party, she'd always choose Blake.

"Then you don't have a date?"

"No," she admitted softly, embarrassment sending her rummaging back in the box.

The guy Sarah was in love with had better have a good reason for putting that lost look in her face, Blake thought. "Good, then you can go with me."

Sarah lifted her head. Hope shone in her clear brown eyes as bright as the gold rose in her hand. "You?"

"Me."

He didn't believe in love or marriage or Christmas or miracles, but she did. "I'd love to."

The Williams & Williams Christmas party was in full swing when Blake and Sarah arrived. She was ecstatic on seeing the elegant ballroom in the hotel draped in sparkling lights, life-size angels, and nine-foot wreaths. Twin crystal chandeliers bathed the laughing crowd below her in glittering prisms of light. The walls were covered in silk.

As she expected, their entrance caused hushed whispers to ripple over the ballroom. One after another, people turned to look up at the couple at the top of the wide spiral staircase. Unconsciously, she stepped closer to Blake.

Blake looked down at Sarah and couldn't blame them for staring. Words failed to describe how breathtakingly beautiful she was. She sparkled as much as the gold and white gown she wore. Each minute movement drew attention to the swirls of gold beads and sequins on the front of her dress, accentuating her breasts. The gold mesh top shimmered with her every step.

"I told you you looked sensational in that dress," Blake whispered in Sarah's ear. "From all the open mouths and slack jaws, you'll have to believe me now."

"My guess is, it's shock at seeing us together," Sarah said nervously.

"I thought I had convinced you earlier today not to worry about the fraternization policy," Blake said easily. "Since you're leaving, it would probably seem odd if I *didn't* bring you to the party."

Sarah nodded, but her gaze continued to scan the assembled guests. Last night she had been so happy Blake had asked her to the party, she hadn't even thought about the fraternization policy—until she arrived home. It had taken her all morning to work up enough nerve to call him with her concerns. She worked hard to put just the right amount of controlled politeness in her voice.

As was typical of him, Blake had considered the possible conflict and didn't have any misgivings. Technically he was her boss, but they were also friends, and the party was a company affair. It was only a professional courtesy he was extending to Sarah, who had worked diligently for him for five years.

"I've only been to one office Christmas party, and from what I've heard, you're usually in and out within an hour," Sarah finally said. She had stopped coming to the event after seeing Blake with one of his "dropees." It was difficult enough at the office. "Our being here together was bound to cause a stir."

Blake grinned roguishly. "Why don't we give them a good look, Sarah?"

Her eyes widened, her heart thudded at the sound of her name on his lips.

He looked into her face with mesmerizing black eyes. "If we're going to give them something to talk about, it should be good, don't you think?"

"Yes, I do, Blake." Sarah tried for the same controlled politeness she had used earlier on the phone. First names were a natural progression in friendship. She just wished she wasn't desirous of so much more.

His large hand slid from the small of her back to curve possessively around her waist as he guided her down the stairs and through the crowded room.

Blake's hand on her seemed natural, almost protective, and Sarah didn't think of protesting. She moved easily beside him. She could well imagine what some of the party attendees were saying.

But what did she care what they thought? She had a chance to be with Blake, to hear him laugh, to touch him openly, to see him look at her with frank male appreciation. New Year's Eve was rapidly approaching and then he would be gone from her life forever. At least she'd have her memories of this night.

Blake led her to a round table in the far corner of the ballroom, where his parents and a few business associates were seated. Greetings were given, introductions made.

"I was about to give up on you, Blake," his father said. "It's almost nine-thirty. Usually you come early and leave with the speed of sound."

People around the table nodded their heads in agreement and laughed.

"Just as I was leaving, Jack Reynolds called from Savannah. He wanted to make sure his employees would be taken care of," Blake explained. "It took longer than I thought it would to reassure him."

"So you kept Sarah waiting," Mrs. Williams said, looking elegant and regal in a red gown and diamonds.

"I put him on hold and called her. In fact, she was the one who persuaded me to listen to Reynolds' babbling on for an hour."

All eyes turned to Sarah. "A good relationship between Reynolds and Williams & Williams is vital to a smooth transition. It was more important," Sarah said easily.

Blake saw the wonder and the speculation in the faces at the table. Sarah sounded like the perfect executive's wife. She understood there were times when dinners went cold, parties were missed. Clarissa had never understood. She always felt he had put her last. Sarah had greeted him with a smile when he'd finally arrived, and had interestedly asked for details on his conversation with Reynolds.

"I'm glad you got things ironed out," Mr. Williams said. "It's good seeing both of you again."

"It certainly is," Blake's mother agreed.

"Did you two get the Christmas tree decorated?"

"No. Under strict orders from Sarah's brother, I had to get her home before ten," Blake said, a glint of mischief in his eyes. "Seems after all these years of Sarah working for me, he still doesn't trust me."

Everyone at the table chuckled. Blake ignored Sarah's elbow in his side. "Smart man," said Howard Cummings, the firm's lawyer. "You were always unpredictable where beautiful women were concerned."

Sarah flushed under the older man's praise. "Thank you."

"If you'll excuse us, I think I'll get Sarah something to drink." His hand on her waist, Blake moved them toward one of the four bars set up around the room.

Their progress was slow because people kept approaching them to say hello. Some were simply courtesy greetings, others were none-too-subtle plays in hopes of moving up the corporate ladder. Usually Blake didn't mind the interruptions. He admired aggressive people. He was that way himself. But tonight he could have done without the continuous barrage. Most of the men were sending too many sideways glances at Sarah. He'd always known he was possessive, but he'd never thought of himself as jealous.

Finally, he had had enough. "It doesn't look as if we'll ever make it to the bar. Let's dance."

Sarah glanced at the people crowded around them. "We're no more likely to get to the dance floor than we are to the bar."

"We'll make our own dance floor then," Blake said and pulled her into his arms.

Sarah followed. She gratefully rested her head against his chest. The slow music drifted through the air and she concentrated on shutting out the noise and the people, until there was only her and Blake.

"You aren't going to go to sleep on me, are you?"

Smiling, Sarah lifted her head. "What do *you* think?"

"What I'm thinking doesn't bear repeating." The music stopped. For a long minute they stared at each other, then Blake muttered something under his breath and headed once again for the bar, his expression impenetrable. This time no one stopped him. Nor did he have any difficulty getting a plate of hors d'oeuvres.

Sarah shook her head in amazement as Blake escorted her back to his parents' table. He pulled out a chair for her. "You can scatter people faster than someone yelling fire," she said.

"I just remembered why I never liked coming to these things." Blake took a seat and jerked his tie loose. "Too many people."

"Now, Blake, you need to get into the Christmas spirit," Esther Williams said.

"What little I had, I lost out there." He nodded toward the throng of laughing people.

Ignoring the festive items on the plate, Sarah turned to Blake. "We can leave if you want to."

Protests rose around the table. Patriarch Daniel Williams's was the loudest. "If he wants to go home, let him. Sarah, you stay with us. I'll take you home."

"She came with me and she's leaving with me," Blake said.

"Not if you keep up that attitude," Sarah said. The three women at the table applauded.

Blake looked at the determined sparkle in Sarah's eyes and realized his possessiveness of her was making him act like a spoiled child. He wanted to be the only one to share her laughter, her smile. If that wasn't enough, he still didn't know who her mystery man was. Worse, he was beginning to dislike the guy more with each waking hour. He sighed. "Sorry, I guess I'm just tired."

Instantly contrite, Sarah laid her hand on his larger one for a moment. "So am I. We really can leave if you'd like."

Blake glanced around the table at the frowning faces. "You've made your point. Stop glaring. We'll stay."

"Isn't he a gracious loser?" Sarah asked. Everyone at the table laughed and the tension was broken. Even Blake had to laugh at himself.

Blake opened Sarah's apartment door and handed her the key. "I'm glad we stayed."

"I had a wonderful time."

"So did I."

They both stared at each other, reluctant to part, but not knowing what to say. "Well, since you're not scheduled to come into the office next week, I'll say goodbye now," Sarah finally said.

"I wish you'd stay."

"I wish I could, but sometimes you have to move on." She was silent a moment, then stepped back into the apartment. Her hand gripped the door and she began to swing it shut.

The palm of Blake's hand stopped it. "Wait."

"Yes?"

Blake didn't know what he wanted to say, all he knew was that he didn't want to think about never again seeing her eyes sparkle, her shy smile that caught you unaware when it blossomed. "What about our Christmas tree? We didn't finish decorating it."

"No, we didn't." Sarah held her breath.

"If you don't have any plans for tomorrow, I can pick you up around four; sooner if you want to help me make my rounds."

"Rounds?" she queried.

"You'll see for yourself tomorrow, if you can make it."

Sarah didn't hesitate. "Early morning church service is over by twelve and I'm free after that," she lied, knowing her sister would forgive her sooner or later for backing out on lunch plans they had made.

"Good. I'll pick you up at twelve and we can have lunch. Dress casually."

"I will. Good night, Blake."

"Good night, Sarah."

Dressed in jeans and an oversize red sweater, Sarah was waiting when the doorbell rang. She opened the door to find Blake, wearing a black sweater and black jeans.

"Hi. Come on in," Sarah said.

"Hello. Thanks for helping me out," Blake said.

Picking up her jacket from the couch, Sarah smiled. "You're welcome. I couldn't very well let you decorate our tree without me."

"Is that some slur at my artistic ability?"

"No. It's the truth," Sarah said as Blake helped her with her coat.

"I like hearing you laugh," he said softly. Sarah looked up at him and Blake felt himself sinking in her big brown eyes. If only she wasn't in love with someone else, he mused. If only he wasn't married to the company. If only she was into casual affairs . . .

But Sarah wasn't the type of woman a man loved and forgot. She'd linger. Memories of her would be worse than the ache he now felt. He stepped back. "Where do you want to eat lunch?"

Sarah blinked at the sudden distance in Blake's voice. "I-I don't care."

"As long as it's not barbecue, neither do I."

They settled on a popular soul-food restaurant. After eating, they went directly to Blake's house. Sarah helped Blake load numerous gift packages of food that had been stacked in the kitchen into Blake's BMW, then they delivered the items to two shelters for battered women. So this is what he meant by his "rounds," she thought admiringly.

Sarah looked at the women in the shelters, their scars both seen and unseen, and tears welled in her eyes. They had suffered so much and it wasn't going to get any easier for them. Perhaps the greatest pain was knowing that a man they had loved and trusted had returned their love with emotional and physical abuse.

She looked up to see Blake watching her closely. Without thinking, she went to him and circled her arms around his waist. Blake looked startled, then pleased. His arm curved around her shoulder. He might not love her, Sarah thought, but she knew with everything within her, he'd never intentionally hurt her.

Their next stop was Mrs. Atkinson's mansion. With the help of her chauffeur, they loaded food, clothes, and blankets into Blake's car. They made a total of five additional trips to the shelters. The women seemed to receive the most enjoyment from the packages of personal items. Some of them had left home with only the clothes on their backs. Blake had told her earlier that he had enlisted the aid of other businessmen to provide toys for the children and small gifts for their mothers on Christmas morning.

He tried to be secretive, but Sarah saw the check he handed the director of each shelter. She was discovering another side of Blake. Kind and generous. She loved him now more than ever.

"I feel so foolish," Sarah said as they stood drinking hot chocolate in Blake's kitchen late that afternoon. "I thought I'd give you a little of the Christmas spirit by bringing you a tree, and you have more than anyone I know."

Blake took a sip of chocolate from his mug before answering. "Christmas spirit had nothing to do with it. Those women and children need help year round, not just at Christmas."

"You're right, but how many people do it?"

"It's no big deal." Blake drained his mug, then rinsed and set it in the sink. "You're still up to tackling the tree?"

"More than ever," Sarah said, her mug following Blake's into the sink.

In the den, Blake said, "I had planned on untangling the rest of the lights and testing them, but I didn't get around to it."

"No problem." Sarah dropped to her knees and pulled the rest of the lights from the box. "It'll go faster if we do it together. I hope they all work. These snowflake bulbs would be impossible to replace."

"You're probably right. As I remember, Mama wanted to have a unique tree," Blake said, plugging in the first set of lights. They worked. "One down."

"We'll have this tree up in no time."

Sarah's words of confidence came back to haunt her a number of times that afternoon, as the tree proved difficult to dress. Several of the strands of snowflake lights refused to burn if there were more than three of them connected. The bows were wrinkled and it took her and Blake fifteen minutes to locate the iron. There weren't enough hooks for the crystal icicles, so they decided to use white thread; naturally Blake didn't have any and they had to make a trip to the store. She had even once knocked over the entire tree.

Sarah couldn't remember ever having so many problems with a tree or having so much fun. There was no awkwardness between them. For much of the time they worked in comfortable silence.

By the time Sarah was satisfied with the placement of the last golden bow, it was dark. "Cut off the lights, Blake, and let's see how it looks."

"Cross your fingers." The room lights winked off.

The tree glowed in shimmering gold and white splendor. "Blake, it's beautiful."

He came to stand beside her. "Thanks to your persistence. I would have given up long ago."

"That's because you have no patience."

"I wouldn't say that," he said, his thumb gliding down her cheek. "You'd be surprised how patient I am."

He pushed the tangled curls away from her face, his hand moving to the back of her head, his lips descending on hers. The kiss was long and deep. When finally he pulled away, he said, "You make it hard for me to keep my hands off you."

Sarah moistened her lips and stared at him, her heart beating rapidly. "I-I had no idea."

"I know. Your inexperience drew me to you as much as it protected you from me. But I'm not used to taking cold showers," Blake said bluntly.

Sarah refused to look away from his burning gaze. "I don't remember asking you to."

"You didn't have to," Blake said. "You believe in love. I've known only passion."

She stared at the man she loved helplessly, his beautiful black eyes reflecting the lights of the Christmas tree. "So, you want to add my name to your drop file."

Blake's head jerked upward. "You know better than that."

"I thought I did, but I'm not so sure anymore," she said and pressed her trembling hands to her lower face.

He had hurt her. The thought left as much of a bitter taste in his mouth as the thought of her in love with another man. But if there *was* someone, why had her lips been so soft and yielding under his, matching his hunger? Why was her body so responsive?

He felt the firm pressure of her thighs against his. The embers of desire he had been trying to control ignited. If the fool she was in love with couldn't make her happy or keep her satisfied, he didn't deserve such a passionate, beautiful woman.

Gently, he took her hands, kissed each fingertip, then pressed a warm kiss against her palm.

"I didn't mean to hurt you, Sarah. I'm sorry."

Like someone in a trance, Sarah allowed Blake to pull her into an embrace. His warm breath caressed her cheeks seconds before his lips brushed across her tear-filled eyes. She fought hard not to respond. No matter what he said, she couldn't take another rejection.

Carefully, Blake began to coax from her what she had freely given earlier. The sudden rigidness of her body only made him more determined to wipe the pain from her face. His tongue slowly traced the outer curve of her soft lips.

A shiver rippled along her nerve endings. She closed her eyes against the encroaching desire invading her body. The ease with which Blake was overcoming her defenses caused her to feel utterly helpless. Fully aware of the frank male hardness pressed against her stomach, she closed her eyes tighter in an effort to keep from stepping closer.

"Open your eyes, Sarah."

Cautiously, Sarah obeyed the soft command and saw the intense look of longing in his eyes. He withdrew his arms and took a step backward.

"I was a fool to hurt you. I'll take you home if you want, but if you can forgive me, I'd like for you to stay."

Sarah believed him. Blake had never lied to

her. It was her decision. He'd take her home if she asked and she'd never see him again. She'd be safe, but she'd never know if she could have made him love her. He thought he was jaded; he wasn't. He cared, perhaps more deeply than others. In his own way, he was afraid to reach out. If she took the gamble, she might lose everything, but the lonely alternative was more painful.

"I want to be your friend, Sarah," Blake said. "I don't want to remember you staring at me with tears in your eyes."

Sarah gathered enough courage to ask, "Is that all you want from me, friendship?"

His sad smile twisted her heart. "That's all there can ever be between us. Even if things were different, you aren't into short-term affairs and I'm not into long ones. I forgot that just before, and see what happened? I won't—I refuse to—hurt you again."

Sarah looked into his determined eyes and realized she had lost. A moment ago he had kissed her with all the passion and need she had dreamed of for so long. Now he was a stranger again. She couldn't stand to look at him and see that impersonal mask descend over his eyes. She wasn't that strong.

He wasn't going to change his mind, and to stay would only remind her of what she couldn't have. He still had it in his head that all women were like Clarissa, and nothing she could say or do would change his mind.

"I think I'd better go," Sarah said softly.

Her heart wept as he said, "I'll get your coat."

To Sarah, the thirty-minute ride back to her apartment seemed to last forever. Neither she nor Blake said anything to break the strained silence. At her door, he held out his hand. Careful not to raise her gaze above his determined chin, she placed her brass key-ring in his hand. She didn't want to look into his eyes. Whatever she would see, passion or indifference, either would break the fragile hold she had on her control.

Her hands tightly gripping the strap of her purse, she stood just inside the door as Blake checked her apartment. She prayed she'd be able to look him in the face and act normally when all she wanted to do was cry. She sensed him returning before she saw him coming out of her bedroom. A fragment of an unspoken dream flashed through her mind. She fought the forbidden fantasy just as she fought the tears threatening to fall. Her gaze lifted from his brown leather loafers to his face.

"Are you going to be all right?" Blake asked, his voice strained.

She swallowed until the stinging sensation eased in her throat. "Yes, thank you."

His harsh intake of breath seemed to come from the depths of his soul. "I guess I'll be going then."

Sarah merely nodded. She extended a trembling hand to take back her keys. After a long moment, they were lightly placed in her open palm. She closed her hand and felt the lingering warmth of the metal. Blake's warmth. A warmth she would never know again. She blinked rapidly to keep the tears at bay.

"I wish you all the best. I meant it when I said you were irreplaceable." He walked to the door. "Good night, Sarah." The door closed.

With a splintered cry of pain, Sarah turned away. Tears streaming down her cheeks, she stumbled to the couch. She clutched a throw pillow to her stomach, drew her knees up, and curled into a ball. Great racking sobs shook her body. She had finally gotten her wish for him to see her as a woman. She had offered him her body and he had politely refused it. He wanted a friend. She wanted a lifetime of love.

God, it hurt. Worse, she knew nothing this side of heaven was going to make the pain go away.

Blake stood on the outside of Sarah's door and heard her crying. His hand clenched on the knob. He had caused those tears to fall, with his uncontrollable need to touch her, to kiss her. She had been so full of life and laughter, she had drawn him like a moth to a flame. This time the flame was living and more vibrant than anything he had ever seen. In jeans and a sweater, she made his body ache as much as he had when she was elegantly gowned.

Too late, he had finally come to the realization that it was Sarah who attracted him. It didn't matter what she wore or that she was an efficient secretary. Sarah in all her different moods fascinated him as no other woman ever had. And he had hurt her. With his eyes closed, he placed his other hand on the door.

"Forgive me, sweetheart. I don't know how to make you happy; I seem to only know how to make you sad." Drawing in a deep, shuddering breath, he turned and slowly walked to his car.

Sarah awoke slowly. The first sensation was pain in her eyes, the second was pain in her heart. Her inclination was to shut her eyes and try to find forgetfulness again in sleep. It had certainly seemed the answer last night, when a drop in the room's temperature and cramped muscles had driven her from the couch to her bed. Once there, the tears hadn't stopped. The last thing she remembered was hugging her stuffed bear while tears flowed.

Her swollen eyes narrowed as she searched the bed for the koala bear Blake had given her. Seeing the gray, furry animal she drew it into her arms. Listlessly she stared at the faint sunlight probing through the partially drawn draperies. Christmas Eve. It was going to be a beautiful day. Somehow it didn't seem right that she was so miserable. Sarah winced at the thought.

She had fallen in love with a man who saw love as a liability, but she wasn't going to turn into a bitter woman because of it. She was going to be as strong as the women in the shelter. One of the things she'd learned from Blake was to face problems head-on. Setting the bear aside, she rose. Today, with all she had to do, was going to test how much she had learned.

It had taken Blake two hours and seventeen minutes to work himself from his house to his car to Sarah's apartment, then to her door. He shouldn't have come, he knew. He could offer her nothing but more tears, yet he didn't seem to be able to make his feet move away. He had to make sure she was all right.

When he had arrived home the previous night he had stayed in the den and stared at the Christmas tree. Each bow, each gold garland, each snowflake light, each crystal icicle reminded him of Sarah. She had given so much and he had given her misery in return.

Long slender fingers rubbed the rigid muscles in his neck. He was wound as tight as a clock. Sexual frustration wasn't helping the situation. It had plagued him most of his sleepless night. If he hadn't stopped himself, he was almost positive they would have made love.

She had been as hungry and hot for him as he had been for her. But Blake was experienced enough to know a fantasy lover was no match for the real thing. No doubt, she was thinking about her mystery man. After they kissed, Sarah had looked at him with a mixture of wonder and desire in her big brown eyes. She was probably as inexperienced as he was experienced. She was definitely off-limits. Friendship was all there could be between them. He just wished he didn't want so much more.

Just because he wasn't able to keep his hands to himself was no reason for Sarah to feel guilty or embarrassed about the kiss they had shared. He never wanted her to regret a moment they spent together. To accomplish that, he had to see her again and make her smile, make sure she still believed in miracles.

Before he could change his mind, he rapped on her door. After a long moment, he knocked again. After all the mental gymnastics he had gone through that day, the least she could do was be at home.

An unexpected sense of disappointment and loss assailed him when more seconds ticked by and still his knocking went unanswered. His shoulders slumped. Slowly, he turned away. Suddenly, the door behind him jerked opened and Blake spun back around. His eyes widened. What was this? His meticulous Sarah was utterly transformed. Her face was smeared with flour and what looked like chocolate. Her faded gray sweat suit was stained.

Her wide-eyed stare conveyed her surprise at seeing him. One hand made a futile swipe at the strands of black hair that had fallen from the ponytail on top of her head; the other hand tried frantically to close the door. The flat of his hand stopped the door from swinging shut and earned him a glare from Sarah.

"Good evening, Sarah." Her expression didn't change. This stubborn Sarah was one he was familiar with. "Seems I caught you at a bad time."

"Yes, you did."

Blake felt the temperature surrounding them drop into the freezing range. He wondered if he should wiggle his toes and fingers to see if he had frostbite. "You left this last night."

She looked at the black leather glove in his hand as if it were a two-headed serpent, then lifted her gaze and held out her hand. "Thank you."

He hesitated. Once his excuse to return was gone, the door was going to close. "I only found one. Do you have the other glove?"

"Yes." She took the glove from his hand and began to close the door. "If you'll excu—"

But her words were interrupted by a loud buzzing sound inside, and Sarah turned and ran back into the apartment, leaving the door open. Puzzled, Blake followed. He stopped on entering the kitchen and suddenly understood why Sarah looked so frazzled. The sink was piled high with bowls and pans, and every inch of work space was covered with baking ingredients. He sniffed the air. It was obvious she hadn't gotten to something on time. He took in the dark brown crusts of the pecan pies on the wooden cutting board.

He turned to see Sarah setting a third cake pan beside two others on a cooling rack. Her expression was one of defeat. She was still staring at the cake pans when he walked over to her. He looked from the lopsided cakes to Sarah and saw the silent stream of tears down her cheeks. He wanted nothing more than to take her in his arms, but he knew nothing would be worse for either of them. She had not invited him in, and he was not about to let his actions get him kicked out. Friendly hugs were out, unless she initiated them.

"Will icing help?"

She shook her head.

"I bet they *taste* good."

Sarah finally looked at him, a hint of a smile flickering on her lips.

"You want to ice these or do you want me to tackle the dishes so we can bake another cake?" Blake asked, pulling off his leather jacket and hanging it on the back of one of her kitchen chairs.

How could you do this to me, Blake? I look like something the cat dragged in and you stand there in tailored slacks and a pearl-gray sweater looking gorgeous and tempting and calm while I have a nervous breakdown. And why are you here disrupting my life and making me wish for something that can never be?

"Sarah?" he prompted. "Dishes or another cake?"

"Neither."

Blake began pulling pots and bowls out of the sink. "I don't mind."

The idea that the great Blake Anthony Williams was going to wash dishes stunned her for a few minutes, then she remembered, friendship not love. "I do. That's taking friendship a little too far."

Blake glanced over his shoulder at the determined face of the woman staring back at him. "I don't think that's possible. You went to a lot of trouble to bring me a tree, then helped decorate it. Washing a few dishes is the least I can do."

Her face flushed at the memory of what had happened after they finished decorating the tree. "Th-That won't be necessary. I can do the dishes later."

"What about your cake?" Blake asked, locating the dishwashing detergent under the sink.

"I used the last of my vanilla extract for the cake, I don't have enough pecans to make more pies, I'm out of flour and eggs," she said with forced brightness. "I missed going to the grocery store on Friday."

Blake stopped squirting liquid detergent and turned. "You went looking for my tree Friday."

Sarah took the bottle out of his hand and shut off the water. "It's no big deal. There'll be enough food at my mother's house. No one will miss mine."

"If that's true, then why are you so upset?" He didn't get an answer; he hadn't expected one. Pulling his jacket from the chair, he put it back on. "Give me a list and I'll go to the store and pick up what you need."

"That's not your pro—"

"The list," he insisted.

Sarah was familiar enough with his tone of voice to know he wasn't going to back down. "Blake, most of the grocery stores will be closing in thirty minutes because it's Christmas

Eve. As for the ones that are open, their shelves will probably be bare."

"What were you cooking?"

"Pecan pie, divinity, pineapple cake, and fudge." Maybe when he realized there was nothing he could do, he'd leave.

Blake grinned, a flash of white teeth in his dark, handsome face. "I know a place that has everything you need, the shelves are full, and best of all, the prices are rock-bottom and there's no waiting to check out."

"There is no such place," she scoffed.

"Get your jacket and I'll take you there."

She stepped back. "I'm not going anyplace looking like this."

His gaze swept from her falling ponytail to her pink fuzzy house shoes. "You look like a woman who's been cooking all day. There are hundreds of thousands of women like you all over the country. Wash your face and put on a jacket and let's go. You don't want to let the place close on us."

She looked at him quizzically. His smile was irresistible; all her plans to be firm and protect her heart crumbled. She had cried and moped most of the day, despite her early morning resolution to the contrary. She had ruined everything she tried to cook because she kept thinking about the man, who was now standing before her. A man who offered friendship when she wanted love.

"Give me the name of the store and I'll go myself."

He folded his arms across his wide chest. "The owner is a friend of mine. You can't get in without me."

"Is it a warehouse?"

Blake glanced at his thin gold wristwatch. "Sarah, you better get a move on if we're going to get the things you need."

She looked around the kitchen at the ruined pies, the sunken cakes, the white globs of divinity. The fudge was in the refrigerator, but the last time she checked, it had the consistency of syrup. Everything she attempted to cook had turned out disastrously. That had never happened before. She must have been incredibly distracted; thinking more about Blake than baking. "All right, if you're sure you don't mind."

"Not at all," he said easily. "That's what friends are for."

"What are we doing here?" Sarah asked as Blake stopped in front of his house.

"There's something I want to show you."

She pressed her shoulder blades against the smooth leather seat. "If you don't mind, I'd rather go on to the store. I have a lot of baking to do."

"My point exactly. The sooner you see what

it is I have to show you, the quicker you can get on with your baking." Getting out of the car, he went around and opened her door.

"Blake, I'd rather not." Too many memories both pleasant and unpleasant waited for her inside his house.

"Sarah, in case you've forgotten, it's thirty-four degrees outside." He shivered as he hunched his broad shoulders inside his brown leather jacket.

She got out of the car and started up the curving walkway. Blake wasn't going to give in, and he might start wondering why she was being so stubborn. She had been to his house dozens of times to deliver or pick up things. She even had her own. . . . The thought made her stop abruptly and Blake had to pull up short to keep from careening into her.

"I'll return your house keys when you take me home."

"I'd rather you keep them. Your last day isn't until New Year's Eve and something might come up in the meantime." Stepping around her, he opened the door.

Instead of arguing, she made a mental note to have the keys delivered to him the day after Christmas. Blake wasn't the only one who could be stubborn. She entered the house and stopped just inside the foyer.

"Follow me," Blake said.

Shoving her hands deep inside her coat

pockets, she did as he requested. Out of the corner of her eye she saw the glint of the Christmas tree. Her determination to leave as soon as possible increased. Her brow furrowed as they entered the kitchen. Her puzzlement grew as he began opening all the cabinet doors.

Blake turned to face her. "I may not know where the ironing board or thread is, but I do know Mabel has one of the best-stocked kitchens in Atlanta. Partially thanks to her love of gourmet cooking, but mostly thanks to you since you supplied the entire house. Do you remember when I had that dinner party and Mabel became ill in the middle of things and you came over and finished cooking everything? We had pecan pie for dessert."

If memory served her right, that evening had been perfect. Blake's guests were his old college professor from Howard University in Washington, D.C. and his wife. They had insisted on meeting the cook. Blake had summoned her from the kitchen. Before she knew it, she was sitting across from him and he was praising not only her culinary skills, but also her talents as the decorator of his house and as his secretary.

She had glowed with an inner pride and satisfaction at his words. As the evening lengthened, she began to think that Blake finally saw her as more than his Office Wife. But the next morning at work, he had reverted to the old

Blake. Her charming dinner companion was gone. It had been business as usual.

One of the first things he had asked her to do was send the professor's wife flowers. As an afterthought, he told Sarah to order some for herself to show his appreciation. She had almost thrown her steno pad at his retreating back. No matter how hard she tried, she wasn't able to make the transition from home to office as easily as he was. She loved him too much.

"I wish you would have told me what you planned," Sarah said tiredly. "You would have saved both of us a lot of trouble. Will you please take me home now?"

Blake's expression hardened. "Why are you being so stubborn? I'm trying to help and you won't even look to see if I have the things you need."

She sighed. That was her problem. Blake was exactly what she needed. "You're the one being stubborn. Can't you get it through your head that I don't need your help?"

"It's the kiss isn't it?"

"I told you before tha—"

"I'm not talking about the first kiss, I'm talking about the one last night." He took a step closer to her rigidly held body. "The one that set my body afire and almost made me forget you're off limits."

"Did I ask to be off limits?" she questioned hotly.

Blake could tell by her expression that she had spoken on impulse. This was the time to be completely honest, Blake realized.

"Sarah, I want you now, but I can't promise you how I'll feel two months from now," he admitted truthfully and felt like a lowlife when she winced. "You aren't the type of woman to go into a relationship knowing it has no future. The only thing I'm committed to is Williams and Williams. I know I can be a good friend to you. I'm not sure about anything else."

"I hope you believe in long-distance friendships then, Blake."

"Why?" he asked, not liking the smile playing around her tempting little mouth.

"Because after the cruise, I'm moving permanently."

A chill of apprehension ran down his spine. "Where?"

"New Orleans."

"New Orleans!" he exclaimed incredulously.

"Yep. My timing couldn't be better," she informed him brightly. "I'll be there in time for the carnival season and Mardi Gras."

"You *can't* go."

She crossed her arms over her chest. "I beg your pardon?"

He wanted to shake her. She was running away to forget some jerk and she had been a living flame in Blake's arms. If she'd just stop and think, she'd realize she couldn't be in love with this mystery guy. "It's because of th—"

"It is *not* because of what happened last night," she said, cutting him off. "I've given this a lot of thought. A move is just what I need to give me a new perspective on life and New Orleans is perfect. It's far enough away to give me an exciting change and close enough at five hundred miles for me to come home to visit."

"But you'll be in a strange city, away from your friends and family," Blake argued.

"Actually, my father is from Baton Rouge, and I've been to New Orleans a couple of times to visit my cousin, Lizzette. She has this fantastic place near the French Quarter and I'll be living with her until I can find a place of my own. My new job is only a short distance away."

"You have another job?" Blake shouted.

"Certainly. You don't think I'd make a move like this without a job, do you?"

Instead of answering her question, he asked one of his own. "With whom?"

She named a large communications company with offices in most major cities. "With the glowing reference you gave me, I had no problems."

"I didn't give you any reference."

A smile lit her face. "Yes, you did. Only you

thought it was for a communications group I wanted to join. It was, but as an employee."

He had to clench his hands to keep from shaking some sense into her beautiful, smiling head. "Does your mother or Randle or any of your family know you're moving?"

"They have nothing to say about it," she told him.

And you have nothing to say about it.

His eyes narrowed. "You're pushing all the wrong buttons, Sarah."

"Let me know when I push the right one."

He started toward her. She backed up until her hips pressed against the island counter. The lower half of his body pressed intimately against hers. He watched her eyes widen and knew she felt the rigid hardness forming against her lower belly. "I think you just did."

"B-Blake."

"Yes, Sarah," he said, his head slowly descending toward hers.

"D-don't you think we better get busy, if we're going to finish?"

His mouth hovered a fraction of an inch from her lips. "That's what I had in mind."

She gulped. "I-I meant the baking."

"Sarah," Blake moaned.

"Blake, please," she whispered.

Black eyes studied her wide brown ones a long time before he straightened and stepped back. He had no control when it came to her.

He took a deep breath. "What do you want to tackle first?"

Sarah studied the rigid way he held his body, the slight flaring of his nostrils, and realized he wasn't as indifferent as he appeared. He wanted her. He just wasn't going to let his emotions overrule what he thought was best for her. She didn't agree with him, but baiting him wasn't going to help matters. She could only push him so far, before he pushed back. Hard.

"I'm sorry," she said softly. "I didn't get much sleep last night."

"Neither did I, and we won't tonight either if we don't get started."

Sarah offered a shy smile, grateful Blake was willing to let the matter drop and move on. "I'll get the things out of the cabinets while you find a sack to put them in."

"Why can't you cook here?"

"Here?" She turned to face him with a bottle of vanilla extract in her hand.

"The kitchen is clean and so are the pans. Most importantly, I have a double oven," Blake reasoned. "Since I didn't see a cookbook or any recipes in your kitchen, I thought you might know them by heart."

"I do, but this is asking too much."

"I'm the one asking you. You can be finished in half the time and get to bed at a reasonable hour. Besides, I can wash everything as you go, so when we're finished, we're finished."

She didn't hesitate further. Both of them needed to put the previous night behind them. "You've got yourself a deal—friend." She sent him a teasing smile and he returned it in full measure.

They worked as well together in the kitchen as they had in the office and on the Christmas tree. They also sang well together to the oldies-but-goodies Christmas songs on the radio. But Blake soon found out Sarah was unwilling to accept his help on some things. She had to measure everything herself, for example.

She also didn't want him touching her pie crust dough. Too much handling or too much flour, she told him, kept the crust from being light and flaky. She did consent to letting him watch the candy thermometer for the divinity and fudge.

Even with the restraints she imposed on him, Blake thoroughly enjoyed himself. Most of all he enjoyed the sight of Sarah scurrying around in his kitchen. Because of his mother's busy schedule and the large number of people that usually stopped by for the Christmas holidays, their cook had always prepared everything for their family gatherings. He had never seen firsthand how much time and effort it took to prepare large amounts of food.

Clarissa, his first wife, had been a decent cook, but he didn't remember wanting to keep her company in the kitchen or volunteering to wash the dishes for her. He didn't consider himself a chauvinist; he'd just never thought of sharing the household duties, since Clarissa didn't work outside the home.

But helping Sarah in the kitchen seemed the most natural thing in the world to him. He had a feeling even if she had to stay up all night, she'd cook every dish she set before her family and friends for Christmas.

Licking the fudge-covered wooden spoon, he watched Sarah place the heavy pan of half walnut/half pecan fudge in the refrigerator, then turn back to the pineapple cake icing gently bubbling on the stove. She had been delighted to see his prized ten-pound can of assorted shelled nuts. He had enjoyed her obvious pleasure, until she'd mentioned that since she knew how much he liked pecans, she was going to send him some pralines from New Orleans.

His appetite vanished. He didn't want her to go, but he had no right to ask her to stay. He tossed the saucepan and the spoon in the dishwater. Water splashed on the floor.

She glanced over her shoulder. "What happened?"

"It slipped," he told her.

"You're probably tired from washing all those dishes. I can't thank you enough." Cutting off the stove, she began icing the bottom layer of the pineapple cake. "I certainly don't look forward to facing mine."

"We'll have them licked in no time," Blake said.

She spun around from the cake to see him wiping up the floor with a handful of paper towels. "You've done enough."

"I won't be able to sleep, worrying about you and those dishes," Blake said. Putting the soiled paper towels in the trash, he stood. "We'll drop these things off at your mother's, then we'll take care of your kitchen."

Panic gripped her. "We're not going anywhere near my mother."

"You're dripping," Blake calmly observed.

She moved the dripping spoon back over the pan. Her mother would jump to all the wrong conclusions if they showed up together. Thanks to Randle's big mouth, she already thought there was something romantic going on between Sarah and Blake. "Did you hear me, Blake?"

"I heard you, but it doesn't make any sense to take these things to your house when you just have to take them to your mother's tomorrow. Another paper towel in hand, he cleaned up the pineapple icing.

"It may not make sense, but my parents are

probably asleep, and I don't want to wake them."

Blake pushed to his feet. He was within a foot of her. They had been much closer while they were cooking, but never for more than a couple of seconds. They were at five and counting. "Do you know, when you're nervous, your eyelashes flutter?"

Long eyelashes fluttered.

"Your family seems like a close and outgoing one. I can't imagine your parents not having one or two guests over on Christmas Eve," Blake said thoughtfully. "And didn't you tell me the night we were decorating the Christmas tree, your parents' house was the place your nieces and nephews toys were stashed? I bet someone is reading bicycle instructions as we speak."

Sarah cursed her loose tongue and Blake's perceptiveness. "I don't want to go over there," she insisted stubbornly, and went back to icing the cake.

"What's the matter? Afraid your mother and father will give me the same assessing looks my parents have been giving you?"

She whipped back around. "You saw them?"

"Every time. Both of them like you. Believe me, they've never asked any of my dates to stay and join them if I wanted to leave."

"B-But I wasn't a date." She added more icing. "We're just friends."

"I told them that, but they looked at me the way parents do when they think you're lying and they aren't going to dignify the remark with a response," Blake said. He wished he could see Sarah's face, specifically her eyelashes.

Setting the icing aside, she added the second layer of the cake. "We're friends." *And I love you so much I ache inside.*

"We're friends." *And I care about you so much I get angry just thinking about you leaving me.*

"Parents get strange ideas sometimes," Sarah said softly.

Abandoning the dishes completely, Blake leaned against the counter where Sarah was working. "Mine want more grandchildren. I thought they'd have collective strokes when Carter and his wife told them they weren't going to have any children. Then they jumped on me for not remarrying. Dianne's daughter only made them want more. She'll probably get the pep talk about having another child while she's here for the holidays."

"If you ever remarry, do you plan to have any children?" Sarah asked.

Blake started to give his pat answer that he wasn't getting married again, then he looked down just as Sarah looked up. He felt as if someone hit him in the stomach with an iron fist. Longing and need shimmered in her beautiful eyes. For the first time, he actually thought about children. The picture that formed in his mind wasn't of himself, but of tiny, laughing replicas of Sarah. The imaginary fist slammed into his midsection again. "With the right woman, I can't imagine not having children."

"I want children, too," she admitted softly.

Another picture popped into his mind: Sarah in bed with a faceless stranger. The image filled him with so much rage, he wanted to howl in fury.

"Blake? Are you all right?"

The slender hand on his arm jerked him back to the reality. "You're not going to New Orleans!" he shouted at her.

She blinked, apparently disconcerted by the seeming shift in conversation. For a few seconds her hand lingered, then she went back to her cake. "It's for the best."

"You can't tell me you want to leave everyone you love!"

"Sometimes the things that are for the best aren't always the easiest," she insisted.

Blake watched her add the third and final layer of the cake with hands that shook. She didn't want to go. She was running from a man who had hurt her. Just like *he* had hurt her—

His chest suddenly tightened and for a long moment, Blake couldn't breathe. His body shook so hard he had to grab the counter and hold on. He couldn't be right. What he was thinking was so wild and preposterous it was crazy.

Yet, as air worked its way into his lungs, the idea gained credence. Any way he turned things over in his mind, he came up with the same conclusion. The truth had been staring him in the face and he'd been too blind to see.

His beautiful, sweet, sensitive Sarah loved him.

He should have known. She was too honest to love one man and make love with another. If he hadn't been so wrapped up in trying to find a way to keep her, he would have guessed sooner. Sarah loved him.

A fierce pride lit within him that somehow he had managed to win her love. He wanted to click his heels with joy and weep at the unfairness of it all at the same time. She could never be his. Sarah deserved marriage. But marriage was the one thing he couldn't give her. He was already married to Williams & Williams.

The thought of coming home from a business trip and finding her packed and crying caused bile to rise in his throat. The tears she shed last night would be infinitesimal compared with the ones she'd shed if things didn't work out between them.

Only he didn't think Sarah would leave. She'd stay with him through anything, and hide her tears just as she had hidden her love for him. He couldn't do that to her.

For them there could never be a happy ending. He could never let on that he had guessed her secret, and he knew what she meant about the best things not being the easiest. He had to be strong enough to let her go on New Year's Eve and trust that when he did, Sarah would meet a loving man to marry and father her children.

"Well, how does it look?" she asked and glanced up. Her smile faltered. Concern lined her face. "Blake, are you all right?"

He opened his mouth to speak but his throat was suddenly dry.

"Blake," she cried frantically, pressing her palm to his forehead.

He closed his eyes, then just as quickly opened them when he felt her arm slide around his waist. She guided him toward a chair. "I'm all right, Sarah."

Large, brown eyes stared up at him. "You scared me."

Not half as much as you're scaring me. "Sorry, guess I should have taken your advice and eaten a sandwich when you did."

"I told you you were going to ruin your appetite sneaking that divinity," she scolded.

"So you did." He gently pulled away. She felt too good.

"Sit in that chair. You aren't moving from

it until you've eaten something." Going to the refrigerator, she took out the ingredients for a ham and cheese omelet. Her heart was pounding so fast and hard in her chest, she had to keep taking deep breaths. Blake had looked so stunned and shocked, her first thought was that he was having a heart attack.

She stopped slicing ham and glanced over her shoulder to reassure herself he was all right. He was simply staring at her with the oddest expression she had ever seen. "Blake, are you sure we shouldn't call a doctor?"

"There's nothing wrong with me that you can't cure," he said.

She grabbed the cheese. "I'll have you something in a minute."

The sound of his forced laughter had her turning back to face him. "It's nothing. Something just struck me as funny," he quickly explained.

She worked faster. She didn't begin to relax until Blake took his first bite of food. She watched him eat every crumb, then insisted he drink a glass of milk. He wanted scotch. They compromised and he had some of each.

"Thanks, Sarah. That was probably the best meal I've ever eaten."

"That's because you were so hungry," she told him. Picking up the empty plate, she returned to the sink. "It's my turn to do the dishes and I don't want you to move."

"I told you I'm fine."

"You didn't look fine earlier." Letting the cooling water out of the sink, she ran in hot water. "You've been working too hard. The holidays are just in time to give you a rest."

"I wish I could stop the whole thing."

"Why would you want to do that?" she asked, busily washing a glass.

"When they're gone, you'll be gone with them," Blake said, unaware of the mixture of anger and need in his voice until he heard the words out loud.

Sarah's shoulders jerked. He cursed himself. He was going to have to do a better job of keeping his feelings hidden and helping her with her decision. Sarah's happiness was what counted, even if he wanted to act childish and stomp and scream for her to stay. "Made any plans for your birthday yet?"

"Not really. My family usually has everyone over for an early dinner because it's New Year's Eve. That gives everyone a chance to go to any other parties they want. Mama hasn't said anything, but we usually plan everything on Christmas day," she said and set a glass on the dish rack.

"Had you planned to go to any parties afterward?"

She shook her head. "I'll be too busy packing and doing last-minute checks. The ship docks back in Miami on Sunday and I'm catching a flight straight to New Orleans. I have a week to find a place to live permanently before I start work. Luckily, my apartment lease isn't up for another month, so hopefully I can find something I like and move my furniture in one trip."

"What about your car?"

"Lizzette and her fiancé are flying up early in the morning and driving my car back." She put the last dish on the rack. "I can't wait to meet fiancé number seven and see if he's the man who can get her to the altar."

"Number seven!"

Laughing at the astonishment in his voice, Sarah began drying the dishes. "Lizzette is stunning. If that isn't enough, she has a voice like velvet molasses. The last time I visited, there were actually four men trying to carry my luggage at the airport for me. They were all looking at Lizzette."

"She doesn't sound as if she's a good influence," Blake said. The men might not have noticed Sarah then, but they would this time.

"You sound like I did, until I met her at a family reunion three years ago in Baton Rouge," Sarah told him. "The men, not Lizzette, always insisted on the engagement because they're afraid of losing her. But when she walks, she always gives the ring back."

"Why does she say yes and then change her mind?"

Putting up the last dish, Sarah faced him. "Because she's twenty-seven and wants a home and family. She keeps hoping each man is the one, but they never pass the final test."

"What test is that?"

Sarah's eyelashes fluttered. "I can't tell you."

Blake rose and came to stand in front of her. "You're eyelashes are at it again."

Stepping around him, she took the fudge out of the refrigerator. Blake stepped in front of her. She took a step backward. "I'm not saying another word on the subject."

"Sarah, from the way you're acting, I've already narrowed the possibilities to around one thing." Blake smiled devilishly. "But is it before, during, or after?"

Her mouth gaped. She dropped the fudge. Half anticipating her reaction, he was ready to catch the heavy pan. He sat it on the counter. "Since you're fond of Lizzette and I know how you feel abou—"

"Blake, you're going to be wearing a pineapple cake if you don't stop."

"On one condition."

"All right."

"You're giving in pretty easy," he said.

"That's because I know a friend would never take undue advantage of another friend."

Blake lifted a dark brow. Sarah thought she had turned the tables on him, but this was one time she had backed herself into a corner.

"Just like a friend would always help out another friend. That's why I'm asking you to spend New Year's Eve with me."

"What!"

"Every year my parents have a New Year's Eve party. Every year I drop by for a few minutes, then I cut out. Last year I promised to stay until the new year. Since it's your birthday, I want to celebrate both of them with you," he said reasonably.

"I told you I have a lot of things to do." She began cutting the fudge.

"So take the rest of the week off."

"I can't. I have to train my replacement."

Blake caught her shoulders and gently turned her to him. "If you train her for a year, she isn't going to be you."

"She's anxious to learn," Sarah insisted.

"I'm grateful for her enthusiasm, but right now we're talking about a combination New Year's Eve and birthday party. I don't want anything to interfere with that."

He also didn't want to think about going to work and seeing someone in Sarah's chair and knowing she wasn't coming back. "I can pick you up around ten and have you home by one. What time is your flight?"

"Nine," she answered reluctantly.

"I could come back at eight and take you to the airport. What do you say if we ring out the old year and bring in the new one together?"

"My family will probably want to take me to the airport."

"We'll all take you."

She twisted uneasily, the warmth of his large hands burning through her sweatshirt. She wanted to be with him so much, but all he wanted was friendship and she couldn't stop herself from wanting more. "Don't you want to spend the time with someone else?"

His thumb absently stroked her shoulder. "No. I want to spend the time with you. I hate that you had to leave before I fully appreciated you. I'll miss you."

Her hand covered his briefly. "I'll miss you, too."

"If things don't work out in New Orleans, remember you can always come back here, or go to the new office in Savannah, or I'll help you find another job anyplace you want to go," Blake told her.

"It *has* to work out," she said sadly. "I can't live on dreams any more." Moving from beneath his hands, she began to cut the fudge again.

"Are you sure about this, Sarah?" Randle said, his arm thrown around his sister's slim shoulders as they stood in their mother's kitchen on Christmas Day.

Slowly she nodded. She had told her family

of her plans to move immediately after dinner. As expected, her mother had been the most vocal against her going. When she couldn't get Sarah to change her mind, her mother had begun to cry. Sarah's own eyes had filled and her throat tightened, just as they were doing now, two hours later.

Her brother handed her a tissue, then pulled her into his arms. "One question. Is there any reason to break every bone in your boss's body?"

Tear-stained eyes lifted. She and Randle had always been the closest in the family. They were eighteen months apart and she had been following her only big brother around for as long as she could remember. The family called them the "notorious twos." He was always smoothing the way for her, just as he had done earlier with her mother. This time, however, there was nothing he could do to help.

"Unfortunately, there isn't," she finally said.

Understanding lit Randle's brown eyes and kicked up one side of his well-shaped mouth. "Damn, sis. I thought you had better sense."

"It snuck up on me." She sniffed and dabbed at her eyes. "I thought I admired his mind."

Randle blinked, then laughed. Grabbing her around the waist, he twirled her in his arms much as he had done in their youth, then set her on her feet. "You're going to make it, and I'm going to miss you like crazy."

Holding onto his arms to balance herself, she smiled up into his handsome face. "All you're going to do is miss my pecan pie."

"It's you, and try to remember, not all men are as stupid as your boss."

"He's the smartest, kindest man I know," Sarah said in Blake's defense. "He helped me bake the pecan pies you practically inhaled. And, despite my insistence otherwise, he helped me clean up my kitchen."

"Blake Williams cleaned up a kitchen!"

"Two to be exact," Sarah said with satisfaction. "His and mine. If it wasn't for him, you wouldn't have had any pie. I burned the first two."

Randle frowned thoughtfully. "That doesn't sound like a man who isn't interested in a woman."

Sarah tucked her head. "I didn't say he wasn't interested."

"Hold on a minute. It sounds as if we're getting back to breaking bones," Randle said with feeling.

"Blake decided we should only be friends," Sarah said miserably. "He doesn't think he can be committed to anything except Williams & Williams."

"I hope he said this *before* I had cause to go looking for him."

"He did. Blake is an honorable man."

"He's a *man,*" Randle said succinctly.

Hands on her hips, Sarah glared at her brother. "And what is that saying about you?"

"Listen, no man is messing with my sister."

She rolled her eyes. "You're just like Blake. Every woman is somebody's sister or daughter."

"You had this discussion with Blake?"

"Yes."

"Mind helping me out and telling me how he got out of this corner I've boxed myself in to?"

She held herself with controlled rigidity. "He said Williams & Williams is the only wife he'll ever have."

Instantly Randle pulled her into his arms again. "Maybe I should pay him a visit anyway for making you so miserable."

Clutching her brother, she fought back tears. "I did this, not Blake."

"But you're unhappy."

Raising her head, she looked into identical brown eyes. "You don't love someone on the condition they'll love you in return. You take your chances, then hope and pray for happily-ever-after. Sometimes it doesn't work out that way. I once told Blake love is a gift and when it's returned, it's a miracle. No matter what, I'll always believe that. It's not his fault he doesn't believe in miracles."

Randle pulled her back into his arms and

said nothing, not even when tears wet the front of his shirt.

Late Christmas night, Blake sat in his office staring at the blue phone. He had picked it up several times in the past hour, had even dialed the first three digits of Sarah's phone number, then hung up. Friends called friends, especially on Christmas, and wished them well. So what was the harm in calling Sarah? He just wanted to know if she had a good time with her family. If she thought number seven was going to be lucky for Lizzette.

He almost smiled as he remembered the shocked expression on Sarah's face when he asked her the "before, during or after" question. She was so innocent in a lot of ways and at the same time so wise. But for them, there would never be a before, during, or after. He'd never hold her in his arms and watch her turn to fire, never hear her whimper with need and know she called out only to him, never lose himself in the heat of her body.

Teeth clamped tight, Blake closed his eyes for a long moment and forced his mind away from the erotic images of the two of them together. Thoughts like that weren't going to help him through the next several days. Trouble was, he wasn't used to being noble. What he wanted he went after. Depravation was something he wasn't used to dealing with. From the thoughtful looks and questions his family had given him all day, he wasn't handling things very well.

He didn't blame them. He had been inattentive and somber all day, except with his niece, Kerri. That had probably puzzled his family. He didn't usually spend a lot of time with children. However, today, seeing Kerri, he couldn't keep from thinking one day Sarah would have children and they wouldn't be his.

Somehow Kerri's smile and her warm little body had helped him get through the day. She had gone to sleep in his arms, clutching the African doll Sarah had picked out for her Christmas present.

He had had no idea what to get his three-year-old niece, and again, Sarah had come through for him. Then, as now, he wondered if someone had come through with presents for *her.*

Blake's college roommate, Devon always complained that since his 'birthday was in December, he either received Christmas presents or birthday presents, never both. Sarah deserved both. She also deserved a man who could give her the home and children she wanted. Rising from his chair, he went to stand in front of the Christmas tree.

The gold and white sparkling splendor would always remind him of Sarah and the gold gown she had worn to the office Christmas party. She had been glowing. Yet, it hadn't taken long for him to make her unhappy. He wasn't going to do that to her again. He'd keep away from her until he picked her up for his parent's New Year's Eve party, and no matter how much his gut twisted, he was going to keep a smile on his face and let her go when the time came.

Sarah took her purse out of her office desk with shaking fingers. December thirty-first. Her last day at work. She felt as if part of her was being ripped away. No matter how much she originally thought leaving was for the best, she couldn't keep from wishing she hadn't handed in her resignation or keep from remembering that Blake had told her she could come back. It was tempting to take him up on his offer. But although they had become closer, they were never going to be more than friends.

She glanced at his closed door. She hadn't seen or talked with him since Christmas Eve. Although she hadn't expected him to be in that day, she had foolishly thought he would stop by the office on her last day. Especially since some of the other department heads involved with the reorganization of Reynolds in Savannah had been at work.

Proves how a woman in love can make herself

believe anything. Apparently, he liked loose friendships.

"Be happy," she whispered, and left. The door to the elevator opened almost immediately. She stepped on, pushed the first floor button, and glanced at her watch: 5:07. Most of the people in the building, including her replacement and her two ex-assistants, were already gone.

Everyone had someone to head home to except her. She didn't even know if Blake still planned on taking her to his parents' house that night. And in the aftermath of the announcement of her move, her mother hadn't mentioned her coming over for dinner.

The way things were going, Randle would probably be late picking her up again. Maybe she should have rented a car after Lizzette and her soon-to-be ex-fiancé drove hers back to New Orleans. Lizzette told her he had failed her test, but had decided not to tell him until after they returned. With all the men in the world, you'd think there would be two just right for both Lizzette and her. Feeling disheartened and alone, Sarah stepped off the elevator.

"Surprise!" Cameras flashed and people applauded.

Stunned, Sarah stared around the lobby at the smiling faces of employees, her parents, her three sisters, and Randle. Her mouth gaped.

The first person to reach her was her mother. "You thought we'd forgotten your birthday didn't you?"

"Never thought it for a moment," Sarah said, hugging her mother and grinning up at her father.

The next couple of hours in the office cafeteria were filled with laughter and tears. But the one person she wanted to see never showed. Finally, most of the people were gone, the food eaten, her presents opened, her thanks given. Randle was taking the last of her gifts to his truck and she was talking with her assistant Janet.

"Thanks for everything. It was a wonderful surprise party. The bracelet you and Gloria gave me is beautiful," Sarah said, once again admiring the intricate knots linking the loops of the gold bracelet.

"Actually, Mr. Williams picked it out," Janet admitted grudgingly. "He helped with the party, too."

"Bla . . . Mr. Williams?"

"I called him when more and more people said they wanted to come. People really like you," Janet said. "I would have thought Mr. Williams would want to be here to wish you well."

Sarah's hand dug deeper in her coat pocket. "Mr. Williams is a busy man."

Janet shook her head. "So are the other department heads, and they came. I guess he got fed up with not being able to figure out the name of the man you're interested in."

Panic assailed Sarah. "Wh-what did you say?"

The young woman's eyes rounded. Both hands covered her mouth. "Oh my goodness! I never meant for you to find out. I wouldn't hurt you for anything. I only told Mr. Williams because I thought he could help." Her words tumbled out.

"Perhaps you better tell me what you told Mr. Williams and why you thought his help was needed," Sarah said with more calm than she was feeling.

With halting words and downcast eyes, Janet related her conversation with Blake. She finished by saying, "After word circulated that you two had gone out together and you started dressing differently, I thought he was helping you get the attention of the man you were in love with. I just assumed that his plan didn't work when he started helping us plan your going-away party. But I can't figure out why he helped with the arrangements and then didn't show."

Sarah did. Blake wanted her to remember Williams & Williams if things didn't work out as planned in New Orleans. Closing her eyes, Sarah sat down in a chair. What a fool she had been. Blake hadn't wanted her; he had wanted to keep a secretary. But at least he didn't know he was the man she loved. She couldn't have faced that.

"Ms. Marshall, I'm sorry. Please don't be mad," Janet pleaded. "I just wanted you to stay."

"Did-did you tell anyone else about this?"

Janet shook her braid-covered head frantically. "No. Never. I'd never do anything to hurt you." Tears crested in the younger woman's eyes. "I only told him in confidence because you seemed so unhappy the day you got sick."

At least no one else knew what a fool she had been. "Could you do me two favors?"

"Anything."

"Please don't tell anyone else about any of this."

Janet squatted down in front of Sarah and covered her clenched hands with hers. "I swear."

"Next, tell Randle I want to do some thinking and I'll take a cab home."

"I have a ca—"

"Please," Sarah said, her voice whispery thin.

Nodding, Janet rose and left.

Sarah wanted nothing more than to lay

down on the tiled floor and cry. Instead, she slowly pushed to her feet. She wanted, needed to be alone. A few people were still congregated at the front door of the building; out the back door was the parking lot and Randle. She headed for the elevator. It slid open immediately and she quickly stepped on.

"Have you seen or heard from Sarah?" Randle asked as soon as Blake opened his front door.

Blake tensed. His hand gripped the doorknob. "No. What's the matter? Is Sarah all right?"

Randle's shoulders slumped. "She asked Janet to tell me she was getting a cab home from the party, but no one has seen or heard from her since. That was three hours ago."

Fear cut through Blake. "Why the hell did you let her take a cab in the first place?"

"Don't you start blaming me," Randle shouted back. "You're the reason she's been so miserable lately. Sarah told Janet that she wanted to be alone, that she had some thinking to do. We both know you're at the top of the list."

Blake accepted his words as the truth. "I never meant to hurt her. Why do you think I stayed away?"

"Well, you did hurt her, and if you ever go

near her again I'm going to smash that face of yours."

"Do what you want. The important thing now is making sure Sarah is all right. I'm going to call Janet and see if she can tell us anything else." Turning away from the door, Blake went into his office. In a matter of moments, he had Janet's phone number on his computer screen and he was dialing her number.

"Janet, this is Mr. Will—" He didn't finish, he simply held the phone to his ear, then moments later slowly put it down.

"What did she say? What happened?" Randle asked frantically.

"She said because she trusted me I made the sweetest woman in the world cry and she hopes I'm proud of myself. Then she slammed the phone down." All Blake could think of was that somehow Sarah must have learned about his talk with Janet. Considering how upset the young woman was, she had probably let the information slip and Sarah had believed the worst.

The beeper at Randle's waist went off. He jerked it up. "She's home. I left Antoine to watch her apartment. We agreed on a number code to use if she returned."

"Does the code indicate how she's doing?"

"No. I told him she had something heavy on her mind and to stay put if he saw her."

Randle started from the room. "But I'll know that in twenty minutes."

"I'll know in eighteen," Blake said roughly.

Abruptly Randle stopped and spun around. "I don't want you near her again."

"I'm going," Blake said with chilling finality.

"Don't you have other plans?" Randle's angry gaze swept Blake's tall tuxedo-clad frame.

"We're wasting time. Close the front door on your way out." Blake stepped around the other man and headed for the garage at a fast pace. He needed to get to Sarah and make sure she understood. No one, not even her brother, was going to stop him.

Blake reached Sarah's apartment in seventeen and a half minutes. Slamming the car door, he took the stairs two at a time to her door, then rang the doorbell.

A broad finger jabbed him in the back. He ignored it and rang the doorbell again. The finger jabbed again. "Randle, your sister needs to know what I've got to say."

"It's Antoine," came the deep voice. "Randle phoned. He wants you to back off."

"I don't care what Randle said, or you either," Blake told him as he rang the bell again. "I'm not leaving until I've seen Sarah. Why doesn't she answer this damn door?"

"She may be asleep," Antoine stated, his brown face creased in a frown. "I caught a glimpse of her face under the security light. She looked like it was all she could do to put one foot in front of the other."

"And I know the reason," came a third voice. "Leave, Williams."

Blake turned to face Sarah's brother. "The only way you're going to get me from this door is by force, and if someone calls the police we'll both end up in jail and we still won't know if Sarah is all right."

"He's right," Antoine said. "She's not answering her door."

Randle rapped on the door. "Sarah, it's Randle. Open the door, sis."

The three men shared a worried look, then Randle pulled out his own key to Sarah's apartment and unlocked the door. His arm shot out to stop Blake's headlong flight. "She might be in the shower or something. Wait here with Antoine."

Blake waited for about thirty seconds, then started through the door. Another arm stopped him. "Get out of the way."

"You heard Randle."

"If that were your woman in there and our places were reversed, would you be out here?"

"Since when is Sarah your woman?"

"Since I stopped being stupid and admitted it," Blake said. Pushing Antoine's arm out of the way, he entered the apartment. He simultaneously dreaded and anticipated each step.

What he found in the bedroom caused pain to rip though him.

Brother and sister sat side by side on her bed. Randle had his arms wrapped around Sarah as he rocked her back and forth. By the way her shoulders shook, Blake knew she was sobbing.

He shut his eyes. He had never wanted to see her cry because of him. He had hurt her in so many ways and all he wanted to do was love her.

The sudden knowledge hit him full in the chest. He loved her. Hands clenched by his side, Blake watched helplessly as Randle tried to comfort her. If he stayed, he would only make her cry again. But, dear lord, how could he walk away from his heart?

Something gray fell from Sarah's lap onto the floor. Instantly, Blake recognized the koala bear he had given her. His heart contracted. Without thought he started toward her. He pulled her out of Randle's arms and into his. Her body instantly stiffened.

"Sarah, please—" His voice broke and it was a long moment before he could continue. "Please forgive me."

"G-Go away."

He kissed the top of her head on hearing the hoarseness in her voice. "A man can't walk away from his soul. We've got a lot to discuss, but for now just know that I never meant to hurt you. I love you."

"No more lies," she cried, and pushed to her feet. She wrapped her arms around her waist, and kept her back to him. "The only reason you took me out was to pawn me off on someone else. Janet told me everything."

"At first, yes, then I began to care about you."

"You only care about a secretary to run your life and your office," Sarah told him.

"You're not going to listen, are you?"

"No."

"We both know how I can get you to change your mind," Blake said and started for her.

She spun toward him. Her eyes widened in alarm. "Stay away from me. Randle, make him go."

Randle looked from his sister to Blake's face, which was now stained with tears he didn't try to hide. He hesitated for a moment. "If I call in the morning and she's crying, I'm coming looking for you."

"She won't be," Blake said and kept advancing on Sarah.

"Randle!" Sarah wailed.

"A man doesn't shed tears on a woman he doesn't care about." Randle shut the bedroom door firmly behind him.

"My brother may buy that act of yours, but I don't," Sarah told him. "Get out of here."

"Come here, Sarah, my love."

"Stop calling me that." Her back was pressed against the dresser.

"Never. You'll always be my love," he said softly.

"I trusted you once, but never again. Just go away." Closing her eyes, she pressed her trembling hands ineffectually against his wide chest.

"I can't, Sarah. Believe me, I've tried," he told her, his voice infinitely tender.

She shook her head. "I won't be like those women at the shelter who keep going back into the same hopeless situation, wishing and praying for a miracle."

"You don't have to. You already have your miracle. I love you."

Her eyelids lifted and fluttered. Hope she didn't want to feel shone in her tear-stained brown eyes.

"You see, I was trying to be noble for once." His fingers stroked the bracelet on her arm. "The gold loops are linked by braided forget-me-knots. Even though you were going, I didn't want you to forget me. I thought I could let you go until Randle told me you were missing." He held up his shaking hands. "You see what you did to me."

"I-I needed to think."

"Sometimes thinking can get you into trouble." His lips brushed fleetingly against hers. "Do you know the only way I could keep the promise to myself of staying away from you was to come by every morning and see you before you went to work? Then, I'd wonder all day what was under that long black coat of yours, then I'd fantasize about taking it and everything beneath slowly off and seeing for myself. Can I see for myself, sweet Sarah?"

She swallowed and her eyelashes fluttered.

"No, I guess I'd better not if we're going to make it to my parents' party."

"Party?"

He kissed her lips again. "Have you forgotten our date?"

"How can you possibly think I'm going anyplace with you?"

"Because you love me, too."

At his words, Sarah gasped.

Blake smiled tenderly. "I've known it was me since Christmas Eve. It wasn't food I needed. I realized you couldn't let one man make love to you and be in love with another. You had to be in love with me, and if it's half as much as I love you, it will last a dozen lifetimes."

"You . . . you want to have an affair, is that it?" she said uncertainly.

"I want marriage."

Now Sarah was the one who looked stunned. "I-I thought you didn't want to get married again."

He smoothed the hair from her face. "That

was before I fell in love with you. Please forgive me and put me out of my misery and say you love me too."

Her face glowed. "I do. I do. I love you so much!"

"Honey." Blake kissed her with hungry urgency. It was a long time before he lifted his head. "Then you'll marry me?"

She beamed. "Yes."

She received another kiss. "I still have to be gone a lot, do you think you can handle that?"

"Yes, because I'm going to make sure you want to hurry home."

Blake grinned. "Stop tempting me and go get dressed."

"Do we have to?"

"Yes. I want everyone to know you're mine."

Immensely pleased, Sarah rose on tiptoe and kissed him. "How long do you think we'll stay?"

"Not long, and afterward we're going to my house and open that bottle of champagne you gave me when I moved in."

"You didn't share it with *her?*"

He kissed the pout from her face. "No. I didn't want to share it with anyone but you. Strange, now that I think back, there were a lot of times I'd get an idea or think of something that I'd want to share with you. Now all I'll have to do is roll over in bed."

"Blake," Sarah admonished, but she was

smiling. Pushing out of his arms, she spied her suitcase. "Oh goodness, the cruise! I don't want to leave you."

"Why don't I reimburse you and we'll give it to Janet," Blake said. "We owe her a lot."

"That's a wonderful idea!"

Blake walked to the bedroom door. "I think it's safer if I wait outside."

"Chicken," Sarah said and hurried to get dressed. The sooner they left, the sooner they could get to Blake's house and be alone.

Almost two hours later, Sarah and Blake stood in front of "their" Christmas tree. Each held a glass of champagne. The strands of snowflake lights entwined around the branches of the tree provided the sole illumination in the house. Sarah snuggled closer to the man she loved with all her heart and soul and thought how fortunate she was.

Blake's parents had been elated by their engagement, as had her parents and Randle. Janet had been thrilled for them both and overjoyed about the cruise. Luckily, Sarah had requested a private cabin and they were able to get a seat on the plane for Janet's husband. Jamaal's grandmother was going to babysit. It was turning out to be the perfect New Year's Eve, complete with her miracle.

"Our tree is beautiful," Sarah said.

His hand around her waist tightened. "I thought about taking it down, but it was the only part of you I had left."

She pressed closer. "Loving you and not being able to tell you of my love was the hardest thing I have ever done."

"I know, but hearing you say you love me is the best gift I will ever receive. And now I have something for you." He took the champagne from her hand and set both glasses on the cocktail table. "There's a gift somewhere on the tree for you."

Sarah's eyes sparkled as much as the crystal icicles. She glanced from Blake's grinning face to the white and gold glittering tree, then her eyes darkened. "I don't have anything for you."

Warm lips settled against hers. Immediately she melted into Blake's arms, reveling in the freedom to touch and taste him. She was still clinging to him when he slowly lifted his head.

"You can't buy, beg, borrow, or steal what you give me, Sarah, my love," Blake said softly, love and sincerity shining in his black eyes.

Tears glittered in Sarah's eyes. "I feel the same way. I love you."

"I love you too." His hands on her red-velvet-covered shoulders, he turned her to the tree. "Now find your gift."

It took Sarah less than fifteen seconds to locate the small, gold package wrapped in gold foil, suspended from a gold ribbon. Her hands shook as she pulled the paper away to reveal a gold gift box. Her heart pounding, she lifted the top and took out a black velvet ring box. She looked from the box to Blake's loving face, then back to the box. Slowly, she lifted the lid.

Her breath caught in her throat. Her entire body trembled.

"May I?" Blake lifted the three karat, heart-shaped diamond ring set in a slim platinum band and slid it on the ring finger of Sarah's left hand.

"Blake, it's beautiful. But when? How?"

"My parents are the close friends of a jeweler who was happy to bring out a selection of rings, my sister wrapped it for me, and my brother and his wife came over and tied it on the tree." Blake smiled into her astonished face and picked up their glasses of champagne. "They're all anxious for you to be in the family."

Sarah took the crystal glass. "So am I. The only unhappy person is going to be my almost-boss when I call him with the news."

"He'll just have to find a replacement. You're not leaving me," Blake said possessively. "If he has any problems with your resignation, tell him to talk to me."

"My magnificent rogue," Sarah said and kissed Blake's tightly compressed lips. "I'm not leaving you. In fact I plan to make sure all the women at Williams & Williams know that although I'm not there, you're mine."

Blake's eyebrows arched. "How do you plan to do that?"

"You'll see," Sarah promised, then proceeded to slide one arm sensuously around his neck, press the lower half of her body against his, and kiss him until they were both breathless and hungry for each other.

"We better make that toast now," Blake said, his voice rough. "In ten minutes when the clock strikes twelve, neither one of us will notice or care."

Sarah's body heated, but she met his searing gaze unflinchingly. "I know." Lizzette's seven fiancés might not have passed the test, but Sarah had no doubt Blake would.

"I love you, sweet Sarah."

"I love you, too, Blake."

He raised his fluted glass. "To my own special miracle, Sarah Elaine Marshall."

Warmth coursed though her. Their glasses clinked. She sipped slowly, her eyes on Blake, his on hers.

Once again he took their glasses, then pulled her into his arms. "I'll do everything in my power to keep you happy, I promise."

"I promise the same thing. And you might as well know, I plan to go with you on your out-of-town trips if you have to be gone overnight," Sarah said, then tucked her head. "At least until we have a baby."

Unsteady fingers lifted her chin. "You'll make a fantastic mother. Our children are going to be very lucky."

"They'll be lucky because they'll have you. One of the most painful things in loving you was knowing some other woman was going to have your child."

"No, sweet Sarah. Only you. Just you," he said solemnly as he captured her lips in a tender kiss. Gentle hands explored the curves of her body, then settled on the rounded curve of her hip, molding her against his muscled hardness.

Faintly she heard the rasp of the zipper at the back of her dress, then cool air as the dress slid to the floor. Wanting to feel the warmth of his skin beneath her fingertips, she unbuttoned his shirt and slid it off his shoulders. She kissed his chest. He shivered.

"I knew you'd be a living flame in my arms and you'd burn only for me." His seeking lips left hers, then traced a path down her throat and along her bare shoulder, then slanted downward to the swell of her breasts.

Her head thrown back, she invited his mouth to take his pleasure and give in return. Her strapless bra fell away and was instantly replaced by his warm hand.

Letting the weight of her breast fill his

cupped palm, he kneaded gently, his thumb circling the sensitive peak until her breast grew taut and heavy. He took that which craved his touch inside his mouth, nibbling, suckling, tugging.

A deep tremor shook her body. Moaning softly, she clutched Blake to steady her spiraling senses. Her restless cries brought his mouth to hers once again, quieting her feverish movements.

Powerful arms lifted her effortlessly and carried her down to the plush softness of the carpeted floor in front of the Christmas tree. He finished undressing them quickly. The snowflake lights shone upon their entwined bodies.

Crystal icicles clinked as Sarah's restless hand accidentally hit a tree branch. Blake took her hand and slid it down his body to the part of him that ached for her. Her hand clenched around the pulsating hardness and her desire for him grew.

He paused and stared down into her heavy-lidded eyes. "From this moment on, we belong to each other."

"To each other."

His mouth took possession of hers and he proceeded to prove his words with a mixture of passionate tenderness and heated savagery. His ultimate possession sent her body and soul soaring. She clutched him tighter and knew he soared with her.

Both cried out in mingled satisfaction as the clock struck twelve.

Both found their miracle on New Year's Eve in each other's arms. A miracle that would last a lifetime.

TIMELESS LOVE

Look for these historical romances in the Arabesque line:

BLACK PEARL by Francine Craft (0236-0, $4.99)

CLARA'S PROMISE by Shirley Hailstock (0147-X, $4.99)

MIDNIGHT MOON by Mildred Riley (0200-X; $4.99)

SUNSHINE AND SHADOWS by Roberta Gayle (0136-4, $4.99)